AVALON

Ceril N Domace

CERIL N DOMACE

First Printing: 2022
ISBN: 987-1-7364301-3-2
Edited by Tiffany Kaye with Writers Untapped and Jenn Jarret with Jenn Jarret Editing Services
Book Cover Design by ebooklaunch.com

For information about purchasing and permissions, contact Ceril N Domace at cerilndomace@gmail.com
www.cerilndomace.com

ALSO BY:

The Fae Queen's Court

Haven

CHAPTER ONE

In Which an Acquaintance Comes to Call

"The function of away teams is threefold. First and foremost, they protect the fae and faeborn that live outside the havens. Second, they retrieve supplies and materials we can't produce on our own. Third, they're our eyes and ears in the world outside our borders. They're our early warning system and our first line of protection, the practical arm of our military. Without them, we would be blind, and any fae outside the havens would be beyond our reach."
— Excerpt from A Corps Member's Duty *by Stephen Andrews-Conway, Lord Aelfric*

Tension followed Owen out of town like dust behind his motorcycle, tying his shoulders in knots even Houdini wouldn't be able to undo. He wasn't sure why. The mission had gone well, and the medicine was safely tucked in the saddlebags. Sure, there'd been a brief moment where he'd thought the contact was going to shoot him—Owen was on the FBI's Most Wanted list—but fortunately, she didn't trust the news where fae were concerned.

The Society Against Fae Emigration, or SAFE as it was better known, and the Committee for Fae Relations had done their best to blacken his name when he'd taken his kids and fled to Tearmann after his wife, Tiffany, had changed—never mind that he'd done it to protect them from those same groups. They'd labeled him everything from a kidnapper to a murderer and put his face on every television in the world so everyone else knew it too.

It made doing this job . . . difficult. Whatever aid that Beira—Queen Titania as he was technically supposed to refer to her outside of

Tearmann—had thought he'd give to the away teams as an active Corpsman had vanished the day they realized how many people believed those stories. The only people who were happy to see him now were fae and their families. Refugees. People like him and his family.

Shaking his head, he turned his attention back to the road. It was getting late, and he didn't want to miss his turn because he was reminiscing. Better to save that for the debrief.

Some tension bled away into the brisk October air at the sight of the farmhouse peeking over the golden and amber trees. That farmhouse was the only inhabited building for miles around, which made it perfect for clandestine gatherings. Its owners, Samuel and Mary O'Riley, had remodeled the barn into a guesthouse when they'd retired, and promptly offered it up to fae away teams. They'd even offered Samuel's old motorcycle for supply runs. By far, it was the most comfortable safehouse Owen had ever been in.

Mary was waiting for him on the porch, fiddling with her bracelets, an eclectic collection of rainbow beads and colorful flag charms one of her grandchildren had made her. Her stout figure and muscular form defied the nearly sixty years she'd walked this earth. That, combined with the graying red hair she tucked away in a neat bun, reminded Owen of Danica Moore, a dragon who was one of the first people he'd met in Tearmann. Owen honestly thought the earth might give way if they ever happened to cross paths. He shuddered at the thought.

She started speaking as soon as he turned off the engine. "Food and your report are going to have to wait. Percill's here early. Give me the bag and head into the house. He's waiting in the kitchen."

Owen almost bit his tongue. "What?" he asked, stumbling off the motorcycle in his rush to run up to her. "He wasn't supposed to be here for another half hour."

"Something spooked him. He got here just before you did, ripping down my driveway like hell itself was at his heels. Scared poor Petunia something awful. We had to lock her in the basement." Mary, normally unfazed by anything short of the actual apocalypse, shot a worried look toward the kitchen window and reached out a shaking hand to take the saddlebags.

Owen passed them over without complaint and resisted the urge to shiver. If Mary and Samuel were the sort of people who faced down the end of the world without flinching, then Percill Wilson was the one who made the denizens of hell run back to their holes in terror. If something had spooked him, they should all be worried.

Percill was one of the battleborn, human soldiers and civilians who had been turned into fae during the Battle of Breckenridge by the queen over fifty years ago—the one and only time that anyone had managed to control the Changing process. No one knew how she'd done it, not even her, but by the time it was over, the Rocky Mountains had been on fire from Montana to New Mexico, and there weren't any humans left in a fifty-mile radius of the battle.

Where the fae may look strange, the battleborn were grotesque. They were something out of Owen's worst nightmares, distorted reflections of the fae and covered in sores and tumors. What was worse, the battleborn blamed the queen and the fae for what had happened to them. Even the friendliest of the battleborn were hesitant to associate with fae without being compensated for their time. Percill was not one of the friendly ones.

If all that weren't enough, Percill was a monster by anyone's standards. Technically, he was still human like Owen and didn't need blood, but he'd started drinking once he'd left safehouse duty and refused to stop. Even as the foreign blood rotted his body out from under him, even as everything that made him human was stripped away, he continued to indulge his thirst. To make matters worse, he'd fixated on Owen and lingered over their every interaction like he was savoring Owen's blood already.

His age and the blood had turned Percill into a walking corpse. His skin stretched over his bones, outlining each in all their grotesque glory. When he smiled, his fangs dug into his lower lip, already marked with the scars of hundreds of eerie grins. His bald head, with its sunken, burning eyes, completed the image of a body waiting for death to catch up.

Owen slowed his walk as he entered the house and tried to force his shoulders to relax. Meeting Percill was unpleasant for anyone, but especially for him. It was just his luck that the man refused to meet with anyone else. Apparently, they were "practically kin."

Owen thanked any deity that was out there that that wasn't true. Being that Owen was only a faeborn vampire—unturned and still human—and that Percill was battleborn, neither were really vampires.

"Ah, Mr. Williams," Percill said in a voice that glided over Owen like oil. "I was beginning to think you weren't coming. That would have been very rude after I went to all this effort to meet with you."

"Enough, Percill. We don't have time for your games, you came here for a reason, now spit it out," Owen said. Percill's thoughts slid against his own like a worm seeking entry through any crack they could find.

Battleborn vampires may not have been as powerful as the queen or even the weakest of the founders, but they had a broader reach. While the queen could control all fae, and the founders could control each member of their respective species, the most powerful of Percill's ilk only needed a single moment's distraction to dominate another's mind, whether they were human or fae.

Owen was one of the few immune to the effect. According to Beira, all vampires were, regardless of whether they'd been turned or not. That meant he was stuck with the job even if Percill hadn't insisted on making Owen his contact. Still, Owen was grateful that so few battleborn vampires had survived the Battle of Breckenridge. Percill was bad enough.

Percill frowned, but his will withdrew. "I have news for your leaders," he said, his tongue flicking out to lick the blood from his lips. "News of your enemies' movements, yes, and of the locations of your captive friends. News of SAFE and many important documents that our friends would like to see in your hands, yes?"

Owen almost swallowed his tongue, and the effort to keep from letting out a shout almost broke him.

SAFE was notoriously anti-fae. Half the illicit research facilities in the world that experimented on captive fae did so with their backing, and the rest hung on their every word. Tiffany had spent some time as one of their lab rats, and Owen wouldn't wish that fate on anyone, not even Percill.

The raid that saved her and her fellow captives was what led to the Battle of Tearmann, when SAFE had invaded and tried to destroy the fae capital. He'd never forgive them for what they'd done to her or anything that had followed.

Small fingers, so still and so white. Something beating that shouldn't be seen slowing to a stop, never to start again.

Taking a deep breath through his nose, Owen bit back a snarl and buried his hands in his pockets before Percill could see how they shook. Now was not the time to think about that.

Beyond what they'd done to his family, SAFE had taken prisoners, and it didn't take a genius to figure out what they wanted with them. Every mission for every away team since then was secondary to getting the prisoners back.

But he couldn't let Percill know that. If he did, Percill would raise his price, and the fae could scarcely afford to pay anything more.

"What do you want?" Owen asked in a cool voice. His nails dug into his palm, and the pain was enough to keep his mind clear.

"My price is but a pittance compared to what your people will gain." Percill's smile grew wider, and his fangs pricked his lip. "You will not refuse me this time."

Owen mentally cursed. "As I've told you a thousand times before," he said, pulling his nails free before he started to bleed, "as the queen has told you and the rest of your kind, there is nothing that is worth my blood."

Somehow, Percill and the other battleborn vampires had learned Owen was a faeborn vampire after the Battle of Tearmann, and they'd demanded he be turned or that they be given his blood. For some reason, they were convinced it would make them full vampires like the queen. The thought of one of that ilk by Beira's side—with access to the deep well of power that let her control the other fae and bound their fate to hers—made Owen consider allowing Beira to change him just to avoid the risk.

"You won't be swayed?" Percill asked, turning away from Owen. "Pity. The price will be higher now and more painful to your cause."

"What else do you want?" Owen asked through a forced smile.

"I want more freedom to travel in your lands when I wish to visit my people," Percill said as he turned back. He held up one hand and examined his poorly kept nails like doing so would convince Owen that his first request was the better one. "I also need a larger allowance for my work and that I be taken along when you attempt your rescue. The blood of the people there will sate me while you so cruelly deny me, Owen Williams."

He drew his lips back in a parody of a smile that didn't reach his silvery gray eyes. His last meal still stained his teeth red, and even from across the table, Owen could smell the rot on his breath. His voice was like ice, cold and unforgiving, but a lustful gleam in his eye whispered that he was already dreaming of the feast.

It made Owen sick to his stomach, but he couldn't let Percill know. Looking weak before a man like him didn't pay. Those who did wound up paying a price beyond their imagining.

"I have the authority to grant you safe travel and to increase your allowance," Owen said, swallowing back bile. "I can even get you on the team sent to rescue the captives, but I cannot authorize murder or the desecration of the dead. You'll have to take that request before the queen."

Percill slammed his hands down on the kitchen table hard enough for the wood under his hands to splinter and crack. "Have I not proven my worth? I brought you what you have been searching for these past months, and this is how I am repaid?"

Brown eyes met silver ones without blinking. Owen couldn't flinch, couldn't look away. "That's your choice. We can meet all your demands barring one right now, and a simple conversation will resolve the last one. You can take my offer or leave it."

Percill's features contorted into a sneer, but he nodded and removed his hands from the table. "Very well. I will need to personally deliver the information anyway," he said, picking splinters from his palms, "so the meeting will not take me too far out of my way."

Owen caught himself before he released a relieved sigh. "Excellent, will you be riding with us, or can you get there yourself?" He hoped that Percill wouldn't come with them. The flight would be unbearable enough without him staring at Owen all night.

"No, I have my own methods for crossing the border." He pulled on a jacket that was more rags than it was cloth. "I will meet you in the capital in two days' time. Prepare the queen for my arrival." Without waiting for Owen's response, he turned and stalked out of the kitchen.

CHAPTER TWO

In Which Owen Reports

"It is essential that the away teams are a branch of the military instead of an independent group. As a military branch, they'll have rules and a clear line of authority for oversight and accountability. We cannot afford the cost of running two separate organizations, not now. We don't have the support systems necessary to run them nor the time to develop them. Our people are dying out there and they need us. We can't abandon them while we fight over who controls what."
—Excerpt from the Council Transcript Archives

Samuel was waiting for Owen on a bench in the hall outside the kitchen. "What did he want, Owen?" he asked gruffly. His hands shook as he worked his whittling knife back and forth, carving feathers onto a bird. A bucket on the floor caught the shavings as he worked. "He's supposed to wait till nightfall. If someone saw him . . ."

"He had information that couldn't wait. Is everyone out in the barn?" Owen massaged the back of his neck. He'd left to pick up the medicines before dawn, and his body wasn't thanking him for the long, cold wait or the early morning.

Standing, Samuel set down his whittling kit and strode to the front window. Percill was already out of sight, but the dark cloud he had left behind still lingered. "Yes, Natalie called everyone in already. Mary is helping them pack up." He ran a hand through his already wild gray beard. If it weren't for the way he dwarfed Owen, Samuel wouldn't have looked out of place in a dwarf clan. "Whatever he had to say must've been important then, the way he came tearing in here."

"You have no idea how important it is," Owen muttered, yanking the front door open. "Believe me when I say the rush was warranted. Now, if you'll excuse me, I need to talk to Natalie about what Percill said."

"Tell her I'm going to check the perimeter again," Samuel said, following Owen out of the house. "If that blasted man got through without tripping any of the alarms, then who knows what state they're in."

"Will do."

Natalie had requisitioned a room in the back of the barn as her office, and that was where Owen found her. It might have been a tack room before the remodel, but the myriad of hooks and shelves now held the few supplies that hadn't been packed yet. Natalie sat at a small table in the back of the room, poring over a map of the area and comparing it to the papers she held in her hand.

"Corporal Williams reporting, Captain Freeman," Owen said, rapping his knuckles on the doorframe.

"Come in, Corporal Williams." Natalie glanced up, and her gills flared out as she peered into the hall behind him like she was worried he had brought the whole team with him. "Give me a moment."

Owen waited for her to finish organizing her papers—they'd only been here a week, he had no idea where she'd gotten so many—and nod before he spoke. Rushing Natalie was never beneficial. It only stressed her out, and her scales were practically falling off as it was.

"Captain," he said when she finally nodded, "as you know, the contact was late. Since the sighting of Private Evans . . ."

The debrief took Owen almost a half hour. He covered how many patrols he'd seen, why had it taken him so long to get back, had anyone recognized him . . . standard stuff mostly, but Natalie left no stone unturned. She didn't like that the contact had recognized him, but she had to admit he couldn't have done anything differently.

He didn't have a chance to tell her about Percill until the very end. Or maybe she intentionally hadn't brought it up, based on the look she gave him when Owen mentioned his name. No matter how important Percill's work was to the fae cause, he still unsettled everyone who knew him.

"Well then, what did he say?" Natalie snapped, rubbing the bridge of her nose when Owen took too long to answer. Her scales faded from their normal emerald to something closer to olive. "He looked excited when he came in, and that's never a good sign."

“He upset Samuel,” Owen said, conscious of the order of things. Natalie would be ecstatic about the captives, but if he didn’t get the other details out of the way first, they’d be forgotten. “Samuel was worried that if Percill was able to get past without setting off any of the alarms, someone else might as well, so he went to check the perimeter.”

“Well, he’s right to do so. Percill probably smashed some of the cameras out of spite.” Her thick hair spines bristled like a porcupine, never a good sign where sirens were concerned. Poison-tipped claws and trips to the sirens tended to follow. “Did he at least give a reason for it?”

“He knows where the last captives are being kept.”

Natalie’s hand slowly fell away from her forehead, and her eyes widened. Her worry and fear slid off her shoulders as her hands covered her mouth, and her gills flapped while she tried to catch her breath. “He knows . . . Where are they? What did he say? When can we get them?”

Owen’s grin couldn’t be contained any longer, Percill be damned. “He didn’t say, only that he had to drop off the information in person.”

“Are you sure he was telling the truth?” Natalie asked in a strangled voice. “He wouldn’t lie about this, would he? No, not if he’s willing to tell her himself. Even he wouldn’t dare lie to her.” She picked up her bag and darted to the door. “Come on, Williams, we need to leave now. We have to tell command. This is too important to wait for sundown, too important to wait at all.”

Owen hurried after her, hardly able to keep pace with her bounding steps. She sent him to gather anyone in the common areas while she helped pack the last of their things onto their dragon, Thaddeus Green. The living area wasn’t big enough to hold him, which restricted him to the unfurnished garage.

“Owen,” Jason called from the couch when Owen walked into the living room. “I was about to send out a search party when Mary told us you were here.”

Jason was a shade and one of Owen’s oldest friends among the fae. He’d been on the team that brought Owen’s family to Tearmann. If it weren’t for him, Owen would’ve been dead ten times over.

“Very funny,” Owen said, scanning the room. Fortunately, they’d cleaned a few nights ago, so there wasn’t much to do. “Get up. There’s been a change of plans. Is your ankle healed enough to search the lofts?”

Jason flopped back into his chair and groaned theatrically, somehow managing to knock his brown hair loose of its bun even as it slowly faded to match the pillows. "Oh, it's awful. The pain, you could never understand. I may never walk again."

"That's what you get for jumping off the roof." At any other time, Owen would've played along, but they didn't have time, and he had to bite back a few choice words.

"Hey, I slipped. I didn't jump."

"Whatever," Owen said over his shoulder as he gathered a load of blankets in his arms. Normally he'd fold them, but dumping them in the linen closet would have to do for now.

Owen spared a few seconds to make sure Jason was headed toward the loft before he finished checking the common areas. Jason had been acting strange since the Battle of Tearmann. Owen didn't know the whole story, but he'd heard Jason had lost someone. He didn't like to talk about it, and Owen hadn't wanted to ask.

Two of the civilians, Seung Choi and his wife, Henna, were in the kitchen finishing the dishes. They were quick to drop what they were doing when Owen told them to. They sprinted out, likely thrilled to finally be heading to the haven. Having someone you love turn suddenly and painfully into something not human had that effect on people. Owen knew from personal experience.

Owen met Jason as he was coming down from the loft, carrying a battered blanket that belonged to their trainee, a third-gen gryphon named John Evans. He'd been banished to the garage after some campers caught sight of him while he'd been hunting the other night. It was kind of Jason to grab it.

"Is that everyone?" Owen asked as they turned down the hallway leading to the garage.

"It should be," Jason said, pushing the garage door open. "The team's been sticking close to Thaddeus since Evans was seen. You're the only one who's been outside in the last three days."

Thaddeus was a third-generation dragon with scales as black as night. Mostly that meant he was the size of a house, strong enough to carry an elephant, and equipped with night camouflage most dragons would kill for. They were lucky the garage was massive—two stories tall and almost twice as wide with doors to match—or Thaddeus never would've been able to get inside in the first place. As it was, his wings scraped the walls, and his head bumped into the ceiling.

The harpies, Tony and Isaac, were attaching the gondola straps around Thaddeus's legs. They, like Jason, had been on the team that brought the Williams to Tearmann.

Tony was a first-generation harpy with all that entailed. From his tattered wings—monstrosities extending down from what used to be his arms—to his beak, which looked more like a large nose than anything found on a bird, nothing about him looked like it fit together.

Comparatively, Isaac, a third-generation harpy, was a work of art, like something that wouldn't be out of place in a fantasy novel from before the first fae were made. He had the advantage of proper arms, separate from his wings, and eyes that could pick out a field mouse scurrying to its hole from a half mile away.

Natalie shouted for the others to get moving, and Owen rushed over to help with the gondola.

The gondolas, a marvel of fae engineering, were each sculpted to hang under the stomach of a specific dragon. By nature, dragons and the foot-long spikes running down their spines weren't meant for saddles, and Thaddeus was no exception.

His gondola was long and deep, an oak-and-steel box that hovered barely a foot off the ground when Thaddeus stood to his full height. Ropes and chains wrapped around each leg, his neck, and twice around his middle on either side of his primary wings. If it wasn't secured tightly, he'd never get off the ground.

That meant that Owen could only really make sure the straps were in the right place. When he'd done what he could, the harpies finished fastening the straps. After they'd double- and triple-checked each joint, latch, and strap, they gave the signal to start loading.

Their original mission—prior to finding the Chois, including their son, Ryan, newly angelic and terrified—had been to pick up supplies. They'd been successful, too, so the ride home would be cramped.

They were down to ten boxes when Samuel ran into the garage like a pack of wolves were at his back, disheveled and out of breath. "Captain Freeman," he yelled as soon as he came within earshot, "you have to leave now; you have to go. Someone turned us in!"

CHAPTER THREE

In Which There Is a Familiar Flight

"We sent a team to bring in a centaur, a kid from Chicago. The team got him, but we couldn't get him out in time. The cops shot him while we were trying to get out of the city, and he bled out in the back of the van. I tried to make it better, make the pain go away, but I couldn't. There was too much. Damn it, we almost made it. If we had been quicker getting to the van, quicker packing up, quicker getting him in the first place, he'd have survived. If we can't protect our people, why do we fight in the first place?"
—Excerpt from the journals of Captain Zubin Khoroushi

For the long moment it took for Samuel's words to fade and disappear, no one moved or spoke. They'd been betrayed and turned in. It felt like all the air had been sucked out of the room, but as the last echoes faded away, they sprang into action. Now wasn't the time to panic.

Shoving his load at Jason, Owen scanned the garage for the Chois. Natalie had wanted them out of the way while they loaded—there they were. Mrs. Choi was smoothing out Ryan's feathers by the back door. Distantly, Owen could hear Natalie interrogating Samuel and yelling for the flyers to get in position.

They all had their parts to play right now, and his was making sure the civilians were in place.

Jason managed to cram the last of the boxes in a haphazard pile just inside the gondola at the same time Owen herded the Chois in. They'd need to organize the mess later, but they could do that in the air. There was no telling how long it would be before they could get another haul like this, and they couldn't afford to leave anything behind.

"Williams," Natalie roared, coming to a stumbling halt. "Get the gun and strap yourself onto Green. You're shotgun on this one."

Gritting his teeth, Owen swallowed his protest and shoved past her. He hated riding shotgun. It meant hours stuck outside in the cold and whatever weather they were cursed with, keeping watch, and providing cover fire. Unfortunately, he was a better shot than Jason, and the flyers had their hands full, so the job was his more times than it wasn't.

The gun, a bolt-action rifle they'd "liberated" on a supply run a few months ago, was always the last thing to be packed. They even had a gun cabinet for it this time, and Owen couldn't help but be thankful that Samuel hadn't locked it. He yanked it open, swung the gun over his shoulder, grabbed the ammunition bag, and then sprinted back to Thaddeus.

Ignoring the stitch in his side, he made a running jump, caught the bottom of the rungs to the shotgun saddle as the slam of the gondola door rang through the garage, and Thaddeus started to move. Gasping for breath, Owen pulled himself into the shell and tied himself into it. The last thing he wanted to do was fall off if Thaddeus made a bad turn.

With a great wail, the garage door jerked up, and Evans, Tony, and Isaac flew out before it was even halfway open. Swearing, Owen scrambled to fasten the last of the ties as Thaddeus shambled after them.

The trees flashed red and blue, and a chorus of earsplitting sirens shattered what should've been a quiet autumn evening. As Owen gripped the rifle, Thaddeus crouched down, and a SWAT van swerved into view.

The wind screamed past as Thaddeus leaped up, his beating wings a counterpoint to the pounding in Owen's ears. Catching his breath, Owen readjusted his goggles and thumbed off the safety. Armored and armed officers poured out the back of police vans, and they weren't even twenty feet off the ground yet.

Time froze as the two groups faced each other, the fae in the air and the humans on the ground. A single shot, skidding off the bottom of the gondola, broke the stalemate.

One shot turned into a hail, bouncing off Thaddeus's scales and the gondola like popcorn as the flyers danced in the air above them, and Owen squeezed off shots in between each beat of Thaddeus's wings.

In turns, Isaac, Tony, and Evans dive-bombed the crowd, grabbing weapons and knocking people over. In the chaos, Owen aimed for anyone who aimed anywhere but Thaddeus's nigh-impenetrable scales.

In theory, this wouldn't last long. The fae were in their element in the air, and even weighed down like he was, Thaddeus was a strong flyer. In a minute or so, he'd be out of range, and the other flyers could catch up to him without worrying about leaving the gondola exposed.

Theory rarely worked out in practice.

A scream, somehow louder than the gunfire and the sirens, broke through Owen's battle haze. He knew that voice.

Swinging his head around so fast his neck cracked, he found the source. One of the officers had a hand on Evans's foreleg and was pulling him down. His wings flapped heavily behind him, struggling to stay up even as other hands reached for his free legs to pull him farther down. Owen fired at the officer holding Evans without thinking.

The shot was enough for Evans to pull free with a scream that chilled Owen to the bone.

They needed to get out of here. Now, before the officers thought to aim for someone's wings.

Thaddeus seemed to agree, because he pulled himself higher and the others followed. Gradually, the farmhouse, the garage, and the chaos beneath them fell out of range of even Owen's long scope, and he packed the gun away. They'd managed to escape, but not without damage. "Natalie," he said into his long-neglected earpiece. "Evans was hit. We need to stop."

"We can't stop until we get to a safe spot, Owen. You know that. The police are bound to have alerted every department within a hundred miles, if not everyone from here to the border. Ask if he can latch onto the net. If he can't, see if Isaac is willing to hold you while you patch him up." Her voice crackled with static. In the background, the Choi family's worried voices mixed with Jason's much calmer one.

"Understood," he said through gritted teeth. Evans was barely keeping up. Owen might be able to get a bandage or a tourniquet on the wound, but his hands were no replacement for siren song, and that was a lot of blood. "I'll keep you informed."

Switching the earpiece off, Owen cupped a hand over his mouth and shouted for Isaac.

The wind stole half of his words, but enough of them got through for Isaac to shepherd Evans above Thaddeus. As they approached, Owen bit back a curse. Evan's foreleg was soaked in so much blood he couldn't have guessed the feathers there were white.

They needed to hurry.

The net dangling over Thaddeus's back and spines would hold him. It was supposed to hold all the flyers on longer journeys, but latching onto it was difficult in the best of situations. One wrong move could send the one trying to land tumbling off the dragon or, worse, onto the dragon's wings, injuring one or both of them.

Evans's first attempt missed—his claws skimmed the rope just as Thaddeus's updraft caught him. The second and third tries had the same result, with Evans getting caught in a strong gust of wind that knocked him off his path each time. Drops of red stained the leather and cloth he was trying to catch, drops that got bigger with each passing moment. The fourth try struck true, and the talons on Evans's good legs caught in the net.

Now it was Owen's turn. He grabbed the leather pouch with their first aid kit and fastened it to his belt before he untied himself. Shotgun couldn't always reach the gondola when injured, and they needed to be able to take care of themselves. He figured he'd be forgiven for using the supplies on someone else. He only hoped it had enough bandages.

He held his breath as he slowly freed his legs from the saddle—the only thing keeping him from falling off. Any time shotgun moved was a dangerous process. Theoretically, the harness would catch him if he fell. Realistically, Owen was not a small man, and he didn't have much faith in the ability of two small chains to hold his weight.

Owen went through the procedure as fast as he dared. His heartbeat roared in his ears so loud it almost drowned out the wind as he undid the safety chains. His hands shook so much that hooking the secondary safety chains took three tries, and it took four to unstrap his legs. A single mistake would send him plummeting to his death, and the harpies wouldn't be able to catch him.

When he was sure each line was in the right place, he climbed out of the saddle, gripped the safety chain so hard his knuckles turned white, and began the dangerous journey back to Evans.

Each step was a battle between him, the wind, and Thaddeus's every move. The smallest adjustment, the briefest change in the wind threatened to bowl him over. If there'd been room, he'd have crawled. Each precarious step threatened to send him tumbling down, but he couldn't stop.

As he drew closer to Evans, fear of something else entirely replaced his fear of falling. That was too much blood. It stained Evans's feathers and glistened on Thaddeus's scales in the dying sunlight. Too much blood.

Lifeless fingers. A beating muscle in a sea of red. A chorus that couldn't turn back time.

Unbidden, the chain slipped from Owen's fingers as he reared back. The world slowed, each breath and movement lasting a million years as Owen's focus narrowed to a growing sea of red.

Don't be sad; I'm going to see Mom now.

David had said that, his dying words. Only he wouldn't see Tiffany because she was still alive, and now Owen was falling and he couldn't breathe.

Take care of each other.

Take care of them? No, he couldn't. Not when he saw David each time Dorothy smiled at him, or Jen turned to laugh with someone who wasn't there anymore. He can't, he can't, he can't—

The chain held even though his feet didn't, and Owen couldn't help but be grateful for the stinging of his cheek as he pulled his face from Thaddeus's side. The fall had shocked sense back into him. Now he needed to keep it there.

His hands shook and his heart stuttered, but Owen crossed the narrow distance left between them as fast as he could. His stomach churned as he approached, the running wind not quite enough to steal away the growing smell of fresh blood.

The relief of fastening the third safety chain gave him enough peace of mind to properly focus on the quietly sobbing and bleeding gryphon that was waiting for him. "Evans," he shouted over the wind, looking anywhere but at the wound. "Evans, let me see the wound. I can help."

Evans shook his head, tears shining in his eye for a fraction of a second before the wind tore them away. "Owen, get Natalie," he gasped. "I need her. My arm, it hurts."

"Natalie can't get up here, Evans, and we can't land. Let me look at it, I might be able to stop the bleeding." Owen ran a hand through Evans's feathers and swore. Evans was going into shock.

"No, I need Natalie," Evans said, sobbing while pulling his injured leg closer. "She can fix me—"

"Evans, I know you're scared, but Natalie can't climb out here. I can patch you up enough for her to look at it when we land, but for now we have to stop the bleeding." The wind was another concern Owen hadn't considered. It wasn't a problem for Owen now that he was fastened into position, but if he didn't tie Evans down, he was going to fall off. His grip was going slack already.

Evans shook his head again, his eyes shut tight against the pain. The blood dripped through Evan's talons, staining the white feathers of his foreleg red and clumping in the black fur on his chest.

"Evans, please," Owen yelled, "I promise we can fix this, you need to let me see it."

Evan's eyes snapped open, and the wind stole his tears away. Owen's heart caught in his chest. Blue eyes, David's eyes. He had to . . . He needed to . . .

Take care of them.

Slowly, Evans extended his injured leg, exposing the wound in all its bloody glory. A knife had slashed down his arm, leaving a laceration that stretched from his shoulder past his elbow. Blood-soaked feathers dripped down onto talons barely holding him in place.

Owen breathed words of comfort as he examined the wound and tried not to let memory overwhelm him. It was deep. Too deep. Flashes of white mixed with the red, and the odds that nothing vital had been hit were slim—but he couldn't let Evans know that. He was scared. Owen had to help him.

Bloody hell, he wished Natalie were here. The medical training that sirens received was better than his field training, even if she wasn't good at healing.

Hands shaking, Owen opened the first aid kit and pulled out a sealed vial. With luck, it would keep the wound free of infection until Natalie or, better yet, one of the capital's healers could look at it. He couldn't waste a single drop, not with a wound this size.

He soaked the bandages with the ointment and wrapped the injured leg as tight as he dared once he'd packed the wound. Pressure and packing were the way to go, and they had to keep the wound closed. It was the only way to stop the bleeding. Blood soaked through the first layer of bandages and then the second. He had enough bandages to wrap the wound four times, and still the white turned red.

But it would have to do for now. Evans was on the verge of unconsciousness and about to fall off Thaddeus. Already, his claws were loose, and his back leg had fallen away completely.

Owen used all but two of the seven straps meant to secure passengers to hold Evans in place. Tony and Isaac would have to be content with one apiece.

When he had satisfied himself that Evans was as safe as he could be, Owen began the slow journey back to the shotgun saddle, pausing every few steps to look back. He wanted to stay, to keep helping, but he couldn't. The first aid kit was almost empty, and he had a job to do.

"Natalie," Owen shouted into his earpiece after he had tied himself back in his saddle, "Evans's injury is more severe than we thought. We need to stop."

His earpiece crackled, the sound barely louder than the wind. "We're going to be airborne for a few hours. How bad is it exactly?"

"He lost a lot of blood. I got it bandaged and put the ointment on, but I'm not sure it was enough. He passed out as I was strapping him in."

"We can't stop. Keep an eye on him, and I'll let you know when the police chatter dies down enough for us to land. Tell me if something changes."

Owen shut off his earpiece and swore loudly as he glanced behind him again. The light of the setting sun lit Evans up in a way that might have been beautiful if it hadn't highlighted the bloodstains. He forced himself to look away. In a few hours, they would stop, and Natalie would look at Evans. Just a few more hours.

***

Owen's thick jacket and face mask were both coated in a thin layer of hoarfrost by the time they finally landed in a forested area somewhere in northern Minnesota. The sun had set two hours ago, and with it came a biting wind that sucked all the warmth from Owen's bones.

Tingling and numb, Owen's legs gave way beneath him when he slipped off Thaddeus, and he crumpled to the ground. Pins and needles attacked his fingers as he tried to breathe life back into them.

Natalie met Owen when he stumbled off Thaddeus. "Where is he? Do we need a sling?" she asked, each word clipped and harsh.

The harpies had started unstrapping Evans as soon as Thaddeus's wings folded in, and Owen pointed toward them without speaking. Distantly, he knew he should be more concerned, but the wind had ripped away all feeling an hour ago.

"By the queen's throne," Natalie whispered. Her scales faded as the blood drained away, and her hands came up to cover her mouth.

Owen looked up—and bit back a curse. The harpies had gotten Evans down, and he looked half a corpse. Fresh blood painted Tony's gray feathers almost black as he frantically tried to retie bandages that had come undone. They needed to get Evans inside, now.

Adrenaline flooded Owen's limbs, pushing away the exhaustion and cold like the sun burning off the fog as he leaped to his feet. Natalie caught his arm, dragging him back to her before he got more than two steps away.

"This is beyond what I can heal by myself," she snapped, shoving him toward the gondola. "Tell the others to hurry; we need to get him to Tearmann." Owen forgotten, she sprinted to Evans's side, already singing at the top of her lungs.

A part of him wanted to go help with Evans anyway, but he forced himself to move the other way. Natalie and the harpies were stronger than him. He'd just get in the way, he told himself as he stumbled to the gondola, his legs choosing now to remember they were half frozen.

With bundles of toilet paper in hand, the Chois were exiting the gondola when he reached it. Mr. Choi caught Owen's arm as he tried to squeeze past.

"Excuse me, sir, but why have we stopped?" he asked, his eyes darting into the darkness beyond Owen's shoulder when a shriek cut the still night air.

"Our gryphon was injured," Owen said gruffly, pulling his arm free. It wasn't a very good explanation, but they'd see soon enough, and Owen didn't have the time or energy to talk when the warm gondola was right there.

Jason was in the process of stacking boxes on the left side of the gondola, presumably to make room for Evans. He looked about as tired as Owen felt.

"Captain wants you—" Exhaustion cracked Owen's jaws open in a yawn halfway through, and shivers rendered the rest almost incomprehensible. "Wants you up top, ASAP."

Nodding, Jason set his load on an already precarious pile, then grabbed a thick fur coat and a pair of goggles from a hook on the far wall. "Understood," he said with a tight, tired smile. "I'll see you when we land."

With Jason gone, Owen turned his attention to the mess he'd left behind. Despite the unsteady nature of the piles, most of the work had already been done. The only thing left—beside straightening the piles—was to raise the bench on the right side of the gondola, which took seconds.

Less than a minute after Jason had left, Natalie threw open the double doors, still singing a wordless tune under her breath. Shooting Owen a grateful look, she led Evans in and settled him on the ground near the medicine cabinet.

He guessed the rest was up to him. Despite the ache in his bones—each step its own burning agony as he regained feeling—and the nausea twisting his stomach, he darted out of the gondola.

Mr. and Mrs. Choi were arguing in quick, clipped Korean under a tree close to the gondola—reluctant, even now, to get too far from their saviors—and their raised voices made Owen's head pound.

He sympathized with them. Really, he did. It hadn't been that long ago that he'd been in their shoes, but there wasn't time for this.

Taking a deep breath, he grabbed Mr. Choi's shoulder and spun him around. "Get back inside," he ordered in a hoarse voice, and glared when Mr. Choi looked like he might protest. Ordinarily, he'd be kinder about it, but ordinarily they didn't have someone bleeding to death in the back of the gondola. "We're leaving in two minutes."

Sometimes Owen wished he had Jason's or Isaac's ease with the civilians, but a single, well-placed glare did more to stop people arguing at short notice than a hundred jokes. Seeing how Mr. Choi ushered his family back to the gondola without argument, a little harshness was fine by Owen.

The harpies and Jason didn't need any directing. Experience and worry directed their steps, and they were already in position when Owen turned around.

From there, Owen's exhaustion took over, and one thing blended into another. Natalie's voice—more useful for hypnosis than healing—bled into his subconscious like blood in water, broken only by screams that barely managed to scrape the haze.

He drifted, a leaf somehow finding peace on turbulent water. Safe. Warm. Calm.

"—ral Williams." A voice, distant as a breeze, briefly broke through the buzz between his ears. "Corporal—hear me?"

Gasping, Owen's eyes shot open and he fell forward. His bad leg—never the same since he'd broken it—spasmed from the new pressure. The last of Natalie's song hovered at the edge of his hearing, tempting him back into its arms with promises of ease and comfort that almost broke him.

"Corporal Williams," a soft voice whispered, shaking the last of the song free from his head.

A matching hand, gentle and careful, settled on his shoulder, and he forced his head up. Mrs. Choi crouched in front of him, her eyes darting between him and Evans, whose soft weeping still broke the silence every few seconds.

"Sorry," he whispered hoarsely, pushing her hand away as subtly as he dared. Each move and sound, from the drag of cloth on his skin to the quiet creak of the gondola around him, scraped against his nerves like nails on a chalkboard. "Is everything okay?"

Mrs. Choi huffed. "I was about to ask you that." Her eyes lingered more on Evans with each pass, roving in an almost clinical way.

Owen didn't want to look. He knew what he'd see. Bloody bandages. Natalie slowly losing her voice. Evans lying still and lifeless.

"How was he hurt?" Mrs. Choi asked. She looked a half step from going over to check herself. "What's she doing?"

Owen bit back a sigh. "A knife. He caught it in his foreleg during the escape," he said quietly. He didn't want to think about this. "Natalie is trying to sing it shut."

She hummed, harmonizing with Natalie in a way Owen doubted she intended. "It doesn't look like she's having much luck." She didn't seem to be talking to Owen anymore, muttering more to herself than anyone else. "A wound like that will need stiches, maybe even surgery."

Owen tilted his head, biting back a caustic remark. "Sounds like you have experience here. You a medic?"

She shrugged, still not looking at Owen. "A vet," she said finally, her fingers twitching as if to grab tools. "I specialize in exotic and large animals."

The breath caught in Owen's throat, and he struggled to swallow around it. "Can you help him?" he asked quietly. She wasn't a doctor, but Evans wasn't human.

The barest movement, a fraction of a nod, had him on his feet, ignoring the ache in his bones, and over to Natalie. He didn't look down, not once, as he relayed the news to Natalie. He couldn't.

Blood on white sheets, the smell filling his nose, staining everything—

Taking a deep breath, Owen signaled Mrs.—No, Dr. Choi—to come forward with a shaking hand. "What do you need?"

CHAPTER FOUR

In Which Things Go from Bad to Worse

"Are you sure we can't do something to make the gondolas more maneuverable? This design leaves them too open to attack. Dani said that most of the dragons couldn't even roll in flight with them on. Also, I know you said that these are only supposed to be for cargo, but can't we put in harnesses? Dragons can't exactly walk into the grocery store and ask for ten pounds of potatoes."
—Excerpt from the letters of Rick Burns, Lord Fafnir

After a while, even Dr. Choi admitted they couldn't do much more. Natalie's singing had managed to make the wound shallower, and Dr. Choi stitched up what was left. After giving Evans enough painkillers to down a horse, they went their separate ways. Natalie retreated to a corner near where Evans had curled up like a cat, still humming under her breath, and Dr. Choi to the warmth and safety of sleep in her husband's arms.

Owen wanted to sleep. His every muscle ached, screaming with each movement, and a headache ripped his concentration to shreds, but every time he closed his eyes, all he saw was a sea of red that chased him back to reality.

The angel boy, Ryan, was perhaps as eager for a distraction from his exhaustion as Owen was and provided a ready stream of questions whenever Owen had the energy to focus on them.

In a way, he reminded Owen of his own kids. The Change wasn't easy on anyone. It was painful, literally tearing the body apart from the molecules up and rebuilding them as it saw fit. Arthur, a siren, and Jen, a werewolf, had struggled for weeks after they'd Changed—fighting with new muscles and limbs that didn't fit on their bodies—to relearn how to navigate an already strange world.

Angels had it worse than most. Werewolves might have to cover their noses in crowds, and sirens might need to watch their voices, but angels became walking weapons from the time their wings sprouted to the day they died. Their bodies produced energy they could manipulate and throw, destroying buildings and lives if they weren't careful.

But it was his wings that were bothering Ryan the most. No matter how he sat or lay down, he couldn't move without them brushing against something and triggering a small light show, which played havoc with Owen's headache.

Ryan had wanted to try flying to see if that would exhaust them enough that he could rest, but the harpies put a firm stop to that. Ryan was, as Tony put it, still a fledgling with down-covered wings. His wings wouldn't be strong enough for flight for weeks. Even then, he was too young to fly alone.

Owen was happy to distract him. He told stories about Tearmann and the people who lived there, about his own journey north and his children, and about what it meant to be an angel. About how the Chois would travel to the Nead, the angel nest, after they were processed in Tearmann so Ryan could learn to control his abilities. Anything and everything he could think of that would lessen the fear Ryan was feeling. Once, a lifetime ago, Jason had done the same for Owen's children.

Halfway through a story that had Ryan failing to muffle his laughter, Thaddeus dove and threw his passengers and anything not nailed down around the gondola. Owen's breath exploded out of his chest as he slammed into the far wall, narrowly avoiding crushing Ryan. Fighting to breathe, Owen wrapped one arm around Ryan, pulled him close, and flung the other out. He latched onto something—a cabinet, a net, in the chaos he couldn't tell—and held on as tightly as he could.

"Jason," Natalie yelled, barely audible over the screaming and the blood rushing in Owen's ears like a tsunami. "What's happening?"

Jason's voice crackled through his earpiece in the same moment a tight swerve almost ripped Owen free of his perch.

"—border guard helicopter. Hold on, y'all, things are gonna get rough!" Jason swore, his voice almost three octaves higher than normal.

If he'd had the breath, Owen would've sworn too. No one was supposed to be here. They'd been told it was clear. Gritting his teeth, he anchored his feet against the wall and held on for dear life.

None too soon, Thaddeus started spinning. Next to Owen, Evans feebly held onto one of the cabinets with all four legs, Natalie clinging to his chest as she desperately shoved flying luggage away before it hit him. Somewhere behind Owen, the Chois begged for answers in a tearful mix of Korean and English.

Thaddeus leveled out—Owen let himself hope they'd escaped—only to start zigzagging a half second later, up and down, left and right. Through the thick walls, the beat of helicopter blades and gunfire grew louder.

By now, Jason's voice was a continuous hum in Owen's ear, accompaniment to the screams. Tony and Isaac were trying to distract the soldiers in the helicopter, darting as close as they dared before pulling back, always moving.

Owen didn't envy Jason. At these speeds he could barely move, let alone fire. The only thing he could do was watch.

"I can see the border tower, Nat. We can make it," Jason said over the screaming of the wind. "We're maybe ten minutes out if we can hold them off—wait, no, Isaac, don't—" A scream, so loud Owen didn't need his earpiece to hear it, almost deafened him. "Natalie, he's rushing the helicopter, Isaac, no—"

An explosion shook the gondola with a fury that knocked Owen loose of his perch. The world dissolved into agony as Thaddeus released an unholy screech and fell.

***

As he levered his eyes open, the bitter taste of iron coated Owen's teeth, weighing down his tongue like a magnet and pouring down his throat with all the force of a waterfall. Thick cloth choked each breath until spots danced behind his closed eyes, and he strained for air.

No, not cloth. Fur.

The fur shifted beneath him as a shuddering breath wracked its body, and a familiar voice whimpered. Evans, he was lying on Evans.

They weren't falling anymore.

Thaddeus's flight was level, albeit shaky. Each slow flap—perhaps minutes, perhaps hours apart—came with agonizing groans and labored breathing that made the gondola creak and crack.

As the world blinked into focus, the bits of Owen's mind running loose found their way home. He pushed himself up and swallowed bile. The room spun, and each swaying bounce sent it tumbling again.

After a heartbeat's fear of blindness, he realized that the lamps were out. A faint light filtered through a porthole, highlighting just enough that he silently cursed. The gondola was in shambles. Books, medicines, foodstuffs, and god alone knew what else covered the floor, loose of the boxes and cabinets that should've been their prisons. His jeans were soaked, and he didn't want to think about what he'd been lying in.

Natalie emerged from a pile of detritus by the door like a whale breaching the surface. "Is everyone all right?" she asked in a ragged voice.

Owen's answer got caught in his throat, tangled in flesh suddenly dry as sandpaper, as Dr. Choi and Ryan made agreeing noises. Dimly, he waved in a way he hoped looked affirmative as he forced himself to his knees.

"What happened?" he managed to ask. One hand tenderly probed the back of his head, and he couldn't help a relieved sigh when it came back clean.

"Owen, thank god." Natalie shoved his hand aside and yanked his head forward to look for herself. "Good, you're not bleeding. Check on Evans while I try to raise Jason. He's not answering his comms." Then she was gone as suddenly as she'd arrived.

Owen blinked after her. She hadn't answered his question. He fought through the fog lingering over his thoughts to decipher her words. A sound from behind him, a mix of a groan and whimper, connected the last of the dots.

Right, Evans. He'd probably banged his leg into something when they were falling.

Turning sent his stomach into a violent roil that he failed to control. Wiping the vomit from his lips, he hoped he hadn't been sick on anything important and reached toward Evans.

His fingers skimmed over what might have been a leg and came away wet. Bringing them to his nose confirmed what his sinking heart already suspected. Blood. Fresh, too. A popped stitch?

Biting back a curse, he swallowed back fresh bile, levered himself to his feet, and pointedly ignored the way his jeans clung to his skin. It was too dark to see properly. He needed to relight the lamp.

As if conceding to the anxiety slowly flooding his veins, his stomach settled. His foot slid through something sticky, and his heart sank lower. *Don't think about it,* he told himself. The lamp, he needed to light the lamp.

Not for the first time, he sent thanks to any deity listening that this was one of the newer gondolas, and he didn't need to worry about finding a match in this mess. It took a few fumbling tries, but the ignitor eventually caught the wick and released a flood of light.

As fast as he dared, Owen turned back to Evans and almost swallowed his tongue. Whatever he'd expected—a popped stitch, a fresh injury, or a bloody beak—this was worse.

A pool of drying blood had formed around Evans and stuck his fur into chunks. Owen didn't need to look down to know what color his jeans had turned. The trail of red footprints leading right to him was answer enough.

Miraculously it looked like some of the bandages had escaped the bloodbath—

Bile rose in his throat, and if he'd had anything left, he'd have vomited again. That was bone. He lurched back, his foot catching on a half-shattered crate, and collapsed to the ground. *Blood and white and things that shouldn't be seen. How could anyone lose that much blood and survive?*

"Natalie," he whispered, each breath as loud as gunfire in his ears. *David's battered body, blood staining white sheets.*

"Natalie," he said again. *The choir dying off, the echo fading with a final breath drawn much too early.*

"Natalie, get over here." Even as the words left his mouth, he knew he should be moving too. They'd need bandages and medicine, and Natalie wouldn't be able to stop singing to search for them. He should move, should push away the blood pounding through his ears, should look away from the nauseating mix of white and red and black.

But his limbs shook so much they wouldn't have been able to hold him up even if he did manage to find his feet. Black spots swirled in his vision as his lungs screamed for air he couldn't find amid the blood choking him.

Natalie pushed past him, Dr. Choi on her heels. They kept saying things, their requests turning into demands quieter than the roar between Owen's ears. Eventually, even that was drowned out when Evans's quiet whimpers turned into deafening screams.

He was awake, the small protection of unconsciousness taken from him with nothing offered in its place. He was awake and Owen wasn't doing anything.

Somehow, in between the roaring and fire now filling his veins, Owen regained his feet and stumbled toward them. Natalie's sung demands, a coarse melody broken every time Evans moved, and Dr. Choi's barked ones meant nothing. Owen collapsed by Evans's head, away from the break, and stroked the feathers there.

Words poured out of his mouth, empty promises that everything would be all right. They would be home soon. Someone was coming to help. Evans looked at him with David's eyes and begged him to stop the pain.

Blood on white sheets.

He needed to help.

Pumping that he shouldn't see, which finally stopped and was somehow worse.

He didn't even realize he was singing until halfway through the second verse. A lullaby. David's favorite.

Oh, the Spring, it is a coming,
And the trees are softly blooming,
And the wild mountain thyme blooms along the purple heather.
Will ye go, laddie, go? And we will all go together
To pick wild mountain thyme all along the purple heather.
Will ye go, laddie, go?

Evans's thrashing slowed, and his screams turned into quiet sobs as Owen sang and combed his fingers through his knotty and ratted fur. Natalie joined in with a mismatched harmony, faltering over the unfamiliar words whenever Dr. Choi nudged her for help.

Owen was so consumed by the melody, by each slow breath Evans took under his fingers, that he didn't realize Thaddeus had landed.

***

Blinking in the early afternoon light, Owen shivered as he stumbled outside like a drunken man. Natalie had all but thrown him out once they'd stopped the bleeding, and he'd barely had time to change. It might not be winter yet, but blood-soaked denim wasn't the most insulating fabric, and the wind was happy to leach the heat from his bones.

Somehow, his heart sank lower when he got his first look at Thaddeus. If he'd been less exhausted, he'd have leaped into action, but his legs shook with the effort of supporting him. As it was, he let loose a string of the foulest curses he knew and stumbled forward.

There would be no recovery from this. Thaddeus's left wing was a ruin that lay on the ground like a rag. The membrane hung in tattered strands between two of the digits, and there were more holes large enough to stick a hand through than Owen could count. Somehow, Thaddeus was still standing, but judging from the way his limbs shook, he wouldn't be for much longer. They needed to get the gondola off before he collapsed on top of it.

Jason was already hard at work, fighting with a strap that had gotten tangled, and Tony was at his side. Blood and chunks of unimaginable things covered both of them.

Owen joined them, slipping under Thaddeus to undo what he could. The harness was a loss at this point, so he didn't care that he had to cut a few straps when blood made his hands too slippery to undo them. The equipment could be replaced; Thaddeus could not. They had to get it off him so he could rest, so they could treat the wound before it worsened.

With the last strap undone, Thaddeus stumbled away and collapsed. The impact brought Natalie out of the gondola, still wiping blood from her hands, and her cursing made Owen's look like something a child would say. Distantly, Owen noticed that dying patches of grass poked through the holes. Bits of yellow and green amid the red and black.

Even with Dr. Choi's help, there wasn't much Natalie could do beyond stitching the smaller holes closed and hoping the bleeding would stop. The average healer was good for patching cuts and repairing broken bones, but even the best couldn't regrow something that wasn't there anymore. Natalie was far from the best.

As Natalie's raspy and brittle voice drifted around the clearing, Owen examined their surroundings. He couldn't do anything else, and no one could blame him if he didn't want to look at Thaddeus any longer.

If he'd been hoping for a village nearby, he was sorely disappointed. They'd landed in a clearing by a fifty-foot cliff surrounded by dense pine trees. In the distance, maybe three miles by his guess, he could barely make out the border tower. His heart sank.

There weren't any villages within thirty miles of the border. Not since SAFE destroyed the village by the border tower at least. They were on their own.

Sucking in a breath, Owen turned and started back toward the others. Jason was camped out a few feet from the gondola, angrily muttering to himself as he dug through the emergency bag. Swearing, he threw it to the ground as Owen walked up.

"What's the plan?" Owen asked, wiping his bloody hands on his jeans.

Jason rubbed a hand over his eyes and swore again. Parts of his face and hands flickered and disappeared with each movement. "Someone has to get help," he muttered, his voice as rough as sandpaper. Tracks in the blood and dust streaked down his face. "The radio didn't survive the crash, and Tony doesn't want to leave the gondola without a flyer if someone pursues us over the border."

"What about Isaac?" Owen asked, glancing toward the gondola as he rubbed his hands together. Tony was perched on top, squinting into the distance like he might see something new.

"What do you mean?" Jason asked in a level voice. His hands came up, wrapping in Owen's coat and squeezing. Then fire roared in his voice, rage barely contained by the thinnest veneer of civility. "What do you mean 'What about Isaac'?"

Clearly, Owen was missing something. He strained at the foggy edges of the day, searching for information that slipped away whenever he thought he had a firm grip on it.

"I haven't seen him since we landed. The last thing I remember is falling," Owen said quickly. His head ached, pounding like even thinking about the last hour had opened the wound again. "I remember hearing his name, but I got knocked out."

The fire bled from Jason's voice, leaving a dumb struck ruin in its wake. "She didn't tell you?" he asked in a shaky voice. His hands fell to his side, and for a moment Owen was worried Jason was about to fall over.

"Tell me what?" Ice crept into Owen's limbs, a cold far worse than a thousand hours in the shotgun saddle. "What happened?"

They'd all been screaming. No one was supposed to be at this part of the border, it was supposed to be clear. Jason had . . . Jason had said . . . Isaac wouldn't . . .

"No," Owen whispered. His knees crumpled beneath him while the ground rushed up to meet him. "He . . ."

"He didn't make it."

CHAPTER FIVE

In Which Owen Meets the Locals

"Tearmann says there's no guarantee they'll be able to get soldiers out here if something happens, so they want the head of each village to put together a militia to do their job for them. Sounds like a load of crock to me—what are they using all those dragons for? Well, I can't do anything about what the capital can or can't do, but I'll get started on the team. Maybe they can do something about our predator problem while they're at it."
—Excerpt from the journals of Georg Steensen, head of Glenhold Village

Snow muffled everything. Sounds, colors, feelings. One inch became two and then three, drowning out the world underneath a blanket of white.

And Owen walked, following Jason's slowly disappearing tracks. Jason was more familiar with fae trail signs, so he got to lead. For once, he was disturbingly visible in his bright orange coat. In a choice between freezing to death in the October chill or using his blending to scout unseen, the decision had been easy.

Natalie had sent them to find a supply cache Jason swore used to be at the base of the border tower. She'd managed to stem Thaddeus's bleeding, but they were almost out of bandages, and every stray wind was a threat that might get it started again. Normally, they'd send a flyer, but Tony was headed east to find help, and since Isaac . . . Well, they didn't have another option.

Owen's heart stuttered as the cutting loss ripped him open again. He still couldn't believe it. Isaac had . . . Owen had known him for almost a year. He'd been on the team that had taken the Williams to Tearmann. They'd been on dozens of missions together. They'd been friends.

Shaking his head, Owen took a deep breath that chilled his lungs. He couldn't think about that now. He needed to keep moving. The storm was getting thicker, and if he wasn't careful, he'd lose track of Jason entirely.

As if summoned, Jason and his bright orange coat popped out of the blizzard to Owen's left, and Owen's foot caught a hidden root.

"Bloody hell, Jason, I've told you not to do that," Owen snapped, rubbing his chest to calm his pounding heart. His foot twinged. Blast, he could've broken his ankle. Jason should know better than to surprise him.

Jason shrugged without looking at Owen, scanning the woods around them like he expected someone to jump out at him for once. "Sorry, I forgot. I thought I'd tell you that I recognize some of the landmarks—"

"What about them?" Owen snapped, keeping his eyes firmly fixed in front of him. He didn't want to look at Jason right now. Jason didn't seem to care about Isaac being gone or the whole mission turning on end. Besides, they shouldn't stop moving. Even if the temperature wasn't rapidly dropping, they didn't have time to waste.

"We're near the ruins of Glenhold," Jason replied as if Owen hadn't spoken. "The cache should be just outside the town. That's about a half mile away." He paused, tilted his head, and cast a sidelong glance at Owen. "What's wrong with you?"

"What's wrong with me?" His jaw dropped, and anger and grief seethed in his stomach. He spun to face Jason, venom dripping from his stomach. "What's wrong with you?"

Owen should stop, but the fire burning inside him raged with a furor that threatened to consume him. What right did Jason have to act like Isaac's death meant nothing? He'd been friends with Isaac's family for almost a decade.

"You're just—working. Like it never happened, like everything is fine," Owen said, snarling. His fists shook, and it took everything he had to keep them at his side. "Doesn't Isaac deserve more than that?"

The breath exploded from Owen's lungs as Jason slammed him into a pine with enough force to knock the snow and ice off the branches onto them.

"Don't you dare say that," Jason hissed. His hand tightened on Owen's jacket, closing so tight the fabric tore. "You don't know loss like

I do." His voice dropped to a harsh whisper as a strange light burned behind his eyes. "I've been losing people for longer than you've been alive." Jason's voice shook, cracking and breaking as though struggling to hold back a flood. The fist not pinning Owen to a tree crashed into the wood by his head with a loud thud. "My parents, my fiancé, my friends—everyone who ever loved me is gone." He swallowed and blinked rapidly. "But I can't let that hold me back. There are people counting on us, and I won't fail them too."

As suddenly as it had come, the fire faded away, trapped behind a wall of ice, and he dropped Owen. "Come on, the ruins should be this way."

***

Owen and Jason walked in silence, the ghost of their argument hanging in the air between them. As they drew closer to what was left of Glenhold, small signs of its former inhabitants appeared around them. A fence here, a well there, and the remains of a charred farmhouse. The trees thinned, and Jason found where the road used to be. Snow-covered as it was, walking along it was easier than continuing through the forest and tripping over every root from here to the capital.

Owen shivered when they passed through the outer walls and into the village proper. He'd never been one to believe in ghost stories, but walking here was enough to make him wonder.

Owen had never been to Glenhold before its destruction—or any of the border villages—but after SAFE's invasion and the subsequent Battle of Tearmann, it had become something of a rallying cry. It had started as a semipermanent camp for the border guards but grew as guards settled in the area with their families. Those families had built the colorful cabins that filled the village, which in turn became traditional for aboveground settlements all over the haven.

The burned husks of those cabins stared at them as they walked down the main road. Faded paint peeled from buildings that were once well tended, doors hung from broken hinges, and everywhere the belongings of the former inhabitants poked out of the snow.

A doll dangled by her apron straps in a window, an assortment of gardening equipment leaned in a line against a low wall, and sun-bleached washing hung on lines, waiting eternally to be taken in. Shattered windows glared out accusations to any who passed. *Why didn't you save them, why did they have to die, why, why, why—*

The wind blew through holes in the walls and brought with it the faint scent of ash. Like a whisper on the breeze, Owen could almost hear what the village had sounded like before everything had gone wrong. Beyond the red house on the corner, he could've sworn he saw a woman's face and—over there, by the well, an elven child disappeared between blinks. The trees that grew in a circle around the town moved against the wind, and occasionally the air in the distance shimmered like a mirage.

"Jason," he whispered. His fingers inched toward his pistol as he squinted toward the trees. "I don't think we're alone."

To his great relief, Jason was also glancing around. "I think you're right," he said in a low voice, laying a hand on the knife sheathed on his belt. "If it's who I think it is, things are about to get a lot more difficult."

Instead of calling out for whoever was following them, Jason darted off the main road. Cutting through what used to be a garden, he headed for the outskirts of town at a clipped pace Owen's numb legs could barely match.

"Jason," Owen hissed through gritted teeth when he caught up. "What's going on? Who is it?"

"Someone with a very good reason to be angry at the capital, and with me in particular," he answered, scarcely louder than a whisper. The rustling from the trees was louder here now that the wind had died down. "Jedidiah Ashwind, my old general. I didn't think he was still in the area."

Owen's breath caught in his chest. "Can't he help us?" he asked in an equally hushed voice. Fae helped each other. "He must have some way to contact the capital or one of the other villages."

"No," Jason said, a sneer curling his lips. "He made that clear the last time I saw him." He tensed once they reached the far side of the village. The trees there pushed up against the border wall like they were the only thing holding it up, and hung over it like storm clouds. "I just hope he'll let us access the cache without raising a fuss."

Owen nearly stopped, the breath caught in his lungs as a knot settled into his stomach. The fae didn't turn their backs on each other. Even sworn enemies would offer each other a place at their fire in winter.

"Why?" he whispered, the word escaping in a puff of air that barely carried it forward. The back of his neck prickled as they clambered through a gap in the wall, and he ignored how the branches above them rustled.

Jason's voice dropped so low Owen could barely hear it. "Most of his family died when Glenhold fell." A crash in the distance—possibly a falling branch or a bit of the ruins giving in to the elements—had his hands twitching on his knife, but they kept searching. "He blames the capital for not having the troops here to stop it."

Jason let out a sarcastic little cheer and darted forward, cutting off any further questions. Dropping to the ground with more energy and ease than Owen had been able to muster for hours, Jason wriggled into a narrow gap in the roots of a towering pine.

A root cave. Owen shouldn't have been surprised; trolls had settled the area after all. They'd built shelters into the roots of half the trees around Tearmann. Huffing quietly, he stomped his feet and hoped Jason hurried. He might be kitted out for the cold but that didn't mean he wanted to stay out any longer than he had to, especially with another storm coming.

Judging by Jason's swearing and panting, it was slowgoing. Owen, idle outside the cave, shivered and debated helping, but if Jason was struggling to move, there was no way Owen would fit in there. Those caves weren't built for someone his size.

The wind chose that moment to pick up, finding each crack and break in his gear and leaching the heat away. The creaking and groaning branches provided an eerie countermelody to Jason's cursing.

"Got it!" Jason's voice echoed oddly, muted by the snow, the roots, and the ground. "Give me a hand. The damn thing's almost as big as me."

The process of extricating what Jason had found—a chest almost as wide as the cave—started with Owen pulling with all his might and ended with him flat on his back, courtesy of a hidden root and gravity.

While Owen contemplated the branches swaying above him, the snow seeping through his clothes, and the decisions that led him here, Jason managed to free himself.

"Queen's throne, you'd think they'd make that big—"

Even if Jason hadn't sucked in a breath and quietly sworn, Owen would've shoved himself to his feet at the way Jason had frozen, hand on his dagger. "What?" His head snapped in the direction Jason was looking, and the blood drained from his face. "Bloody hell."

The trees had moved. Or rather, the trolls had, and their eyes promised murder. They'd packed their trunk-like bodies so tightly together that a cat couldn't slip between. In their branches, on their shoulders, and peeking through the cracks between them were dozens of fae, each armed to the teeth and aiming at them.

"Ashwind." Somehow, Jason managed to make the name sound like a curse. "I wish I could say it's nice to see you again."

"Likewise, Sergeant Lucien." An elderly first-gen troll with birch bark skin pulled away from the crowd and laughed. His lips twisted as he tilted his head to one side. "I thought you'd know better than to come back here."

Jason walked forward, the snow crunching underfoot. "We had a bit of trouble on the border." He slowly raised his hands in the air. "Let us take what we need, and we'll get out of your hair."

Owen's fingers twitched to grab the pistol nestled on his hip, but instead he followed suit. None of Ashwind's crowd lowered their weapons.

Ashwind snorted and lowered his bow. "Was that your group on the border?" He handed his bow to an elf behind him and took a step forward with a shake of his head. "Nice piece of work there. Pity about that harpy, though. I told you those hypocrites up in the capital were going to send your lot to their deaths."

Snarling, Jason stormed forward and stopped inches from Ashwind. "Isaac's death was the humans' fault, not the council's." His fists shook, and Owen's shoulders ached with the memory of their power. Jason was holding himself back but not well. "They do everything they can to get us home," he hissed through clenched teeth, "all of us."

Ashwind sneered. "Yes, and while they fret over those stupid enough to be outside the haven, they forget about those already here. We don't get as much as a passing glance." The crowd gathered around them muttered in agreement. Several shot burning looks at Owen, who shrunk back.

Good thing he hadn't spoken much. The last thing he wanted to do here was draw attention to himself, and his accent was a dead giveaway that he wasn't havenborn. He doubted this lot would be any friendlier when they realized he was human.

"That wasn't our fault. We couldn't even get anyone out to check on the border villages until—"

"Until your precious queen had drunk her fill and sent the dragons to rescue her people, leaving us alone and unprotected," Ashwind said. He closed the distance between them and loomed over Jason like a tsunami. "How many people would've lived if she'd sent someone to check the border villages?" He swung his arms wide, and fire burned behind his wooden eyes. "How many of *our families* might have made it if she hadn't been so eager to bring the damn hostages to the capital?"

Owen's breath caught, and for a moment he forgot how to breathe. The queen hadn't been the only one to want the hostages back, he wanted to yell. The entire capital had looked the other way when the Corps bent regulations to get them home without decontamination and debriefing.

Ashwind hadn't been the only one to lose someone because of that mistake.

"We. Didn't. Know." Jason drew his fist back, bringing the attention of every bowman in the area to him. The real concern of Jason getting himself killed dashed any relief Owen felt about them not aiming at him anymore. Jason's voice grew hollow and his eyes vacant. "We sent gryphons—"

"It wasn't enough." The group behind Ashwind shifted. Some pulled knives from their belts and stepped forward, but Ashwind stopped them with a raised hand, his hard eyes still glaring daggers at Jason. "She chose those outsiders over her people," he said firmly, enunciating like he was speaking to a small child. "We're the ones who fought to be here, not them. Let the outsiders save themselves."

Snarls, grunts, hooting shouts, and yells filled the forest in a way that was louder than a group their size should've been able to produce as Ashwind's followers made their agreement known. Owen's stomach twisted with an emotion he couldn't identify, that wasn't his, and he took another step back, praying there weren't any roots behind him. Elves, dammit, they had elves.

"Jason, we should get what we need and leave," Owen muttered, daring to speak for the first time. Three of Ashwind's followers had been inching closer to them, rope in hand, and the rest didn't seem far behind. Meanwhile, Jason and Ashwind were locked in a staring match where blinking might cost Owen and Jason their lives. "Or just leave."

Jason gave no indication he'd heard Owen or even that he realized the crowd was turning against them even more.

Finally, just when Owen was debating pulling Jason back himself, Jason uncurled his fists. "Look, Ashwind, just let us go," he said in a low voice. "We can argue what happened later, but we need these supplies." He gestured at the crate behind them. "We were assigned a supply run, but it turned into a rescue mission. We don't have enough food or blankets for our team and our passengers. You have to know that. Who knows when our harpy will get back. Please, let us take what we need, and we'll leave."

It almost worked. For a few seconds, Ashwind stroked his chin and looked at the two of them. The crowd behind him whispered angry retorts, and several caressed their weapons thoughtfully. Owen was starting to wonder if they should make a run for it when Ashwind smiled. "A pretty tale you tell. If I didn't know better, I'd almost believe it, but the queen wouldn't put one of her blood bags at risk for a simple supply run."

Owen inhaled as ice flooded his veins. "How do you know who I am?" he asked, trying to summon some of the surety and strength he used whenever he had to talk to Percill. The shock had long worn off, and his limbs felt like ice. It didn't lend itself to a solid defense.

"I have my sources." Ashwind rolled his shoulders, and the scratching noise of his barklike skin rang unusually loud in the clearing. "Now, why don't you tell us why you really went outside?" A large, feral grin spread across his face as he stared at Owen and Jason, like a cat that had the mouse right where he wanted it.

"Ashwind, leave him out of this," Jason snapped, his fists clenching and unclenching at his side. "He had nothing to do with the attack."

"Didn't he?" Ashwind asked. "He and his family were the last ones brought in through normal procedures, and his wife was the one who led SAFE right to us." With each word his voice deepened, like the forest itself was breaking open to speak. "The queen didn't even have the courtesy to bleed her dry for what she did. People, our families are dead because of her, and the damned queen lets her live."

"Don't pretend we didn't suffer," Owen shouted, finding his fire amid the ice and snow. He marched within arm's reach of Ashwind, taking the place Jason formerly occupied, and stared his death in the eye. "Our son died because of SAFE."

"Your son?" Ashwind spat and met Owen's forceful glare with one of his own. "Is the death of one boy supposed to make up for every person who buried their spouse, every other parent that lost their child, or the countless orphans that now walk those halls?" He pushed even closer to Owen, and a dark fire burned in his eyes. "If I had my way, she would've been forced to feel the suffering of everyone who lost someone to those monsters. She would've lost what we lost, felt what we felt."

Around them, fear, hurt, grief, and anger—a towering inferno of rage—filled the air. Low muttering in Fead, the language of the Fae, filled the crowd as the elves among Ashwind's followers fed their emotions back into the crowd.

Jason grabbed Owen's arm and yanked him back. "Ashwind, this isn't helping anyone. Calm down, we can still work this out."

Ashwind's eyes gleamed with a mad light while he stalked forward. The crowd moved with him, circling until even the smallest escape route was blocked.

"Can we, Lucien?" Ashwind asked in a dark voice. His fingers stroked his knife and lingered on the hilt like he was imagining plunging it into Owen's chest. "The queen will never listen to us or our grievances. But"—a sickly leer crossed his face as he cast his eyes over Owen—"if we had a hostage, someone she values, someone she needs, then she would have to."

Owen's heart sank to the ground, and he almost followed it. Somehow, he doubted he'd come through that experience in one piece. Beira didn't value him like that anymore. They hadn't been friends in months. They hadn't even spoken since their fight, and he hadn't donated since he'd joined the Corps.

"Are you crazy?" Jason hissed. "Kidnapping an innocent man, one of the queen's donors, isn't the way to get what you want. Let us go, we'll talk to the queen, ask her to meet with you—"

"Meet with us? Meet with us?" Ashwind spat again, and the spittle missed Owen by mere inches. "We've been trying to speak with her for months. She's ignored our messages and killed everyone we've sent to negotiate with her."

Owen almost swallowed his tongue. “That’s impossible,” he whispered.

At the same time, Jason asked, “What are you talking about?” His head tilted to one side, blocking Owen’s view of Ashwind. “There’s been no word from any of the Regulars since y’all disappeared.” A growl from beyond the line of trolls quickly multiplied into a chorus, and Jason reached a hand back as if to confirm Owen was still there. “Even if she wanted to hurt one of you, she couldn’t, you know that.”

She couldn’t. The queen swore an oath of protection to each and every fae that passed into her borders. She couldn’t break it any more than one of the fae could break a promise to her. To kill one of them would be as good as committing suicide.

“Hang her vows, I’ve seen the bodies, seen her handiwork,” Ashwind said through gritted teeth, and the crowd roared in agreement. “Their throats were ripped out, and they were bloodless. I remember the war, Lucien. I remember what the battlefield looked like after she was done. No one kills like a vampire.”

“Ashwind—”

“Enough, Lucien. You won’t win this,” Ashwind said, a hand poised in the air to beckon the other fae forward. “Now, it seems to me that you only have two options. We can’t let you go, so either you surrender or you try to fight us off.” He crossed the last few feet between the two groups, stopping inches from Jason. “I can’t promise you that you or the human won’t get hurt if you try to resist. The Regulars have been itching for a fight for months now, and they can get uppity at times like this. Out of control, one might say. One of you may even get killed. But . . .” He paused, a sly grin that looked too cunning for someone with eyes that mad crossing his lips. “If you stand down, I will personally guarantee your survival until all this is over. What’ll it be, eh, Lucien?”

***

There hadn’t been a choice. Two men—and one of those a human—against a fae horde? Impossible. Even without the elves and the sirens, they would have been hard-pressed to escape with their lives, let alone with the supplies they had been sent to get. Jason had been upset about it, but in the end, he’d allowed the Regulars to blindfold them and bind their hands.

Ashwind told them to pick out what they needed from the supply cache and sent two of the Regulars to carry it back to the crash site. Ostensibly, they were also supposed to be acting as his official representatives, but Owen wondered if they weren't also sent to remind the Corps that the Regulars had had the opportunity to capture the entire team but didn't.

Jason and Owen were tossed over the backs of two werewolves and carried away from the cache. Each bouncing, lurching step reminded Owen how he had been knocked out a few hours prior, and vomit threatened each time he jolted up and down. He soon lost track of how long they'd been traveling, distracted as he was by the dual states of his stomach and head.

His stomach, at least, was glad when they stopped, and someone forced him to his feet. A hand around his arm dragged him into a warm space, out of the biting wind, and threw him to the floor. Jason's muffled cursing preceded his entrance but stopped when he landed on Owen with a thud. The door slammed shut, cutting them off from the world outside.

CHAPTER SIX

In Which He Demands His Freedom

LADY AILELL: Look, according to the Accords, no fae can live outside the council's control. That means that the battleborn can't be independent, even if they have their own city.

QUEEN TITANIA: They're not fae, Ailell.

LADY AILELL: The humans don't know that. They think the Change didn't work because it was forced.

QUEEN TITANIA: I never intended for that to happen. I wanted to stop the fighting.

LADY AILELL: It doesn't matter what you intended. What matters is what the UN would do if they found out the council let the battleborn live outside our control.

QUEEN TITANIA: They have a right. They're not fae, so they are exempt from the ruling of the Accords. They can have their city.

LADY AILELL: But—

QUEEN TITANIA: My word on this is final, Ailell.

—Excerpt from the Council Transcript Archives

Owen didn't try to get up. Shivers wracked his body as he curled farther into the fur rug beneath him, searching desperately for even a scrap of the heat he'd lost to the biting wind.

"Owen, are you all right?" Jason asked from Owen's left. There was a shuffling noise, and a warm lump shoved itself into Owen's side.

Owen sucked in a breath through his nose and forced his teeth to stop chattering. "I'm fine. Cold and sore, but fine." Once upon a time, Owen might've been embarrassed by how quickly he pressed his back to Jason, but any scruples had died when he'd lost feeling in his extremities. "You?"

"Oh, I'm wonderful," Jason muttered. "Betrayal always leaves a lovely taste in my mouth."

"That's a little harsh, isn't it?" It took every ounce of his will, but Owen forced himself to uncurl and inched as close as he could to Jason without crushing him. "He'd have to be on our side to betray us. Besides, he's just throwing his weight around."

"He kidnapped us," Jason said, enunciating each word like he was talking to a slow child. "He kidnapped us, and he actively wants to kill you. The only reason we're still alive is he needs hostages."

"How—"

"He told me himself," Jason snapped. He pulled away and must have turned over, because his chin settled on Owen's shoulder, close to his ear. "Listen to me, Jedidiah Ashwind does not lie, and he does not exaggerate. He wanted to give the queen your head as a welcoming present, and trust me, if he said it, he meant it."

That made Owen pause. The last time he'd heard Jason speak like that, they'd just found out SAFE was accusing Owen of murdering Tiffany.

He swallowed and shuffled onto his back. "If that's the case, what happens next?"

Pressing closer, Jason shrugged as a shiver wracked his body from head to toe. "I d-don't know," he managed to say. "A year ago, he'd have helped us, no questions asked. Now though . . . I dunno. I heard him say something about meeting someone, and then he walked off."

"That doesn't bode well for us," Owen muttered. His legs ached—agonizing pain arched up them with every move now that the feeling was slowly returning. "How long before the queen gets here, do you think?" They'd crashed almost a half day's flight from the capital, and Ashwind couldn't have taken them far, not if he wanted to stay close to Glenhold.

"Well, we went northwest as far as I could tell," Jason said, interrupting Owen's musing. "We should still be in the haven, but by my guess, we have at least twelve hours ahead of us."

The conversation died as the issue of getting warm took precedence. They may have been out of the wind, but they didn't have a fire, and the rug did little to shield them from the stone beneath it. Cor, but he wished they had a blanket. Or that their hands were untied, but the Regulars were masters of knots, and pulling just made things tighter.

After a few minutes of silence, Jason spoke. Or rather, tried to speak. His face was still buried in Owen's neck so all that came out was a muffled mess. He pulled back and tried again. "Did you hear that Aaron's wife finally gave birth?"

"Yes . . ." Owen said slowly, turning his head toward Jason's voice. "And?"

Jason shrugged against Owen's back. "Figure we might as well talk about something while we wait. I don't know about you, but I'm too cold to sleep."

"And you can't think of anything better to talk about? Say . . . how we're going to get out of here?"

"There's no point." Jason's chin dug into Owen's shoulder as he shifted again. "There are miles of wilderness between us and any of the villages this far north. We'd freeze to death before we found anyone who could help us, or one of the werewolves would run us down—"

"I get it," Owen snapped. Groaning, he slumped back into Jason and tried not to feel a little petty victory when that had made Jason's chin slip off his shoulder. "What are we supposed to do then? Wait for morning?"

"What else?" Jason sighed and pulled away from Owen, who tried not to mourn the heat. "Our best bet is to conserve our energy and hope things work out."

Owen wanted to argue, but his words turned to ash in his mouth. Jason was right. They were trapped.

It was Owen's turn to sigh, and the sound that came out was nearly a cry. It shouldn't be like this. Ashwind should've helped them without questions—it's what the fae did. They should be home by now, preparing for their next mission, not stuck here, prisoners of someone else's grief.

White and red and his hand going limp, dear god, he couldn't be gone—

No. No, he wasn't going to think about that.

"Let's get the blindfolds off at least," Owen muttered gruffly as he turned onto his side. His wrists screamed as he wriggled close to Jason, but he forced himself to keep going until Jason's front pressed into his back. Pain was good; it meant the feeling was coming back. If it also served to chase away ghosts, well, he wasn't going to complain.

"Fine by me."

Of course, Owen hadn't stopped to think about how they were actually going to get the blindfolds off until Jason had already started nuzzling at his neck.

"Watch my ear," Owen hissed, yanking his head back before Jason's teeth could close over it again.

"'m sowry, 'm e' widdle busy a' 'he mowment," Jason said, having finally managed to grab hold of Owen's blindfold with his mouth. "Ah a'mos ga' i'."

True to his word, Jason yanked the blindfold up with one move, and Owen blinked in the dim light. They were in a gray cave with walls blackened by years of lamp and candlelight. A single lamp hung from a hook on the far wall, and flickering light peeked in through a gap below the low door that was the only way in or out of their cell.

"Owen," Jason said, interrupting his examination of the room, "unless there's something important going on, get mine off now."

"Oh, sorry," Owen said. He bit back a curse as he landed awkwardly on his arm as he turned. "Just let me—bloody hell, Jason, what'd they do to you?"

What he could see of Jason's face was either bruised or bleeding. Small trailing scratches covered one cheek, each at least three inches long and still bleeding. A small cut near his hairline had scabbed over but had stained the blond hair around it black. His lower lip had split open, and dried blood trailed down his chin.

Jason shrugged, a painful-looking gesture. "I may have gotten mouthy, and my ride didn't appreciate it. It doesn't look that bad, does it?"

Owen had to work his jaw to get to the point where he could speak without sputtering. "It looks like they beat you with their claws out. How didn't I notice this earlier?" He pulled back some more to look for any other obvious injuries.

"Owen, I'm fine. They slapped me around a little, that's all." Jason smile was not comforting as it reopened the cut on his lip. "Get my blindfold off, all right?"

Owen nodded, forgetting that Jason couldn't see him. The blindfold was encrusted with dried blood. If he wanted to do this without reopening anything, he'd need to be careful. A fresh wave of anger bubbled in Owen's chest that none of the sirens had offered to sing the wounds closed. Head wounds bled a lot.

"Stop worrying," Jason said quietly. He smiled and his teeth shone red in the dim light, but somehow, he managed to make it look gentle. "Grab it with your teeth and pull it down. Don't worry about me, I've had worse."

"All right, all right, give me a moment," Owen said, dragging himself closer. He leaned forward and nuzzled Jason's ears in much the same way as Jason had done to him. It took two tries to get a decent grip on the blindfold with his teeth, and the coppery taste of Jason's blood almost made him drop it again, but he managed to keep ahold of it.

"Thanks," Jason said, squinting up at Owen. He made his own cursory overview of the room they were trapped in. "Wow, they certainly didn't go out of their way to make this feel welcoming, did they?" he asked, eyebrow raised as he turned back to Owen. "I mean, you'd almost think we weren't wanted."

"At least we're out of the wind, and they gave us the rug. I'd hate to think of how cold it would be if we had to lie on the stone or worse, outside," Owen answered, and glanced at the door again. The wind had picked up, howling like a werewolf in the night, and he shivered. Thank heaven for small mercies.

"Ugh, don't remind me. I get colder just thinking about it." Jason pushed himself up on his elbows and winced. "By the throne, I think that wolf cracked a rib when she kicked me."

Owen forced himself into a sitting position. "I assume it's not serious, otherwise you wouldn't have waited to tell me, right?"

Jason collapsed back on the ground and rolled on his side to face Owen. "Psh, it's not that bad, I've been beaten up worse training with Abey." An explosive shiver coursed through his body, and he groaned. "Hey, would you mind getting over here? It's not getting warmer, and I can't pull myself up like you have."

"Oh, of course, sorry," Owen said as he shifted into a position where he could lie down without falling on Jason. "There, is that better?"

"Much." Jason shuffled as close as he could and buried his face in Owen's jacket. "Now we can finish our conversation from earlier."

"What, about you hiding your injuries?"

Jason made a face. "My injuries? No, those are boring, old news. We've already talked about those. I want to hear about your family."

"Jason, you've heard everything about my family, all the news," Owen said. His eyebrow almost disappeared into his shaggy hair. "You had dinner with us the night before the team left. You know as much as I do."

"But Owen," Jason whined. "That's not the fun stuff! The only things I know about your family are the boring stuff you tell everyone: the headline to the article, the back-cover blurb, the front window display. I want to know the good stuff, the juicy watercooler gossip I can tell all my friends. I've been living vicariously through you, and I need my fix." He finished his tirade by turning his head and opening his eyes as wide as possible, lips curled in a pout. The effect was somewhat ruined by the blood smeared over his face.

"No." Even though Owen was smiling, his stomach tied into knots. He didn't want to talk about his family now. It was bad enough he and Jason were prisoners; the last thing he wanted to think about was the ones he'd left behind.

"Are you sure?" Jason asked, smiling broadly, albeit painfully. "We could make bets on what Ashley and Dorothy turn into, or whether Arthur finally asks out that second-gen he's had his eye on, or how—"

"No. I'm sure, let's talk about something else," Owen said, no longer smiling. His eyebrows furrowed together as he stared at Jason. "Like how you almost broke your leg trying to impress Natalie last week."

The cell was blessedly quiet as Jason grumbled. It didn't last.

"She reminds me of my fiancé. That's why I was trying to impress her." Jason's voice was gentler than Owen could ever remember it being, his eyes half-lidded as he stared into nothingness. "When Natalie gets mad, when she gets upset with me for doing something stupid, she gets the same look in her eye that my fiancé did. When she raises her voice, it's like I can close my eyes and be back in our crappy apartment in New York, back before the war, before everything went to hell."

It didn't feel right to interrupt, to tell Jason he didn't have to explain if he didn't want to. Not now, after Owen had asked him about it in the first place. Jason's fingers tangled in and out of Owen's shirt as his voice shook.

He turned his head still farther away, most of his voice disappearing into the rug. "It's been years, decades, but I never really moved on. They were the one for me, you know?"

Humming, Owen slid down until he could look Jason in the eye. "What happened to them?" he asked quietly.

Jason turned his face back to him, wearing a bittersweet smile. "They tried to help me when I Changed. They were a nurse, they thought they could help." His breath hitched and he blinked tears away. "That was right at the beginning, right before people started experimenting on fae. We were a couple of kids; we didn't know what was happening. We'd only heard these crazy rumors about people turning into monsters, like in some cheap horror flick." His voice broke, and he turned away from Owen with his shoulders hunched. "I hurt them, hurt them bad. They had to go to the hospital, and the staff threw me out when I tried to see them."

"What did you do?"

"I ran." He glanced at Owen, the ghost of a pitiful smile turning the corner of his lip up. "I didn't want to get arrested, but I got picked up in the Heights a week later. I spent the next two years in a hellhole disguised as a research facility before I was broken out. I never saw them again." His eyes darted away and refocused on the floor as he tried to contain a shudder. "I heard they survived, but I couldn't . . ."

Owen's stomach twisted and knotted. He shouldn't be surprised that Jason . . . well. Few fae and fewer veterans had happy stories about how they'd Changed. Anyone who lived among the fae got used to tragedy.

"Tiffany's birthday is tomorrow," Owen found himself whispering, "the twenty-seventh that is, since it might be tomorrow already." His throat closed around the words, and for a moment he wished he was anywhere else but here. "I was hoping to get home in time to surprise her," he managed hoarsely. "She blames herself for—" He choked on his tongue, bile and iron almost drowning him.

She blamed herself for blood on white sheets and blue eyes glazing over. For shards of white that shouldn't be seen. For a heartbeat stilled long before its time.

Jason shifted and said in a low voice, "It's not her fault. That's what SAFE does. They get in your head, make you think they're on your side. It happened often enough during the war."

A sigh huffed out as Owen ducked his head into Jason's shoulder. "Not like this. Not—Tiffany knows that, but it doesn't change anything for her. She thinks that because she didn't try harder to tell people about the collars, it's her fault. She may as well have killed David herself as far as she's concerned."

"But the queen herself said it wasn't her fault," Jason said. "It was all over the haven. The other hostages knew, too, and no one's blaming them."

Owen laughed, a sharp, bitter sound that tore through his chest. "It wasn't enough. Blast, it wasn't her fault—" It was his, he'd told her, screamed at her till his throat nearly bled. "But she doesn't believe it. She's dying, this is killing her, and I can't do anything except sit around and wait for it to happen." He bit back a curse and dug his fingernails into his palm. "Do you know what it's like for her now?" His fists shook, but the aching agony of frozen limbs warming couldn't distract him, couldn't keep him calm. "She's so scared of losing us she won't let the kids out of her sight. She wouldn't let Arthur join the Corps, even as a healer, until he was seventeen and she couldn't stop it anymore. She won't stop trying to make me quit."

He couldn't quit. She didn't understand that. He couldn't quit until the fae were safe and no one had to be afraid of dying like David had.

"Owen—" Jason said, but Owen plowed right over him.

"What's worse is she doesn't go out anymore. She's afraid to. Everywhere she goes, she says people are staring at her, blaming her." An animalistic noise ripped from the depths of his being and found its way out of his throat. "I'm losing her, and I couldn't sit by and watch it—"

"Owen, snap out of it," Jason ordered, and grunted as he pushed himself to his elbow.

Owen's mouth clacked shut, and he took several deep breaths through his nose. This was why he hadn't wanted to talk about it. He got worked up, started shouting, and the next thing he knew, he was punching someone. Again.

"Sorry," he finally managed to say, forcing his hands to relax. "I just—I can't. The way she acts, I might as well have buried her with

David." It *hurt*, but it was true. She'd become a wraith, a shadow of the woman she used to be, and she refused to do more than haunt the wreckage of what their lives had been.

Jason awkwardly patted his hand on Owen's stomach, a poor attempt at comfort. "Hey, it's all right, things will get better. I promise."

"No, it won't, you don't—" His jaw snapped shut, and he breathed deeply through his nose. Everyone said that, and it wasn't nearly as helpful as they thought.

"Talk to the queen if it's really all that bad," Jason suggested quietly. "You know she'd do something if you asked."

Owen buried his head in Jason's back to resist screaming at the emotional horror show bubbling up inside him like a poison. "You don't understand," he said through gritted teeth. "I did go see Beira. I asked her to help, to talk to Tiff, but she wouldn't."

"What? Why?" Jason's shoulders tensed like he wanted to grab Owen and shake him. "She wouldn't do that, not unless . . ."

"She didn't think she could help," Owen whispered. He pulled his head up, turned on his back, and stared at the gray ceiling.

He'd begged Beira, pleaded with her on his knees to do something, and she . . . she refused to do anything. He had never understood what it meant to be stone-faced until he saw how Beira, who was supposed to be his friend, had looked that day. It had led to the first true fight they'd had in the time they'd known each other.

For over an hour he'd argued and screamed himself hoarse. It ended with him storming out of her office, throwing curses and profanities over his shoulder, and her solid, infuriatingly logical arguments following him out the door like a foul smell.

That had been the end of their friendship. They'd only spoken twice since. He had left the capital the following morning, desperate for the distraction the away missions would provide him, and unable to stand another minute of watching Tiffany self-destruct. In the months since, he was only home during his scant leave between missions and barely even then.

Damn Jason, he thought as he bit back another animalistic scream. If Jason hadn't dug, hadn't made him feel like he had to be open, too, all of this would've stayed buried where it belonged.

“I’m sorry.” Jason’s voice was quiet, a whisper Owen barely heard. “I shouldn’t have pried.”

“No,” Owen whispered hoarsely, “you shouldn’t have.”

Jason lay there silently shivering until Owen calmed enough to come close again. They both fell into silence. They’d each delved places they shouldn’t have gone and poked at wounds that hadn’t yet healed.

Owen fought the pull of his eyelids as time wore on. Their lamp flickered and died, and their world narrowed to the tiny fraction of light bleeding through cracks in the door.

Time crept by him, unnoticed as each breath brought a battle to stay awake. Over and over again his eyes would fly open after a minute or two’s rest, and he’d resolve to stay awake this time. The night passed in fragments of captured sleep, until the cell door slammed into the wall.

CHAPTER SEVEN

In Which Friends Are Enemies

"If it weren't for Colonel Ashwind, every person in this camp would be dead by now. He raised the alarm before the commandos could torch our supplies last spring, led raids on enemy facilities, and spent weeks training the surveillance corps to his standards. His experience with the research centers gave him an edge most of the commanding officers don't have. He'll do anything to protect his troops, be they fae or human. Pardon the language, but hell, after the Battle of Billings, I can't think of anyone under his command who wouldn't follow him into hell and fully expect him to bring them back out again."
—Excerpt from the transcript of Colonel Jedidiah Ashwind's Court-Martial

Owen shivered as the wind found every gap in his clothing. Blast, it was like daggers made of ice.

Ashwind's soldiers had dragged them from their cell an hour ago, blindfolded them again, and carried them to . . . wherever here was. The meeting point presumably.

Owen shifted to avoid a rock digging into his knee, careful not to disturb Jason, who'd been weakly leaning into him, a fever searing even Owen through both their clothes since they'd been dumped here. Someone greeted Ashwind, so Owen assumed the meeting was about to start. None too soon, in his opinion. They'd been kneeling in the snow for the last twenty minutes.

"Any sign of them yet?" Ashwind's rough voice came from Owen's left.

"None, Colonel Ashwind," a female voice said from behind Owen. One of their guards.

Ashwind snorted and came closer to them, his footsteps crunching in the snow. "Figures they'd make us wait. Have the captives given you any trouble?"

"None here, sir," the woman said.

Her voice had a rough quality to it that made Owen think she was a werewolf. A lot could change in shifting, but werewolves always sounded like they were growling. Even Jen did, and she was only first-gen.

"Good. Let me know—" Heavy wings flapped in the distance, cutting him off.

"They're here," Ashwind muttered. Snow crunched underfoot as he moved behind Owen and Jason. "Best get in position before she sees you."

His last words were almost drowned out by wings, and the ground shook from the impact of landing. All sound stopped once the wings stilled and no one moved. Owen hardly dared to breathe. And then . . .

"Colonel Ashwind," Beira said in a voice like ice. The words sounded like a curse and cut deeper into Owen than the wind.

The familiar sound of her voice filled Owen with a relief that made his head spin. Beira was here. She'd get them out.

"Queen Titania," Ashwind said, matching her tone word-for-word. "I appreciate you coming so promptly. Some of my men have experienced your courtesy lately and were concerned you'd send your lackeys instead."

"I'm not here to fight, Colonel," she said, somehow managing to sound bored and respectful at the same time. "Just to get my people back."

"Your people, of course." Ashwind scoffed. His hand tightened around Owen's shoulder. "They're all you ever care about."

Ashwind's voice was choked off and rough, like he was speaking through his teeth. The urge to pull away, to retreat from the fingers digging deep bruises into Owen's shoulder was almost as impossible to resist as it was to achieve. From the way Jason stiffened against him, Owen would wager he was getting the same treatment.

"You were one of my people once, one of my most loyal supporters," Beira said in a voice so soft it was a wonder Owen could hear it. "'The first to battle, the last to bed.' That was the motto of the Regulars, wasn't it?"

"Then I learned where your values lie," Ashwind growled. Owen's shoulder creaked under the pressure of his fingers. Jason let out a quiet gasp. "You don't care for anyone who lives outside of the citadels and certainly not for those on the borders."

"We didn't know they were coming," Beira said, sharp and brittle. "There was no way to stop what happened."

"Course there was, you chose not to follow regulation." Wooden fingers dug deeper, twisting into the gap of Owen's shoulder, and he whimpered into his gag. However faint it was, the sound was enough to break Ashwind's concentration, and his hand dropped from Owen's shoulder. "My apologies, you didn't come here to answer for your crimes."

Beira made a noise like a protest, but she bit it off. "Whether any crimes committed can be attributed to me is up for debate, but you are right," she said, the words edged with caution like she'd just remembered Owen and Jason were there. "Release them. I brought what you wanted."

"Oh, release them? While I must thank you for the goods you've brought, which my soldiers will unload without any trouble from your dragons, I have to say no."

"I could order you to," Beira said mildly. A wave of power, tickling Owen's throat like a cough, soaked the area around them. Like poison in a well.

Owen wished he could see. Beira had one of the best poker faces of anyone he'd met, but they'd been friends long enough for him to see through some of her tricks. Without his eyes, he couldn't even begin to guess what she was playing at.

"You won't, though." Ashwind chuckled, and the sound was like a knife tearing through flesh. "You can't, not if you want any chance in hell of bringing the battleborn back into the fold."

The battleborn? Owen frowned around his gag and tilted his head. The battleborn had been independent for decades. Besides, Beira had been the one to push for it in the council; she wouldn't want them back.

"You'd be surprised what I can do. It's been a long time since the war."

"Not that long, and my memory is as sharp as ever."

The dragons, at least three if the footsteps behind Beira were enough to go by, growled. One snarled something to Beira in the draconic dialect of Fead, and she was quick to rebuke them in the same tongue.

"Nonetheless, I need them back," Beira said after a final snarled word to the dragon. "Corporal Williams's children were quite insistent on the matter, and these two have become a pair where his youngest is concerned."

"And I'd be happy to," Ashwind said, an unseen sneer twisting his words into something ugly to Owen's ears. "Far be it for me to withhold a father from his children. You just need to agree to my terms."

"And what would those be?" Beira said. "We've already brought you food, equipment, and medicines we can scarcely afford to lose."

Ashwind's hands came to rest on Owen's shoulders, too close to his neck for his comfort as the fresh bruises still stung.

"We want independence," he growled. His hands shook almost imperceptibly around Owen's neck. "The battleborn president has already given us permission to join them, provided we have proof you'll leave us alone once we cross their borders."

His hands closed around Owen's throat and tightened until he struggled to breathe. His stomach twisted and his body shook. No, please, not here. He needed to see his family again.

Beira snarled, and the dragons surged forward. The thunder of their steps was enough to jar Owen's teeth and bring snow crashing down on their heads. The hands still on his shoulder were the only thing that kept him up. Jason was not so fortunate and let out a sharp cry when he collapsed into the snow.

"No, get back. I may not want to kill him now, but I will. Get back."

Sparks lit up Owen's blindfold even as he struggled to pull away. The gag ripped at the corners of his mouth while he twisted, searching for just a little more air. His heart pounded in his ears so loudly he missed Beira's answer.

Beira's voice was much closer when Ashwind's hands loosened, and Owen could breathe again. "You know I can't do that." Her voice was calm, but the weight of her words—a physical presence that bore down on him like a vise—took almost as much of Owen's breath away as Ashwind's hands. She was commanding Ashwind.

It shouldn't bother him this much, but the air he kept desperately sucking in didn't seem to reach his lungs. He wasn't fae. She shouldn't be able to affect him this much.

But he was faeborn.

"I'm pushing the limits enough with Daingneach and the battleborn already," Beira continued, heedless of Owen's struggle. "The Accords clearly state that no fae can live outside my control—"

"And Paxton is inside your borders. The same loophole that lets them live freely applies here."

"It's not that simple," Beira snapped. "I have no legal control there and little control over the battleborn in any case. I wouldn't be able to protect you if something were to happen to you there."

"Like you were able to protect us from SAFE?" Ashwind snarled. His hands tightened around Owen's throat again and pressed against his windpipe. Owen couldn't decide if he was grateful for the blindfold or not, because—while he couldn't see his vision going dark—the dizziness was so much worse in the pitch black. "My family was slaughtered while under your protection. You were too weak to keep us safe, even in your own lands."

"Ashwind, I can't allow this." From any other person, Owen would have said the words sounded desperate. From Beira, they were as certain as ice in winter. "Ask for anything, soldiers, weapons, technology, and I will grant it to the best of my abilities, but this is too much."

"Then it appears we are at an impasse," Ashwind said, his hands finally leaving Owen's throat. Owen hunched forward and sucked in greedy breaths. "Guards, take the prisoners back to base."

"No," Beira yelled, the dragon's roars echoing her words and the ringing in Owen's ears.

They couldn't go back, Owen wanted to scream. Jason was right, Ashwind might be calmer now, but if either of them stepped the wrong way, he'd kill them without hesitation.

Arms like steel picked Owen up and threw him over their shoulder as Jason let out a muffled yell.

"Wait," Beira said in a low voice.

The person carrying Owen paused, but their hands tightened around his middle.

Owen's breath stopped on its own accord. Please, he silently begged, they couldn't go back. They'd never leave again.

She bit off a sigh. "I cannot approve of this on my own," she finally said. "But I will give you an audience in front of the council." This time she did sound desperate, a crack in her wall that threatened to bring everything down. "If they approve of the measures you're taking to keep the other Regulars safe, I won't fight it."

Owen's heart restarted as he remembered how to breathe again. She'd given in. Somehow, even though he'd mostly known she'd do what it took to keep them safe, he hadn't expected that.

Ashwind scoffed, but tellingly, he didn't order the guards to keep moving. "We've tried sending people to argue our case in front of the council. After we found the third's head three feet from his body, we figured you didn't want to talk to us."

"You'll be safe, I promise you," Beira said, the words bearing all the weight of one of her oaths. "No one will hurt you or hinder you when you and your emissaries come to my gate, I swear."

"You swear, do you?" Ashwind said with a growl. His voice quieted as he stomped toward her, but Owen could still make out his words. "Do you swear on the blood of the lost, on the crown that you wear, on the faith of your people, and on your own name? Do you swear we will have nothing to fear from any who bear your colors?"

Owen almost swallowed his tongue as the clearing fell into silence. Beira wasn't exempt from the limits of her own power. A vow like that, by her people and her name and with the weight of a command, would bind her tighter than any chain. She wouldn't be free of it until it was fulfilled in letter and spirit.

"I swear, by my name, my crown, and the faith of my people, you will be safe. Please, release them." The words rang like they were going to the ears of every fae in Tearmann. The cracks of desperation had disappeared, hidden by a promise that would never be broken.

For one, heart-stopping moment, Owen was worried Ashwind would refuse the vow despite its strength. One second bled into two, and then—

"Put them down."

And now Owen could breathe.

CHAPTER EIGHT

In Which Owen Goes Home

LORD AELFRIC: Why the fuck did you do that? We'll never be able to catch them now. Those fuckers know where we are, we'll have to move camp. Fuck that, we'll have to move everything, change all our plans.

QUEEN TITANIA: I trust them, Stephen. They said they'd help, and I gave them my word we'd let them go.

LORD AELFRIC: Your word? Your word is worth enough for you to put everything we've built at risk?

QUEEN TITANIA: I can't explain it, and I don't expect you to believe me, but I couldn't stop them. I couldn't, I tried, but I promised them, and something made me—

LORD AELFRIC: Yeah, right. Well, when we're all dead, I hope you feel good about yourself.

—Excerpt from the War Council Transcript Archives

Owen wrapped his hands around a steaming thermos of tea and breathed in the sweet scent of chamomile. He'd been right; Beira had chosen three of the largest dragons to come to the meeting. One, a female with blue scales, wore the gondola Owen, Jason, and two sirens were now riding. Beira rode on the largest dragon, a green-scaled brute longer than a bus and almost thirty feet tall. The third dragon, a male with pearl scales, kept a lookout. Owen occasionally caught glimpses of sunshine flickering off his scales through the windows as he dove in and out of the clouds.

The sirens said he'd been lucky. Beyond minor frostbite in his toes, some bruising, a concussion, and a slight fever, he'd escaped unharmed.

Jason, however . . . well, Owen wasn't surprised when the sirens handed Owen a thermos and shoved him aside.

Somewhere along the line—and Jason hadn't yet admitted where—he'd cracked two ribs, broken a third clean through, and received a concussion one of the sirens had admiringly described as "epic." All that was in addition to the cuts and bruises that had turned his face into a lost Picasso painting. Judging by the frantic overture their singing had taken, Owen didn't think Jason would be out of their clutches for a while.

Sipping on his tea—and thank the throne, whoever brewed it had some idea what they were doing—Owen slumped by a window and watched the scenery fly by. This far from Tearmann proper, there wasn't much to see beyond trees and the occasional bit of farmland.

It wasn't until he could see home that the last of the tension bled from his shoulders. The mountain grew and grew, its snow-covered peak and the scars SAFE left behind as familiar to Owen as the names of his children.

Home. They'd made it.

Gryphons and harpies and dragons alike filled the skies; some darted off to places unknown, loaded down with mail and goods; others swarmed the incoming dragons, no doubt calling for news or gossip; still others seemed to take no notice of them, simply enjoying the sun on their wings before winter trapped them inside.

On the ground far below, wagons and pedestrians jockeyed for passage through the east gate. The last traders of the season had found their way inside, and Owen didn't doubt that the market would be filled with their hawking before long.

If he'd been able, Owen would've called the dragons to stop and stayed like that forever. This was why he did what he did. These people and this place had taken in his family when they'd had nothing, and he'd die before he let that debt go unpaid.

But the Eyries called to them, and the hubbub of life outside disappeared into the cool darkness of the Corps entrance.

A lifetime ago, Owen had landed in this same cave with his family. It looked different now—SAFE had practically reduced it to rubble, and restoring the murals and carvings that covered the walls had been a low priority with winter coming—but it still took Owen's breath away.

Back then, he'd stumbled out of the gondola, half asleep and clutching Dorothy's hand, and been struck dumb by what he saw. A grand cathedral of silence he'd called it, a hole in the world where the only thing left was him and his family.

Their landing brought three more sirens into the gondola, and the choir carried Jason's pallet out before Owen could get a word in edgewise.

Forcing himself to his feet, Owen set aside his thermos and moved to follow them. His legs burned beneath him as he shuffled out of the gondola.

"You should go home."

Of course, Beira was waiting for him. He didn't see her dragon, but he didn't put it past her to have leaped off him the moment they were over the entrance. She might deny it, but she had a flair for the dramatic that even Lord Orpheus couldn't match.

Sighing deeply, Owen turned to face her. A thickening fog had settled between his ears, and finding any words was an unbearable struggle. "We need to be debriefed," he finally managed. Pointing vaguely in the direction the sirens had taken Jason, he stumbled forward. He needed to stay close. Needed to stay near Jason and find out what had happened to the others. It'd be easier on all of them if Natalie didn't have to hunt him down. After, he could go home after they were done.

Beira caught his wrist in an icy hand and frowned as she studied his face.

He frowned too. She shouldn't feel so cold. Had she been eating properly?

"She won't mind waiting until you've had some rest." She paused and her frown deepened. For a moment, he wondered if she was going to change her mind. That was her thinking face.

"Go home," she finally said, half a command and half a request. "Your family almost lost you."

She squeezed his wrist once before dropping it. It might have been comforting once, but now, as she disappeared into the shadows of the Eyries, it felt like he was being sent to bed without supper.

Alone now that Beira and the sirens were gone, every ache and pain Owen had been ignoring flared up tenfold. The aching pit in his stomach fought with his leaden eyelids and the beat of a headache trying to rip his brain apart.

He had a job to do, he wanted to scream at his aching limbs. Jason was in no shape to tell Natalie what had happened—hell, he might not even remember half of it. No, he couldn't go home yet, he couldn't.

But . . . but . . .

He was so tired.

His feet led him to a group of gryphons, and he struggled through the thick haze that settled over his tongue to convince one to carry him to the lower floors. He didn't remember the flight or the walk home or greeting his neighbors.

One moment he was watching the ground rush up to him, the wind stealing his breath away, and then he was outside a familiar pine door. "Williams" was engraved on a copper plate at eye level, and a small bouquet of flowers that had been refilled every week since the Battle of Tearmann sat by the door.

He wanted to go in, but his feet stuck to the ground, and his wrist froze inches from the doorknob. Muffled voices drifted through the two inches of wood that separated him from his family. He could picture the scene that would greet him if he could make his arm finish its move forward, his wrist turn the handle.

Toto would notice him first and come barreling to greet him. Ashley, or perhaps Jen, would follow to see what had drawn him to the door. He couldn't account for Arthur; he'd hardly been in the apartment since David died, but Tiffany would be in the kitchen, wrestling with dinner even though she couldn't cook, or in the dining room, playing with Dorothy. She'd see him, push past the others, and—

The door opened and Arthur barreled out, shouting over his shoulder, "I won't do it. I can't sit—" They collided with an almost comedic thump and fell to the floor in a tangle of limbs.

Shoving Owen away, Arthur jumped up, his lips tugged back into an ugly snarl. "Watch it—"

His sneer melted away, and his eyes widened like a child at Christmas. His mouth moved soundlessly. His hand inched toward Owen, still on the floor and blinking up at him, like he was afraid Owen was a trick of the light.

"Dad?" he said in a small voice.

Something tight unraveled in Owen's chest, and he smiled as relief flooded his aching limbs. "Hey."

And Arthur—hair spikes flaring up and scales flushed red—collided with him again, wrapping him in a hug so tight Owen struggled to breathe. "Dad, you're alive." His voice was wet and wrecked, and his arms shook like he still didn't believe Owen was there, even while he was touching him. "We thought . . . Captain Freeman said . . ."

"Arthur, please, the captain said to wait—"

Owen's eyes shot up, and if he'd had the energy, he'd have cried.

Tiffany collapsed against the door, a clawed hand over her mouth. Her eyes were as wide as saucers and shone like starlight. She tried to speak, but the words dissolved into hitching sobs.

Pushing Arthur away, he made himself stand. "Sorry I'm late," he said in a low voice, smiling tiredly.

The world disappeared into a flurry of feathers as she rushed at him, and her wings wrapped around him like a cocoon. Her claws dug into him, but he couldn't feel the pain. Wrapping his arms around any part of her he could reach, Owen let his head fall into her shoulders as he released a shaky breath.

They should go inside. Arthur was yelling for the girls to come out, and a crowd had to be gathering around them, but Owen couldn't bring himself to move. Time stood still and so did he. The world could wait a bit longer.

***

When Owen emerged from the shelter of Tiffany's wings, Ashley dragged him into the apartment and shoved him toward the shower. When he'd gotten out—clean and loose-limbed—Arthur and Ashley had disappeared. Tiffany said something about them going on errands before she'd forced Owen into his armchair. His limbs ached, leaden with exhaustion that had him seriously considering the merits of falling asleep standing up, so he went without complaint.

Tiffany ran around the apartment, dragging chairs from the dining room and the bedrooms and hurriedly tidying up while Owen watched in a daze. He tried to help and even got halfway up before she shoved him back down again. Toto, it seemed, took her side and plopped down on Owen's feet without any prompting.

Arthur and Ashley returned from their respective missions not long after, bringing Dorothy and Jen with them. Tiffany sent Arthur off again to get food from the community cafeterias, and he brought back enough cookies, cakes, and pastries to feed a small army; and three of his friends to help carry it all.

The evening passed in a blur.

Friends came and went in front of Owen. Eoire, Aaron, Abey, and his old coworkers bled together as they came, one after another. Food passed through his lips untasted. Conversation flowed like wine, but he couldn't remember a word of it. The arching music of a violin hummed above it all, a beautiful sound he barely heard over the buzzing in his ears.

The guests left long after Owen's last clear memory of the evening. One moment he'd been speaking with Andrew, and the next, Tiffany was pulling him to their room, one arm wrapped around his waist to keep him standing. Their bed called to him like a siren, but more persuasive. He collapsed into the soft mattress and pulled the blanket over his head, mind already gone to the field of dreams and body not far behind.

He was home.

CHAPTER NINE

In Which Owen Makes a Promise

"Half of my flight has been injured on these missions in the last six months, and three of them will never fly again. At this rate, we won't have enough flyers to do the winter hunting, and yet, do I receive the reports I was promised explaining their condition? No, I'm left in the dark. I was given this position to protect my people, and if I am not allowed to do that, I will be forced to withdraw the Visok Peak flight from the Corps. Give me an explanation for their injuries, or find yourself different flyers."
—Excerpt from the letters of Wingmaster Inmasul

Owen stared at the ceiling above him. There wasn't much to see except for a single strand of iron working its way over the bed. A workman's chisel had worn it smooth decades ago, and specks remained from some previous attempt to lighten the room by painting it yellow.

He'd look somewhere else, but he didn't have the energy. A fever that had been waiting for his guard to drop had claimed him as he'd slept and kept him in its clutches for the last three days.

Tiffany had panicked when he wouldn't wake, or so he was told. She'd made quite a sight, barging into the neighborhood clinic, him hanging in her arms like a rag doll. His nurse, a gentle second-gen elf who'd come in not long after he woke, had told him the story in a half-hearted attempt to cheer him up. She'd reassured him Tiffany had hardly left his side, but something important had called her away.

If Owen had had the energy, he would have snapped at her. Of course, it would've been something important that had called his family away. He may have been fever addled, but he had known that much.

"Are they keeping you here too?"

Owen shot up with a yelp and instantly regretted it as each of his bruises came to life in one fiery chorus. "Who's there?" he hissed through clenched teeth.

The speaker stepped into the room. No, *stepped* wasn't the right word. *Limped* or *stumbled*, perhaps. Fell, the speaker fell into the room, jet-black fur and white feathers tumbling over each other in a great heap of limbs, wings, and tail.

"Evans?" Owen said, his eyebrows shooting up. The sirens should've seen to him ages ago. He pushed himself up farther and bit back a whimper as his body screamed at him. "What are you still doing here?" Had Evans gotten sick too? Fae were hardy, but he'd been injured, and infection bowed to no species.

"Sorry," Evans hissed from his pile on the floor, "I didn't mean to scare you." Slowly, he folded his wings back and pushed himself up on all fours.

Owen eased himself back onto his pillows, giving in to the screaming of his various aches. "You didn't, I was just surprised."

Evans hummed, and the click-click-click of each step echoed through the room as he edged closer. "I heard you got captured," he said while settling his head on the edge of Owen's bed. If it weren't for the panting he was trying to hide, he might have looked nonchalant. "No one told me you were back yet. Did they hurt you too?"

"No," Owen said, turning back to the ceiling. He didn't want to think about the Regulars or his time with them. "I was lucky."

"Then why are you here? Major Rodriguez should have fixed you by now."

Owen huffed, the air passing his lips in a tired rush. "I got sick after we got back." He tilted his head back to Evans. "Besides, Aaron's out on patrol. He won't be back for another week."

Aaron Rodriguez was one of the few sirens blessed with the ability to heal humans. He'd led the team that brought Owen's family to Tearmann, and Owen had been fortunate enough to work with him on his first few missions. The healers had been trying to pry him from the Corps for almost a decade now.

"Oh," Evans said in a quiet voice, and pulled back from Owen. "I thought . . ." Evans sat at Owen's bedside and gripped the mattress with his foreleg to stabilize himself. "We're the only ones here, you know. The healers don't like to keep people here if they're healthy. They let Jason go a few hours after he came in, and he was hurt pretty bad, so I thought . . ."

"You thought I was hurt too."

Evan's head bowed, and his talons dug into the mattress. "They don't leave people here," he said in a low voice. "They heal everyone. You've been here for three days, and I heard you screaming. No one screams like that unless they're hurt."

Evans turned away, and for the first time, Owen caught sight of the damage he'd caused by landing on Evans. His breath caught in his chest, and his heart leaped to his throat.

Evans's right foreleg was gone. The only sign of what had been there before was a small patch of skin, a scar the size of Owen's hand, and a small ring of white feathers.

He had done that. If he'd had a few more bandages or more medical training or if he'd held on tighter before the crash—

"It doesn't hurt anymore," Evans said, breaking Owen free of the endless cycle of self-recrimination. "The doctor said she'd find someone to make me a prosthetic, but I can't leave yet."

Owen tore his eyes away from the scar and fixated them on Evans's face. "You can't leave?"

Evans shook his head. "No, they don't want me to be by myself if something goes wrong. I live in the barracks, and most of my roommates are deployed, so . . ."

"You're stuck here," Owen said quietly. Besides that, Evans didn't have any family that could take him in. It was why he'd joined the Corps so young.

Evans shrugged, and his wing came down to cover the scar. "For now at least," he said glumly. "If I can find someone to stay with me, they'll release me. Besides, I won't be able to stay in the barracks much longer."

Ah, right. Amputees couldn't be active duty, and even though the domestic branch had plenty of positions available, Owen doubted Evans qualified for any of them. He was too inexperienced. Too young.

"I'm sorry." He was, truly. This wasn't Evans's fault this happened, but he'd be stuck with the consequences for the rest of his life.

"Don't—" Evans said with a snarl, shooting to his feet with the grace of a newborn calf. "Don't feel sorry for me."

"Evans, wait—"

By the time Owen dragged himself up and to the door, Evans was long gone, and even the echoes had died away.

"Damn it," Owen hissed under his breath. He ached too much to chase after him, and even if he did, what would he say? "*Sorry I ruined your life because I didn't strap myself to the wall?* or *Sorry for reminding you that your situation is my fault?*

No, damn it. Pressing his head to the cool wood of the doorframe, Owen let out a shaky sigh and sank to the floor. Once his legs stopped burning, he'd limp his way back to bed.

Evans was stuck here until he recovered enough to work, and Owen couldn't do anything about it, no matter how much he wanted to fix it. Even with the Corps stipend, Evans wasn't going to be able to afford an apartment. Tearmann was overflowing with refugees and newcomers squabbling for a haven-sponsored apartment, and each of them had their own problems. They wouldn't want a newly disabled veteran hanging around while they tried to rebuild their lives.

His only shot at getting out of here was the desperate hope some generous soul would open up their home to him. That, or move out of the capital entirely.

His eyes shot open. If he could convince Tiffany, maybe he could help.

***

"No, Owen, we can't do that to the kids." The tips of Tiffany's claws dragged over some of his bruises as she helped ease him into a shirt.

Suppressing a wince, Owen tugged the hem the rest of the way down. The doctors were finally satisfied he'd recovered and had agreed to release him. Arthur was supposed to be home tonight; the last thing Owen wanted to do was give the doctors any reason to keep him in the hospital longer.

"Tiff, he doesn't have anywhere else to go." He didn't say that the boys' room had been practically empty since Arthur moved out. "He can't stay in the barracks anymore, and it's killing him to stay here."

"It doesn't matter, Owen, there's too much going on," Tiffany said, her hands hovering in the air to catch him if he lost his balance. "Between Dorothy's flying lessons and Jen's pack meetings, we don't have time for it. Besides, Ashley wants her own room again and . . ."

Owen's heart soared, and a smile came unbidden to his face. He still couldn't believe it. Dorothy was a *gryphon*, with wings that promised to be just as glorious as her mother's.

It hurt him—made his heart ache—that he'd been too sick to be there for her while she Changed, but she'd survived, and she was thriving. He'd never have to worry about her being taken away again.

"Think about how good this would be for Dorothy." *And for you,* he didn't say. Besides, Ashley could barely look at David's old bed without bursting into tears. "She'd have someone else to watch her, another gryphon, and you'd have someone to fly with."

That was a low blow, judging by the way Tiffany flinched, but he pressed on. She'd barely left the ground since she'd come here, and she'd have to get comfortable with flying sooner or later. Evans was perfect for that since . . . Well, he needed to relearn how to fly anyway.

Tiffany's jaw tightened as her tail slashed the air behind her. "No."

Owen almost swore. "It wouldn't be for very long; he just needs a place to stay until he gets his feet back under him." It wasn't like he was asking for Tiffany to house the whole Corps in their apartment, just one person. It wasn't even like they hadn't done this before. One of her coworkers had stayed with them for a month once, and he hadn't complained about it.

"I know why you're doing this, Owen, and it won't work." All the fire left her voice as her wings drooped. "It won't make you feel better."

"This isn't about me, Tiff." It was. It was his fault Evans was here, and he needed to make up for it. "He needs help, we can't leave him here."

Tiffany walked away without acknowledging he had spoken, but stopped at the doorway, her wings drawn tight to her. Her voice could've cut steel.

"David's dead, Owen. You need to accept it."

Owen froze, three steps behind Tiffany.

Blood on white sheets, blue eyes glazing over to a chorus of death.

Blinking back tears, he shook the memory away, but it clung to him like a spider's web. It had been ten months, damn it. *Don't be sad,* David had told him, but he couldn't.

"This has nothing to do with David." The words that scraped through his throat flooded up from a well that had been overflowing since he'd buried his son, and they almost drowned him.

"Doesn't it, though?" she asked, her fists shaking at her side. "You found someone to take David's place, and you're so eager to fill the hole you don't even realize what you're doing." If Owen's words came from a well, Tiffany's were from a long-dry reservoir, long since burned out by the heat of the sun.

And suddenly, Owen understood.

"I'm not your father," he said quietly, like it would break her, "and David isn't your brother."

Tiffany turned on her heel, fire spitting from her eyes. "You're doing exactly what Dad did, you think I don't know it when I see it?"

"Tiff—"

"He never had time for me after Mom and Daniel died, I practically had to raise myself," she said, her wings flaring out as she stalked toward Owen. "And then—" Her voice cracked. "And when I brought you home, he had time. He took you fishing, taught you to box and shoot, everything he couldn't bring himself to do after my brother . . ." Her hands curled into shaking fists as her eyes brimmed with tears, and Owen's heart sank.

He wanted to take her into his arms, to comfort her, but every screaming instinct in his bones froze him in place.

"You were a replacement for Daniel, you knew that, and you worshiped him for it." She stumbled back into the wall with a guttural sob. "I won't—I can't do that to my babies, Owen. I can't."

His mouth opened and closed, but try as he might, nothing came out. He hadn't meant it like that, but now that he'd spoken it out loud, he wondered how he'd thought she could see it as anything but him trying to fill the gap David left behind.

Sighing, he took her hands in his and wiped her tears away. "He needs our help, Tiff," he said in a low voice, biting back every screaming emotion that wanted him to lash out. "I'm not trying to replace anyone. What can I do to make you believe that?"

Tiffany stared at him, her tears slowing to a stop. "You have to quit, Owen." The words were rough and hoarse and hollow. "These missions have almost killed you more times than I can count, and this time it wasn't even humans that hurt you. Go to the queen, tell her you quit, and I'll let him stay."

Owen heard the words but didn't want to understand them. The Corps had been his life for months now. He couldn't quit, he had a job to do, and—he'd almost died. Thaddeus and Evans had been crippled, and Isaac was killed. He and Jason were captured.

"You're right," he said in a low voice as he settled at her side. "It's not fair to you or the children, but Tiff, you have to understand. I can't do that. I can't sit around waiting for things to happen." He'd done enough waiting before the battle, watching and learning. He thought he'd figured things out by then.

Blood on white sheets.

He hadn't gone home after the battle, safe in the knowledge that the kids were home and under their neighbor's watchful eye, when the messenger found him outside a clinic nursing his injuries. The agony of walking on a broken leg had been a drop in the ocean of what was to come.

Tiffany scoffed and lifted her head to peer at him with damp eyes. "You did it before, you can do it again."

He wanted to argue. He should have. This job was important to him. He played an important role in protecting the fae. His work kept them safe, fed, and healthy. He had thousands of arguments he could make, and maybe, if he fought long enough, Tiffany would agree. But that wasn't what was at stake here. How long had she spent trying to put their family back together while he'd been deployed? How many times had he come back bleeding and battered from a mission gone wrong?

She was right, and he was arguing to put off the inevitable. He'd been a homemaker before, and he could do it again. If worst came to worst, he could always work as a carpenter again.

"I'll do it. I promise I'll quit. But please, let me take care of Evans."

CHAPTER TEN

In Which the Game Is Set

LORD BRESS: I honestly think the only person not concerned about battleborn vampires is Beira.

LADY ERI: She understands how little of a threat they pose, James.

LORD BRESS: But Uncle Stephen said they can control fae like we do, except they can control humans too.

LORD CHIRON: Lord Aelfric gives them too much credit. Even the weakest elf is stronger than them, and he knows that.

LORD AELFRIC: Don't underestimate their power. Some of my greatest victories were the result of touching someone in the right way, Chiron. Remember, they still look human, and humans trust people who look like them.

—Excerpt from the Council Transcript Archives

The next two days passed in a blur of cleaning out the boys' old room, settling Evans in, and frantically assembling Owen's resignation paperwork. The girls had taken to Evans easier than Owen could've imagined. Five minutes after Evans had walked through the door, Dorothy had him playing dolls with her while Ashley practiced violin.

Jen . . . she'd spent the last two days holed up in her room, buried under a pile of David's old clothes. He should talk to her, but he didn't want to start anything he couldn't finish. His life wasn't his own while the Corps still held his leash, and he just didn't have the time.

"Corporal Williams . . . Owen, wait a moment. I need to speak with you." Beira's voice, soft as a whisper but hard enough to crush diamonds, cut through the milling crowd like a knife.

Wind rattled the windows overlooking the valley floor as the others filtered out, Jason leading a shell-shocked Natalie by the arm. Their debriefing had turned into a disciplinary hearing over her handling of Evans's injuries and . . . everything else. She was lucky she'd escaped with a demotion; General Ziad had wanted to press charges in civilian court for negligence.

The others had long since gone, and even the echoes of their voices had fallen silent before he found the nerve to approach. But still, Beira didn't turn from the window. The world below, cloaked in mist the sun hadn't managed to burn away, had drawn her in entirely, and Owen could understand why.

Beyond the mountain and the trees, the Toad and Liard rivers met in a flurry of rapids. Small lights fought back the fog as the riverboats began their long trade journeys. Still, past that, the threatening clouds that would bring the first real blizzard of the year loomed over the horizon.

But she hadn't asked him to stay so they could admire the scenery.

"I had an interesting meeting the other day," Beira said as calmly as if she were relating an anecdote over tea. "Percill Wilson came to see me, and he was quite perturbed that you had the audacity to get hospitalized."

"I explained everything in my report, Your Majesty," he answered without taking his eyes from the window. He wasn't really looking at the valley—beautiful as it was—but he didn't want to look at her either. It was one thing to submit a report or answer questions with her staring him down; it was another to talk one-on-one. Facing her reflection was painful enough.

It had been six months since he'd stormed out of her office, sending curses flying over his shoulder like bullets. Six months they'd gone without acknowledging each other's existence outside of work. Six months he'd spent fighting to protect their people. Six months where his family had suffered because she refused to do anything. And now, the morning after he and Tiffany submitted his resignation paperwork, the one person who could put a stop to it wanted to speak with him.

They'd been friends before all that. She'd been a rock while his world had fallen apart more times than he wanted to count. Without her, he honestly wasn't sure he'd have survived losing David. She'd found him a place in the Corps, helped Jen join a pack, been a willing ear whenever he needed it . . . but she hadn't been willing to help him run from his problems at home any longer.

He was grown enough to admit he'd missed her since their fight.

"Apparently, we were both supposed to be there. He said you should've made the arrangements."

That . . . wasn't surprising. Percill had a way of doing things that he expected everyone else to abide by.

Clasping his hands behind his back, Owen dug his nails into his wrist and was glad Beira couldn't see them. "What was I supposed to do?" he asked evenly. "I didn't plan to almost die."

Beira shrugged, and her reflection remained infuriatingly tranquil. If it was possible, her icy veneer had gotten even better in the last few months. At this rate, she'd soon resemble the emotionless boulder Dani accused her of being whenever they fought.

"I explained your situation, but he seemed to feel you'd done it to spite him." Her words had a wryness to them, like it was the punchline to a joke only the two of them understood.

Once, it might have made him smile.

Sighing, Beira glanced at him from the corner of her eye. "But that's not why I called you here."

"Your Majesty?" he asked carefully, far calmer than he would have liked. He knew that voice. It was the one that had chased his curses out the door. Blood pounded in his ears as loud as the market at noon, and his stomach quivered.

"Percill is refusing to hand over his information without a guarantee that you'll be on the mission to save the captives."

The world fell away under Owen's feet as his head whipped around. "What?" The room spun, and his breath caught in his chest. "I'm retired," he said dumbly. "I promised Tiffany I was done."

"I know. Your paperwork ended up on my desk this morning." Somehow, she was even more emotionless than before.

"Then you know I can't. Beira, I promised Tiffany—the last mission almost killed me." Half-formed explanations and excuses tripped off his tongue, and none made an impact. "Besides, humans—and civilians—aren't allowed on rescue missions."

"I know." Her eyes became ice that froze the words in Owen's chest even if her face remained unchanged. "We don't have a choice. You know why."

And it broke his heart, but he did. They couldn't leave the captives. Any price was worth it. Even a broken promise.

"So, my resignation was denied?" The words caught on his tongue like a foul taste.

"Not denied," Beira said, her façade breaking for a moment as her lips turned down before it went back up again. "Delayed. We need you. Percill won't work with anyone else."

"Delayed? For how long?" he asked in a shaking voice. His hands fell to his sides in tight fists as each word shot from his mouth like an arrow. It bordered on mutinous, but he couldn't stop himself. The future that waited for him now stretched into oblivion. "He's never going to stop now that you gave in to him. One mission turns to two turns to three until he gets what he wants."

He should stop, but the racing of his heart and the screaming in his ears wouldn't let him. He'd had to deal with Percill for months now. He knew the sort of man Percill was and the sort of man he wasn't. He was a hunter with his prey in his sights. A con man seconds from his goal. A thief with his hands on the crown jewels. If she gave him an inch, he'd take the throne.

"It's one mission," Beira said, like Owen had never spoken at all. "If he's right, we'll have all our people back, and he'll have lost his leverage." She took a step forward, hand outstretched toward him, then fell back without touching him. "I'm sorry, but we have to risk it." She turned, words still flowing from her mouth, but he couldn't hear them.

"It's so easy for you, isn't it?" he asked. He swallowed, desperately wishing for something to drown himself in. His fists shook, and all the air seemed to have fled the room. This wasn't fair. How dare she do this when she'd spent months trying to make him step down. "You have no idea what you're sending me into."

Colonel Ashwind had been right, he realized with a start. She only cared about her people.

He didn't realize he'd said that last bit aloud until Beira spoke.

"You're one of my people too." With that, her calm veneer shattered.

Beira's hands shoved Owen against the window. His head slammed into the glass with a loud crack, and his feet kicked uselessly beneath him. One hand wrapped tightly into his uniform, holding him a foot from the ground like he weighed nothing.

"That man, that *monster,* is everything I don't want to be," she hissed, lifting him higher still. Her eyes burned with the fury of a lightning storm, and her voice thundered off the walls. "I read every report Lieutenant Freeman sent. I know what he wants from you. I know how he revels in destruction, how his every step is soaked with blood."

The glass cracked behind him as he struggled to catch his breath, and a chill sank into his bones while the wind howled in the background.

"He asked me, again, to turn you," she hissed. Her lips pulled back in a smile that didn't reach her eyes, eyes that burned with every emotion she hadn't let herself show before now. "You're right, he won't ever give up. We could deny him for a thousand years, and he'd still ask again as the clock ran down on the thousandth year."

All at once, her hand loosened, and Owen plummeted to the ground, gasping for breath. He tried to speak, to find words to calm the storm he'd unleashed, but she pulled away before he could. Through watery eyes, he watched her, the fire in her eyes burning brighter than he'd ever seen it.

"I allowed him to keep his wretched life because the information he brought was more valuable than my own comfort. I have a duty to our people, Owen, and so do you." Her voice boomed, bouncing off the walls in a way he'd only heard once before. It pushed on him, adding the weight of his vow to his shoulders and demanding he bear the strain. "You took my vow when you joined the Corps, and I will not allow you to relinquish it yet."

All at once, the pressure vanished and Beira visibly shrunk. Her hands came up to cover her face, and they shook.

"You are going on this mission, Owen," she whispered. Her shoulders—her entire body—trembled as her skin paled to a color whiter than snow. "It's your choice whether it's as a prisoner or a captain. Report to my office in two days' time, or I'll have you dragged there."

***

The halls echoed with his footsteps as Owen trudged toward the elevators. "You've really got yourself into a mess this time, Williams," he muttered. "You promised Tiffany you were done." He'd promised everyone.

Dorothy's eyes had lit up like the night sky when she'd heard. The others had been glad too—Ashley even smiled for the first time in months—but Dorothy had been effervescent in her glee. Filing his resignation paperwork had done more to bring his family joy than anything he'd done since they came to Tearmann, and now he had to rip that away from them.

As the elevator began its slow journey down, he crumpled to the floor and let out a shaky sigh. This wasn't his fault, he told the guilt squeezing his chest like a vise. He'd done everything right, filed all the paperwork and everything.

It was really Beira's fault, he thought savagely as he made his way through the tunnels leading to the residential district. She was the one who wouldn't let him retire. She was making him go on this mission. If she'd stood up to Percill, everything would've been fine.

The halls got more crowded the lower he went, which did nothing for his foul mood. Between the lunchtime market rush and a construction detour on the third floor, it felt like half the haven had crammed into the central cavern. Hawkers and shoppers alike screamed at each other just to be heard over the din, and each step became a battle to avoid someone's wing or tail.

Between one move and the next, the crowd swallowed Owen. A centaur, arguing with someone on her back, knocked Owen into a troll, who shoved him into a pack of werewolves, and from there, it was a struggle to keep on his feet, let alone regain control.

With a thud, Owen slammed into something hard that drove the air from his lungs. Rubbing the back of his head, he spun around, a curse ready on his lips, and—froze.

Blood on white sheets, eyes going dim and closing. Holes. God, so many holes. Don't be sad, I'll get to see Mom again.

The world narrowed as Owen's heartbeat roared in his ears, drowning out even the loudest hawker. *Daviddaviddavid*—his lungs screamed for air that didn't come, no matter how hard he gasped. No, he couldn't be here. That was halfway across the market. That was the reason he never came this way.

But he knew that face, knew that shaggy hair he'd fought to tame a thousand times, held that hand through flu shots and across streets. It couldn't be anyone's but his. The memorial statues were scattered through the market. Why did he have to run into this one? Black spots danced in front of his eyes, and his hands shook. God, why couldn't he leave, why wasn't he leaving—

Don't be sad, David had said, like Owen could be anything else with a dead son in his arms. Like the world hadn't come crashing down and broken their family.

Sound and breath came back to the world in the same moment. A stray wing slammed into Owen's back, knocking him over, and he welcomed it. Without waiting for an apology, he stumbled back, heedless of any tails, wings, or feet in his path. His feet took him away, and he weaved through shoppers and stalls like he could outrun the past.

When he finally stopped, his trembling legs crumpled beneath him, and he could barely drag himself to a wall. Pressing a hand to the burning stitch in his side, he breathed deeply through his nose, counting slowly to himself.

This couldn't keep happening.

These . . . incidents, panic attacks had started a month or so after they'd buried David, not long after his first away mission. The first ended with him curled into a ball on the bathroom floor, soaked in sweat and missing the hours between breakfast and lunch. From there, things had only gotten worse.

Being home turned into a harrowing trial, one that tore open half-healed wounds and trapped him in a cage of expectations. Everyone—even Jen—was handling their loss better than he was, and the shame cut him open inside.

The missions had helped. Away from home, fewer things reminded him of what he'd lost, and he learned to avoid anything that triggered the attacks on the rare occasion he was home.

Beira had found him one of the few times he hadn't been able to avoid one.

He didn't remember what had triggered it, but when he'd come back to himself, they were in her office, and she was rubbing his back while softly counting between breaths. At the time, he'd appreciated it.

Beira had a way about her that made people open up. She listened without judging, waiting until she had all the facts before speaking. She'd done it this time too.

He hadn't meant to, but before he knew it, he was laying all his woes out before her. Everything, from how he couldn't sleep to how his family was falling apart to how he barely recognized Tiffany sometimes. That hurt the most.

He'd asked her for advice, desperate for something to soothe the screaming in his chest, and she'd obliged.

You need to stop running, she'd said, as calm as if she were asking him what tea he'd like. *It's your family, and things will only get worse if you neglect things like this.*

From there, she launched onto a campaign to get him to resign. Every meeting, every conversation ended with the same damned question.

Why don't you resign?

Because he couldn't, he'd told her. Because his work was important. Because nothing would change if he stayed home. Because nothing he tried worked anyway. A thousand excuses and a thousand reasons why he couldn't face what his life had become.

That was what made all this hurt so badly.

Sighing, he pressed his head to the cool wall behind him and forced his eyes open. This tunnel was empty and barely used, if its bare walls were anything to go by. Any place that saw much traffic tended to get covered in murals and carvings before the year was out.

The noise of the market was softer here, muted, and it calmed his heart. The last thing he wanted right now was to deal with some well-meaning pedestrian asking if he needed help. Still, if anyone had seen him run in here, he wouldn't be able to avoid that if he didn't get moving.

With a groan, he shoved himself to his feet and ignored how his legs shook.

The tunnel eventually let out near the southern Grand Staircase, and Owen slipped into it as quietly as a shade. It was crowded here, but not as crowded as the market, and his mind wandered while his feet guided him along the familiar path home.

Beira really had tried to get him to retire for months, doing everything short of directly ordering him to. Hell, she'd have thrown him a party if he'd retired a week ago. And if he'd been retired, Percill wouldn't have been able to move her. None of this was her fault.

Percill . . . he was really the one to blame. His obsession with Owen was the reason Beira had delayed his resignation and why he had to look Tiffany in the eyes and tell her he had to do one more mission.

But he couldn't tell Tiffany that, and the thought left a foul taste in his mouth. His feet faltered when he caught sight of their front door. Percill's very existence was on a need-to-know basis. Two-thirds of the Corps didn't know about him, and Tiffany was a civilian. Cor, she'd think Owen had gone behind her back, had voided his resignation paperwork for one more shot at glory.

If he was lucky, he'd end up on the couch for a month if she didn't kick him out entirely. She wouldn't make Evans leave, not when they'd already welcomed him into their home, but she could do a million things to make Owen miserable.

Squaring his shoulders, he turned the doorknob and tried to ignore the sinking in his stomach. Better to deal with it now and avoid any accusations of him trying to hide it from her.

Tiffany narrowed her eyes at him the moment he stepped foot through the door, and Owen was grateful the kids were gone. One look, and she shook her head. A second, and he opened his mouth to explain before she assumed the worst, but it was too late.

"You said you quit," Tiffany said in a voice that would've chilled an active volcano. Her tail lashed around her ankles while she aggressively scrubbed the lunch dishes. "You promised me."

"I know," he said softly, leaning against the doorframe. His chest ached. "But the queen wouldn't—"

"Wouldn't let you?" Tiffany scoffed, and threw her rag into the soapy water. "The same woman who believes in free will so strongly that she let the battleborn establish their own country even though it practically violates an international treaty? *She* wouldn't let you?"

Wincing, Owen took a deep breath and raked a hand through his hair. "It's more complicated than that, Tiff," he said tiredly. "She didn't have a choice." Percill hadn't given her one, just like she hadn't given him one. "The informant will only help if I'm there." It sounded hollow even to his ears.

"Why you? Tell me that at least." She turned, wiping her damp hands on her apron, and then crossed her arms. "There's nothing you can do that hundreds of other Corpsfolk couldn't do better."

He ran a hand through his hair again and wished things were different. If Percill didn't insist on so much secrecy, if this mission had come a month ago, if he'd never met the man in the first place . . . If, if, if. So many *ifs* that wouldn't change anything and weren't going to help him.

"The informant insisted," he finally managed, swallowing the lump in his throat. "I can't say more. It's confidential."

"Confidential?" Her voice dropped to scarcely louder than a whisper. Would she curse at him? Yell?

But she held her tongue and spun to face the sink in silence. Her hands shook as she dunked them into the soapy water. "You promised me you were done," she said evenly. "But you lied to me, admit it."

That stung. Swallowing hard, he stepped forward, a hand raised to touch her shoulder, but thought better of it. Water soaked into his jacket as he leaned against the edge of the counter, but the kitchen was too small to go anywhere else and still be able to look her in the eye. "I've never lied to you, Tiff," he said quietly as she furiously scrubbed a pot.

He hadn't. Almost twenty years they'd been together and he'd never so much as fibbed about brushing his teeth.

"I promise, I'm telling the truth."

She snorted and set the pot out to dry. "That's not an answer," she snapped, yanking the plug free as she did.

The gurgling of the water down the drain was the only sound other than her deep breathing. Eventually, silence fell, and a horrible feeling settled into Owen's gut. He should say something, but he couldn't figure out what.

"I need an explanation, Owen," she finally said, resting her hands on the sink. "I can't take this at your word. You've been sneaking around for months. Even the kids have noticed. I don't want to assume the worst, but . . ." A quiet sob burst through her lips, and both hands shot up to cover her mouth.

Owen recoiled like he'd been struck and almost fell over. No, she couldn't . . . he wouldn't, but . . . he could understand it, and he had to swallow bile.

"I'm not . . ." he whispered. "Tiff, I wouldn't do that to you, to the kids." It wasn't enough. Before, back when they'd all been humans and the fae were something he read about in the news, she'd known that. Now, she didn't know him well enough to know better. They'd both changed too much for that.

He'd spend up to a week home after a mission, then be gone for two. He told stories about what he'd done but not where he'd been or what he'd seen. The kids had pulled away—Dorothy didn't come to him when she got hurt, Ashley barely spoke at all, Jen had practically moved out, and—and his family had fallen apart.

But he couldn't tell her why, no matter how much keeping it from her tore at his heart. The rules existed for a reason, even if he didn't understand them and no matter how much they hurt the ones he loved. Even if he told her, he doubted she'd believe him, and it wouldn't change anything he had to do. Percill wouldn't be dissuaded, and Beira had made his options painfully clear.

"Tiff, I really don't have a choice here. I promise, it's just one more mission."

In the silence that followed, a speck of dust hitting the floor would have sounded like cannon fire. Tiffany's sigh was significantly louder than a speck of dust.

"Is that how we're doing this?" Tiffany asked. Her voice shook, and she wouldn't meet his eyes. "One more mission? And how many more informants are going to insist you need to be there after that? Two? A dozen? Just admit you don't want to retire, or come up with something better if you're going to lie to me." Her wings quivered behind her, and he ached to hold her, to comfort her like he'd have done before he joined the Corps, but he didn't have the right to do that anymore. Not when she thought he'd...

Owen swallowed. His head spun, his chest tightened, and he almost blurted the truth out right then and there.

Tiffany's eyes, her bright blue eyes that had been David's, grew damp and watery. "I think you should stay somewhere else for the time being. It's not like you're here much anyway." She turned away, toward the living room, and took Owen's heart with her.

"I have a meeting with her in two days," he found himself saying, tongue thick with confusion and pain. "You can ask her yourself, all right?" He'd never brought anyone besides Dorothy to his meetings with Beira before. It definitely crossed a line, but he couldn't bring himself to care. Tiffany would never believe him otherwise. She'd never forgive him anyway, a small part of him whispered. She thought he'd broken his promise. She thought worse.

Tiffany stopped, one foot in the living room and one in the kitchen. "Come with you?" she said without turning around. Her voice cracked. "You think that's all it'll take? An invitation to one of your 'meetings'?"

"No—" The implication almost made Owen sick.

She turned. Her eyes were still damp, but a fire had been lit behind them. She stalked toward him, a predatory gleam holding him still. "Well, I will go with you," Tiffany said, holding her head high, "and we'll see what the queen has to say about this."

***

Tiffany didn't eat dinner with them that night. A blanket and pillow and three days' worth of Owen's clothing had been unceremoniously dumped on the bathroom floor while he'd been cleaning up. The locked bedroom door had driven the message home. Owen was in the doghouse.

"Are you and Mommy fighting, Daddy?" Dorothy asked. She'd been in the middle of telling him, in detail, about everything that had happened while he'd been gone and hadn't seemed likely to stop while she still had breath. Jen, it seemed, had competition for the title of family chatterbox. "Jingyi said his daddy had to sleep on the couch for a whole year when he called his mommy a name." Her brown eyes widened to the size of saucers, and she clapped her hands over her mouth. "Did you call Mommy a bad name?" she asked in a hushed voice.

Owen resisted the urge to sigh when Arthur, home for one more night before he had to return to the barracks, snickered as he walked past. "No. She and I just need a little time apart, that's all." And he needed to find his way back into her good graces. "Now, why don't you finish your story?" He patted the sofa next to him and got a mouthful of feathers for his trouble when she leaped onto the couch.

Dorothy's downy wing pulled away without her noticing its brief residence in his mouth. "Jingyi wants me to come to his birthday party next week, but I don't want to go. He played a mean trick on Toby, and we're not friends anymore."

"Oh?" Owen asked, relieved Dorothy was young enough to be distracted so easily. "What did he do?" The others might not have been as blunt about what he and Tiffany had argued about, but they wouldn't stop asking until they knew.

Dorothy squealed and bounced in her seat. "Oh, it was so bad," she said with a frown so severe it wouldn't have looked out of place on a prison warden. "Mr. Abnell said Toby's recital braids were nice, and Jingyi got jealous, 'cause he forgot to paint his scales."

"Really? What happened next?" Owen asked. The door to the boys' room shut with an audible bang, likely Arthur's attempt to escape a story Owen was sure he'd already heard a thousand times. It left him alone with Dorothy, and he was glad of it. She was growing up too fast.

"Well, first he asked to borrow my scissors, 'cause he broke his, and then guess what he did? Guess, Daddy, guess!"

"I don't know. What?" Owen asked as he pulled his blanket out from under his pillow. He draped it over the two of them, and Dorothy snuggled into his side. Her tiny claws dug into his legs like pinpricks.

"He cut Toby's picture all up! There were so many pieces even Mr. Abnell couldn't fix it." Dorothy's lower lip quivered, and her tail twitched beside her. The feathery tuft hit Owen's leg every few seconds, a move so reminiscent of Tiffany his throat swelled. "Toby was so sad Mr. Abnell had to send him home, 'cause he was going to give it to his nana. Sophie, Henry and me wanted to make him feel better, so we all painted pictures for him. That way he can choose which one he likes best and give it to his nana just like he wanted to." Her whole face lit up as she smiled.

"What happened next?"

"Jingyi had to say sorry and . . ."

Dorothy had a way of speaking that made him feel like he'd been there. Her words had a life to them that drew him in, even when they were nonsensical to the point of being incomprehensible. She was full of life, and that was what Owen needed right now.

So he let himself get lost in her stories. One bled into another over and over again until long past her bedtime. Dorothy drifted off between one word and the next, halfway through a story that could have been about a duel to the death or Arthur's last visit home. They'd sort of blurred together toward the end.

He should take her to bed. It was late, and she had to be up early tomorrow, but he couldn't make himself move her. It had been months since he'd been able to do this, to spend enough time with Dorothy—with any of them—that she fell asleep. He should move her. She wasn't the only person who needed to be up early. And yet . . .

She'd changed since he'd last been home and not just physically. The physical differences were the most obvious, of course, but that didn't make the hidden ones any less important.

Glossy black fur covered her from head to paw and all the way to the tip of her tail. Her wings were large and cumbersome, and not an hour went by when she didn't knock them into something, but he'd been assured she'd grow into them. Downy white fluff mixed with the beginning of proper primary, secondary, and tertial feathers. Her tail—oh, her tail—was an interesting mix of down, feather, and fur. It had a mind of its own, and Dorothy had taken to holding it in her hand to keep from tripping over it.

But . . . the physical differences were only the start. She'd blossomed while he'd been gone, and he kept kicking himself for missing it. What good had he done that was worth missing his children growing up? He'd missed her Changing, for crying out loud. She'd been hurting, probably worse than she'd ever been hurt in her life, and he hadn't been there.

Dorothy mumbled something in her sleep and turned to bury her head in his leg. Owen brushed a hand through her hair and was more grateful than he'd like to admit that it hadn't been cut. It was rougher than it used to be, but the hair on her head was still finer than her fur.

Tiffany's hair, her beautiful hair, hadn't made it. She'd always worn it long, down almost to her waist. He wasn't sure if it'd been cut by SAFE or if it'd fallen out like Arthur's had, but her hair was gone.

Dorothy's thumb had found its way into her mouth, and she looked younger than she was. She wouldn't remember their house, the house her grandfather had built, or riding in a car or airplanes or anything of their life before coming here. She . . .

She needed to go to bed. It was late, and staying up later to worry about things she'd never experience wouldn't make those things happen.

As he hefted Dorothy in his arms, he realized she was lighter than he'd expected. So light, he could balance her on one arm and corral her wings with the other. Truth be told, her wings were the hardest thing to manage. He told himself he wouldn't break them if he touched them, but the hollow bones felt so fragile under his hand.

She woke up while he was putting her to bed. It wasn't much, just long enough to wish him goodnight before she burrowed herself in her blankets, but it made Owen smile. He wasn't getting everything wrong. He cast his eyes around the rest of the darkened room, at the dark shapes that were Jen and Ashley. This was what was important, and he'd neglected it for too long while chasing after something he'd never reach.

CHAPTER ELEVEN

In Which Owen Is Vindicated

LORD CHIRON: What good would a draft do for our society?

QUEEN TITANIA: It's not a draft.

LORD CHIRON: Sure, Your Majesty, it's a mandatory reserve.

LORD AELFRIC: The mandatory reserve will ensure the away teams have the people they need to accomplish their objectives.

LORD CHIRON: We already fought one war and our people are tired. We will never have peace if your warmongering keeps us perched on the precipice of annihilation—

QUEEN TITANIA: The mandatory reserve will remain in place until the volunteer corps are large enough to cover the shortfall, Chiron. Aelfric, see to it that the appropriate people are informed—and stop antagonizing him.

—Excerpt from the Council Transcript Archives

Tearmann was built inside a mountain range with all the spacing issues that it entailed, carved up like a six-layered cake to make use of every inch.

In theory, it made sense to utilize space like that, but in practice, it made Owen want to rip his hair out. There used to be more shortcuts back before the Battle of Tearmann, but after a stray grenade turned the convenient staircase between the second and third floors into a deathtrap, he had to walk halfway around the market just to get to the political district on the third floor.

Tiffany was going to kill him.

He'd said he'd meet her there. He wouldn't be long, so just wait outside the queen's office. He just had to run by the Foodbank—the organization that monitored humans in the havens and organized Beira's blood donors—and let them know his retirement had been postponed and to not put him back in rotation yet.

He should've known better, and from the way Tiffany was tapping a clawed foot and scowling, she thought that too.

Tiffany shook her head. "I almost thought you weren't going to come." She didn't look at him. Instead her eyes roved over the hall like she expected someone to jump out at her. She tangled her hands into her knit shawl and swallowed.

Skidding to a halt at her side, he smiled ruefully. "Sorry," he managed to gasp, clutching the stitch in his side, "I—hit an unexpected detour."

Technically, he was still on time. Early even, but Tiffany didn't know that. If he could get her in and out before the real meeting started, he probably wouldn't get in trouble for bringing her here to begin with.

"Shall we go in?" he asked, offering his arm to her. She didn't take it. Keeping close to the wall, she moved toward Beira's secretary.

"She's not going to let me in, Owen," she said under her breath. She frowned as she tugged her shawl tighter over her shoulders. "This is a waste of time."

"It'll be fine, Tiff. I promise." Silently, he prayed Beira wouldn't make a liar of him. He hadn't approved this with her, but her anger would be nothing compared to the storm Tiffany would unleash if she thought he'd lied to her again.

Beira's secretary, a blond elf who hadn't liked Owen even before he and Beira had fallen out, raised an eyebrow at Tiffany. "Meetings by appointment only, Corporal Williams." She wasn't as powerful an empath as David had been, or even as strong as Eoire was, but her disapproval was palpable. Owen could taste it, like sewage sitting at the back of his throat.

"It's captain now, Ms. Henninger," he said, trying to sound and feel more confident than he actually was. Lying to elves was hard. He needed to feel like he believed what he was saying as well as sound like it. "And we have one. Captain Williams and guest, at two." Technically, Owen's was the only name there, but it shouldn't matter. He'd done this before. Twice. With Dorothy.

Ms. Henninger frowned, a perfect match to the one Tiffany still wore. Taking her gaze off Owen for a bare second, she glanced at something behind her desk. "It seems you're correct," she said as her eyes returned to drilling holes in Owen's forehead. "She's still with her one o'clock, though."

The *you'll have to wait* was heavily implied, but Owen stepped forward like he hadn't a care in the world. "It's fine," Owen said. "We'll wait in the council chamber." He grabbed Tiffany's arm and pulled her behind him.

It was a small miracle Ms. Henninger didn't try to stop them. Beira's visitors were supposed to wait at the desk until they were called in. The fact that he didn't have to was a testament to how often he'd done this before their falling out. Score one for old habits and fast movement.

Prompt as she usually was, it was still five minutes before two by the time Beira's door opened, and the gryphon she'd been meeting with rushed out.

"I know you're lurking around out there, Owen," Beira called, her voice lacking its usual energy as it drifted into the council room. "Come in before anything else goes wrong. Otherwise, we'll have to put this off for another week."

Once, Owen might have asked her what was wrong and joked about the number of things that required the queen's personal attention. Beira would've laughed and called him something foul before launching into a tirade about whatever was bothering her. He'd have been able to breeze in, one of the few who wasn't a founder that who could do that.

They hadn't been that close in a while.

Beira was paging through a book, her back to the door, as they entered, and gave no indication she'd heard them. Owen sucked in a breath. Even from behind, she didn't look good. Her clothes, which had once fit well, hung off her shoulders, swallowing an already skeletal frame. Tension sat coiled in her shoulders and neck and made each movement look stiff.

"Your Majesty," he said awkwardly. The title didn't sit right in his mouth. He could count the number of times he'd used it outside of briefings or meetings on one hand. When they'd been friends, he hadn't needed to, and afterward, he hadn't had cause.

"Mrs. Williams, I don't seem to recall inviting you to this meeting," Beira said without turning around. An edge to her words had Owen wondering if their argument was replaying in her mind as well.

"Owen said you wouldn't let him retire."

Well, Tiffany had never been one to beat around the bush. All the same, any chance of Owen escaping this without getting in trouble for bringing her to a meeting that should—technically and practically speaking—be confidential vanished.

The book snapped shut, and Beira set it in its place with clinical precision. "Your husband took an oath to defend the haven and its people when he joined the Corps. He is subject to their rules now, one of which is obeying the orders of his superiors." She turned and fixed a blank stare on Tiffany. "I am his superior and I gave him an order."

Tiffany's wings bristled, and her shawl fell to the floor. "He resigned," she snarled, surging forward to slam her hands down on Beira's desk. If Owen hadn't been more concerned with the looming and ever-increasing possibility of getting court-martialed, he'd have been touched at how fast her anger had turned from him to Beira. It vindicated him, at the very least. "He's not a part of the Corps anymore."

Beira glanced at Owen and back. "His resignation was delayed." Her eyebrow arched as she sank into her chair. "Owen should have told you."

Owen shrunk back against the wall. He'd managed to avoid being drawn into this so far and—even if this was his fault—he wanted it to stay that way.

Fortunately, Tiffany didn't take the bait. Her claws dug into the wood, leaving deep scratches in their wake. "You've had him on your leash for months, and just when I get him untangled, you pull him back in."

Beira rubbed her temples and closed her eyes. "It's more complicated than that."

"Yes, everything is classified." Tiffany's lips pressed together as her claws dug into the wood in a way that made Owen flinch. That would be a nightmare to repair. "He did tell me that."

"I was under the impression this was supposed to be a private meeting."

That oily voice sent chills down Owen's spine as he and Tiffany whirled around. A figure, surrounded by shadows that seemed unwilling to flee under the light, stood in the doorway. Owen's heart jumped to his throat, and he made an aborted attempt to step in front of Tiffany. He knew that figure.

"Percill. You're early." Beira was, as ever, a beacon a serenity while things went wrong.

Without indicating that he'd heard her, Percill stepped into the light and approached Owen. "Mr. Williams, I see you decided to come this time. It was quite upsetting to hear you wouldn't be attending our last meeting." A skeletal smile exposed red-stained teeth as he set a hand on Owen's shoulder. "You're lucky the queen convinced me to wait."

Owen swallowed and forced his hands to unclench. Tensing like that put the ball in Percill's court. "I got held up." That was one way to put being kidnapped, held for ransom, and then spending three days in the hospital, but he refused to admit that. Percill was a shark who smelled blood.

"Of course, I'd expect no less of you," Percill said in a soft voice. His eyes slid from Owen to Tiffany. "Ah, this must be your wife. I've heard so much about you, my dear."

Tiffany glanced at Owen while Percill bent down to kiss her hand. "I can't say the same about you," she said in a shaky voice. Her ears lay flat against her head as she pulled her hand away and discreetly wiped it on her leg.

Raising an eyebrow, Percill took a step back. "Is that so? I met your family on their journey to the haven, and your husband and I have been working together for months."

"Enough, Percill," Beira said. "We have work to do."

Owen appreciated the rebuke beneath her words. He didn't care for the calculating way Percill was looking at Tiffany, or how the ever-present oily touch of his thoughts had disappeared once he'd seen her. It was bad enough he had Owen in his sights; he didn't need to get his claws into Tiffany too.

"Mrs. Williams, I'm sorry, but we'll have to continue this meeting at a different time. Say, three o'clock tomorrow?"

Turning back to Beira, Tiffany nodded. "Three works," she said in a shaky whisper. Her wings pulled in tight around her body as she picked up her shawl. "I'll leave you to it, then. I . . . I should be getting home. The girls will be home from school soon."

"No, please stay," Percill said, pulling a chair out from the front of Beira's desk. His smile grew even wider but didn't touch his empty eyes. "You might find our discussions interesting."

"She's not a Corps member, Percill," Beira said. She folded her hands in front of her. "This meeting is confidential."

Percill chuckled. "Exceptions can be made. This does concern her, after all."

Owen bristled, and his fists clenched again. The oily presence was back, and it wanted Tiffany there. Blast, she needed to get out. If Percill wanted her for something, they couldn't let him get it.

"No, she's right," Tiffany said, and edged around Percill to get to the door. "I should go."

"Wait," Beira said, rising half from her seat before Tiffany moved more than two steps. "What do you mean, Percill?" Gone was the serenity, and in its place was calculating focus that turned her eyes to ice.

"These places are always built in the same fashion." Percill's pale, almost translucent skin stretched over his hands as he tapped his forehead. "She knows more about the facility than my contacts, and what's more, they won't expect a captive to return. Besides . . ." He smiled, but it lacked even the cursory warmth of a corpse. "You and Mr. Williams trust her."

Beira wouldn't agree. This was a matter for the Corps to deal with, and there were members who'd survived as captives; they'd be as familiar with the research centers as Tiffany was. They didn't need her to get involved. Percill just wanted to mess with Owen.

But as the seconds ticked by and she made no move to send Tiffany away, Owen's heart sank. "Beira, you can't seriously . . ." He couldn't even bring himself to finish. The thought of putting Tiffany in the line of fire—leaving her where Percill could get his slimy fingers into her—was more than he could bear.

"She can stay for now, but if you can't provide a more concrete reason for her presence within the next ten minutes, there will be consequences."

"Certainly, Your Majesty." Another smile that didn't reach his eyes spread fresh blood over Percill's teeth as his fangs pierced through his lower lip. "Rest assured, she is perfect for what I have in mind."

The air disappeared from Owen's lungs like a black hole had opened up in his chest. They were supposed to get Tiffany away from here. She couldn't—Beira couldn't be serious. She'd been the one to warn him to keep Percill and all the battleborn vampires away from his family in the first place.

"Captain Williams, sit down," Beira said in an even, measured tone. "I won't ask you again."

He blinked, and the room came back into focus. Tiffany was now sitting in front of Percill, and his hands rested on her shoulders. No, resting wasn't the right word. They were holding her there—if her many failed attempts to nudge him away were any indication.

"Please, Captain Williams. I don't have all day," Percill said, removing one hand from Tiffany's shoulder to gesture at the spare chair. "Sit."

Owen's throat closed over any response he could have made as he shuffled forward. His knees turned to wood and refused to bend when he went to sit, but the threatening groan the chair made when he fell into it went unnoticed as Beira and Percill began speaking.

He didn't know what they said. His breathing drowned out their words, and what filtered through could have come through a wind tunnel for all he could understand. His focus narrowed in on Tiffany, still trapped by a monster. A monster he hadn't been able to protect her from. A monster he'd put in her path to begin with.

Owen had broken his one rule for dealing with Percill. He'd flinched. He'd exposed his weakness, and now all his vulnerabilities had become toys for a master manipulator. The bitter taste of bile almost made him gag. It didn't matter what they said or what plans they'd made.

Percill was in control.

***

Tiffany's voice snapped Owen back to attention and returned air to his lungs.

"...for that long. It was bad enough when it was just Owen that was gone all the time."

"Mrs. Williams, surely you understand that your aid is needed here." A note of exasperation in Percill's voice made Owen oddly proud. He'd never known Tiffany to let anyone push her around for long, and Percill was no exception.

"It's only one mission, Mrs. Williams," Beira said. One side of her mouth pulled back into an almost imperceptible smirk as she scribbled something in her notepad. "Afterward you and your husband would be released from the Corps."

"You said the same thing when you first pushed me to join the Corps, Your Majesty," Owen croaked. He swallowed and tried again. "We both know how that ended."

One mission turned to two and three. By the fifth, the one that ended with scars running down the length of his back, Owen had been the one pushing for more missions while Beira tried to convince him to stay home. The thing she'd offered as a temporary escape had become the tool he'd used to run from a wound that would never heal. He saw that now.

Beira's breath hitched. It wasn't much, practically unnoticeable if he hadn't known what to look for, but there nonetheless. "I fail to see how that is relevant, Captain Williams. This is a special circumstance." Her fingers tightened on her pen, only loosening when the metal bent under the pressure. "She's being drafted. Once the mission is completed, she is free to do as she pleases."

"It doesn't matter in any case," Percill said. By now, he'd moved behind Beira's oak desk and stood at her left shoulder. "She's one member of your team. A team, I may remind you, I have given you permission to choose." The lamp behind him chose that moment to sputter out, casting him into darkness, and yet—his eyes shone like they had absorbed its light. "If you wish to free the captive fae, you must listen to me. Without my information, you have no hope of succeeding."

"Believe me, we're well aware of that," Tiffany said. Her voice was calm—almost civil—but her body language was anything but. Her tail lashed back and forth, hitting Owen every rotation, and her claws had already driven deep gouges into her armrests.

Beira coughed to draw everyone's attention back to her. "I hate to cut the meeting short, but I have another appointment, and I still need to discuss the team with Captain Williams."

Frowning, Percill pulled away from Beira and said, "Of course, but I can't help but think it would be more beneficial if I was here . . ."

"We'll send you the list," Beira said dryly. She stood and, taking Percill by the arm, walked him to the door. "Rest assured, we'll keep you updated."

Perhaps sensing that Beira wasn't going to give in, Percill went without a fuss, and the tension noticeably dropped once the oak door clicked shut behind him.

Beira leaned against the door and let out a sigh while her shoulders slumped, and all traces of her serenity faded away. "Well, that was a train wreck," she muttered.

"What exactly was that?" Tiffany asked in a small voice. "What was he? Why was he so interested in me?" She hadn't pulled her claws from their wooden resting place yet and, if the way her fur and feathers were still ruffled was any sign, wasn't going to anytime soon.

"That," Beira said, rubbing the bridge of her nose, "was Percill Wilson. He's the long arm of my information ring in the U.S. Without him, we'd lose half of our teams."

He did much more than that, Owen wanted to say. In the time since he'd removed himself from safehouse duty, Percill had established himself as a force to be reckoned with. He'd set up more safehouses, trained more allies, and brought in more supplies than people who'd been running the borders for decades. His methods were maybe questionable, but his results weren't.

"When did you tune back in, Owen?" Beira asked, shaking Owen from his thoughts. "When you spoke or earlier?" She crossed the room and pulled three glasses from one of the cupboards behind her desk. Her hand hovered between her whiskey decanter and her ever-present pitcher of tepid water before she filled each glass with water.

Owen's heart skipped a beat. Blast, it was too much to hope no one had noticed. "Just before I spoke," he admitted quietly.

"So you missed the bulk of the meeting," she said, then sighed deeply. "Wonderful. Well, at least Percill didn't seem to notice."

"Excuse me, what are you talking about?" Tiffany asked. Her eyes darted between Owen and Beira as her ears perked up.

Beira turned around, three water glasses in hand and her eyebrow arched. "Your husband was dissociating and likely had an anxiety attack as well. Don't try to deny it, you don't live the kind of life I have without becoming familiar with the signs. Here, finish this." She shoved one glass at Owen, the second at Tiffany, and set the third on her desk. "I'd offer whiskey, but we're going to need to keep our wits about us for now."

Beira waited until they'd emptied their glasses to speak again. She set hers aside, leaned forward, and folded her hands. "Now, I'm not going to give you a blow-by-blow of the meeting, Owen—I'll leave that to Tiffany—but there are a few things we need to get sorted before I can let you leave."

"Can't this wait?" Owen didn't know why, but he was struggling to keep his eyes open. His whole body had gone numb, and his mind drifted between thoughts. "It's past three."

"And it'll be later still before we're done."

Owen looked at Beira through bleary eyes. Putting the words he needed together took a colossal effort, and opening his mouth an even bigger effort, and—

"Then we better get started," Tiffany said. She leaned forward, resting her elbows on her knees, and steepled her fingers, an imperfect mirror of Beira.

Beira smiled, and the effect was that of two equally strong wills combining to reach their goals. "To start, you'll need to pick a team of ten or fewer members, including the two of you. The whole of the Corps, reserves and active duty, are available, but I have some recommendations . . ."

And so it went. Beira made a suggestion; Owen shot it down and returned with one of his own. Even Tiffany, who seemed to have fully accepted her role in these events, had more than a few ideas. And even once they'd sorted out the team, they had more to discuss.

They talked until a clock, buried somewhere on Beira's overloaded bookshelves, chimed six times. Swearing and apologizing for keeping them so long, she ushered them out and promised to notify the proper people before their next meeting.

With the echoes of a slammed door reverberating through the council chamber, Owen instinctively searched for Tiffany's hand. Her claws dug into his knuckles as her fingers wound around his and squeezed.

They'd decided on four people for their—*Owen's*—team. Two he'd worked with before and wouldn't hesitate to trust with his life. Of the other two, one was a stranger and the other, he knew from experience, didn't have full control over her abilities. Beira would choose a dragon to transport them, and Owen trusted her judgment, but the whole situation made him queasy.

Tiffany squeezed his hand again. She smiled tightly when Owen looked at her. She gently tugged him after her, and something knotted inside Owen came undone.

Whatever happened, at least she believed him now.

CHAPTER TWELVE

In Which a Bridge Is Repaired

"Werewolf packs are the core of the fae foster care system. In practical terms, this is because any orphaned, lost, or neglected child that finds their way to a werewolf will end up with thirty odd caretakers fully prepared to do whatever it takes to keep them safe regardless of what anyone else says about it. Rather than fight them on it, the Founders Council decided to formalize the process. They can smell abuse and fear, you know, so generally any child that ends up in their ranks will be better taken care of than if they were at home. As a result, a werewolf's testimony about a given parent's care toward their child is generally seen as enough to decide custody agreements one way or the other."
—Excerpt from A History of the Havens *by Anthony Freedman, Lord Chiron*

It was six in the evening, and the population of Tearmann was on the move. Exhausted workers rushed to finish their errands before the shops closed for the night, and the lamplighters began their work of refilling empty oil jars and replacing spent wicks. In a few hours, they would snuff out three out of every four lamps—plunging most of the city into a void—but for now, the world was full of life.

Owen's hand tightened around Tiffany's as they walked down the crowded halls. The people around them had no idea what their rulers did behind the scenes, the deals they made with demons to ensure their protection, and he envied them for it. They had a queen who would move mountains to keep them safe. A queen who would sacrifice anything for the greater good.

Anything.

"Owen," Tiffany whispered, barely loud enough to be heard over the chaos. "What are we going to do? We only have a month."

A month? That was news to him. Blast, he'd missed too much. That didn't leave much time for training or planning. "I'm not sure," he muttered, scanning the hallway. The Grand Staircase would be crowded at this hour; they'd be lucky if they got home in under a half hour, and they were late enough as it was. "We'll figure something out."

Sighing, Tiffany pulled Owen forward, clearing a path through the crowd with her wings and her will. "We don't have time to figure something out. We can't leave the kids alone for a week."

"Arthur and Ashley could watch them," Owen suggested as he ducked under a centaur's wildly gesticulating arm. "They're old enough."

"That's no good." Tiffany finally released his hand as they breached the crowd and entered the surprisingly empty Grand Staircase. "Between his training and that Kordonowy girl, he won't have time. Besides, he's only seventeen."

His hand felt empty and cold, and he shoved it in his pocket without thinking too hard on that. She'd been kind to him so far, but he wouldn't assume she'd forgiven him. With all he'd done—and hadn't done—he wouldn't.

"Can't we ask him to move back in for a few weeks?" he asked. The lamplighters hadn't gotten here yet, and a full third of the lamps had gone out. "I'm sure the Corps would let him if he asked."

"No, they wouldn't. They let him come home for your party, so they won't let him take another leave right away." Her voice took on a sharp edge that bounced back on them like a shout. She hadn't wanted Arthur to join the Corps in the first place. "He needs to be near the hospital for his training. It's why he moved out in the first place, remember?"

"And our apartment was too far away." Owen did remember that argument. The whole bloody neighborhood did. He'd just returned from a mission in Texas and had almost turned around to beg for a new one to avoid being caught in the cross fire. Unfortunately, Jen had seen him, and he'd had no choice in the matter.

"Hurry up, dear. We should've been home an hour ago." Her wings caught the ever-present updraft as she spoke, and she glided down a few steps to their floor.

"Easier said than done," Owen muttered, skipping steps to keep up with her. It was too bloody dark for this. One wrong step and he'd break his leg again. That was probably why no one was using the staircase right now, come to think of it.

Their discussion continued as they walked through the housing district and all the way to their front door. Their neighbors were crossed off the list for being too busy, Owen's old boss got shot down because he and his wife had their hands full with their grandchild, and even leaving them with the werewolves was soundly rejected because of a laundry list of issues, most centered on Dorothy. Her wings were still growing in, but that hadn't stopped her from trying to use them. In the short time he'd been home, Owen had stopped her from jumping off three tables, the Grand Staircase, Evans, and—

Owen stopped, hand on the doorknob. "Tiff," he said without turning his head. "What about Evans?"

***

"So, you want me to babysit?" Evans asked, taking a clean plate from Owen.

It had been a stroke of luck that Owen and Tiffany had returned home before Evans and the girls went to the cafeteria and nothing short of a miracle that they had food in the kitchen for Owen to cook with. They'd never have been able to have a coherent conversation in the cafeteria at this time of day.

"Out of the way," Tiffany ordered, then pushed Owen aside so she could dump her load of dishes in the sink. "We'd pay you, of course," she continued, dunking her hands into the soapy water, "and it's only for a week,"

"I can do dishes, Tiff. Cooking doesn't remove my ability to use a sponge," Owen said, but obediently shuffled away anyway.

"It's not a question of if you can do them," Tiffany returned in the same fashion. "It's if you'll do them before Dorothy distracts you again."

"Be that as it may—"

"Hate to interrupt," Evans said, looking very much like he didn't mind interrupting at all. "But I'm tired, so . . ."

Duly scolded, Tiffany shoved her hands into the soapy water and got to work. "Like I said, it's only a week, and we'll have a month to get ready for it." Without looking, she pushed a battered red pot in Evans's direction. "Here, this one goes in the cabinet over there."

Evans, despite repeated assurances from Tiffany and Owen that he didn't have to do any chores, had latched onto helping with the dishes as a way of paying them back for letting him stay. Like most gryphons, he hated feeling like a burden. He and Tiffany definitely had that in common. Apparently, that desire didn't extend to childcare. "Why can't you ask one of the neighbors?" he asked, shuffling across the kitchen on his hind legs. His prosthetic arm may have provided balance, but he hadn't mastered using it to hold things yet, and his pride forbade him from asking for help. He set the pot on the counter and pulled the cabinet door open with his flesh arm. "Or even better, just let Ashley do it."

In another life, that would've been the perfect solution. In the eyes of the fae, thirteen was more than old enough to watch their siblings alone, even for weeks at a time, but they couldn't dump that responsibility onto her on top of therapy, school, and everything else she dealt with as the only human in her family.

"It's complicated," Owen whispered, glancing into the living room. Ashley was reading a book to Dorothy while Jen pretended not to listen. His heart panged, and he wished he could be in there with them. "We don't want to put that much pressure on her. She hasn't been the same since . . ." *Blood on whi*—no, now was not the time. He couldn't do that here. Speaking past the lump in his throat, he turned back to Evans. "We'd thought that since you were living here anyway—"

"I could keep an eye on them." Evans sighed and carefully eased the load of plates he'd balanced on his prosthetic onto the counter. "I mean, I suppose I could. Dot wants to learn how to fly and, no offense meant, but you two are way out of your league there."

Any other time—discussing anything else—Owen might have laughed at the face Evans made. Beaks made frowning practically impossible, but he had managed it.

"To be fair, Tiff's wings came out fully formed," Owen tried to joke. His lips pulled back in a facsimile of a smile that he hoped didn't look forced. "We didn't have to deal with her jumping off things."

"Fledglings'll do that," Evans said, dropping to his haunches as he took another pot from Tiffany. "She needs to work her muscles so they grow properly. Since she can't play any flying games with you, she's trying to do it on her own."

Owen threw his hands in the air. "See? You're already taking care of them. You'd be perfect." Sighing, he ran a hand through his hair as his stomach twisted into knots. He should've known that. With Jen, he'd spent hours with their werewolf neighbors, asking questions and taking notes. The boys had had teachers to show them how to use their abilities, teachers who'd been more than happy to talk with him. But with Dorothy . . . He hadn't even been there for her Change. "Look, Tiff says Dorothy's not jumping off things as often since you started taking her out every day. And—and Jen, she's home. Even Ashley smiles more."

Keeping the bitterness from his voice took more work than he had expected. He wasn't the reason the girls were doing better, and he knew it.

"They'd do all that, and more, if you two were home more often," Evans said in a low voice. He drew his wings closer around his body and rubbed the spot where his prosthetic met his flesh. "Especially you, Captain."

Owen's breath caught and his smile fell. Damn him, did Evans have to throw it back in his face? "It's not like that . . ." he hissed, harsher than he meant to be.

Tiffany wiped her hands on a rag and abandoned the dishes for her husband's side. "One week and then we can come home for good." Her still damp hand found Owen's and squeezed. "Can you help us or not?"

Evans sighed and his shoulders deflated. "I can manage a week." His wings pulled around his body tightly, like armor, as his gaze dropped to the floor. "I'm just not so certain about the kids."

***

Owen let the door to the girls' room close with a soft click and rested his head against the cool wood. His skull hadn't pounded this badly since the last time he'd sampled the pubs of England and Wales.

"You okay?" Tiffany asked softly. Her footsteps came to a stop behind him.

He answered without lifting his head off the door or opening his eyes. "I'm tired. I'll be fine." Each word—hell, each sound was like a hammer slamming into his brain. To be honest, all he wanted to do right now was crawl into bed and sleep for a few days, but he'd have to wait for Tiff and Ashley to go to bed to claim his spot on the couch.

Tiffany snorted, and the noise scraped Owen's nerves like electric feedback. "You've got a headache, don't you?"

Wordlessly, Owen nodded, and the bright whirl of colors behind his eyes made him wish he hadn't.

Sighing, Tiffany reached up and laid a hand on Owen's forehead. "Well, you don't have a fever, so it must be stress. How are you sleeping?"

On a lumpy couch that should've been thrown out four years before the Williams got it, he didn't say. It was his fault he'd been banished to the couch, and complaining about it wouldn't fix it. "Poorly," he finally managed to rasp, lifting his head away from the door.

Tiffany tsked and pulled away. "Follow me, I just put a kettle on. You look like you could use some tea."

The promise of tea was more than enough to convince Owen to follow Tiffany into the kitchen instead of hiding himself away somewhere dark and quiet. She shoved him toward the kitchen table and ordered him to sit down before he passed out, then dimmed the lights and puttered around the kitchen, pulling two mugs and their tea tin out of the cupboard.

"Here you go," Tiffany said once the tea had finished. "We're out of ginseng, I'm afraid, so you'll have to settle for chamomile."

Her voice still grated over his nerves, but Owen found he didn't mind so much. Tea always worked wonders to improve his mood, even if they were out of his preferred flavor.

They sat in silence, watching the tea steep. Tiffany's leg bounced under the table while one clawed finger traced paths in the wood.

"You know, I wasn't really mad at you," she said after a few moments. She stared into her mug like Owen wasn't there. "It's just . . . I was so happy you were retiring. You almost *died.*" Her voice cracked and it broke Owen's heart. "When you came home, spouting that nonsense about the queen not letting you retire, I lost my temper."

She'd almost kicked him out. "It's okay," he whispered back. A lifetime ago, he'd have taken her hand at this point in the conversation. "I can't say I didn't deserve it. Besides, I'd have done the same thing in your position."

Tiffany snorted and picked up her tea. "No, you wouldn't," she said bitterly. "You're too much of a gentleman for that. You'd storm out and make a fuss, but you wouldn't have threatened me like that."

"What can I say?" He chuckled and immediately regretted it. "Your dad did a good job beating the prat out of me when he taught me to box."

"This isn't funny, Owen," she snarled, slamming her mug down. The tea sloshed over the sides and all over her hand, but she ignored it. "I'm trying to apologize."

"And I'm trying to say you don't have to," he answered, his voice even despite how his hands shook. This was all his fault. She wasn't the one to blame here. "I was acting like an ass. If anything, I should be apologizing to you."

"To me?" Tiffany said with a bit off laugh. "What'd you do that you'd need to apologize for? I shouldn't have doubted you. You haven't broken a promise to me in the nineteen years we've been married, and you wouldn't start now."

"I dragged you into this," Owen said in a low voice, mindful of Ashley and Evans sitting in the living room not too far away. "If it hadn't been for me, Percill would never have seen you."

Snorting, she picked up her tea again and took a long sip. "I dragged myself into it. I should've believed you and not gone to that blasted meeting." She frowned into her mug and whispered, "If I had, we wouldn't be having this conversation now."

She sighed while her wings drooped, and she rubbed her eyes. "Look, I'm not trying to assign blame for what happened today. I should have believed you, and I need to apologize for that. Are you going to let me or not?"

His chest ached as if he were hearing those words again. "I told you," he said. "It's not your fault. I don't blame you." He raised a hand to cut Tiffany off before she could protest, then continued, "I've already forgiven you, so you don't have to apologize."

"Can I do it anyway?" she whispered, her voice wobbling. Her hands tightened around her mug like it would keep her stable.

"Only if you'll let me apologize too." He had more blame here. Besides, she hadn't been wrong. He'd promised he was done with the missions, and if their positions had been reversed, he'd have blown up too, despite what she thought.

A small smile lifted Tiffany's lips enough for her fangs to show, and she whispered, "I'm sorry for not believing you and for trying to kick you out. I don't have any excuses, and I never should have done it. I can only swear it won't happen again and hope you'll forgive me."

Owen took a large, bracing sip of his tea and ignored the twisting in his stomach. "I still don't blame you," he said in a low voice. "I'm sorry for putting you in that position. I made a promise I couldn't keep, and now we're both screwed. When we get out of this, I promise I'll do better."

They finished their tea in silence and slowly, the way it should be drank, savoring each sip. One mug became two to avoid wasting the last of the hot water and the time they had together. At some point, Owen's hand met Tiffany's, and he laced his fingers through her tea-soaked ones. He kept them there until they'd drained the last of the dregs, and the bottoms of their mugs were bone dry.

Ashley and Evans had long since gone to bed. Owen's headache had subsided, but it would return with a vengeance if he didn't get some sleep. Reluctantly, he untangled his hand and stood. "I'm headed to bed. I'll see you in the morning."

Tiffany caught his arm as he turned toward the living room and the couch that awaited him there. "Wait," she said, gathering the mugs in her other hand. "I'm coming too. Give me a moment to finish here, and we can go together."

His jaw dropped, and he slowly turned to her. "Then I'm not . . . ?" It'd be more than fair if she needed her space tonight after everything that had happened, even if she'd forgiven him.

Tiffany made a face. "Do you think I want to deal with your whining in the morning about how much your back hurts? Besides, it's cold in our room when it's just me."

He couldn't stop the smile that split his face in two even if he'd wanted to. She'd let him in, even after everything he'd done. "You think it's cold?" he shot back, stepping clear of her wings as she moved to the sink. "Imagine what it's like for me. I don't have fur."

Laughing, Tiffany flicked water at him as she rinsed out the mugs. "That explains why you keep stealing the blankets."

Their bickering continued into their room with shots being exchanged in equal volleys. Ordinarily, Owen might have been concerned about how fast Tiffany had recovered—it usually meant they weren't done talking about whatever had caused the fight—but Tiffany was smiling. A real smile that showed her myriad of pointed teeth in all their glory that he hadn't gotten to see in months. He could take the teasing to see that again.

CHAPTER THIRTEEN

In Which Owen Visits His Son

"For obvious reasons, we can't bury people in winter, and for even more obvious reasons, we can't wait until the ground thaws to bury them properly. We haven't had many people die of old age—or even many die of natural causes—so it's not an immediate concern, but we do need to deal with it, and soon. Look at it this way, there are humans here, and they, at the very least, need a place to lay their dead. Bury or burn, it needs to be handled."

—Excerpt from A Grave Situation *by Lindon Clark of Lyon Avenue*

The stone was cold and drank in the lamplight like water devoured fire. The walls were blank, free of the color that consumed the rest of the capital. They'd been left in their natural state—untouched and unformed by any human tool—apart from one.

Owen laid six withered wildflowers on the threshold of David's tomb, all that could be found at short notice this late in the year. "I'm sorry it took so long for me to visit," he whispered, kneeling in front of the flowers. In time, the rock digging into his knees would be worn smooth, but for now, it was a reminder that he didn't visit enough.

This was the first time he'd been here since they'd buried David, and not much had changed. Someone—Dorothy, if he was any judge—had painted a few dozen flowers across the base, and a rose carved from granite rested on the mantel.

Owen's heart panged and he tore his eyes away.

The climate here didn't favor roses, so the fae carved them out of stone for dead loved ones. Traditionally, they were handmade, but they could be bought in the market if one knew where to look and didn't care how it reflected on them.

Owen's still sat in his desk at home, practically untouched.

"Your mom and I are going on a mission in a few weeks," he whispered around the knot in his throat. "The queen's sending us to Arizona."

He never knew what to say when he visited graves. It didn't feel right to talk to their residents like they were still there or like they wouldn't know what was going on if they were, but he didn't want to sit in silence either.

Sighing, he ran a hand through his hair, and his fingers caught in the tangles. "We got someone to look after your sisters since Arthur won't be able to get leave, but I'm worried about Ashley. I'm not sure how she'll handle both of us being gone." He could hear her crying most nights after Dorothy and Jen fell asleep. He'd told himself that he was respecting her privacy by not checking in on her, that she just needed space, but he wasn't sure now.

"Jen misses you," he whispered, feeling stupid for saying something so obvious. "She joined a pack while I was gone and—and that's helping. Her teachers even say she might pass her classes this year." Tiffany had said the pack master had been to Owen's welcome back party, but he didn't remember meeting her. One more thing he had missed. One more place someone else had needed to pick up his slack.

He reached out a hand and traced David's name in the granite. Being here hurt less than he'd expected, like a weight had lifted from his chest. The letters blurred and tears rolled down his cheeks when he blinked. He shouldn't have taken so long to come back.

"And Dorothy finally Changed," he whispered in a shaky voice, dropping his hand again and wiping at his eyes. "She's a gryphon, like your mom. She talks as much as Jen, though." As much as Jen *used to.* She didn't talk much now, not to him at least.

"Jason's already started a betting pool on what Ashley Changes into." Ashley was the only one left now, he realized with a jolt. The lone human in their family of fantastic creatures. Well, Ashley and Owen, but Owen knew what he was, and he would never Change.

The weight in his chest got lighter the longer he spoke, and he wondered how he'd lived with it for so long. It was like seeing sunlight for the first time after a long winter, the first breath of air after a rainstorm. He still felt a little silly talking to the air, but he didn't want to lose that feeling so he kept going.

He told David's tombstone about his last mission, about how he had gotten captured and sick, and about his new mission. He talked about everything that had happened since David had closed his eyes for the last time, until his voice rasped and his throat screamed for water. He wished he'd thought to bring a canteen.

A scraping noise from the hall broke him from his trance and sent him jumping to his feet. He stumbled on numb knees as he spun around. It was stupid to feel like this—this was his son's tomb; he had every right to be there—but the thought of someone overhearing him made the weight settle on his chest like it'd never left.

He'd managed to regain his feet when the source of the scraping turned the corner, and froze.

"Jen, Ashley," he said in a haggard voice. "I didn't know you were coming."

Didn't think they'd come was more like it. Hell, it had taken him almost a year to force himself here. Still, he could've asked.

"We always come to see him before school," Ashley whispered, her eyes just this side of dead. She held a chunk of granite—a rose with half the petals painted red.

Owen's stomach twisted at the thought of his untouched rose, and he stuffed his hands in his pockets like that would hide that he didn't have it with him. "I'll wait for you, then," he offered, blinking hard to chase tears away. "I can walk you to school."

The offer felt hollow, a half-hearted platitude that didn't even begin to make up for everything he'd done. For the months he'd spent away, for the distance between them that had grown so great he hadn't known about this ritual, for leaving them to figure out their grief on their own.

Ashley nodded and walked past Owen without changing her expression. Jen trailed after her. Her steps had a certain reluctance—like she wanted to be anywhere and nowhere else but here. Her rose was less finished than Ashley's, but the outer petals had started to take shape.

Owen sat outside the door to the tomb. He could've gone back inside, tried to support the girls, but the nagging feeling that he'd be interrupting something wouldn't leave him alone. His fingers itched. Blast, he should've brought his rose.

A numbing wind—the product of an unseen ventilation shaft or window off in the distance—howled past Owen. The lamp flickered and shadows danced to the rhythm of two echoing chisels. The wind, the chisels, and the ever-encroaching shadows were Owen's only company.

Five minutes turned to ten and then twenty. A tombkeeper passed by at the half-hour mark, relighting lamps and depriving Owen of the company of his shadows. She glided past Owen like a ghost, and the girls emerged in her wake. Jen stormed out and shoved her rose into her schoolbag so roughly she jostled Ashley's—now entirely red—rose, almost undoing her work.

"Come on, we're going to be late," Jen said with a growl. She stalked past Owen, her tail slicing through the air like a knife through butter, and disappeared around the next corner.

Owen and Ashley followed at a slower pace. They walked in silence, occasionally catching glimpses of Jen before she vanished again.

"Do you want me to take that home for you?" Owen asked when they left the catacombs behind. In the distance, the low din of the morning market echoed toward them. "I have time before my meeting."

Red stained Ashley's fingertips as they tightened around the rose. "No, I want to visit him after school," she whispered without lifting her gaze from the paving stones.

"Is Jen going with you again?" he asked, desperate to hold on to this scrap of her attention for as long as he could. They weren't too far from the stairway up to the school now, and it'd be crowded enough at this hour that they wouldn't be able to talk.

"No. Her pack is going to a spring a few miles away after school." She paused, glanced at Owen, and smiled as if to reassure him. "I don't mind, though; I like it when it's just him and me."

Owen's chest tightened a little. He'd never seen a smile so empty. "Well, do you mind if I come?" he asked cautiously. "My rose is little more than a rock right now, and I'd appreciate the company while I work on it." He wouldn't have understood what she meant yesterday, but he did now. It was why he'd left so early this morning, sneaking out like a thief in the night to see something he had all the right in the world to visit.

The hallway had filled up in the last few minutes. The rush of people running to work and school had come so gradually he almost hadn't noticed how he'd had to start fighting for space.

Ashley stopped so suddenly a harpy almost knocked her over. Her small smile, a real one, did more to ease Owen's worries than a hundred large and empty ones. "Yes—I mean, no—I don't mind if you come." Her fingers eased their grip on the rose but left prints behind that marred the paint. "I'm almost done with my rose. I could help you with yours."

A part of Owen wondered if she was offering to avoid finishing hers. Completed roses were left at the tombs as a sign their owner's mourning had come to an end, and—barring the fresh marks in the paint—Ashley's was perfect.

Despite his worries about how Ashley was or wasn't dealing with her grief, smiling back was easier now. "I'd appreciate that," he said around the lump in his throat. His smile quivered, but it eased the weight in his chest like talking to David had. "I'm going to need help to finish it."

He shouldn't need the help. He was a carpenter, he knew how to carve—hang the difference between wood and stone—but whenever he sat down to work on it, he couldn't bring himself to make a single mark. It didn't seem right. Something so cold and dead wasn't enough to honor such a vibrant life.

He waved as Ashley disappeared into the crowd. His cheeks hurt from smiling, but he didn't try to stop. This could be his chance to start fixing things with Ashley. And from there, everyone else he'd hurt.

***

His meeting—well, less of a meeting and more of an informal explanation for the conscription notices Aaron and Jason had received that morning—didn't take as long as he'd expected. Or hoped for, at any rate.

The notices were his fault after all. He'd been the one to suggest them. Jason because there wasn't anyone in the Corps that he trusted more, Aaron because of his healing abilities. If Aaron had been on the last mission, Evans might not have lost his leg.

He wasn't sure what he'd been expecting. Blame, maybe? Jason was still recovering, and Aaron had retired from active duty because he wanted to be home for his wife and daughters. Neither of them should be out in the field, but he wasn't going without them.

But no, they hadn't blamed him. They were Corpsfolk, through and through, and they knew their duty. Until the day they set down their uniform for good, they lived at the beck and call of the Corps. Aaron had even said that he'd have done the same thing in Owen's position.

Jason just laughed and asked how Owen had expected to stop him from coming.

Once they'd returned to their lives—Aaron to his daughters, and Jason to the "sweet, sweet embrace of bed"—Owen didn't have anything to do. Until his meeting with Beira and his new teammates tomorrow, he was on his own. He could go home, but since Dorothy had started kindergarten and Tiff was back at work, only a lump of rock was there, waiting to be carved into a rose.

He wasn't ready to get it yet.

So, with nothing better to do and six hours before he was supposed to meet Ashley, Owen let his feet wander. Through the halls, caverns, and chambers of the third floor they led him. Past the political district and the office behind the council chamber, where Owen's future had been decided. Past the market and the Grand Staircases that were the lifeline of the city. Past the catacombs and the offices where the Williams had registered a lifetime ago.

His feet stopped as slow, methodical chanting breached the fog that had swallowed him. Carved reliefs covered every inch of the walls here. Some were half familiar, the stories they told tugging on the back of Owen's mind. A werewolf led a parade of animals marching in twos onto a ship already overflowing with life. An elf slept among lions without being harmed. A crowd of fae and humans alike stood before a man high in the clouds, their arms raised in adulation as wretched figures were swept into a fiery chasm.

Idly, he wondered how the carvers had chosen which species to assign these figures. As far as he knew, Bible stories didn't feature fae. The few that did weren't necessarily flattering. That being said, he couldn't deny the appropriateness of each change. People will make space for themselves if they're denied it, he supposed.

The chanting came from a room halfway down the hall with a curtain drawn over the entry. A plaque on the wall next to it informed Owen that this was the Mosque of the Havens. Roughly one hundred feet south was another doorway. That one was open, and a handful of people were praying in front of an altar. The plaque beside it read "Cornerstone Christian Church." He passed three more churches, two mosques, and an Olympian temple, most no larger than the council chamber, before he came to the end of the hall.

More accurately, he came to a wooden door, roughly fifteen feet tall and half that wide, that split the hall from the space beyond. Carvings covered every inch of it, ones like he'd have made when he was first learning carpentry. Uneven and rough figures hadn't so much been carved as hacked out with a dull butter knife. Most were missing limbs, and a few were hardly more than suggestions in the wood. That door didn't have a plaque. Instead, "St. Alban's Cathedral" was carved in a rough hand into the stone above the door.

He wanted to go inside. He didn't know why—none of the other churches or even the temple had drawn more than a passing glance—but he didn't fight it.

The door pushed open at a light touch.

It was empty. And dark.

Stepping quietly to muffle any echoes, he walked down the center aisle and past rows of trenches, each wide enough for him to sit cross-legged in. Lamps lined the wall, but less than half were lit. The cathedral drowned in a mire of flickering shadows and the cavernous echoes of the smallest crackling flame.

Owen slowed to a stop a few feet from the stairs leading to the altar. A single red lamp hung above the tabernacle, casting a bloody pall over the area. He squinted, trying to make out the details of the rose window carved into the wall behind the tabernacle, but was unwilling to step onto the altar itself for a better look.

"I didn't think you believed."

Owen's eyes fell shut. He should be surprised, shocked even that she was here, but he just felt numb. He'd almost expected this. "I didn't see you there," he said, turning to face the figure emerging from the shadows. "I thought you had meetings all day."

Beira shrugged as she came to a halt outside the red circle of light. The shadows clung to her and turned her dress—likely a pleasant blue in better light—into something close to black. "My meeting let out early, and well, my youngest great-granddaughter is getting baptized today. I thought I'd come down and get things set up."

Owen let out a bark of laughter. "Your youngest? You have more than one?" Distantly, he'd known Beira had a son, a harpy she'd adopted during the Fae War, but he'd assumed he was childless. That or he didn't speak with Beira anymore.

"Three now. This is my grandson's firstborn." Beira's half smile filled with pride. She turned away and walked to a column half-hidden in the darkness. Three clicks echoed in the silence as sparks flared and caught, flooding the area with more noise and light than it should.

"Really?" Owen said without moving from his place by the altar. "I didn't know you had so much family." He wondered if he had a right to the tightness in his chest, to the hurt that had him digging his nails into his palm. They hadn't been close for months, but they'd known each other for almost a year now. Long enough for talk about children and grandchildren to have been filed away with how she liked her tea.

Beira laughed as light bloomed in front of her, and she moved on to another column. By now, half the lamps were lit, and a pleasant glow filled the nave. He couldn't yet make out the wall carvings beyond vague shapes in the shadows, but he could see her without squinting. "Not many that weren't raised here do. My son never took my name."

"Why?" Owen asked, finally moving to catch up with Beira.

She shrugged and fiddled with her flint and steel as she turn to face him. "Conner didn't want to live in my shadow, and I . . . I wanted him to be safe." Her smile didn't fall, but a darkness slipped behind it that hadn't been there before. A weight she hadn't been able to shed in the long years of her life.

Owen wanted to ask her what dangers she was worried about in Tearmann, in the very heart of fae power, but something about the way her fists clenched at her side made him hold back.

Instead, he cast his eyes around for a convenient change of subject. "You know I've never been in this part of the city," he said, and gestured at a carving he could only barely see. He thought it might be a saint of some sort. "I didn't think the religious district was so large or quite so . . . decorated."

Beira's fists relaxed, and she went back to lighting the lamps. "The political district is bigger, but the caverns here are some of the finest in the city."

"Why is that?"

Three more clicks echoed through the caverns, and another lamp flared to life before she answered. "It started with a crucifix in a cavern not far from here, then grew from there. People would come by after they finished work for the day and . . . add things. A carving here, a lamp there."

"All this from a crucifix?" Owen wasn't religious, not in any sense of the word, but that seemed like a bit much. Even if a few of the big religions—the Catholics, Jews, and most Muslims among them—had accepted the fae, hundreds still thought that the fae were demons at best and a sign of the end times at worst. That didn't create a welcoming environment.

Beira lit the last lamp and shrugged as she walked back to Owen. The room wasn't entirely lit—lamps would never be as bright as electric light—but he suspected that would change when the great chandeliers were lit. Still, it was bright enough to reveal the carvings and statues in their full glory.

And glory was the right word for it. The carvings brought lifeless rock alive in a near-perfect facsimile of life. Granite and limestone became cloth, soft skin, and fur. Angels, both biblical and fae, flew across the ceilings on wings that threatened to take them soaring off the stone and into existence.

The trenches were pews, hidden for the flow of the cathedral. Words carved by believing hands covered them. Bible verses, psalms, entreating prayers, and the names of those that had passed. "*Pater noster qui es in coelis*," "protect Angela Marie," "*requiem in pacem*, and pray for us, Grandma Ines," "*Santa María, Madre de Dios*, please protect our brothers."

"Impressive, isn't it?" Beira said, spinning with her hands out. "The life's work of some of our sculptors."

Owen whistled. "It certainly is," he said under his breath.

Why then, was the doorway to all this beauty little more than a scrap of wood for students to practice on? Hell, when he'd been an apprentice, he'd have been embarrassed to show someone that, let alone have it on display. "Why the door?" he asked. "It doesn't really match the decor, does it?"

Beira chuckled softly. "That's a . . . reminder. One Father Johnson and I couldn't bring ourselves to replace."

"A reminder of what?"

Beira didn't answer. Instead, she walked forward and laid a hand on the back of the door in question. It was bare on this side. Unmarred and without a single scratch. Besides the smooth floor, it was the plainest thing in here.

"Most of us didn't have anything more than the clothes on our backs when we first came here," she finally said without turning around. Her words echoed, turning over and over on themselves the longer she spoke. "Everything you see, we had to make for ourselves."

She turned and rested against the door, then raised a hand to count on her fingers. "Our homes, our food, our clothes, and, yes, our places of worship—all came from nothing." Tilting her head, she crossed her arms and stared at Owen. "This door is hideous, and clearly, we can do better. So, why do you think we keep it?"

Owen shrugged. He had an idea—more than an idea. For the same reason business owners kept the first dollar they ever made, or basketball players kept the ball they made their thousandth shot with.

Beira pushed off the door, walked over to the last pew, and—patting the ground next to her in invitation—sat. "It was a gift from a local sculptor, you know." Seeing Owen's raised eyebrows at this apparently unrelated non sequitur, she scoffed and rolled her eyes. "Don't give me that look. Omar knew exactly what it looked like when he donated it."

"He must not have like you very much, then," Owen said before he could stop himself.

Beira threw back her head and let out a bark of laughter. "If only," she said lightly. "No, if anything, he liked us too much." A small, proud smile turned up the corners of her lips. "No, Omar was blinded during the war. He'd been a sculptor but didn't trust himself to work with stone once he'd healed. This"—she pointed to the door—"was his first project after losing his sight. He's done other things since then, even recovered enough to work with stone again, but he's proudest of this."

Owen's brow furrowed. "Why?" he asked, slumping down onto the pew next to Beira. His feet almost disappeared into the shadows of the trench, the light of the lamps not quite enough to reach this far. The Memorare, written in German, laced across the stone next to his hand with a signed prayer for someone named Dai. Owen couldn't decipher how it made him feel, but he moved his hand away from it to quell the odd stirring in his stomach.

"He calls it a visible reminder that we need to appreciate what we have, even if it looks bad. The fact that he's never seen it himself never fails to make him laugh." As she spoke, she absentmindedly pulled her braid over her shoulder and started twisting it. Her smile faded the longer she stared into nothing, and she seemed to be wrestling with something.

It didn't make sense to Owen. It might be a donation from someone Beira respected, but that didn't change the fact that it may as well be kindling for all the aesthetic value it had. A place like this, even if he didn't agree with the church or what it represented, deserved a door as beautiful as it was. Deserved to be represented by something that would show observers how the fae had made something beautiful amid their desolation.

"Omar and people like him are the ones who built this district," Beira said in a soft whisper. She drew her legs up and rested her chin on them as her eyes drifted closed. "If they didn't believe, if they didn't see doing it as a worthy cause, these caves would still be bare." She shrugged, tossed her braid back over her shoulder, and leaned back. She looked more at ease here than Owen had ever seen her. He almost expected her to start humming or some other such nonsense.

But did he see it that way? "Even a blind sculptor had skills that would be better used elsewhere," he muttered under his breath.

"Maybe so, but Omar always said it's one of his favorite projects."

As Beira spoke, Owen realized—to his horror—that she'd heard him. Cor, that sounded even worse now that he thought about it. The urge to duck his head, to look anywhere else but at Beira, was almost as overwhelming as the flame turning his cheeks bright red. "I didn't mean . . ."

Beira's shoulders relaxed a fraction, and she sighed. "No, you meant it. I know you don't believe." Letting out a huff of air, she flopped onto the floor and pillowed her arms under her head. "You're not the first person who's made a comment like that, and not just about the door. You've seen some of the murals, right?"

"Yeah," he finally said, tracing a half-faded petition with the tips of his fingers. "I know he must have thought it was worth it, but . . . there had to be other things he could've done. Dug ditches, assembled lamps, or something. You can't feed people with a church."

She laughed again, harsher this time. "Not if you do it wrong," she muttered while rubbing her eyes. "Look at it this way, enough people thought this place was worth it that they preferred to work here instead of digging ditches or assembling lamps. No one was forced to work on this."

Owen nodded, the foul taste of a point gone unheard turning his stomach, but he was unwilling to push the argument.

As the silence between them grew, Beira sat up and crossed her legs. "At any rate, what brings you here?" Her body tensed as an unseen weight settled across her shoulders. He hadn't even noticed how much softer she had seemed here until it was gone. "I wasn't joking when I said I wasn't expecting to see you here. Were you looking for me?"

It occurred to Owen that he didn't have a reason for being here. He'd been wandering, yes, but one didn't usually wander into the religious district without cause. It ended in a dead end and didn't have any connecting tunnels that went somewhere useful. There were three staircases, yes, but those only connected to the housing district on the second floor. No wonder Beira assumed he'd come looking for her.

"I, uh, got lost," he admitted after the space between her question and his response stretched to an unwieldy length. "I wasn't paying attention to where I was going and ended up here."

Beira laughed and shook her head. "And you thought you'd come in." Her voice held no judgment, but Owen couldn't help but notice that the knot in her shoulders hadn't gone anywhere. "Well, if you aren't doing anything, you're welcome to stay for the baptism," she said, jarring Owen from his thoughts. She got to her feet and extended a hand to help him to his. "My daughter-in-law throws one hell of a reception."

Owen let her help him up without responding. "No, but thank you," he said once he'd regained his feet. "Even if I was Catholic, I promised Ashley I'd visit David with her after school."

Beira glanced at her watch and laughed. "You'd better get going, then; school gets out soon."

Owen glanced at his own watch and managed to resist swearing by the skin of his teeth. Blast, it was almost three, and he was halfway across the mountain. A large part of him thought running in a place of worship was rude, but he'd be a liar if he said he didn't. Beira's laughter chased him through that hideous door as he tore out of the church and into the hall.

***

He crossed the mountain in record time and even managed to stop by the apartment for his rose. He may have skidded to a stop outside the high school two minutes before class let out for the day, but he was here. Between the aching stitch in his side that was pleading for a break and his screaming lungs, being upright at all was a miracle, but if he sat down, he would miss Ashley, and he'd missed enough time with her for a hundred lifetimes.

The scant minutes before the end of the school day passed before he caught his breath. Still, as kids of all species and generations poured out doors, through windows, and off balconies, it seemed like an eternity.

Owen had chosen a place by the southern stairs to wait for Ashley. Most students had jobs or apprenticeships after school and would take the northern stairs or the eastern halls to get to the business district. The south stairs were a direct shot to the housing districts and let out in a hall not far from the catacombs. With luck, Ashley would head this way, and he'd catch her before she got too far.

The first wave of students came and went, mostly to work as he'd predicted, but he didn't see Ashley. The second and third waves of students were equally bereft of anyone who could've been mistaken for his daughter.

Finally, long after the last stragglers had disappeared and as he started to wonder if he'd missed a message, she trudged out the doors, walking like all the troubles in the world were in her backpack.

"Ash!" he yelled, and waved his hands wildly. "I'm over here." That was louder than it needed to be—the hall was empty except for them—but he'd needed to do something, anything, to get that expression off her face.

Ashley's head shot up, and even from this distance, her relieved smile shone like the sun. "Dad," she yelled as she jogged over to him. "I was worried you weren't going to come." The weight in her backpack hadn't disappeared, but she was moving like it wasn't bothering her as much.

Despite the sick feeling in his stomach—he hadn't been gone long enough for her to stop believing his promises, had he?—he put on a matching grin and swung his arm around her shoulders. He needed to start somewhere, he told himself. He'd messed this up enough. "Of course I came," he said, very conscious of how strained his smile felt. "I promised I would."

Ashley didn't seem to notice. She pulled away enough to link their arms together and led him toward the catacombs. If her words seemed quick and her actions wild, Owen didn't comment. He was out of sorts himself after all. How could he blame her for feeling the same way?

CHAPTER FOURTEEN

In Which They Plan

"We have an army despite not calling it one. The Tearmann Accords forbid the formation of a fae military—one of our concessions before they would grant us a homeland. However, because our founders aren't complete idiots, they created the next best thing. The Corps, officially the Siren Corps, are an aid group. They retrieve fae trapped in hostile situations and supplies we can't produce on our own. The fact that they operate under a military-style charter, receive the best combat training we can offer, and are our first response in the event of an attack are technicalities brushed aside under the assumption we live in an untamed part of the world. It would seem humans forgot that animals and nature don't hold the same fear for us that they do them."
—Excerpt from Of Corps and Combat *by Professor Alan Jacobs*

A message from Beira was waiting for Owen when he and Ashley had gotten home last night. Never one to waste words, the only thing she'd written was a time and place. Specifically, "the Holstad Conference Room at 0900." Tiffany had gotten one, too, except hers said "0800" and one of them had to get Dorothy to class.

If Owen had been the uncharitable sort, he'd have been more vocal about how often he'd had to climb up to the Eyries in recent weeks. At the very least, Beira could have arranged for someone to fly them up here; those stairs didn't get any shorter the more they were climbed.

"Owen! Good morning," Jason called from across the room, drawing the eye of every worker, passerby, and official in the room with his boisterous waving. As usual, he was abominably cheerful for the hour and his circumstances.

"Morning, Jason, how're you?" Owen called back as he jogged over.

Jason pulled a face and waved a hand dismissively. "Psh, I'm fine. Sirens healed me up almost as good as new." He was paler than was healthy. His tan, which he somehow managed to maintain year-round even under hundreds of tons of earth, wasn't as vibrant as usual. But otherwise, he did look all right. At least until he started swaying.

Owen rushed forward and barely managed to catch Jason before he fell over. "Cor almighty, I thought you said you were fine." He grunted and readjusted his grip. For such a small person, Jason weighed a ton.

Jason smiled despite his skin shifting between a sickening gray and a color outside the visible spectrum. "I am," he said, and swallowed like he was trying to not throw up. "I'm . . . I'm still tired from being healed. Takes a lot out of a person, you know."

Owen arched an eyebrow. "You're sure you're not hungover? You seemed fine at the hearing."

"That—" He pushed away, and while his legs shook under him, he didn't fall over again. "Was the product of endorphins and enough coffee to drown a dragon."

Owen made a mental note to stay close as Jason lurched away. Jason would be fine, he told himself even as his stomach tightened into a knot of nerves. He'd been going on missions for longer than Owen had been alive and would keep going on them until long after Owen was dead.

But all the same, Owen had to be realistic. Even Beira didn't dare overrule the medics. They were only a few weeks from departure, and if Jason could barely stand despite the treatment of the finest healers in Tearmann, he'd be more of a liability in the field than any help. Going on this mission without him . . . wouldn't be pleasant.

So he followed Jason down the hall, churning his fears over in his mind and half listening to a conversation Jason had no problem continuing without Owen's input.

"... be a week or so more before I'm back in fighting form, but the sirens are confident there won't be any lasting consequences . . ."

A week less of training time, a week before they would learn if he could do this.

"... of course, they wanted me to stay in the hospital, but I told them I could recover from healing-induced exhaustion just as well at home as there . . ."

Even if he was healed, his stamina would've taken a hit. If he was strong enough to go on this mission, would he be able to perform at a level Owen was used to?

"...excited for this. I've been going stir-crazy in my apartment, haven't you?"

Blast, he wasn't sure he could do this without Jason.

"Furthermore—oh, hey, we're here," Jason said, ramming his elbow into Owen's side.

Disorientated by the air leaving his lungs, Owen didn't immediately realize Jason was right. The Holstad Conference Room was one of the largest in the mountain because it wasn't a room at all. It was a large, open-air cave almost a hundred feet wide and twice as deep. Owen had only been in there once, for a terrifyingly in-depth seminar on dragon harnesses.

They weren't the first ones here either. Aaron, Tiffany, and a dwarf woman whom Owen thought he should've recognized were waiting outside. The dwarf, a stout redhead with a delicately braided beard that went to her waist, gestured animatedly as she spoke with Tiffany, who had her wings wrapped around her like a blanket. Based on Aaron's bored and confused expression and what the echoes whispered, they must have been talking about computers.

That meant the dwarf was Jane Ayers, the closest thing the fae had to a hacker. Considering Owen could count on one hand the number of his neighbors who knew the difference between a laptop and a cell phone, that was saying something. She'd fallen in love with computers when she'd been in London and spent the next three years studying them. The only reason she'd come home was because her visa expired.

Despite her credentials, Owen had argued against having her on the team. Tiffany had been a programmer—a security expert in fact—back home; they should have chosen another fighter. Beira overruled him. Percill would expect them to send someone to deal with the electric and digital security, she'd said. Since she "didn't trust Percill to plan a dinner party without trying to turn it to his advantage," she wanted Jane as a red herring. Apparently, he didn't know about Tiffany's background, and Beira wanted to keep it that way.

Aaron saw them first and, probably desperate for a rescue, yelled, "You're late."

Jason laughed and sashayed across to Aaron to hook an arm over his shoulder. Owen tried very hard not to wonder whether he did that for support or because he enjoyed irritating Aaron. Knowing Jason, probably both.

"Aaron, Aaron, Aaron, when have you ever known me to be so rude as to be late?" Jason said, pinching Aaron's cheek. "We're right on time, as always."

Jane snorted and crossed her arms, somehow looking down her nose at Jason despite being two feet shorter. "You're lucky they didn't start early." If it weren't for the smile tugging up her lips, she'd have sounded cruel. As it was, it came off just this side of good-natured.

As Jason let himself get drawn into a bickering match with Aaron and Jane, Owen pulled Tiffany aside.

"How'd it go?" he asked in a hushed voice.

Rubbing her arms, she shivered and pulled her wings in tighter. "They had me sign some papers and sent me out. Eoire's in there now." She glanced over her shoulder at the unopened door and shook her head. "For Pete's sake, I'm still freezing. I don't see why we couldn't have this meeting in her office."

"We're supposed to meet our dragon today." Owen glanced around to check if anyone else was in the hall. There wasn't, so he supposed the officials were already inside. "Wait, what papers?"

She shrugged and finally stopped rubbing her arms. "Contract stuff. I think they're trying to cover their rear if something goes wrong. Jane said she had to do it too."

Right. The Corps ran on an improbable amount of paperwork. He should've expected that.

The door opened before he could ask anything else, and a familiar redhead poked out. "They say you can come in," Eoire said quietly, a wave of exhaustion and agitation following her words like a flood. Except for the deep bags under her eyes, she'd hardly changed since Owen first met her. She still wore the same braids—albeit slightly worse for wear, like she'd slept in them—the same horrifically stained leather apron, and the same plain but serviceable clothing.

She held the door open and smiled tiredly at Owen as he and Tiffany walked through. He bit back a yawn, returned her smile, and made a mental note to check up on her.

Once he'd actually gotten into the conference room, he stopped dead, his jaw practically on the floor.

Settling onto a small outcropping in the middle of the room was a creature as large as a dragon but like nothing he'd ever seen. Massive wings folded awkwardly around a wormlike body that didn't seem built to have them while its tail wrapped around the outcropping. It only had two legs that he could see, and they hardly looked thick enough to support the weight they were under. It . . . it didn't even have scales. Splotchy calico patches covered its skin from the tip of its tail to its unsettlingly smooth face.

A loud curse in Spanish broke Owen's concentration, and he whipped his head around to see Aaron pressed back against the door. "*Madre de Dios*, why is *that* here?"

The creature snarled and tossed its massive head—longer and slimmer than a dragon's but also lacking the signature headspikes. "Attending a meeting, same as you," it said, flapping its wings, which looked nearly fifty feet wide, to keep balance. "Queen Titania invited me because you need to get somewhere fast and quiet." It settled its wings to grip the stone floor with fingerlike protrusions sticking out from its elbows.

"Peace, Gayle. Peace, Rodriguez," Beira said without looking up from the papers she was sorting into a folder. She was sitting at a table that hardly had enough space for their party. In all the commotion, Owen hadn't noticed her there. "I invited Miss Stern, there's no reason to be concerned."

A sound almost like a growl burst out of Aaron's throat as he pressed his hands against his thigh, careful to keep his claws from his own skin. "But she's battleborn, ma'am," he hissed through his teeth. "Why is she here?"

Owen had never seen Aaron this shaken, and they'd ridden shotgun through a thunderstorm together. He looked one wrong move from launching himself—poisoned-tipped claws first—at Gayle.

Beira looked up, an unimpressed look curling her lips down. "Because she's the fastest and stealthiest flyer we have now that Mr. Green is retired." The words were colder than he'd ever heard her use on one of her people. So cold they made the air seem warm. "Do we have a problem here?"

Aaron removed his hand from his side and curled his fingers into his palm. "No, Your Majesty. There's no problem." Each step looked like it physically pained him, and the seat he took was as far as he could get from Gayle while still being at the same table.

Gayle snorted, then made a noise close to laughter as she readjusted herself. "Besides, I'm a halfling, not battleborn, thank you very much. I have as much right to be here as you do."

That may not have helped her case. Halflings weren't looked down on by the general population, but their parents were. Throwing more confusion into a gene pool already drowning in uncertainty wasn't highly looked upon.

Combined with the general disdain the battleborn and the fae held for each other, it was a miracle she'd been born in the first place. Something in Aaron settled a bit at that news, even if he still seemed reluctant to get closer to her than necessary.

Either ignoring or unaware of the tension, Beira pulled a battered set of blueprints from her never-ending stack of paperwork and spread them on the table. As she did, her lips pursed, and a flicker of resignation flashed through her eyes.

"There is one more matter we should discuss before we get started," she said in a tired voice. "Despite the council's and my best efforts to persuade him otherwise, Jedidiah Ashwind has demanded a place on this expedition and will not be swayed."

The uproar was almost loud enough to bring the cavern down around their ears. The memory of Ashwind's hospitality was too near for Owen to want him anywhere near this mission, and the others agreed with him. Even Gayle didn't like it.

"He's an extremist, everyone knows that," she yelled, a puff of steam from her nostrils obscuring her face. "The battleborn don't even like dealing with him these days."

Owen couldn't help but think that was a good point. The battleborn were as isolationist as possible in the havens, and if they didn't like someone who agreed with them, neither should the fae. "He's a loose rocket, Your Majesty," he snarled, having gotten to his feet at some point. "We can't trust him to have the back of anyone he considers a monarchist."

And the only one Ashwind wouldn't consider a monarchist straight out was Gayle. That left the rest of them with a troll-shaped blind spot.

"The halfling's right," Aaron said. It looked painful for him to agree with Gayle. "He's a radical."

"Silence." Beira's voice was a near whisper, but her words rebounded off the walls and back to them again. All fae jaws snapped shut, and even Gayle, who was only half fae, fell silent.

"Ashwind wants to see with his own eyes if the captives are real," Beira said once hers was the only voice. Her face had darkened, somehow hidden in shadow despite the lamps keeping each corner of the cave lit. "He has agreed to cease his secession campaign until the matter is settled."

"And what will he do once it is?" Owen asked, uncomfortably aware of the others' eyes on him. The order for silence may have only lasted as long as the last of the echoes, but none of them dared speak. "What if he wants to take hostages again?"

Beira nodded and settled back into her chair. The sourceless shadows disappeared, but their weight didn't. "If the captives are real and in a position of suffering, he has agreed to retake his place in the military."

The air seemed to leave everyone's lungs as they gasped simultaneously. Jason found enough of his voice to whisper, "The military? We haven't had a military since you signed the Accords."

Beira's nod confirmed what Jason didn't want to say. The fae may have been teetering on the edge of war for almost a year, but neither side had formalized it. Officially reforming the army was more than a violation of the Accords. It was an outright declaration of war. One the rest of the world wouldn't be able to ignore.

"The council and I realized we need to consider the possibility." Beira's breath caught on the last word. She looked up, but not at any of them. Her eyes focused on something past Owen's shoulder. "Jedidiah Ashwind may have been forcibly retired, but he was one of our best soldiers. Bringing him back into the fold would reinvigorate our forces. Even if that weren't the case, we can't afford to have a hostile force sitting on our southern border." The corners of her lips turned down. "We need him."

Owen wished he couldn't see her point. The odds of this blowing up in their faces were catastrophically high, and they needed all the help they could get—or at the very least have the fewest forces working against them. If getting Ashwind to see sense meant bringing him with them, they didn't have a choice.

Gritting his teeth, Owen sat down again, then took a deep breath to speak. Tiffany beat him to the punch.

"How closely will we have to work together?" she asked in a quiet but firm voice, equal to what Beira had been using earlier. She was calmer than Owen would've thought. Her tail and wings were practically statues. "Do we have to train together?"

Beira shook her head. "No, even he admitted it would be too much to expect that. We haven't finished working out the details, but I'll keep you informed."

Beira politely waited for another question or an argument, but none were forthcoming. Adding Ashwind didn't change much, but at the same time, it felt like the mission had been turned on its head. Something abstract had just become real, and it pulled on Owen like Ashwind himself was hanging around his neck.

That weight stayed with them as they went through the blueprints Percill had gotten for them. They were . . . extensive.

Owen whistled under his breath. This place was a veritable fortress. Three floors and two basements, all locked behind a concrete-and-steel wall ten feet thick. Without these plans they wouldn't have a shot in hell of getting in there.

Percill did good work, however much it pained Owen to admit it. In addition to the blueprints, he'd sent pages and pages of notes detailing everything from security features to staff rotations. They only had five weeks before SAFE moved the captives, so they had to hurry.

Having all this made planning easy. Well, not easy, but more certain.

They'd break in on a Friday, the last day before SAFE moved the captives. Percill said they could get past the gate guard by hiding in the back of the weekly delivery trucks. Supposedly, the night staff didn't bother to search them the way they were supposed to. Once Owen's team was in, they'd need to navigate the labyrinth of hallways in the main building and get the captives back out before the delivery trucks left again.

Simple in theory, but theory rarely played out that way in practice.

Still, they had a plan now. That alone made trekking up here worth it. Sure, it might change a dozen times between now and next week, but at least they had something to change.

The real issue now was training. None of them were at the same place, practically speaking.

Ashwind was Ashwind. No doubt he didn't need any survival or combat training, but Owen couldn't say the same for anyone else. He and Jason were both still active duty but were also still recovering, Aaron was a Corps member who'd been a desk officer for almost a year, Eoire and Jane were in shape but didn't have any combat training, and Tiffany . . . Well, her father had taught her to box and shoot like he'd taught Owen, but she didn't have any experience fighting in her current form, and she still had trouble flying. The only one they didn't need to worry about was Gayle.

She'd been a drop supervisor and go-between for Paxton and Tearmann for years. Besides practically growing up hopping the border, she'd trained with the battleborn and the Corps for most of her life, a perk of being the daughter of a flight commander and a squad leader. If it weren't for her unique biology, she'd be perfect. That being said, the same things that made her fast and stealthy also made wearing a traditional combat gondola damn near impossible.

"I've spoken with the engineers, and they've agreed to fabricate something custom for you, but I'm afraid it won't be very comfortable for your passengers," Beira said, spreading a new set of blueprints onto the table.

The design was simple and basic, likely something the engineers wouldn't even admit to creating if they'd had more time, but looked functional.

To compensate for her only having two legs, the engineers wanted to wind a harness around her neck, sized precisely to keep it from sliding into her wing joints. Small compartments bound together with stretchy cloth instead of one large compartment would increase maneuverability, and a streamlined shotgun shell set at the base of her throat would increase visibility and cover a weak point. It wouldn't be comfortable, but theoretically it would work.

"How many compartments are there?" Aaron asked begrudgingly. His sharp eyes gleamed as they darted over the plans, examining each section with the eye of a master strategist. He may not like Gayle, but he'd been in the Corps for a decade. Ignorance killed as many fae as bullets, and he needed to depend on her and her equipment in the field.

"Six for your group, two for permanent storage, and eight for injured captives," Beira said while turning the blueprints toward him. "If you can get the healthy ones to the drop-off point, we'll have trucks waiting to bring them to a safehouse until they can recover. If not, we're packing a net that should be able to hold them under the gondola until we can meet you closer to the Canadian border."

"What do we do if there are more captives than we anticipated?" Owen said, rubbing his chin. Even under ideal conditions and presuming most of the captives could fly, they'd be pushing Gayle's weight limit. There was no way she could carry as much as a standard dragon.

"Percill says he can guarantee fewer than twelve captives." Beira sighed deeply as she massaged her temples. "Much as I hate to rely on him, he's never outright lied to us before. We'll have a team on standby just in case, but they're on an unrelated mission, so hopefully, you won't need to bring them in."

As Beira rolled up the blueprints and stuck them back in their storage tube, she said, "Regardless, your main concern is getting them out. Miss Stern can carry up to a hundred and fifty percent of her standard capacity for roughly fifty miles, which is far enough away for the support team to find you."

The conversation then turned to logistics. Schedules, supplies, and more exit strategies than Owen thought were necessary or feasible. No one could plan like Beira when she set her mind to something.

Lunch came and went, and someone had stoked a fire when they realized they wouldn't be leaving before they froze to death. Things only wound down about two hours after Owen's throat started aching like he'd used it as sandpaper.

"Well, if that's everything, you're dismissed," Beira said, glancing around the circle. No one met her eyes or tried to get a word in. "Report to your trainers tomorrow."

CHAPTER FIFTEEN

In Which Owen Prepares

"Humans have their place on away missions—for one, they blend in even better than shades—but only a moron would say they fight better than us. The fae are faster and stronger, and we have the sirens to heal us if we get hurt. Of course, in an ideal situation the humans wouldn't have an opportunity to fight, but sometimes it can't be avoided. With this in mind, we developed this guide to teach humans how to fight with fae. Once you're used to us, fighting other humans will seem like a walk in the park."
—Excerpt from Human vs. Fae Combat Preparation *by Lord Keme and Lord Aelfric*

Owen spit out sand as he pushed himself off the training room floor for the third time in ten minutes and the tenth in under an hour. The taste was distressingly familiar.

He'd been flattered when Lord Keme, the undisputed champion of hand-to-hand combat and small-team tactics among the fae, had offered to give him some pointers on his technique. Now, three days into what had turned into the most physically and mentally exhausting exercise regime of his life, he wished he could go back in time and punch himself in the face.

Owen didn't collapse to the ground as soon as Keme left the room to get the equipment for the next part of their workout, but it was a near thing. His arms and legs burned like he'd run a half-marathon, and his lungs were screaming.

"You know he's not trying to kill you, right?" Jason asked from across the room, where he was lounging against the wall.

Owen grunted, too tired to give Jason a withering glare, and wiped his forehead with his already sweat-soaked shirt. "Are you sure he knows that?"

Owen wasn't the only one lucky enough to get a partner. Aaron and Jason had been drilling together all morning, which made Aaron's absence even more noticeable. "Did you chase Aaron off?"

Laughing, Jason jumped off the bench he'd been lounging on and crossed the room to sit by Owen. "I'm not that lucky. No, the bastard's gone to get some equipment for our next exercise. Says I'm flickering like a crappy motel sign." He slouched and crossed his arms over his chest. "It's not like I've been doing this longer than he's been alive or anything, but what do I know?"

Owen could understand that. Jason had better control over his blending than most first-gens, but his flickering had gotten them in trouble more than a half dozen times.

"It's been ages since you've been on a mission of this magnitude, Lucien, and you're getting sloppy," Keme said, storming into the room like a hurricane was on his heels. "I've seen Rodriguez's reports. Your average blend time is up to almost thirty seconds."

"I was hurt, sir," Jason said. He didn't bother to stand, but his hands tightened a minuscule amount. "Another week and I'll be back on the top of my game, same as always."

Keme grunted as he set a bag of books on the floor. "I don't doubt it, but that's no excuse to let up on your training." As he spoke, he handed Owen one yoga mat and laid out his own. "You have no idea what you'll face once you're deployed, and you need to be prepared for anything."

Yoga wasn't Owen's thing—he wasn't very flexible—but Keme went easier on him when they discussed strategy while doing something. Also, it let them cram in more training time if they didn't have to set aside time to stretch.

And so, in the child's position, they discussed *The Art of War* and its impact on logistical planning. In the warrior's pose Keme framed riddles for Owen, who answered them when they shifted to a pyramid. They went from pose to pose and through different scenarios until Owen's mind was as worn out and stretched as his body. Finally, when Owen felt his brain would burst, Keme returned them to the starting position.

"All right, I'll see you tomorrow morning, Williams." Keme didn't even seem winded from their marathon training session—seven hours broken only by lunch and water breaks—which seemed unfair to Owen. Hang that Keme had almost seventy years' experience and had only slightly modified his routine to include Owen, a man should be exhausted after that much work. "We're starting reconnaissance tactics tomorrow so Lord Aelfric is joining us."

Owen waved half-heartedly from where he'd collapsed into a lump on the floor. Tomorrow was supposed to be his recovery day, and his aching bones insisted he take advantage of it. He wasn't a young man anymore, even if Keme didn't seem to realize that. Sitting in a dimly lit room going over dusty military strategy books wasn't quite sleeping until noon, but it would have to do.

Tiffany would've enjoyed it. She was never happier than when she spent an afternoon buried in old books or when whatever overly complicated plan of hers bore fruit on game night.

Unfortunately, she wouldn't be there. Between her flying lessons and relearning how to fight, practically every second of her day was spoken for. The only time he got to see her was at dinner, and even then, they were both too tired to do anything more than collapse into bed once Dorothy went to sleep.

A battered green canteen, dripping with condensation, appeared at his shoulder, and he took it and drained it without hesitation. "Thanks," he muttered hoarsely once the canteen was empty.

"No problem."

Hold on. Jason wasn't a baritone.

Owen squinted in the direction the voice and canteen had come from. "You're not Jason." A quick look around showed that Jason wasn't even here anymore.

Laughing, Arthur offered a hand to help Owen up. His training uniform, an eclectic mix of winter camouflage and thick furs, stank to high heaven, and his ivory scales caught the light in a headache-inducing way. "Good catch."

"What are you doing here?" he asked bluntly. He could've been nicer, but he didn't have the energy to do that and stand, even with Arthur's help. Besides, this room was reserved for Owen's daily butt-kicking session. Arthur shouldn't even be here.

Arthur shrugged, and the black fabric of his undershirt pulled taut against his shoulders. "Training's done. I thought I'd do my civic duty and see if any senior citizens needed help getting home."

"Cheeky brat," Owen muttered without any heat.

Joke as he might, he was glad for the company as they headed out. As little as he'd seen Tiffany recently, he'd seen Arthur even less. He hadn't even been home since Evans moved in.

They chatted as they walked, taking back hallways and stairs to avoid the crush on the Grand Staircases. Mostly inconsequential things—Arthur's new girlfriend, a siren he'd met in the Corps dorms, among them—but inevitably they circled back to their respective training.

"So you're done for the day?" Arthur asked as they made their way up the last staircase to their floor. They were on the wrong side of the mountain, but at least things were horizontal now.

Owen grunted, and he stopped at the landing to catch his breath. He was glad this hall was empty because he had to grab onto the wall to keep from falling over. His legs burned. He'd have to talk with Lord Keme tomorrow. All the training in the world was useless if the training crippled him.

"Mostly," he finally said. "I'm meeting with some of the engineers tonight. They've got a working model of the new gondola."

And he had to be there while they tested it. He'd be lucky if he got home by midnight, and he'd still have to go back again tomorrow night. Such was the life of a captain, apparently.

"What about you?" he asked, shoving thoughts of the plethora of evening meetings waiting for him out of his mind. "How's boot camp going?"

"Really well, actually." Arthur's hand drifted toward the private insignia on his left shoulder as a note of pride entered his voice. "My instructors say I'm almost ready to go into the field."

"Already?" His stomach twisted. It hadn't been that long, had it? Sirens usually got six months of training before they deployed. Arthur had only moved out a bit ago. "It's only been, what, three months?"

"Four." Arthur grinned so widely he was practically preening.

"Impressive," Owen managed to say. His chest felt hollow and tight. Cor, Arthur was only seventeen. Evans wasn't much older, and he'd lost his foreleg on his first mission—Isaac *died* and he'd served for years. "You'll probably end up on border duty for a while, though."

God, he hoped so. Even Owen served a few weeks on the border before his first away mission. It took a real prodigy or a major emergency to get sent on an away mission before six months. Even then, they had to be specially requested by a team captain before they could leave the haven.

"Probably," Arthur muttered petulantly, scuffing his boots on the floor. "At least, that's what my instructors say."

"They know what they're doing." Owen sighed and pushed himself off the wall. "Come on, let's get home."

That hadn't been the distraction he'd wanted it to be. Now new tensions were swirling around in his stomach like a whirlpool.

Arthur followed without comment for almost five minutes. A few more hallways and Owen could rest his aching legs.

"How's Mom's training going?"

"Good, as far as I can tell." She seemed to be enjoying it at least. Or if she wasn't, she hadn't told Owen about it. "Her flying instructor says she's made a lot of progress."

The halls slowly filled as they got closer to the apartment. The housing levels were never really empty, but the distant chatter made Owen pick up the pace.

"Must be tough, starting from zero."

"Hm," Owen hummed.

Not quite zero. She may not have been in the ring in years, but she still knew how to throw a punch. The only difference now was that she was a lot stronger than she used to be. Also, of course, the wings and the claws.

"It just seems weird. Civilians normally aren't allowed on rescues. You'd think they'd want someone with more experience."

"Oh?" Owen said over his shoulder, trying to sound light. "You have someone better in mind?"

"As a matter of fact . . ." Arthur said, grabbing onto Owen's arm and pulling him to a stop. "Yes."

He had a sinking feeling; he knew where this was going. Arthur never met his eyes when he was asking for something he knew he shouldn't, and he hadn't looked at Owen since before they'd left the gym. "Who?"

"Me."

Fuck.

"No." The swirling feeling in his stomach turned into a hurricane, and he wanted to be sick. Arthur was too young, too inexperienced, and too vulnerable. He hadn't even finished boot camp, let alone their specialized training, and he should know better than to even suggest it. "Absolutely not."

"Why not? I'm almost done with boot camp, and if I went, Mom could stay home."

"Arthur, no. You're too young." *Blood on white sheets, leaking through bandages and soaking Owen's hands. God, it was everywhere.* "Your mother's an adult, and the Corps decided she was essential for this mission."

No. Not the Corps. Percill had wanted her. That was the only reason she was there. The urge to peer into the dark corners of the hall, checking each nook and cranny like even thinking about Percill in front of Arthur would bring him here, hit Owen like a tidal wave.

Arthur threw his hands in the air. "You're not listening—"

"It's out of the question." He couldn't even consider it. Even if there was room for another teammate, the thought of Percill anywhere near the kids was enough to make his heart stop. Percill already had Tiffany and Owen. Like hell was he getting Arthur too. "There's—well, she has to come. You can't just push your way onto a dangerous mission because I'm in charge."

Arthur should know that. The away teams weren't drawn from a hat. There was a rhyme and reason to each placement, and messing with that to bolster someone's ego could jeopardize the mission and get someone killed. If Arthur thought he should be exempt from that rule, then maybe he didn't understand enough about the world to be in the Corps after all.

"But what about the girls?" Arthur asked pointedly. He crossed his arms and glared at Owen like a child who'd just been denied a sweet. "Who's going to take care of them if you don't come back?" The unspoken "again" rang between them like a church bell.

He wanted to scream. Tiffany and he had discussed this, and he still didn't have a good answer. Arthur was too young to give up his career to take care of his sisters, and most of the people Owen trusted to help were coming with him on what very well might turn into a suicide mission. On any other mission, with any other team, Owen would've been thrilled to have Arthur with him, but not here and not now.

"I said no. Drop. It." The words hurt as they came out, like they were pulled from the deepest depths of his soul, pushed up by oceans of blood. He couldn't lose Arthur too.

Arthur glared at him, eyes narrow slits and teeth bared, before he nodded. "Fine," he hissed, hair spikes bristling. "I'll drop it. Let's go home."

***

Arthur didn't stay for dinner that night.

One week, then two flowed by, following the same pattern. Owen woke, saw the kids off to school, went to his training sessions, then collapsed back into bed after his evening meetings. If he was lucky, Arthur came to find him in the gym after his workouts with a new list of reasons why he should take Tiffany's place on the mission, and he'd graciously accept Owen's counterarguments. If he wasn't lucky, they'd end up screaming at each other while Jason pushed Arthur one direction and Aaron pulled Owen the other.

Keme's training sessions had grown. He had Owen running the sessions now while he supervised. That didn't mean they got any easier. Now, instead of Owen getting his butt handed to him by one person, the whole team got to take turns throwing him into the dirt, and he had to critique them on it.

Well, that wasn't entirely true. Keme's training had come in handy more than once, and Owen could easily hold his own against most of the others on the first match at least. After that, he lost more bouts than he won.

He'd spent more time with Tiffany since the group sessions had started than he had since David died. Even if they were working during it, he got to see her, talk with her. The long hours and backbreaking work weren't so bad when she was there. Hell, if it weren't for the others, it wouldn't be so different from the training her dad had put him through after they got engaged.

One day, a week in, he told her that, and she'd laughed. He'd ridden that high through Jason throwing him into a wall.

Once they finished combat training, everyone converged in the Eyries. The dwarves had finished Gayle's gondola in record time, and the team needed to be able to get into and out of it blindfolded. Literally. More than one Corps member had been blinded in the course of duty.

Last week they'd begun flying in it, and safe to say, Owen had never had a less comfortable ride. The gondola had been designed for stealth and speed, so anything nonessential—that is, anything that could've possibly made it pleasant—had been stripped out. Even the biggest compartment was barely as wide as Tiffany's wings.

They managed though, covering each other's weak spots and finding their place in the new hierarchy. Slowly but surely, the team was coming together.

On his rare afternoons off, he spent an hour or two in front of David's tomb, trying to force himself to work on his rose with Ashley. The last of her petals had long since been painted, and only the toughest taskmaster would say it was anything except perfect, but it still seemed to find its way home with them at the end of the day. And Owen's . . . well, Owen's rose had a few more chips in it. At this rate, he'd finish right around his eightieth birthday.

Each time he picked up his chisel, his hands just froze. The granite sat in his hands, a dead thing that he couldn't bring himself to throw away or change.

He should probably talk to a therapist about that.

He was on his way back from one such carving session three days before they were supposed to leave when he first heard fighting echoing down the corridor. He almost kept going—they were near the center of the city, and the guard would interfere shortly—but stopped in his tracks, heart leaping to his throat, as a familiar snarl echoed down the hall.

He was halfway there before he'd even realized he was moving. The aches and pains and the soreness that had been a constant companion in the last three weeks disappeared as he slid around a corner. An answering growl reverberated through the air and put the speed of Hermes into Owen's step. That sounded like a fully grown werewolf. Blast, he thought Jen had gotten over this; she hadn't gotten in a fight in weeks.

He was so caught up in his thoughts, in the worry and terror that made thinking difficult, that he almost ran past the fight. Breathing hard, he shoved his way through the crowd and—there. Jen had a third-gen werewolf with mottled brown and black fur pinned to the ground, her teeth buried in his shoulder and her claws scrambling for some sort of hold. Three scratches on her upper arm stained her blond fur red, and if he didn't do something now, they'd have company soon.

The werewolf on the ground growled, ripped Jen off his shoulder, threw her to the ground, and advanced with a snarl that hardly seemed to have anything human in it at all. He raised his hand and—

"Stop," Owen yelled, throwing himself between Jen and the other werewolf. "Get away from her!" Reflexively, he shifted into a defensive stance, arm raised to throw the other werewolf aside if he charged.

The werewolf snarled, rose onto his hind legs, and shifted back to human. "She attacked me," he said as soon as he could form words. His skin bulged as his fur receded away and his bones shifted into place. "They all saw it."

His friends, mostly werewolves themselves, muttered in agreement. One, a young siren, started humming under her breath while she poked at the bleeding bite on his shoulder.

"Take it easy—" A blond blur shoved past him, and Owen lunged forward to catch Jen before she made contact.

"You're lying," Jen screamed, swiping at the werewolf and struggling against Owen's grip. "That's not what happened!"

The werewolf yelped. "She did it again," he yelled, darting farther back into the crowd. If Owen hadn't been busy trying to stop Jen, he'd have laughed at how scared he looked. "She's gone feral."

Owen swore and gripped Jen tighter when she dug her claws into his arm—not deep enough to injure, but he was definitely aware they were there. Cor, where were the guards? "Jen, stop," he ordered in his firmest voice.

At first, he didn't think she was going to listen, but after another feeble struggle, she stopped fighting him and growled at the other werewolf.

Just in time, too, as a nude shade wearing a small pouch with the symbol of the guard around her neck turned the corner.

"What's going on here?" she asked Owen, eyes darting around the crowd. Her gaze lingered on the tear and bloodstains that marred the werewolf's shirt from Jen's bite, now completely healed by the guilty-looking siren. Her hand darted to her pouch. "Is anyone injured?"

Owen swore silently this time, but before he could get a word out—

"Nothing," growled the werewolf, rubbing at his healed injury. He made a convincing show of looking innocent and even took full advantage of the werewolf puppy dog eyes as he spoke. "We were goofing around." The crowd all muttered in agreement with him, but he was the only one to meet the guard's eye.

Her eyes flashed back to Owen, who nodded. He should tell the truth. He'd always harped about taking responsibility for one's actions, and this was as far from that as one could get, but he didn't have time to deal with a full guard inquiry. If the injured party was willing to slide it under the rug, he wasn't going to protest. He could deal with Jen once they got home.

"Someone reported fighting. You're sure nothing happened?" Her words lingered in the air, as if they'd be able to sniff out the truth on their own. "All right then, I'll be on my way, but if something happens, let me know."

As she turned the corner, already partially invisible, Owen let out a breath. The crowd of teenagers began to dissipate, likely eager to leave just in case the guard wasn't gone. The werewolf Jen had been fighting with glared at her and snarled once more before shifting back into his wolf form and chasing after his friends.

***

"So," Owen said as they walked back to the apartment, his hand wrapped around Jen's forearm like a vice. "Want to tell me what that was about?" He tried to keep his voice low and calm, but residual worry and fear were ripping apart his insides like a blender. He didn't want to do this here. This hall was a major thoroughfare, but Jen would wall up if he waited.

Jen scowled and ducked her head. "He started it," she muttered in a sulky voice. Her footsteps dragged, and her claws left little white lines in their wake.

Owen took a deep breath and counted to ten, then said, "That's not what I asked, Jen."

She didn't answer, and he didn't dare press her in public. Once they got home, he'd sit her down and get an answer from her even if he had to drag it out of her. As they reached their hall, she muttered something under her breath.

"What did you say?" He glanced around to be sure no one else was in the hall before he knelt in front of her. Leery of her making an escape attempt—she knew the city well enough to hide from him for days if she wanted to—he loosened his grip on her arm but didn't release it.

"He was laughing at me," Jen whispered in a broken voice, eyes glistening. Her ears pressed back against her skull so flat they almost disappeared into her fur. "He said—he said you and Mom were leaving because I couldn't keep my pack safe."

Owen's jaw dropped. Werewolves were social creatures, and failing to protect the pack was one of the worst sins they could commit. He may as well have accused her of killing David herself.

"Tha—that's ridiculous," he whispered numbly, but it was too little too late. Before the words even finished leaving his mouth, she tore her arm free and sprinted to the apartment, quiet sobs echoing behind her.

The sound of a slamming door boomed down the hallway as Owen raced after her. Heads poked out of other doors while he shoved the apartment door open and—with moderately less force than Jen—shut it behind him.

He came into the living room just as Jen threw herself into the armchair so hard it almost toppled over, and drew her knees up to her chest. Her hackles bristled like a hedgehog.

A part of him—the part of him exhausted by constant training and weeks spent on edge—wanted to lash out at Jen for running away, but that would only make things worse.

He inhaled and exhaled three times, counting to ten each time. When he felt calm enough to speak without yelling, he knelt in front of Jen's chair.

"None of this is your fault," he whispered. "We have to go. It's our job." His hand was halfway to her shoulder before he thought better of it. In this mood, she was as likely to snap at him as to let him comfort her.

Jen growled, and she pulled back as far as she could. "You and Mom keep saying that," she said hoarsely, "but you won't tell us why you have to go. You—you were going to stay home. What's so important that you have to leave again?"

"Jen . . ." He sighed. His leg ached, and he scooted closer to the armchair to lean against it.

He didn't know what to say. He'd been so caught up in everything—in Ashley's depression and Arthur's wrath, in training and Tiffany, and in trying to regain some measure of control over his own life—that he'd forgotten about everything else.

Another sigh pushed past his lips as he rubbed his eyes. "Jen, I can't help that I'm going to leave," he whispered, ignoring the niggling voice in his head that warned him to be careful of her sharp teeth and giving in to the urge to rub her shoulder with his free hand. "We have a job to do."

Jen grabbed his hand without raising her head, her claws digging into the soft flesh, and said in a wet voice, "Why can't someone else do it? Ms. . . ." Her voice hitched and turned into a sob. "M-Ms. Dutchske said there are thousands of Corps members. Can't one of them go instead?"

Owen swallowed against the lump in his throat. At some point, his eyes had become suspiciously wet. "I want to stay—believe me, I want it more than anything in the world—but the man we're working with refuses to work with any of them. He said it has to be me." He shouldn't be telling her this, not even as vague as it was. It wasn't allowed, and besides, there was a part of him, bolstered by the memory of what he had pulled Jen out of, that was terrified she would try to find Percill herself if she knew anything more about him.

She'd get herself involved, like Arthur kept trying to. Like Tiffany was. He'd keep Jen safe at the very least.

Jen's lips pulled back, and the growl she let loose was laced with loathing, fear, and a dark, dark rage that chilled Owen's heart. She threw herself into Owen's arms with the fervor of someone seeing a loved one for the last time and buried her face in his neck. "I hate him," she whispered, her whiskers tickling him with each heaving breath. "I wish he was dead, then you wouldn't have to leave."

Owen's breath caught in his chest as his arms automatically closed around her. Jen wanted someone dead. His little girl—who'd never met someone she hadn't become friends with, who never said something she didn't mean—hated someone so much she wanted them dead.

A silent sob sucked the air from his lungs, and no matter how hard he tried, they refused to fill again. She shouldn't hate this much yet. She shouldn't hate this much at all. She was—she was Jen. Good-natured and amiable to a fault, friendly and sociable. But somehow, since they'd come here, she had lost enough of herself that she could hate.

He made himself take a breath, then another, and pulled back. Jen's eyes, shining with as of yet unshed tears, looked at him with a miserable face as she wiped her nose with the back of her arm.

"Jen . . ." He couldn't let this go on, but he didn't know how to stop it. "We have to go, we don't have a choice. We just . . ." They needed more time. Jen, Arthur, Dorothy, and Ashley needed Tiffany and him, but the seconds were ticking past with the tenacity and indomitable will of Niagara Falls. Try as he might, he couldn't hold them back. There were only so many hours in a day. "We need you to hold it together for a little longer, okay? We'll be home soon, and I promise we won't leave again."

The assurance was hollow, and they both knew it, but seeing the light leave Jen's eyes ached like someone had stabbed him.

Her ears drooped as she nodded without looking up. "Okay, Dad," she whispered in a shaky voice, and her hands fell listlessly to her side.

Owen opened his arms for another hug, hoping desperately she'd hear everything he couldn't say, praying she knew he meant it, but it wasn't enough. Her lips trembled, and she darted away, disappearing down the hall and out of the apartment before he could react.

He raced to the door and out into the hall just as Jen vanished around a corner. Heedless of the stares and calls his neighbors sent after him, he tore after her. After charging down three halls, up a flight of stairs, and around more corners than he could count, Owen finally slowed to a halt. His burning lungs and aching legs weren't enough to block out the bitter taste of failure.

He'd lost her.

CHAPTER SIXTEEN

In Which They Leave

"Look, rescue missions are hard even before you leave. You have to have the right team, with the right supplies, at the right time. And when you do leave, you need to be sure you've taken enough medicine and food while still being careful to not overload the dragon. I've been on missions where my team and I had to dump our gear so our ride could get off the ground. Overpacking isn't just annoying, it's potentially lethal. So watch your gear and never take more than necessary."
—Excerpt from the lectures of Sergeant Mike Mann

Try as he might, Owen didn't see Jen before they had to leave. She was always out when he came home and perpetually one step ahead of him when he went looking for her.

He used to think he was a good father. Before all this, when they'd all been human and still lived in Kansas, he'd always known what to say or do to help the kids. Now? Now it felt like he couldn't move without some reminder of all the ways he'd failed. Between Arthur, whom Owen hadn't seen in three days; Ashley, who put on a brave face that couldn't quite hide the broken pieces behind it; and Jen—Owen felt like he was drowning in everything he didn't have time to fix.

"She'll be here, Owen," Tiffany said, laying a hand on Owen's shoulder.

Owen grunted. He'd had squabbles with Jen before, but she'd never stayed angry for longer than an afternoon. No, this felt different. Even if she did show up, it wouldn't be to see him.

Bloody hell, everything had gone to hell since Percill showed back up in his life. Everything that had gone wrong since then could be laid firmly at his feet.

The way Jen's eyes dimmed as the hope drained from them. Arthur's voice gone hoarse from their arguments. Ashley's dead smile, her hands cradled around a rose she refused to finish. If it weren't for Percill, Owen could've stopped all that.

The fifteen-minute warning tore through the background chatter of mechanics.

Tiffany kept looking at him from the corner of her eyes as she stowed her gear and frowned. They'd discuss this later, whether he wanted to or not. Lucky for her, they would be right next to each other until they got to Arizona.

He pushed the thought aside, opened his compartment, and shoved his bag near the bottom. Somehow, it seemed even tighter than it had during training, and the thought of being stuck in there with himself for company made Owen want to turn around and go home.

Familiar shouting made Owen jerk up so fast his head slammed into the compartment lid. He spun on his heel, eyes darting around for the source and . . . there, arguing with Beira. Jedidiah Ashwind had forced his way into the hangar and was yelling so loud Owen was surprised the ceiling hadn't come down.

"—an outrage, we agreed I would stay out of their training, but then I hear about you sneaking out before dawn," Ashwind thundered, looking one wrong move from strangling someone.

Beira kept pace with Ashwind and waved off concerned aides and mechanics. "We weren't sneaking off," she said with the air of one who'd already had this conversation a half dozen times. "We agreed they'd pick you up at the border."

Ashwind snorted, which sounded eerily close to two pieces of wood being rubbed against each other. "As if I'd let one monarchist know where my camp is, let alone a whole group of them." The space where his eyebrows would've been if he'd had them was so furrowed it looked like the Grand Canyon.

By now they were feet from Gayle, and Ashwind was fuming like he was about to explode. He turned on his heel and snarled. "This proves that I was right. You lot can't be trusted." His fingers clenched so tightly they creaked. He opened his mouth as if to speak again—and stopped.

Taking a deep breath, he relaxed his fists enough to run one hand through his winter-thinned scraggly beard. "I'm a man of my word. I promised I'd hold my judgment until the end of this, and I will." His eyes flared again, so full of fire Owen was surprised there wasn't smoke coming from Ashwind's ears. "But I assure you, if this is some kind of trap or your monarchists try to leave me behind again, nothing will stop me from destroying them."

Beira clenched her jaw and nodded. "Of course. I promise I'll get to the bottom of this miscommunication. In the meantime, Captain Williams will show you where to store your things." Her eyes narrowed the barest fraction, and her lips turned up in a smile that could've cut diamond. "You have less than fifteen minutes, best get in place."

Ashwind grunted and turned to face Owen. He, at least, made no pretense at warmth. "Fifty years and she hasn't changed a bit," he grumbled under his breath as he shoved past. "Come on, where's my spot?"

It took Owen a moment to realize he was being spoken to. He swallowed and moved forward in a way he hoped looked calm and collected. He wasn't scared of Ashwind, but only a fool wouldn't be cautious around him.

Beckoning over his shoulder, he led Ashwind to his compartment. It was in the middle of the gondola, but at the bottom of their group and as far from Owen's as was possible.

"I see they spared no effort to make this comfortable," Ashwind muttered as he leaned down to inspect his compartment. It wasn't any smaller than the others, with a door a bare two inches wider than its intended occupant's shoulders, but next to a man of Ashwind's size, it looked tiny. "For heaven's sake, didn't they use any padding? We'll be shaken to pieces long before we get there."

Leaving him to his complaining, Owen went back to his compartment as fast as he dared.

"Daddy!" Dorothy's cry brought an unbidden grin to Owen's face. He spun around and dropped to his knees just in time to catch her fur- and feather-covered form. Her wings wrapped around his shoulders as far as they could reach. A bolt of warmth shot through him, and he hugged her back as tightly as he could. When she pulled back, a fresh wave of tears leaked down onto the wet patch in her fur. "Daddy, do you have to leave again?"

Owen pressed a kiss to her forehead and murmured, "I'm afraid we have to, sweetheart." How many times had he faced those tears? It never got easier. Damn Percill.

Tiffany came up from behind Owen and bent to take Dorothy from him. "We'll be back soon, sweetie, I promise."

Evans and the others caught up at that moment, and instead of trying to comfort Dorothy the way he wanted, Owen turned to face them. Evans darted up first, followed closely by Ashley and—something like lead fell from Owen's heart—Jen.

"I'm sorry, sir," Evans said, awkwardly stumbling over his new prosthetic. "She got away from me."

Ashley threw herself at Owen before he could respond.

"Don't go," she whispered, burying her face in his neck. "Please don't go."

Owen's chest ached as he hugged her back. He pulled away and raised a hand to wipe her face. "It'll be fine," he said, his voice breaking. "Take care of your sisters, and we'll be back before you know it."

"Isn't that my job?"

"Arthur." Owen's head whipped toward Arthur's voice, and he couldn't help the relieved grin that spread over his face. That was all of them; he got to see them one more time. Relief and worry tied his stomach in knots, but he shoved them away. "I thought you couldn't get away from your squad."

Arthur hurried over, dodging around the mechanics and various assistants running around the Eyries, and wrapped Tiffany in a hug. "My captain heard you were leaving, so she let me skip the night patrol debrief to see you off." He was still wearing his combat kit—complete with mud splatters, dead leaves, and a large regulation knife—so he must have skipped the barracks.

Tiffany kissed his cheek. "Thank you for coming," she said when she released him, her eyes wet. "I was worried we wouldn't get to see you before we left."

Ducking his head, Arthur smiled sheepishly and scuffed his foot against the floor. "Eh, I'd have gotten away to see you off no matter what, even if it was to wave." He turned to Owen and sighed. "I still think I should be going with you," he grumbled as he pulled Owen into a hug. "I could help. You know I could."

Owen sighed and shook his head. "We're not having this argument again, Arthur." He didn't want to fight now, not when they'd wasted so much time already.

It didn't help that he did have some good points. He wasn't particularly skilled as a healer or hypnotist, but he was an amazing harmonizer who could boost the abilities of even the most lackluster singer. Furthermore, his combat abilities had blossomed in the last year, and he'd become a decent tracker. If it were any other mission, Owen would've been thrilled to have him, and Arthur knew it.

"I know, I just . . ." Arthur trailed off and, shoving his hands in his pockets, sighed in a way that was eerily reminiscent of Owen.

"You want to help," Owen finished. He could sympathize; he remembered being in Arthur's place at that age. Of course, he'd been trying to get another shift at the grocer's, not trying to join an away mission with a higher than usual risk of dying. "And the best way to do that is to stay here and listen to your superiors. You've already got your next assignment, right? That should keep you busy until we get back."

Arthur grunted but didn't respond, and the bell sounded before Owen could say anything else.

Tiffany sighed and set Dorothy down. "That's five minutes. We'd better get going."

Owen cast one last look at Jen, who hadn't looked up since she'd hugged Tiffany, and bit back a sigh. After a final round of goodbyes, with teary hugs from Dorothy and Ashley and a somber one from Arthur, Owen waved goodbye and turned away. At least she'd come and he'd gotten to see her before they'd left. He could take not getting a hug or a proper goodbye, even if he'd rather walk to Arizona with the whole haven on his back.

A small part of him hoped she'd chase after them, a small part that persisted even as it became more and more unlikely. He didn't hear the hoped-for sound of her feet running to him before he reached Gayle. He didn't hear it as the others got into position or as he climbed into his compartment. He didn't hear it as Beira addressed them and wished them luck on their mission. And he didn't hear it as the compartment door swung shut and Gayle launched herself into the air.

***

Even with all their training, Owen still had to admit the ride was rough. The compartments were so small Owen could touch his hands to either side and his feet to the bottom without stretching. The sides were a mesh netting through which Owen could feel Tiffany's shifting wings and hear Jason joking with Aaron.

"Tiff?" he whispered as quietly as he could for fear of bothering the others. The next four hours would be miserable enough without everyone getting in each other's faces.

"Yes?" she answered in an equally quiet voice. The mesh under his fingers pushed out then retracted. She must have turned around. Her voice, louder and closer now, confirmed it. "What is it?"

Owen started to shrug and only halfway through remembered that she couldn't see it. Instead, he said, "I wanted to check on you. How're you doing?"

Her compartment rustled like her wings were rubbing against the far wall, and she said, "It's a little tight, but we knew that. I'm more concerned about you."

She didn't have to say it for Owen to know what she was talking about. "I didn't expect her to have forgiven me yet," he said softly. "But I'd hoped she'd at least say goodbye." It hurt more than he'd expected, but he knew it was still less than he deserved. "She was right, you know. We shouldn't be here."

"Bit late for that," Tiffany said in a deadpan voice. Past her, there came an agreeing snort that sounded like Jason.

"That's not what I meant," Owen said with more bite than he meant to put in it. He took a deep breath and started again. "If it weren't for Percill, neither of us would be here." As much as it hurt to consider how Jen had learned to hate, Owen understood it.

Tiffany hummed, and her claws poked through the mesh as she tightened her fingers around his. "That's true, if it weren't for him, we wouldn't be here, but . . ."

Owen shifted and brought his other hand up to wrap around the lump where her hand was. "But what?"

Tiffany huffed, and her hands pulled away from his. For several long moments, all he could hear was her shifting around in her compartment. When she finally did speak, she sounded muffled, like she'd buried her face in her arms. "Is it bad that I'm glad about it?" A faint scratching noise hid just under her words like she was running a claw over the floor. "We've spent more time together in the last few weeks than we have in months. You've been gone so much, and even when you were home, you were never . . . home."

Owen bowed his head and wrapped his arms around himself. That was truer than he wanted to admit. "I didn't want to be," he whispered. "It felt empty." He couldn't put it into words. For weeks after the Battle of Tearmann, he'd been stuck in their apartment, left to the empty rooms and the echoes of a silent voice, while everyone else was out working. For months even the thought of spending more time there than he had to made his heart drop like a stone. The rest of the mountain hadn't been much better, and when Beira had offered him a place in the Corps, he hadn't taken much convincing.

Tiffany's voice was louder than he expected when she spoke. "We missed you."

Owen's sigh released something he'd forgotten he even carried, a tiny nugget of grief that had lodged in his heart and destroyed any chance at peace before it was more than a thought. "I missed you too," he whispered, wishing Tiffany would put her hand back so he could hold it.

"Would you have retired if it weren't for Evans?" she whispered.

Owen started to speak but hesitated. Finally, he said, "I'm not sure. Being in the field was better than being home, less empty, but I think I knew it was time. I didn't . . ."

He didn't want them to have to mourn him the way they mourned David. That hadn't been the first mission that ended with him in the hospital, but it had been the worst. He'd lost a friend, almost lost a second, and had inadvertently crippled someone who wasn't much older than Arthur. Someone with David's eyes.

"I'd had enough," he whispered, pushing his fingers against the mesh, searching for Tiffany. "I sat in that cave and I realized that, more than anything in the world, I wanted to be home with you and the kids. I wanted to go home."

Despite everything that remained to be said between them, Owen and Tiffany fell into silence. The hours would've passed unnoticed if it weren't for the growing light shining through the portholes. That and the growing stiffness in everyone's limbs. As such, everyone welcomed Gayle's gradual descent and the way the compartments shifted as she went from horizontal flight to vertical landing.

Owen wasn't the only one who almost fell while exiting his compartment, nor was he the only one to stretch as widely as he could once he'd hit solid ground. All around him, the others tried to relieve the worst of their aches before they had to go back inside.

Even Gayle took the opportunity to shake and move in a way she couldn't while the gondola was occupied. Once she'd finished a series of cat-like stretches, she scratched at the skin behind her harness with a wing tip.

"Ugh, my shoulders ache," she whined.

Jane frowned. "That's weird. The weight distribution is supposed to be even to avoid hurting you. Want me to look at it?"

Gayle nodded vigorously. "Please. It's giving me a neckache, and I'd rather not have to fly with that."

"Wasn't your training supposed to help you get used to flying with passengers?" Owen teased, nonetheless pushing himself to his feet and following Jane. He churned their inventory list over in his head and pondered whether they could shuffle things around to make it easier on Gayle without losing anything.

They weren't supposed to unhook the harness for fear of reattaching it wrong, so Owen searched the compartments while Jane examined Gayle's neck straps. The first seven were simple—open, confirm they were empty, and shut—but the lower eleven were more difficult.

The first held the nets, and they needed to be handled carefully to avoid getting tangled. The second and third were their medical supplies and food, all accounted for as they should be and in the proper place. The fourth held their weapons and gear, which they would wear on the way back to conserve space. The fifth and sixth were supposed to be empty, and the fifth was. The sixth was not.

"Uh, hi, Dad."

Owen blinked. For a moment, he couldn't believe his eyes. Arthur, still in his patrol kit, couldn't be here in the middle of Montana. He was supposed to be on a patrol along the northern border. He couldn't be here.

By the time reality sank in, Owen's stomach had turned to stone, and black spots danced in front of his eyes. With a jolt, he remembered to breathe, and with oxygen came a flurry of emotions too mixed up to describe.

"What are you doing here?" he asked in a low, deceptively calm voice once the fire in his blood had turned from a roar to a furious simmer waiting for the opportunity to flare up again.

"Owen? What's—Arthur!" Tiffany's shriek rang through the clearing and knocked Owen out of his hyper focus on Arthur.

Owen couldn't imagine what Tiffany had expected to find when she came over to see what was holding him up. Still, the horror in her voice was a perfect match to the sinking dread in his heart.

Arthur swallowed and almost fell over in his hurry to stand. Four hours was hard enough without having to stay still and quiet for fear of discovery. His limbs must have felt like lead. If he weren't so furious, Owen might have been sorry for him.

Owen didn't give him any time to adjust and find his land legs. "Do you have any idea what you've done?" he hissed, grabbing Arthur's arm. By now the others had gathered around, and even Gayle had moved to get a better look.

"I—I—" Arthur stuttered, stumbling like he'd have fallen if it weren't for Owen's iron grip on his arm.

But Owen didn't give him time to speak. Plowing over Arthur's feeble protests, Owen laid out every one of the ways he had put the group, their mission, and himself in danger in a calm and low voice, a rigid dichotomy to the storm in his chest that wanted to scream and shout.

Arthur had stowed away on a rescue mission. He hadn't completed their more advanced training—making himself a liability—and they didn't have the gear or the manpower to get him to safety and to complete their mission. Not only was a court-martial likely, it was damn near guaranteed. He'd be lucky if he didn't go to jail, and any future he'd hoped to have in the Corps was gone.

"I wanted to help!" Arthur yelled when Owen paused to take a breath.

Ashwind snorted, a sound echoed by anyone in the clearing who wasn't a Williams. "Of course you did," he said. Until now he'd stood away from the others, silent and willing to let Owen take the lead. "You're a child."

Arthur bristled. "I'm not a kid!" He yanked his arm from Owen. "I'm a full ranking Corps member with as much right to be here as you." His pleasant features distorted into a snarl. "More, even."

Owen barked out a laugh and turned to pace. "If you had orders, yes, but you didn't." Tension ramped up his steps, and he had to fight the burning itch to punch something. "In fact, I'm certain your orders sent you in the opposite direction. So not only did you stow away, but you're also absent without leave, and you abandoned your post. What were you thinking?"

Faced with the waiting stares of not only his parents but the entirety of a highly trained away team, Arthur deflated and shuffled his feet in the dirt. "You weren't listening to me," he muttered, not daring to meet anyone's eyes. "I could help, I know I could."

"How did you get in?" Ashwind asked. He sized Arthur up like he was considering something Owen didn't want to think about. "No matter what I say about you people, the security at the capital is top notch. You shouldn't have been able to get close enough to stow away."

Arthur shrugged and looked up. "I wasn't going to, but when everyone was distracted by the queen and getting into position, I just . . . No one was looking. I saw an open compartment and got in before I could think better of it."

"You saw an opportunity," Ashwind muttered, and rubbed a hand over his mouth. "Did you stop to think about what your presence here would do to the mission?"

"Clearly not," Owen snapped, fighting the urge to pace again and losing. "If he had, he never would've left."

Tiffany, who'd been silent up until now, chose that moment to speak. "What are we supposed to do with him?" Her voice shook, and her fists were clenched at her side like it took everything she had from going to Arthur and trying to comfort him.

"There's nothing we can do," Jason said solemnly, and the others agreed with him in the same manner. "We can't leave him here, or we'll be court-martialed right next to him, and we can't bring him back. At best we can drop him off at the pickup point on the way there."

Ashwind barked a laugh and darted forward to grab Owen's arm. "Hang that, Williams, this is an opportunity." He dropped Owen's arm and turned to Arthur. "You, boy, what's your skill set?"

Arthur blinked, then stuttered a response. "I'm . . . I'm a harmonizer, but I'm a decent song at healing too." Gaining speed and with it, courage, he continued before the others could interrupt him. "I'm a good scout, I can fight and—"

"And he's not coming with us, so drop it, Ashwind," Owen said.

Ashwind raised his brow. "He'd be useful, that's all I'm saying. I say we put him to work. It's what he wants, after all."

No, no, no, no, they couldn't do that. Arthur shouldn't be here, and they shouldn't reward his disobedience. "No," Owen barked. He took a deep breath and started again. "No, he had orders, and he disobeyed them to come with us. We're not rewarding this sort of behavior. Once the mission is over, we'll turn him over to the Corps, and they can deal with him."

Arthur would never forgive him for this, Owen knew that, but he would be safe. And maybe one day, far off in the future, Arthur would understand why he'd done it. For now, it was enough that he wouldn't be in harm's way.

Arthur swallowed but, perhaps realizing that speaking would only make things worse, said nothing. He held Owen's eyes for a few seconds before ducking his chin into his chest.

Owen shook his head and turned to Jane, who had been standing silently in Gayle's shadow. "Can you find a place for him that won't hurt Gayle?"

Jane nodded, her braids and beard bouncing as she rolled up her sleeves. "He's about your size, and you have the next shotgun shift. We'll stick him in your compartment."

"Good," Owen said, turning back to the gondola. "Everyone get in position, and Tiff . . ." He resisted the urge to massage his temples. "Keep an eye on Arthur, won't you?"

CHAPTER SEVENTEEN

In Which It Began Smoothly

"We were completely unprepared, which is the only excuse I have for what happened. Between the weather, the wildfire, and the mob, we didn't have time to double-check that everything was in place. As a result, we were two miles up before we realized we'd left Sergeant Omar behind and had to double back for him. We managed to find him, but by the time we did, the smoke was too thick to see through. A falling tree broke Emma's wing, and we lost Captain Xavier to a fallen power line. We rode Emma out, but something—the shock or an infection—ended up killing her before we could get help. The rest of us managed to get to a safehouse and get out before the fire caught up with us, but it was close."
—Excerpt from Mission Report 14325X83 by Commander Olson

Over the course of their two-day trip to Arizona, Arthur ended up on the receiving end of a tongue lashing that nearly ripped the flesh off his bones, courtesy of Tiffany. Then a similar one from Jason. Then a disappointed one from Eoire and Aaron, who teamed up for maximum guilting. And an incredulous one from Jane, who couldn't believe he'd been able to sneak on. Ashwind mostly stayed out of it, but he did pull Owen aside to argue they should use Arthur since he was there.

Owen, after his initial argument with Arthur, said nothing directly to him. Instead, he spoke around him, ordering Jane to find him a place in the compartments, telling Jason to take him on patrol, and asking Tiffany to keep track of him. It might have been petty, but a part of him—a part crippled with terror because whenever he looked at Arthur, he saw a shadow standing behind him with bright blue eyes—thought he could keep them all safe if he just didn't acknowledge him.

By the time they landed in a dusty canyon approximately ten miles from anything important, Owen had spoken fewer than twenty words to Arthur since climbing into the shotgun shell.

Once free of his compartment, which seemed to get smaller the longer he had to spend in it, Owen stretched and cast an eye over their surroundings. There wasn't much.

The small canyon—more of a crevasse really—was just large enough for their group if Gayle kept her wings pressed tight to her body. She'd had to land on top of the canyon and climb down before she could let them out. An abandoned building, perhaps a barn or warehouse, leaned against the canyon wall like a drunkard. A path, hardly wide enough for a small truck, ran between it and the far wall.

"All right," he said, turning back to Gayle and the others. "Take five, then get your things together. I want to be out of here two hours before sunset." A series of assenting groans answered him, but nonetheless, the others started moving.

Owen was digging his gear—a bulletproof vest, a pistol, a rifle, and three large knives—from his compartment when Arthur grabbed his arm.

"Anything I can do?" His voice was respectful, but his cheeks were stained red with excitement, and he kept glancing toward the equipment lockers.

Owen yanked his arm free with a grunt and gathered his things in his arms. "You're staying with Gayle. You're going to keep watch while she gets the nets in place."

Arthur's hopeful face fell, and he darted in front of Owen. "But I can help," he said, catching Owen's arm again. "You might need an extra pair of hands in there."

"No, Arthur," Owen said. His gear almost slid out of his grasp in his rush to get his arm free. The others were standing a respectable distance away and determinedly not looking at them. Even Tiffany, who barely met Owen's eyes before looking down, didn't try to help. "We can't bring you with us. It's bad enough that you're taking up space here when we need every spare pound for the captives, but we'd be putting ourselves right alongside you at the docket if I let you come."

"But Dad—"

"No, and if you ask me again, you'll be facing more than a court-martial when we get home." Owen stormed off to hide behind Gayle before either of them could say anything they'd regret. Hopefully, that was enough to keep Arthur back until after they left.

Threatening him like that was cruel, especially since Arthur was technically an adult, but they couldn't bring him no matter how much he asked. This was a sensitive mission, and despite being a good singer, Arthur didn't have the training or the maturity. Besides, Gayle really could use a hand, and having him here to help meant they could get out earlier.

Sighing, he set the bundle of gear on the ground and stripped. His clothes worked for travel or urban reconnaissance, but he needed to change into something more . . . circumspect for the mission. For him, that meant tan camouflage under his combat gear.

Jane had the same gear as Owen, but Jason needed to go in naked to take full advantage of his blending, Tiffany wore a modified weapons harness that fit around her wings and a basic bulletproof vest, and Aaron's scales were tough enough that armor would get in the way. Beyond that, everyone but Jason also had a helmet, a suitably adapted headset, and a utility belt or backpack for their weapons and any gear they couldn't hold.

Gearing up didn't take long, and the others were ready before Owen sheathed his last knife and double-checked his spare ammo clips.

They stared at him for a while, no one saying anything, before it occurred to Owen that they were expecting something like a speech. Swallowing, he cursed the bit of himself that had never been comfortable with public speaking.

Gayle curled up on the far side of the canyon, her wings wrapped around her legs but still poking at the walls. The others gathered in front of her, and Ashwind . . . well, Ashwind stood apart from the others, wearing a faded set of combat fatigues and nothing else. A rifle hung over his shoulder, and two knives hung at his waist. Beyond them, sulking by the barn, was Arthur. All were still waiting for him to say something.

"You know what we have to do," Owen said quietly, speaking before he realized he'd meant to. "And you know why we have to do it." He paused and hoped that that might be enough before he sighed and scrounged together enough words to continue. "We've only got one shot at this. If even the slightest thing goes wrong . . ." He dropped his hand to his belt. This wasn't going well. "They need us, the people in there. They don't have a chance without us."

They didn't. The odds of the stars ever aligning like this again were practically nonexistent. If they failed, SAFE would move the captives elsewhere, and the channels Percill had used to find them would be blocked.

"They're depending on us to do our parts, and I know we won't let them down." Slowly, he looked each of them in the eye, studying their faces, searching for any sign of unease or fear. "It may not be ideal or the kind of role we'd prefer, but we're all needed if we want any chance in hell of getting out of here with our lives and mission accomplished."

They were ready. What's more, they could do this. They'd been training for this for weeks. They'd studied the layout and the personnel files Percill had given them. They knew what to expect, and they knew how they planned to beat it.

"Away team, move out." The words had a sort of finality to them. They couldn't go back after this, but they couldn't stay here either. He resisted the urge to look at or speak to Arthur. More than anything, Owen wanted to keep him where he could see him, but he couldn't bring Arthur, and Owen couldn't stay here. And yet . . . he knew that if he looked, it'd be almost impossible to resist him. "Base team," he said with a grunt. "Be on the lookout for us and be ready to leave when we get back."

And so they ran. The seven-mile journey to Percill's meeting point passed in near silence, each focused on keeping their footing and their breath in the dim light.

They slowed when the marker—a dilapidated gas station next to two dying juniper trees—came into view. Owen lifted two fingers to signal for Jason to scout ahead and Eoire to keep an eye on him. He wasn't worried about being seen this far out, but better safe than sorry. Besides, Jason was damn near invisible when he wanted to be, even clothed.

After three eternal minutes of silence, an emotional shift—safety, peace, and rest—from Eoire signaled that Jason had cleared the building. A Fead rune scratched into a side door proved that Jason was already inside. Owen shoved the door open with his shoulder and led the way in.

Jason was sitting on what used to be the checkout counter, already half naked. "If Percill's here, he's become a shade," he said once Owen came into view. "Want me to scout around for him?"

Owen shook his head, then nodded. "Stay within visual range of the door. I don't want to have to go searching for you if he shows up while you're gone."

Grunting, Jason shucked off his pants and disappeared. The only signs of his passage were dusty footsteps on the ground and a small breeze as he passed by.

The others spread out in the gas station, and Owen and Eoire took up sentry positions next to the blacked-out windows. Tiny gaps in the cover were just big enough to peek out while still staying out of the door's line of sight.

They couldn't see much. The same desert they'd tracked through for over an hour, an ill-kept highway, and a few scrubs barely clinging onto life. Every few seconds, Owen tore his eyes away, scanned the room to confirm where his team was, and glanced at his watch. They may have been early, but not by much, and Percill was never late.

Jason appeared next to Owen and almost startled him out of his skin. "Sorry about that," he said in a low voice. "Just thought I'd let you know that something's kicking up dust on the road south of us."

Owen took a deep breath to calm his racing heart and returned to his vigil at the window. "Is it Percill?"

Jason shrugged and settled down next to him. "Could be, there was too much dust to get a clear look. I could make out three covered trucks, and that was it."

Owen could see the dust for himself if he craned his neck. There was a lot of it, a veritable storm. "That's a lot of sand," he whispered, squinting to see if he could make out any details. "Are they even driving on the road?"

Jason chuckled. "The road's half dirt at this point, and the area's too dry to have seen rain in months."

The trucks slowed to a stop outside the parking lot. Jason had been right. They were covered transport units straight out of a war movie. From this angle it was obvious that at least one of them was full of crates and that Percill was climbing out of the middle one.

"There he is." A growl Owen couldn't restrain laced the words. "Everyone get into position. Who's got Jason's clothes?" Not that he would wear them, but they didn't know if they'd be able to come back here once they got the captives. "Wait for my signal to go outside."

Tiffany arched an eyebrow, and her tail lashed in the dirt. "Oh? And what are you going to do?"

Readjusting his backpack, Owen straightened. "I'm going out to meet him."

***

Percill was a snake, even when he was helping them. Owen was reminded of this the second Percill smiled and blood-tipped fangs split his lip open again.

"Captain, you're early."

Owen grunted and resisted the urge to grab his pistol. "We made good time."

Percill nodded and looked behind Owen. "I assume the others are waiting inside?"

"Aye, we didn't want to risk anyone seeing them before you got here." He gestured toward the trucks and raised an eyebrow. "Are those yours?"

Owen thought Percill scowled, but if he had, the expression disappeared in the space of a blink.

"Yes," Percill said, turning away. "The drivers are mine, so I expect no trouble with them."

Owen didn't want to think about what Percill had done to make them his. "Better not waste any time, then," he said, and signaled the others behind his back. "Let's get into position."

Getting into the trucks was almost comical, like something out of Saturday morning cartoons. All three trucks were full of boxes, and Owen's team was to hide in, under, and behind them. One or two of the human-sized teammates could hide in narrow spaces in the back of each truck while Tiffany and Ashwind crammed into mostly empty crates. Jason, as suited his nature, hid in plain sight with one of the drivers.

Owen pretended he didn't see the knife Aaron slipped Jason or hear the whispered instructions to take care of the driver if things went wrong.

They weren't supposed to hurt humans if they could help it, but he didn't blame them for being cautious.

Tiffany was in the truck with Owen, and he couldn't help but be relieved. Beating down the thought that it might be better—from a tactical position—if they didn't travel together, he slumped down against her crate.

Still, as the truck roared to life and started down the highway, being this close to her was reassuring. From the second they'd climbed in here, they'd been on the clock. Everything else—the countless hours of training, the flight down, and the run to the meeting point—had all been preparation for this. From here on out, everything depended on the team and his ability to lead them.

***

The truck ground to a bumpy halt ten minutes later. Owen couldn't see anything from his vantage point, and he couldn't hear much more. He resisted the urge to shift to a position that didn't make him feel like he was sitting on his kidney and damn near stopped breathing to avoid nudging anything. They couldn't afford to make any noise. A creak, a sneeze, anything that couldn't be dismissed as normal truck noises was a risk they couldn't get away with. All that it would take to set the mission on its end was a security guard being a little more nosy than normal.

The truck rolled forward and stopped again, and Owen held his breath. Despite what it looked like, this was the most dangerous part of the mission. They were restrained in an unfamiliar area and completely at the mercy of their surroundings if they did manage to get away.

On the positive side, the facility was supposed to be nearly empty after nightfall. Guards would be at a minimum, and the researchers had all gone home for the weekend. If their luck held, the worst they could expect was an annoyingly high level of electronic security, the only kind that didn't need the weekend off.

Still, even though Tiffany and Jane should be able to override or temporarily disable the security, they wouldn't be able to do that if they couldn't get in at all. Much as he hated to admit it, they needed Percill.

The boxes shifted as the entire truck bounced—likely the victim of a speed bump or a vicious pothole—and Owen bit his tongue to hold back a curse when one landed on his head. They weren't moving very fast, but they must be inside now. At least, he thought as he rubbed the sore spot, he hoped they were. The roads in the facility didn't seem to be any better kept than the ones outside it.

They were good for something, though. The boxes had shifted enough to see a little of what was behind them. Owen breathed a sigh of relief when a glance confirmed all three trucks were past the wall, and he slumped against Tiffany's crate. They'd made it.

CHAPTER EIGHTEEN

In Which Proof Is Found

"As the saying *goes, anything that can go wrong will go wrong and at the worst possible moment. Murphy's Law might be simpler, but I find Finagle's is more true to life. It's why I have six backup plans for any given mission. After all, it's not paranoia if it saves your life often enough."*
—Excerpt from the lectures of General Janette Mulligan

They waited in the trucks until after dusk. The drivers and someone Owen couldn't see started to debate whether it was better to unload now or wait until morning, but Percill's greasy voice compelled the speakers away before they could finish.

It didn't make Owen relax much, but he was man enough to admit that some of the tension in his shoulders disappeared when they left. They were in now, and security in these places was usually focused on keeping people like them out, not in. Once the coast was clear, they would move.

Still, an hour passed by the time Percill finally gave the signal to get out. The loading dock was abandoned by now, as it should be, and far less ominous than Owen would've expected from a secret fae research facility. Smaller, too. Their trucks took up all but one of the loading ports.

But it was empty and safe—once Percill took out the cameras—and that was what mattered.

"Yeesh, it was tighter than a church on Easter in there," Jason said, stretching much too vigorously for someone not wearing anything.

Owen snorted as he helped Tiffany out of the truck. "Don't act like you had any room to complain," he said in a low voice, a note of warning on his tongue. Most of the workers were gone, but not everyone, or this would be easy. “You were up front the whole time.”

“Yeah, but I had to stay blended,” Jason whined, “and I couldn’t move or I might’ve flickered.”

“Oh, how you suffer,” Owen deadpanned, deliberately glancing at Tiffany, who looked one quip from strangling Jason. He stifled a laugh while readjusting his gear, then took a deep breath. “Everyone ready?”

The mood, already low, sank like Owen had tied an anchor to it. Hands and talons alike darted to check their bearer’s gear—and in Jason’s case, toward the person who had his gear—before the others nodded, and they left the safety of the garage proper.

To start, things went like clockwork. Owen barely had to do anything. The halls beyond were practically abandoned and lit by security lights every fifteen or so feet. The stucco walls blended into each other, long stretches of nondescript tan broken only by office doors and the occasional landscape painting.

They met Percill as he was coming out of one of the offices and wiping blood from his lips. As always, the sight of him was as reassuring as a knife to the throat.

Owen set a hand on his pistol. “Did you kill them?” he asked in a low voice, casting a wary eye into the darkened room. Percill had wanted blood for his work here, and he wasn’t the type of man to wait for a meal patiently.

“Of course,” Percill said, fetid and putrid breath washing over Owen like a foul perfume. “We wouldn’t want to risk them escaping. They’d warn the others.”

Of course.

“You should’ve left that up to me to decide,” Owen snapped. “It’s why you put me here, right?”

He left it there when Percill didn’t answer, despite how much he wanted to push it. The queen had given Percill permission to do that, he reminded himself. They didn’t have time to argue about it. Hopefully whosever blood that was actually deserved whatever Percill had done to them. Probably not, though. The important people’s offices were farther inside.

They knew where they were going thanks to Percill’s blueprints, the ones they’d studied for weeks. Left at the first crossing, straight through the next three, left again, then distract Percill while Jane and Tiffany got through the electric lock on the door to the secured part of the facility.

Once in, their precautions tripled. Past that door, the security features went from a standard bank to NASA, and it would only get worse the deeper they went.

Jason scouted each brightly lit hall before they moved forward, searching for anyone who'd decided to work late, and brought Eoire and Aaron in if he found any. The locks gradually changed from simple pass codes to ID verification and then to biometrics, and each time Jane had to call them to a halt while she fiddled with a bit of coding or shut down a new section of cameras, Owen's heart rate skyrocketed. Ashwind mostly stayed back, but the farther down they went, the more stone-faced he became. Even Percill helped more than Owen expected him to and with less general creepiness. Three times, he even took down a guard before the others noticed them coming.

He fed each time. That was probably the worst bit, even if the people here almost certainly deserved it.

It went . . . really smoothly.

Before Owen had time to worry they'd gone wrong somewhere, Jane was on her tiptoes in front of the last door, a steel-and-wire monstrosity with "SPECIMENS ROOM" written across it in large blocky letters. Tiffany whispered furiously under her breath while the others stood watch and Aaron distracted Percill.

Eoire had been able to sense the captives for nearly ten minutes now—their emotional agony so loud it was almost deafening, she said. Her forced calm bled into the air around her like a poison even as her jaw clenched so hard Owen was surprised her teeth didn't crack under the strain.

The quiet hiss of electronics whirling and gears grinding filled the air as the door rumbled open, and Owen's breath caught in his chest. Everything had gone so easy so far. If it was going to go wrong, now was the time. An alarm, a trap, something. There was no way it could be this easy.

The door clanged into the wall with enough force that it echoed down the hall, but otherwise it was silent. No alarm. No obvious trap. Light from the hall spilled into the otherwise dark and silent room. Carefully, Owen signaled Jason forward, and together they walked in, Ashwind at their heels.

Owen turned right after passing the threshold, his hand searching the wall for a switch. It was dark in there. Big, too, if the echoing footsteps were anything to go by. They needed more light.

The twin sounds of Jason and Ashwind cursing filled the room after he flipped the switch. When he looked up, Owen cursed too.

They'd found them.

Over a dozen cells, each barely four feet at their widest, and more than half of them occupied by fae with dead eyes. Fae covered in scars and needle marks. Fae wearing muzzles and blindfolds and bloody shackles, bound like rabid dogs behind doors of steel and glass.

He stumbled back, legs weak, and clapped a hand over his mouth. Cor, he could count their ribs from here.

Unbidden, he thought of Tiffany and he almost threw up. That had been her not so long ago. She'd been in a cell like that, and he'd seen her scars often enough to know that she'd faced the same treatment.

"Wait!" he called hoarsely to Jason, who was already two steps from the closest cell and reaching out. "Secure the room first."

He didn't want to leave them in there for a second longer than he absolutely had to, but they had to follow procedure. Procedures which only existed because, at some point, someone had gotten killed by not doing it. They couldn't blow this now, not when they were so close.

Jason yanked his arm back like he'd been burned. His body flickered, and whole sections faded away at a time, but when he called for the others, his voice was like thunder.

Jane, Tiffany, and Aaron swept past, and Owen reflexively pulled up his rifle. The others would sweep the room; he needed to keep watch.

But if his eyes flicked back to Tiffany, currently lifting Jane up to check on top of a shelf for bugs or trackers, no one would blame him. She was safe. She'd gotten out of this, and they would get the others out of here too.

And once they were out, he was going to beg her forgiveness for leaving her to recover from this on her own. On his knees if he had to.

When Ashwind and Jason finished clearing the room for explosives, Jane announced that she hadn't found anything, and considering what Owen knew of dwarvish subsonic hearing, he was inclined to believe her. They were clear.

The first cell lock was practically putty in Jane's hands. The screech of unoiled hinges sent the elderly first-gen werewolf inside cowering to the back corner of the cell, and Owen almost saw red. What had these monsters done to them?

"Go take care of the other doors," he ordered through gritted teeth. "We're running out of time."

Owen took a deep breath and released it. Calm, he reminded himself. These people had been through enough already, and his face wasn't necessarily the sort of face they wanted to see. Blast, maybe he should've let one of the others handle this.

"It's okay," he said in a low voice, scraping his boots against the ground as he slowly approached. "We're from Tearmann. We've come to get you out of here."

The werewolf flinched at Owen's touch, but Owen kept up a quiet litany of comforting words, half nonsense, half reassurances, as he slowly removed the blindfold and then the muzzle.

"There we go," he whispered as he sat back on his heels. "I don't have a key to the shackles, so we'll have to go outside. Can you stand?" Tiffany or Ashwind would be able to break them if they couldn't find a key.

The werewolf raised a quivering hand to his mouth and stared at Owen with a mix of awe and distrust. "I can stand enough," he said gruffly, the words rough from disuse and abuse. There were bloody holes where his teeth had been.

Owen swallowed thickly and had to look away.

The werewolf pulled his lips back in a garish smile as he stood, shoving off Owen's attempt to help even as he shook so bad it was a marvel he was able to stand at all. "They pulled 'em out 'cause I kept biting people. I didn't let that stop me."

Owen swallowed again and kept a hand out to catch the werewolf as they exited the cell. The others had already freed three more captives—a dazed harpy missing most of her feathers and two shades covered in bandages and ragged clothing so soiled it was practically glued to their skin—and Ashwind was ripping the other cells open.

Owen left the werewolf with Jane, who'd found a key ring and was determinedly trying each key in the shackles, and strode off to help more captive.

As he helped an elf man with glazed eyes out of a cell so small Owen could touch both sides without extending his arms, Owen glanced around the bedraggled group. Jane and Tiffany were passing out weapons to four of the captives—two trolls, a muzzled second-gen dragon, and the harpy. Jason was peeling the shades out of their ragged clothing and grimacing. Ashwind had given his coat to a shirtless elven woman with a baby so young it must have been born here. His face was a dark maze of shadows and wrath that made Owen fear for the next human they came across.

There were ten captives total. The toothless werewolf said there used to be fifteen, but they'd come too late for the rest. He'd frowned and pulled his lips back in a gummy snarl. Two had passed that morning. Vivisection. The scientists didn't seem worried about preserving their subjects anymore.

Owen swallowed and looked away to tamp down the fire raging in his chest. He should focus on the ones he could still help before he worried about the ones he'd failed.

Next to him, Aaron was singing an elf's wounds closed enough for him to walk out under his own power. Most of the captives weren't too badly injured, but that was the third person he'd healed, and at this point Owen was worried Aaron wouldn't be able to walk out by himself. The type of healing some of these people needed was complex, and Aaron was doing it on his own after three days of hard travel.

He tried not to think about how much having Arthur here would've helped.

Crouching down by Aaron, Owen set a hand on his shoulder. "Are you all right?" He didn't look it. His scales had long since turned an ashy gray.

Aaron coughed and pushed himself to his feet. "I've been better—" He coughed again, and the sound was like sandpaper rubbing against glass. "That was the last of them, right?"

"Enough of them." Owen nodded and cast an eye over the rest of the captives. The cuts and bruises left wouldn't immobilize anyone, and they could be healed when they got to safety. "Take a break before we head out again. You won't do anyone any good if you exhaust yourself now."

Huffing, Aaron wrapped his arms around his legs and rest his head on his knees. "I'll be okay," he muttered. "I just need a minute."

Owen shook his head. "I'm going to make the rounds. Wave or groan or something if you need me."

Aaron waved him off with a rude gesture, and Owen let out a huff of laughter.

Ashwind, who'd taken up watch at the door once the last of the captives were out, scowled. "Don't celebrate just yet," he snapped. "We're not out yet."

Owen's face fell, and he fought back some choice language. "What, are you finally taking this seriously?" he finally managed to say. Who was Ashwind to say something like that?

Ashwind shrugged as his hand curled around the hilt of his knife. "This is enough proof for me," he said darkly. "And the Regulars always keep their word."

Owen's breath caught in his chest. That's right. The only reason Ashwind had come was because he hadn't believed there were any captives. While a part of Owen nearly drowned with a flood of petty vindication, the larger part couldn't believe it had taken this long. If he thought he could've gotten away with it without losing his hands, Owen would've shaken Ashwind by his lapels and yelled at him until he was blue in the face.

The fae protected their own. Ashwind should've known that better than anyone.

Owen forced his hands flat against his sides. The weight of his rifle against his side felt like a millstone around his neck. "Good of you to finally catch up with the rest of us."

Ashwind's hands curled into fists at his side, and his jaw tightened.

Then Ashwind laughed, low and long, a sound like branches scraping against a window. "The fears of an old soldier, I'm afraid. You see enemies everywhere after a while." He paused, glancing at Owen out of the corner of his eye, and something softened there. "You'll understand one day." Regret painted those words a sad, dark color. "When you've got as many battles under your belt as I do."

"I won't," Owen snapped, more honest than he'd meant to be.

He'd made a promise and he'd meant it. As soon as they got back to Tearmann, he was hanging up his uniform.

Ashwind snorted. "I said that, too, and look where that landed me. Good soldiers don't step down, especially not with a war biting at their heels."

The silent implication made Owen's stomach turn, and he clenched his jaw. "Percill," he called, deliberately turning away. "Are your drivers ready?"

Percill, who'd been lurking in a shadowed corner near the door since they'd come in, arched an eyebrow and sneered. "I gave them an order, and they know better than to disobey me."

There was a rebuke there, but Owen didn't have time to puzzle it out. They'd been here too long already. "Take Jason and Eoire and make sure of that. I want to be out of here as soon as the others are ready."

Owen had been ready for a fight here, too, but Percill didn't argue. Without a word, he pulled Jason and Eoire free of the others and disappeared into the hallway. Owen shook off the momentary shock that Percill had listened, and turned to the captives.

In short and stilted words, Owen explained the plan. They would go in small groups, two or three captives to a Corps member, and make their way to the loading dock. By the time they got there, the trucks would be ready to leave, and they would load up. The gas station was only a few miles from the facility, and the journey to the meeting point should go smoothly. With luck, Gayle and Arthur would be finished with the netting, and they could take off before sunrise.

The actual escape was, perhaps unsurprisingly, almost easy. They'd taken down most of the guards on their way in—the shades got to the ones they had missed long before the others even noticed them—and Jane's camera hacks held beautifully. It was a breeze, so easy that Owen could've done it with his eyes closed.

As the gate and the facility disappeared behind them in a cloud of dust, Owen let loose a breath he'd been holding for almost a month now.

They'd done it.

The captives—former captives—in Owen's truck blinked like they were coming out of a dream, exchanging disbelieving looks and running shaking hands over the truck. A light slowly dawned in their eyes, one at a time. A single sob turned into a shout of jubilation, then a chorus that echoed in the other trucks.

They'd done it. They were going home.

***

The gas station was, as abandoned buildings tended to be, even creepier at night. A half-full moon lit up the stretching dead branches of the juniper trees and the vulgar graffiti that was somehow more garish at night. In the distance, a crow cawed and took off in a flurry of movement, only to land again on the roof of the gas station and start preening its feathers.

The trucks skidded into the parking lot, and Owen was outside before they came to a stop with the others not far behind. "One, two, three . . ." he counted under his breath, scarcely daring to believe it. Ten, they were all here. And they'd done it without losing anyone on their end.

"We did it!" Tiffany's shout was almost deafening as she scooped Owen up and spun them both around. Her wings enveloped him in a feathery cocoon, and Owen wanted to kiss her so much it took his breath away.

And why shouldn't he? They'd done it. His heart sang as he wrapped his arms around her with just as much force and pressed his lips to hers. The hard part was behind them. In a few short days, Percill wouldn't have any hold on them. His head spun with a wave of relief.

All around them the same situation was playing out. The former captives were caught in a strange mix of tears and laughter as they danced, stretched, and sang for the joy of being free. He should stop them, he knew. They were still too close to the facility to throw out all precautions, but . . . they needed this. He needed this.

This mission had been sitting on his back like a ten-ton bowling ball. He hadn't been able to escape it, not at home, not at work, not even at David's tomb. For the past month he'd lived and breathed the very real risk he or someone on his team would die here, and he still had it easier than the poor bastards they'd pulled out of that hellhole.

They should get moving. Dammit, they had a reprieve, but it wouldn't last forever, and they were pushing their luck already. The former captives—led by the toothless werewolf who introduced himself as Eli—weren't in any shape to run. At a walk, the pickup point was more than two hours away, and that trip wouldn't get any shorter the longer they waited.

Still, it was hard to make himself push Tiffany away and get the others moving. Her wings left him with the reluctance of one who having finally collapsed into bed after a long day, didn't want to leave it.

There was only one more thing to do.

The drivers . . . well, Percill was supposed to handle them. They weren't fae allies, but they were involved nonetheless. Hopefully, they would wake up somewhere tomorrow with no recollection of today's events, but Owen wouldn't put it past Percill to order them to drive off a cliff or worse.

"Where are you sending them?" Owen asked.

Percill answered without turning around, his hands extended in front of him like he was directing an orchestra. "There's a small town roughly twenty miles from here. They'll be found in the morning, alive, thank you very much."

Owen couldn't resist snorting. He held his own hands up in a placating gesture. "Given your track record, you can't blame me for worrying." He turned to watch the trucks, their rear lights now tiny pinpricks of light, before chancing a glance at Percill out of the corner of his eye. "You didn't take as much blood as I thought you would when the queen gave you permission to feed."

A sad smile, the first Owen had seen on Percill that wasn't mocking, curved his lips the barest fraction. "I will not be denied for long," he whispered in a gravelly tone. His hands dropped, and he shook his sleeves down over them. "My price is yet to be paid."

Jason appeared at Owen's shoulder before either of them could say anything else, thankfully wearing shorts now. "We're ready to leave. These folks are in pretty rough shape, but we'll get there."

Owen nodded and, more than a little grateful for an excuse to look elsewhere, turned to Jason. "Any chance you could run ahead and clear the site?"

Jason snorted and rolled his neck. "Do you even need to ask?" And with that, he was gone, off like a shot into the darkness.

Owen watched him go until he couldn't see him anymore, then turned back to Percill, who still stood motionless beside him. "We'll meet you back at Tearmann."

"Perhaps." Shrugging, Percill turned away.

Owen almost asked what he meant, but didn't. That was a rabbit hole he didn't want to venture down. Besides, they still had work to do.

"All right, everyone," he called as loudly as he dared. "We're heading out. Don't wander off, the pickup point is a few miles away from here, and we don't have much time to waste."

Eli called his group to order, and they set out. Their pace was almost glacial compared to how fast they'd managed to make it here, but they were moving. The distance wore away under their feet, tracked only by the moon's slow and almost hypnotic journey across the sky.

That was their undoing. Owen had gotten so caught up in the minute, in the placement of one foot in front of the other and whether Eli's group would need a break soon, that he didn't hear anything until it was too late.

"—ap, it's a trap—"

Owen stopped, the blood draining from his face. "That was Jason," he whispered, precious seconds ticking by before his tired brain was able to process what he was saying. "Bloody hell, everyone, run, scatter!"

The former captives, desperate to stay that way, needed no urging.

Running was a lot harder when sprinting pell-mell through the desert at night. Blast, he should've expected something like this, should've known better. Everything had gone too smoothly, and he'd let his guard down.

His heart pounded in his chest, roaring through his ears with a deafening wail as he pushed his legs even harder. They already had Jason, and Owen wouldn't be able to help him if he got captured or killed. He swore violently between harsh breaths and prayed, despite himself, that some of their attackers would come after him instead of one of the others. He was human. They couldn't do much to him.

The trap found him before he could evade it, an answer to the prayers he hadn't wanted to make. Three figures dressed in black jumped out of the shrubs in front of him. One shot something at him, a net or a rope of some sort, and he threw himself to the side.

He rolled, shoved himself to his feet, then dove at the figure holding the net launcher. Sand filled his mouth as they hit the dirt, and the net launcher skidded into the darkness.

Owen spit and sprang up, already moving to the next one. He couldn't keep this up for long. Exhaustion was already starting to weigh down his limbs, but every second counted. His only shot at escaping this was keeping them disorientated long enough for the others to get away and—

Tiffany screamed.

Owen turned, all thought of the men he'd been fighting abandoned, and sprinted toward that sound. His legs ached and shook with each pounding step, but he couldn't stop, and he couldn't shoot—he might hit Tiffany.

A group of four men had Tiffany surrounded, and two more had trapped her wings in a net. Owen hit them with everything he had.

At this point, he didn't care if he escaped or not. He launched himself into the two holding the net, and his swings were wild and unfocused, fatigue taking his control from him while his lungs screamed for oxygen he couldn't give them. He couldn't regret it, though, because watching Tiffany throw off the ropes and take to the skies was worth anything that would happen to him.

That split second of distraction was enough for one of the men he was fighting to slam something into the back of his head.

His vision went black and his knees gave out. Blood pounded through his ears as he spit out sand and struggled to stand. A dark and screaming shape fell from the sky, a rope wrapped around her wings like a spider's web. He stumbled forward and was hit from behind again. A boot dug into his spine as he howled and screamed, ripping his hands away before they could be bound.

"Tiffany," he screamed, tearing his throat raw. "Tiffany! Tiffany! Tiffany—"

CHAPTER NINETEEN

In Which a Bad Apple Spoils the Batch

"I wish I could say that I knew why she did it. We weren't friends, but we'd known each other for years. She was . . . we were comrades, siblings-in-arms. We'd fought together countless times during the war. I trusted her to have my back, and she trusted me to have hers. When the army attacked, we had no idea how they'd found us, but the camp was in ruins and she was gone. We thought she'd been killed and kept thinking that up until Breckenridge, where I found her in a U.S. uniform. She'd just shot one of our friends."
—*Excerpt from* The Betrayal of Jess King *by Tamu Kamba*

Owen wanted to blink. To look away or turn his attention elsewhere but couldn't muster up the energy.

The far side of his cell was covered in silent monitors, each showing a different cell holding someone he'd failed at a plethora of angles, and he couldn't stop watching.

As far as he could tell, almost everyone had gotten away. Of course, he couldn't be certain. For all he knew, everyone had been captured, and they wanted to dangle the possibility of rescue in front of him like a carrot on a stick. He hadn't actually seen anyone in person since he'd woken up in his cell on what could generously be called a cot and stripped to his underwear. Not anyone whom he wanted to see, at least.

Oh, he'd had plenty of human visitors. Mostly government agents and SAFE researchers.

"You know you're going to prison in the morning," said the besuited man sitting at a small table on the other side of the glass. Apparently, he was Owen's court-appointed lawyer. Owen hadn't requested him, but he'd shown up yesterday and hadn't left.

Owen shrugged but didn't look away from the monitors. Aaron and Jane would be back soon if the pattern held.

The lawyer wasn't a fan of the monitors. He'd tried to get them shut off yesterday—he didn't want them to unduly influence Owen's decision, apparently—but the researchers had refused. He'd fussed and whined and might have succeeded in getting rid of them if Owen weren't glued to them. Whatever he'd hoped to do by turning them off, the researchers' glee at recording Owen's reactions to their work had been more than enough to convince them to keep the monitors right where they were.

On the top left monitor, three expressionless goons in tan jumpsuits dragged Tiffany into her cell. Her glassy eyes narrowed at her captors as they fastened shackles around her arms and legs. Her lips pulled back behind her muzzle while she twisted in their grip, fighting a losing battle that ended exactly how he'd expect. They left her lying awkwardly over her wings, which were tied tightly together so she couldn't escape even if she did manage to get outside.

Owen was going to kill them for that.

Jane and Aaron were normally on the right feeds, but the goons had taken them away about an hour ago. He tried not to think about what was happening to them.

The glint of a lens peeking out between the top two monitors taunted him. A silent reminder that he was being watched just as closely. That they were prepared to capture any scrap of information he might drop like a rat chasing after crumbs.

The microphone crackled with static as the lawyer sighed. "I can't help you if you don't let me, Mr. Williams. You'll go to jail for a very long time unless we can give the judge something to convince him to go easy on you."

They wanted him to turn on the fae. First the FBI, then the researchers, and now this court-ordered bastard. Owen had been with the fae for almost a year and had been sighted on away missions a half dozen times. Clearly, he'd been in someone's confidence. He had to know a lot about the havens and the Corps. If he'd just turn all that information over, they might be able to work out a deal. He could clear his name, advance science, and help protect his former country at the same time.

A win-win as far as those on the other side were concerned.

If the researchers had offered to stop it or to let them go, maybe Owen would've given in. Passed on some nonsense about the generation system or the founders or harpy mating dances. Nothing serious, not details about the Change or anything, but just enough to tell them he might be persuaded to give them more if they sweetened the pot. After all, those were his friends, his teammates, and his *wife* on the other side of those monitors. The only thing he could do was watch while they were hurt over and over and over again, and if there were some way he could free them, he'd take it.

But from the way some of the researchers lingered over the results, they would never willingly give up their new toys. So, he sat and watched and wondered if Tiffany and the others could see him too.

The lawyer sighed, and his chair creaked as he leaned back. A dim reflection in the monitors showed him running his hands through his thin hair. "Look, I have some calls to make, but I'll be back soon. Why don't you think about what I said?" His voice would've been kindly if it hadn't been for the undertone of disgust. His chair scraped against the floor, and the microphone translated the sound into a scream that resonated through the room, almost covering the quiet click of the door shutting behind him a second later.

Only when he left did Owen allow his eyes to fall shut. He kept them closed for a minute, desperate to block out the images that had been permanently emblazoned on the back of his eyelids, before he opened them again.

He'd paced all of yesterday, full of energy that lacked an outlet. It hadn't accomplished anything more than making him intimately familiar with the dimensions of his cell. At three steps long and two wide, it was hardly large enough for his cot and the toilet that had been crammed into the corner.

Two walls were made of plain concrete, one from a glass that had to be bulletproof as it hadn't shattered no matter how often he'd thrown himself at it. As for the fourth one . . .

That was the one with the monitors. The ones Owen had been staring at for hours. Most of the time they showed direct feeds into the other cells, but sometimes they switched to ones from labs. He'd lost count of the experiments he'd had to watch, unable to rip his eyes away for even a moment. Stress tests, blood tests, and more had been administered on an endless cycle that started over every two hours.

Tiffany . . . they treated her like an animal. They'd taken everything from her and hadn't even given her the luxury of a bed. They'd stripped Aaron and dumped him in a glorified aquarium, pulling him out without giving him time to readjust to breathing air and dragging him away. Jane had slightly better conditions, but her indignities weren't any better. They'd shaved her, removing every inch of her hair and sticking her in a cell that was blindingly white even through the monitors. Her eyes, meant for the darkest caverns, must be in agony right now. And Jason . . . well, they shoved him into a flimsy jumpsuit and drugged him into a stupor. Most of the time he was more of a vague suggestion of a person under his jumpsuit than something with actual form.

The door creaked again, but Owen didn't turn to see who'd come in. Three goons were in Jane's cell, dragging her between them. Deep bruises littered her arms and legs. One guard, a tall brunette, leaned down to examine the scratchings Jane had left on the floor before pulling the others out of the cell.

"You could put an end to their suffering," a chillingly familiar voice said from the other side of the glass.

And that was the reason they were here. Percill. He'd been the first one Owen had seen after he'd woken up. He also hadn't been in chains. Owen had said a lot of things in that first ten-minute interview, and none of them had been flattering.

It had all made a horrifying sort of sense. Why getting in and out had been so easy. Why Percill conveniently had all the information they'd need to break in. Without Percill's help, Owen and his team never would've gotten as far as they had. And it was all because they weren't actually rescuing anyone so much as providing fresh subjects for an insatiable pit.

Cor, the only reason SAFE hadn't grabbed Gayle or Arthur was because Beira, in all her wisdom and paranoia, hadn't told Percill where she'd be waiting. Even then, if Jason hadn't spotted their troops, Owen would've blindly led them right to camp.

Closing his eyes again, Owen took a deep breath. His hands twisted in his blanket, and he desperately wished they were wrapped around that man's throat instead.

"Percill," Owen said when he trusted himself enough to speak without trying to break the glass again. "Congratulations again on proving every negative stereotype about your species true." He opened his eyes and turned to look at the man who'd put him and his team here. He didn't bother fighting back his sneer. "Proud of yourself, are you?"

Percill didn't react to Owen's barbs. Pity, he'd been working on them all morning.

"Are you finally going to tell me what they offered you to turn on us?" Owen asked. He couldn't stop thinking back on all the clues Percill had left behind, the hints that he'd waved in front of Owen's face like a red cape in front of a bull. He'd known everything, had blueprints, and the police had conveniently found them right after he'd been at their safehouse. Cor, they should've seen this coming. "Money? Power? Or just the satisfaction of being a traitorous bastard?"

This time, Percill shrugged. "It was necessary." His bloodless lips turned down in a brief frown before straightening again. He stood in the middle of the room like he wished there were more shadows to lurk in. "You understand now. You didn't before."

Owen snorted and rubbed his eyes. "Understand? What exactly am I supposed to understand?"

"Where our people stand in the world." The way he said it was so easy, as if Owen should've known this by now. "As long as the humans outnumber us, places like this will flourish." He took a step forward, now so close to the glass that puffs of condensation formed with each breath. "Our people are crumbling. Infighting divides us, and the queen is too weak to protect us. We can't survive if you refuse to take your place at her side, Owen Williams."

For a moment, Owen struggled to find words. How could Percill just say that so plainly? There were cameras everywhere. He counted three beyond the one directly in his cell, and the researchers had made it clear they caught everything at every angle.

"That's what all this was about?" he asked in a choked voice, hands tightening into fists at his side. "You want my blood?"

Percill sighed in a very put-upon manner and stepped back. "I want peace." He tilted his head and spoke as if Owen were a very small child who didn't understand why he wasn't allowed to eat chocolate for dinner.

"The time where it could be achieved by taking your blood has long since passed. We must have more if we want to prevent the coming bloodshed."

"You—" A disbelieving noise bubbled out of Owen's throat. It started as a chuckle, then developed into a full belly laugh that made it hard to breathe. Tears ran down his cheeks as great howls ripped through him like a tidal wave. "You—you actually believe that, don't you? That's why you did all this?"

Owen couldn't believe it. Everything that had gone wrong—the last month, all the stress and worry and fear, all the times he'd nearly died and the people who did die. Isaac and Evans and Thaddeus. The captives who'd been pawns in a mad scheme. The wasted lives and pain and destruction. And now this: him, a prisoner, and his wife and friends being tortured in the name of science. All because Percill thought—and he laughed, throwing his head back, heedless of the sharp crack it made as it hit the cement.

"It was you, wasn't it?" he asked through relentless giggles. "You were the one killing the Glenhold messengers. You wanted to force Beira's hand." She'd known for years that she was weakening; she'd said as much to him when she'd asked him to let her turn him. Fighting a war was hard enough when your forces were united.

Percill shook his head. "I had no part in that. Although, I will admit to warning the Canadians that you would be approaching the border." His lips turned up in a true smile, one that chilled Owen to his very bones. "I'm not the only one concerned with the future of our people, and some of my kin are . . . more aggressive than I."

Owen almost choked on his laughter. "The only—?" Of course. He smacked his forehead. "You want war," he whispered, blood draining from his face. "You and the other battleborn vampires."

"We want the same thing, Williams," Percill said with a snarl. His teeth ground together, and something black and brackish dripped out of his mouth. "My people might not be true fae, but we are cut from the same cloth as the queen. The difference between us is that we didn't wait for the storm to break to make our moves."

His eyes glowed with an unearthly light, and he bared his teeth in an unholy grimace as black muck slid down his chin like rotten blood. "Look around you, do you think these people will stop if things stay as they are?

Do you think the queen has even the slightest chance of reversing the tide of hatred that's coming for us?"

"No," Owen snapped. He shot to his feet and stalked to the glass like a storm about to break. "I want to go home and not have to worry about me or my family dying." Blood roared in his ears, and the effort it took to refrain from slamming his fists into Percill's face was Herculean. "You and your kind don't want peace. You want something to excuse your warmongering, and the queen's the only thing standing in your way."

Percill raised an eyebrow, regarding him with something that could've been respectful had it not smacked of disgust. "Peace is a distant dream," he said as cold and impersonal as winter's chill. "And it will stay that way unless something changes."

And the only way Percill saw to change it was to destroy everything that had come before it. Even if it killed most of the people he was allegedly trying to protect.

Percill let out a breath that was almost a purr and chuckled. "I have tasted the blood of enough men to tell if they might one day be our brothers." He stepped closer still, almost melding with the glass. "I haven't tasted yours, but I know you will be one of us one day, and my kind and I will be at your side when that day comes."

"No." Owen slammed his fists into the glass on either side of Percill's face. His heartbeat thundered louder than a rocket as images of the world Percill wanted and the role he wanted Owen to play in it repeated in the back of his mind. "I'll die first."

"As I understand it," Percill said, stepping back, "you will." Most of his collar had, by now, been stained black, and the smell was foul even through the glass. He turned, waved, and sauntered to the door. "Do tell the warden I said hello. You'll be his guest for quite some time."

CHAPTER TWENTY

In Which a Part Returns to the Whole

"Most research facilities (and I use the term lightly) were little more than fae-holding centers. Some, undoubtedly, were founded for noble reasons, and the people running them truly wanted to help the fae, but most were not. By the war's end, even the most ardent war supporter admitted most went far beyond the boundaries of ethics and human decency. The damage had been done by then, though, and the fae weren't keen to forgive."
—Excerpt from Facts and Fables: A Study of Fae Internment Facilities *by Anonymous*

To his great surprise, the guards left Owen to ruminate in his cell for the rest of the day and on into the night. No one, not the guards or his hokey lawyer or even the fake journalist, came through those doors to spare him from the endless cycle of abuse on the monitors once Percill had slammed them shut.

Owen slept in fits and bursts that he didn't think lasted for longer than a half hour at a time. It was hard to judge, seeing as nothing changed between him falling asleep and waking except for who was in their cells. They didn't feed him, and the lights never even flickered.

With little else to do, Owen resigned himself to watching the monitors. For recon purposes, he told himself. He needed to know all he could about their captors if he wanted to escape.

However, even the monitors got repetitive after a while. Approximately every fifteen minutes—and he counted every laboriously slow second—someone was taken from their cells and someone was put back. Of course, who was taken and who returned didn't seem to follow any set pattern. Even the fifteen minutes wasn't set in stone. Jason didn't seem to be taken out for more than ten minutes at a time, and Aaron rarely came back in under twenty. The endless observation did have a few benefits. By the third hour, Owen could identify each of the goons assigned to his team's cells.

First, there was Mole, an overweight woman with stringy black hair and a large mole over her right eye. She had a cruel streak and delighted in using excessive force. Tiffany's shackles always seemed to need tightening when Mole was assigned to her.

Then there was Freckles. He was as skinny as a rail and about half as sturdy. He'd carefully swept his flaming red hair into a low ponytail and kept his clothing meticulously neat. He practically dove for the hand sanitizer whenever he had to touch one of the fae.

Jacques was next. That probably wasn't her name, but she looked like a Jacques. A remarkably average woman, Owen wouldn't have noticed her at all if he hadn't spent the last three hours watching her appear on the screen every fifteen minutes. She wasn't fat and she wasn't thin. She wasn't tall and she wasn't short. Her skin was dark, but only in the sense that it might be tan, but it might also be a natural skin tone for half a dozen ethnicities.

The last was Braid, so named for the long brunette braid she threw over her shoulder right before she dragged her colleagues out. A veritable giant, she towered over the others and didn't seem to mind using her bulk to get her way. Owen only saw her occasionally, but he couldn't help wishing she was more involved with his team. She wasn't cruel.

Braid was the one who brought Jason back for the last time that night. Without a clock, Owen couldn't tell the time, but the other three had vanished three or four rotations ago, so he supposed it must be late. One by one, his monitors flickered out, or perhaps the lights in the other cells did. Finally, the lights in his cell switched off, and Owen was plunged into total darkness.

He tried to sleep. Hopefully, morning would come quickly. As depressing as watching the monitors was, it was better than pacing his cell.

Just as his eyes started to drift shut, the door to Owen's cell flew open with a tremendous bang. The lights blinked on as he shot up and squinted toward the door through what felt like the light of an entire sun.

"Food. Put your hands on the far wall." The speaker was a squat, homely sort of man who didn't seem that interested in his surroundings. His beige overalls were stained and ill fitting, just like the ones every other guard wore. Owen couldn't help wondering if they just picked their uniforms out of a big pile on a locker room floor somewhere.

Gesturing with the tray in his hands, the guard spoke again. "I said, get to the wall. I don't have all night."

Owen couldn't quite make out the contents of the tray, but he was willing to wager that it held the same bland and tasteless mush they'd given him yesterday. Still, it was something, and he needed to keep up his strength if he wanted to get out of here.

Behind him, the tray scraped along the floor as the guard shoved it through a tiny slot at the bottom of the glass wall. The slot sliding shut was his cue to turn around, and he was treated to a clear view of the guard's off-center bald spot before the door shut and the lights were turned off again.

A minute's groping in the dark led him to his dinner. It was as bad as he'd expected. A mix of corn mush and oatmeal run through a blender until it was indistinguishable from baby food. It tasted like it, too, but he scraped the last of it up with the rubber spatula they'd given him yesterday. Pity there wasn't more, even if it was disgusting. His stomach felt like it was about to collapse in on itself.

Finished with his meager meal, Owen lay down again. Sleep came slower this time. His stomach had awoken and begged for something more substantial than he'd been able to give it. His mind, too, fought its own battle to keep him from rest.

He couldn't stop thinking about last Christmas. Tiffany's cousins were supposed to come down from Seattle to visit. Owen had spent three days cooking a feast fit for the gods while Tiffany wrangled the kids into cleaning the house like their lives would be over if they left a single speck of dirt behind.

It had all been for naught, though. A blizzard had blown through on Christmas Eve, trapping Tiffany's cousins at the airport and them in their house. To make things worse, the power went out. Most of Owen's wonderful dinner, from the still-cooking turkey to the pies Toto had gorged himself on while they transferred what refrigerated goods they could to the porch, had been ruined. They'd ended up eating chicken noodle soup and what Owen could salvage of the sides.

They'd spent hours huddled in front of the fire, waiting for the power to come back on. Tiffany and Owen took turns telling stories about how they'd met and how Owen followed Tiffany back to America to marry her. The power hadn't come back on by the time the fire died, so they'd all spread out on the king-sized mattress in Owen and Tiffany's room.

It was the happiest Christmas Owen could remember. And the last one they'd been able to celebrate as a family.

A few weeks later, Owen wrecked the car while driving Tiffany to the hospital, and he'd lost her. He'd blamed himself for her death, mourned her, and tried to build a life among the fae. Then he'd lost David, too, and even getting Tiffany back couldn't fix that.

He shivered and turned on his side. Queen's throne, it was cold without the heat from the monitors, and the powers that be hadn't seen fit to give him a blanket.

This was all his fault. He should've been more alert, taken a different path or left Tiffany back at the camp—s*omething,* because he didn't see a way out of this, and now both of them were trapped here.

And the *kids.* Arthur had been right all along. Bad enough Owen had to go, but he'd barely argued when Percill and Beira forced him to bring Tiffany and now . . .

Queen's blood, he'd messed up. Not just now, but ever since David died. He'd left his family to stitch themselves back together by themselves. Left them because he couldn't face them without seeing the gaping hole where David had been.

If he got out of this, he'd do better. Even if Percill got what he wanted, Owen was done. Let the proper fae fight the war; he'd take care of things on the home front. He'd go to therapy, get his old job back, and make up for everything he'd missed while he'd had his head firmly up his ass.

***

Morning could not come soon enough, hang whatever waited for him. Warm memories or not, his cell was cold, his cot was hard, and Owen had tossed and turned for most of the night.

The monitors did, eventually, turn on again. Painful as it might be to watch them, it was still better than staring into the void, waiting for madness to settle in.

Little changed except for a growing collection of cuts, bruises, and other minor injuries on Jane, Tiffany, and Aaron. The same four guards collected and returned them in semi-regular fifteen-minute intervals. Braid stopped to examine the scratches on the cell walls three times and twice to buff some out before anything happened in Owen's cell.

About two hours after the monitors had turned on, the door leading to Owen's cell swung open, and his lawyer, followed by Mole, Freckles, and Jacques, sauntered inside. Freckles carried an orange jumpsuit and handcuffs in front of him like a shield. The other two stayed by the door, souped-up stun guns in one hand and the other on the pistols on their belts.

"Mr. Williams," the lawyer began, already sweating through his cheap suit. "I'm sorry it has to come to this, but the state is ready to take custody of you." His knuckles tightened on his briefcase like he was prepared to use it as a weapon if needed. "If you have anything to say in your defense, now would be the time. I might still be able to work out a deal for you."

Mole grunted and squeezed her stun gun tighter. She looked one wrong move from electrocuting him into next year. "Turn around. Hands against the wall. Now."

Owen didn't answer. Slowly, like he had all the time in the world, he stood and placed his hands on the wall, clearly visible.

The slot slid open, then shut again. "Put the jumpsuit on, then reassume position." Freckles said, his voice shaking like he thought Owen would do something to him through glass he couldn't break.

Slowly, keeping his hands in the air, Owen turned around. As non-threatening as he could manage, he grabbed the jumpsuit and slid it on. "Come on, gents," he said as he put his hands back up and faced the wall again. "I think we can all agree that orange isn't my color."

No one laughed. In fact, Owen could swear he heard one of the stun guns rev up in the silence that followed. He was about to turn around to check if they wanted him to do something else when someone twisted his arms behind his back and slammed his head into the wall.

Owen turned so his face wasn't smooshed into the cement while cold metal snapped around his wrists. "Bit tight," he managed to say as Jacques pulled him away from the wall.

Jacques didn't answer, but Owen didn't mind. She wasn't much of a conversationalist anyway, and that wasn't the point.

The glass had vanished into a newly appeared slit in the floor, which explained why there hadn't been a door before.

The lawyer and Mole left first, him glancing at Owen nervously and her stomping out like she was imagining Owen's face under her boots. Jacques and an increasingly shaky Freckles stuck their stun guns to Owen's spine and marched him after them.

Owen took some comfort in the fact that he recognized this hallway. He'd been down it twice the night of the raid. They were still in the research facility. If he could get to the others . . .

A beige figure turned the corner at the end of the hall and stopped, fifty feet from them.

Mole came to an abrupt halt. "You there," she snapped, "this section of the facility is supposed to be on lockdown. Return to your post."

The figure didn't say anything. One hand reached up, removed the lumpy regulation hat, shook her braid out, and—

"It's one of them," Mole screamed. She dropped her stun gun, and her hands flew to her pistol, but she was too slow.

Eoire charged down the hall, her long legs eating up the distance like an Olympian, and hit Mole with a punch Owen knew from experience was strong enough to knock out an ox. Owen didn't wait to see the result before making his move.

He threw his head back into Freckles's face and felt a twinge of vindication when blood splattered into his hair as Freckles stumbled back with a freshly broken nose. Before he could recover, Owen's foot slammed into Freckles's stomach, and he doubled over.

Owen spun to face Jacques, but Eoire dashed past him like the hounds of hell were at her heels. Three quick hits later and Jacques was on the ground, cradling her broken ribs and crying softly.

"Eoire," Owen said, unable and unwilling to hold back a smile. "Cutting it a bit close there, aren't we?"

Eoire shrugged and threw her braid over her shoulder. "Couldn't be helped, Owen. I needed to be sure the others were ready before I could move, and it's not easy to read runes on the move."

Owen rattled his shackles. "Get these cuffs off me, and I'll forgive you."

Rubbing his wrists after Eoire freed him, Owen nodded toward the lawyer, who was now sobbing on the ground, a small puddle spreading beneath him.

"Bit excessive, don't you think?"

Eoire shrugged. "It keeps them down."

Owen raised an eyebrow. "Are you using fear or anxiety? They seemed pretty worked up even before they got to me." This wasn't his first experience with elven tactics, and he liked it only marginally more as time passed. Eoire's strength and control had improved enough to spare him from the general emotional cloud, but he was still at risk from it, which he hated.

"Anxiety," Eoire said. Leaning down, she picked Mole up and swung her over her shoulder. "It's more effective."

Owen nodded. He'd seen more people paralyzed by slow-growing anxiety than rapid fear. Besides, he thought as he grabbed Jacques under her arms and dragged her into what used to be his cell, it was also something even the weakest elf could project from a distance to devastating effect. Eoire was far from the weakest elf.

The lawyer was easy to wrangle. One glare from Eoire was enough to send him scrambling into the cell, stammering about how they could raise the glass wall. He noticeably relaxed once the wall was up.

"Where are the others?" Owen asked as they went to grab the guards' weapons.

"Down here," Eoire answered, veering left down a small side hall. "They moved them to a different cell block. There are still a few guards besides those three, so be on the lookout." She slowed to a halt in front of a door Owen didn't recognize, and glanced back at him as she punched in the door code. "It's not pretty past here, just so you know."

Owen grunted and gripped his stolen pistol tighter. He could guess what was waiting for them past that door. He'd spent the past two days watching it after all.

She was right. It wasn't pretty.

Bloodstains dotted the floors, a red testament to what happened here. Some of them were old, barely suggestions staining the laminate, but most were still red and fresh.

Owen's legs ached, protesting after days of confinement, but he pushed them faster. They ran into three guards. One, Owen shot between the eyes. Eoire got the second, breaking his neck before he even thought to draw his weapon, and the third dropped his weapon and begged for mercy the second he saw them. They bound his hands behind his back and shoved him into a broom closet.

Sliding through a puddle of blood, Owen followed Eoire around a corner, and his heart almost stopped. There, slumped over in the back of the cell, was a familiar blond lump.

"Tiffany," he breathed, willing her to move—to give him some sign of life. "Tiffany!" His body moved without a conscious command, racing forward and yanking the cell door open. His knees hit the floor with a thud that he barely registered as he desperately reached out to search for a pulse.

A clawed hand emerged from the mass of feathers and closed around Owen's wrist before he made contact. A tired, bruised, and battered Tiffany emerged, folding her wings behind her. "Geez," she whispered. She coughed, and her voice was louder when she spoke again. "You didn't even give me a chance to answer."

Relief flooded Owen's bones, consuming and drowning him with a wave that turned his limbs to jelly. "You're . . . you're . . ." The words jumbled around in his head, tossing and turning and mixing with each until he couldn't think straight.

His world turned into a cascade of golden feathers streaked with dirt as Tiffany wrapped herself, arms and wings, around him. "I'm all right," she whispered into his neck. "We're getting out and we're going home."

Owen had no doubt that the growing salty patch he was making on Tiffany's shoulder had a twin on his own, and still, he couldn't speak. They were going home.

"As touching as this is," Eoire said, her voice enough to remind Owen where they were, "we have to get going before the lockdown ends, and we're going to need some help with Jason."

CHAPTER TWENTY-ONE

In Which Someone Blows Holes in Their Escape

"If an escape is managed, there is a simple three-step path to follow. One, do not stop moving until you confirm that you're not being followed. Two, keep an eye out for anything you can use as a weapon or tool. Three, don't be afraid to throw someone through a wall. You're stronger than them, and they won't hesitate to kill you. Let go of that bit of your conscience that doesn't want to hurt anyone, and do whatever it takes to get out. You can moralize later."
—Excerpt from Keep Calm and Tunnel Out *by Jackson Smyde*

Even with Jane and Owen's help, Jason could barely walk. "What'd they give him?" Owen muttered, readjusting his grip. He hadn't found a way to keep Jason up and moving that didn't feel like he was hauling a sack of potatoes.

"I'm not sure," Eoire whispered, so quiet her words only just reached them. She was pushing out a wave of confusion and apathy so strong Owen struggled to focus even on the outskirts of her attack. With luck, it'd take down anyone in front of them. "A blending suppressant of sorts, but I couldn't get close enough to see."

Jason chose that moment to yell something unintelligible before half his body flickered and vanished. The sight of everything that didn't disappear almost made Owen drop him.

Swallowing back bile, Owen turned his head away. Stripping Jason had been a mistake. He saw that now. He didn't need to know what Jason's lungs looked like, thank you.

"The lockdown can't last much longer," Tiffany said, shoving Owen and Aaron aside so she could take Jason herself. As easy as if she were lifting Dorothy, she swung him over her shoulders and marched forward. "How far to the exit?"

Eoire shrugged and, peeking around the next corner, said, "Maybe fifteen minutes to the garage." Her braid almost clocked Jane in the face as she turned back to them, her mouth set in a grim line. "There's a van that should—"

A distant roar, like a humming at the back of the mind, stopped her in her tracks. It grew louder, buzzing through the air, and she paled. As it drowned out everything else, she yelled and—*boom*—the ground trembled.

Owen stumbled into a wall. The lights flickered, and pieces of ceiling tile rained down like ash upon them. As quick as it had begun, it stopped.

"What was that?" Owen asked under his breath, and scanned the hallway like it'd give some clue. The shattered remnants of the ceiling panels coated the ground with a thick layer of dust. "An earthquake?"

"Dragons," Eoire whispered hoarsely from where she'd curled into a ball against the wall. Her hands clutched at her skull, clasped over her ears. "It's so loud. I can hear them screaming. We have to get—"

Even as she spoke, the roar returned and drowned out everything in its path, echoed by a half dozen just like it. It grew louder, a deafening scream that made Owen clap his hands over his ears, too, before it could deafen him and—

Boom. One explosion. *Boom,* two. *BOOM,* louder than any Owen had heard before, one after the other, and the roar started again. The ground shook, the ceiling caved in, and the hallway plunged into flickering darkness. Owen's foot caught in an unseen pile of rubble, and he fell to the ground. His head buzzed—although whether that was from the blow or the deafening roar, he couldn't tell. The others were splayed out on the ground around him, Tiffany shielding Jason with her wings, Eoire clutching Aaron like he was a lifeline in an unforgiving sea and *screaming,* and Cor, where was Jane, she'd been right beside him—

BOOM. Someone yanked on Owen's jumpsuit. He rolled without thinking, and a chunk of concrete as big as him crashed into where he'd just been and then . . .

The roars stopped. He waited, curled into a ball for ten long seconds. Slowly, he raised his head and let out a quiet curse.

All things considered, they'd been lucky. Half the lights were out, and piles of rubble were everywhere, but no one was hurt any worse than they'd been before.

Whatever caused it, the second explosion had been a lot closer than the first, and if it did this much damage as deep in the facility as they were, they might not be able to reach the garage.

"Careful," Jane said with a grunt, eyes glinting in the semidarkness. "Whatever that was, it's compromised the whole structure."

"Agreed," Owen said hoarsely. This called for a change of plans. "Jane, take the front with me. Everyone else, stay behind us and don't move until we say so. Keep an eye out for anything we can use."

They crept down the hall at a snail's pace. Every step was now a potential deathtrap of live wires, loose rubble, and collapsed rooms. Owen and Jane meticulously searched every inch before they called the others forward. In the distance, the roars continued but without the catastrophic consequences of their earlier peers.

The halls were empty apart from them and the occasional distant alarm, and it was starting to make Owen's hair stand on end.

Even if their escape hadn't set off alarms, the explosions had. The guards should be swarming the halls by now—to escape whatever caused the explosion, if nothing else. He'd already been caught with his guard down once.

"Where is everyone?" Aaron whispered.

Tiffany grunted. "Probably dead. The only reason we survived was because we were at the back of the facility. Anyone up front would've been caught in the blast."

"But we haven't seen anyone—living or dead," Aaron argued, his voice echoing off the shattered concrete in a hypnotically singsong manner.

Eoire's quiet, panicked muttering harmonized with Aaron's voice in a way that made Owen's stomach twist. "I know this place isn't exactly well staffed, but there's no way we were the only ones inside."

Humming in agreement, Owen considered a partially crumbled wall to his left. They couldn't leave the way they came unless they wanted to dig through what looked like half the building, and they didn't have time for that. Someone was going to come looking eventually, and he wanted to be outside when that happened.

"Tiff, Jane," he called over his shoulder, "can you two clear this?" If he was remembering right, the garage was on the other side. The sooner they got out of the complex proper, the better. Hopefully the van Eoire mentioned was still drivable.

Jane inspected the wall and hummed consideringly. "Should be able to. That's not a support wall. Eoire, Aaron, we'll need you too."

Owen gently took Jason from Tiffany and stepped back. Thankfully, Jason seemed more coherent—or at the very least, Owen wasn't treated to any more glimpses of his organs—so hopefully the drugs were wearing off.

It was Eoire he was worried about now. The others were mostly fine. They were walking and working, but she'd been a twitchy mess since the first explosion, and she hadn't been able to say why. She was barely coherent. If she couldn't get herself under control, they'd all suffer her fears with her.

The feeling didn't fade as Jane placed the last lever and got the others to pull. Jane may have been a hacker by trade, but she was raised by dwarves. Construction and destruction were two halves of the same coin in the mind of the average dwarf, and with the strength of four people on her side, Jane got the wall down in one go.

As the dust settled, any success Owen might have felt turned to horror, and his blood ran cold.

Half of the complex was gone, wiped from the earth like it had never been there. A mask of dust, flames, and smoke obscured what little remained. Faint screams tainted the air like the most horrible lullaby ever sung, and beyond that . . .

A white dragon soared over their heads, flames spewing from her jaws toward the soldiers below. The tips of her wings skimmed what was left of the building, each movement creating a miniature tornado.

"Cor almighty," Owen whispered. He fell to his knees, heedless of rubble digging into them. Whole dragon flights and angel choirs dodged around small aircraft, singing a terrible song of wanton destruction and chaos. Far above him, a lone angel, too bright to see clearly, dove into a band of soldiers side by side with a black dragon spewing death from his jaws.

The ground below them had been turned into a field of fire pocketed by great craters. The soldiers that had survived the bombardment of flame and energy fended off harpies and gryphons that ripped flesh, cloth, and metal alike to shreds. And beyond that, in the background, a chorus of howls and siren song that took the strength from Owen's limbs.

And still, far above them all, circled a great green dragon. The figure riding it was too far away to be seen—but Owen knew. Beira had gone to war, and she didn't stand idly by.

Using the dragon as a staging point, she leaped at planes that dared to come within her reach. What she did or damaged was impossible to say, but by the time she leaped off again, the planes had begun fatal descents, flames and smoke spewing off their back ends. Three jumps for three planes.

Dread sank Owen's gut. She couldn't be here. The humans weren't supposed to know she was alive; she'd shown her hand. Queen's throne, they'd nearly escaped themselves, why did she come? She should've trusted him.

"It's war," Jason muttered in a slurred voice. His eyes focused on the ongoing carnage in a way they hadn't inside the facility. "We're going to war again." Despite the shaking in his limbs and the rapid and uncontrolled flickering of his skin, he pushed Owen away and stumbled forward, eyes fixed on the sky. "We have to get out of here, get someone's attention. We can't—"

With a hollow cry, his legs gave out, and Aaron darted outside to catch him.

"Jason, don't move," Aaron sang while batting away Jason's protesting hands to search for damage.

Darting to Jason's other side, Owen took his free arm and scanned their surroundings. They couldn't stay here. The fighting was headed their way, a horrid death song creeping closer and closer the longer they waited. They needed to get out before it swept them up. As if to hammer the point home, the battered body of a woman in combat fatigues crashed to the ground in front of them.

Tiffany swore and pushed past them, shaking out her wings as she went. The explosions and everything she'd gone through didn't seem to have damaged them, which was a blessing. It wouldn't have been the first time someone came out of a research facility with their wings clipped. "We need to get out of here," she yelled. "I'm going to grab someone to help with Jason."

Owen's response, half command and half plea for her to come back, was lost in the wind and rushed takeoff. She disappeared into the smoke, toward the flashes of light, flame, and gunfire before he managed to get the words out.

Swallowing back curses, Owen readjusted his grip on Jason. "Come on," he yelled, jerking his head toward what was left of the loading dock. "We might be able to find a car." The odds were slim, and even slimmer that it would be running, but they needed to get out of the open. With Tiffany gone they were too human to be assured the fae wouldn't attack them and too fae to be sure the humans wouldn't either.

They didn't get far before a scream unlike any Owen had ever heard—rage and pain and fiery, bloody death rolled into one—rent the air and sent chills down his spine. The sound echoed in his eardrums, over and over like a drumline. A bronze dragon high above them writhed in pain, his wings flapping uselessly as he fell through the air like a puppet whose strings had been cut.

Swearing, Owen threw Jason over his shoulders and sprinted toward the slight protection of the shattered garage. He didn't need to look back to be sure the others had followed him. A dragon would only fall like that for one reason, and Owen didn't want to be in the open for the explosive aftermath.

They'd almost made it when the dragon hit the ground. Its impact sent a shock wave that shattered the remaining walls of their shelter. The tremors hadn't stopped before a spark found the leaks in his hydrogen pockets.

***

With a great shuddering gasp, Owen jerked up, and he looked around wildly—unable to remember where he was, how he'd gotten there, or even his own name. An impenetrable gray fog that reeked of ash and blood had enveloped the world.

"—ad, Dad!" said a voice, echoing like the speaker were down a long tunnel.

He should know that voice. Somehow, he knew it should be as familiar to him as his own.

"—ving, we've got to—" It faded in and out, blocked out by a distant roaring wind.

A pair of arms grabbed him under his own and yanked him to his feet. Even as the world spun, Owen searched his memory for the voice, and when he met the eyes of the voice's owner, *he knew.*

"Arthur," he whispered, and everything came rushing back with a sickening vividness. The dragon. His hands came up to grip Arthur's wrists, and he squeezed. The feeling of flesh and cloth under his bloody fingers made him weep. "What are you doing here?" he whispered in a broken staccato. "You were supposed to leave."

His heart ached. If he'd had the breath, Owen would've yelled that Arthur shouldn't be here. Arthur was supposed to stay out of it, to help get the others to Tearmann and stay safe. What would the girls do if all three of them died here? It was bad enough that Owen's mistakes had gotten Tiffany and him captured. He didn't want Arthur's blood on his hands as well.

"Dad, we've got to go," Arthur yelled, breaking through the buzzing that hovered just on the edge of Owen's hearing.

The fighting was almost on top of them, each yell and gunshot as loud in Owen's ears as his own breathing, but he couldn't leave yet. The others . . .

From the corner of his eye, he saw Jane digging Jason free of a pile of rubble, both of them coated in dust and ash. Beyond them, Aaron pulled Eoire to her feet. He couldn't see Tiffany, and his chest hurt.

She'd gotten out of range of the explosion, he told himself. They'd made it this far. She'd had to have gotten out. He'd see her again.

"Arthur, wait, where are—" His foot caught on a rock, and he barely avoided crashing to the ground. His whole body ached, and staying upright was hard enough when he wasn't being dragged. "Where're we going?"

"I'll explain later," Arthur snapped, twisting his head around so fast Owen was surprised his neck didn't snap. "Come on, Gayle's over here."

Over here turned out to be what was left of the western wall, a crumbling ruin barely thirty feet long and ten feet high. The sight of Gayle's black and white calico head over the rubble sent Owen's stomach twisting and turning. She shouldn't be here, either, but she was a way out. She could get Arthur out.

Arthur led them around the last corner while Owen was still processing, and Gayle's head snapped toward them, her lips pulled back in a terrifying smile.

"You found them! I was starting to get worried." Despite the fighting above them—they'd have to fly *through* that, since the only way out was up—she didn't seem worried. Her tail lashed behind her, upending a pile of cement and rebar.

"Course I did," Arthur shot back. His voice cracked and Owen's breath hitched. Arthur was too young for this. He should've sent him home as soon as they had found him.

A yell from Ashwind, who was chained to Gayle's back and armed with a machine gun, got them moving. Gayle, at least, didn't seem any worse for wear. She leaned down, screaming something that the buzzing in Owen's ears and the chaos around them drowned out. Arthur kicked the netting out of the way and ushered the others to the saddle compartments.

She was giving him a status update, he realized as Arthur shoved a still-stumbling Jason into his compartment, and he'd only caught half of it. He turned to face her, took a deep breath, and asked her to start again. As she spoke, Owen's stomach dropped lower and lower until he could've used it for boots.

Ashwind had been the one to lead the others to Gayle, and the one to explain what had happened to those that had stayed behind. He had wanted to launch a rescue and might have convinced Gayle and the others if Arthur hadn't pointed out that the primary mission was to get the captives to safety. They could worry about rescuing the others when they had the Corps' full support for a mission. Beira's war party found them when they were halfway back to the capital. Apparently, Percill hadn't waited to take credit for betraying them, and Beira wasn't going to let SAFE off without any consequences.

A stronger dragon had taken the captives home, and Gayle, Arthur, and Ashwind led the others right to the facility. From there, it had been a bloodbath of angelic bombs, dragon fire, and siren song. They'd destroyed most of the facility in the first wave before the survivors had managed to rally defenders from a nearby air base.

When Gayle paused for breath, another scream rang out. This one was different than the ones before it. Louder, stronger, more pervasive. For countless seconds, it hung in the air like an inescapable toxin. Clapping his hands over his ears, Owen fell to the ground and searched the sky, praying desperately that it wasn't another fallen dragon.

But no. Almost directly above them was a great beam surrounded by a miasma of smoke and flame. Even as he watched, it doubled, tripled in size until it nearly outshone the sun. Barely visible inside it was a woman with her head thrown back and her hair spread around her like a dark halo. Any fae that still had the strength to fly surrounded her in a protective sphere while the ones on the ground sang a deadly song of terror and despair.

Owen's hands fell away from his ears, heedless now of the screaming that hadn't stopped. He'd only heard of this happening once before, when Beira had created the battleborn during the Battle of Breckenridge. The stories said it'd almost killed her, and that it was nearly uncontrollable. She'd been at her strongest then.

"No," he whispered. His breath caught in his chest. "No," he shouted as he pushed himself to his feet. Ignoring his screaming muscles, he rushed forward, toward the light. This couldn't be what killed her. He wouldn't let her die, because he hadn't been able to protect his team. "You can't, you'll die!" Owen swore and turned back to Gayle. "Get me up there," he yelled, almost inaudible even to his own ears. "We need to hurry." They didn't have another choice. If one of the fae had been able to stop her, they would've—Owen wasn't the only one to have heard the stories—but she was too far gone.

Gayle was his only hope. She might be a halfling, but she wasn't full fae. Beira's commands didn't have the same sway with her.

Ignoring the ringing in his ears and the way the world turned on its edge when he turned too fast, Owen scrambled up Gayle's harness, screaming for her to take off.

The sirens joined Beira in an ungodly harmony, a symphony commanding him to *obey submit become* that set Owen's hair on end. It was intoxicating, poisoning his limbs even as he struggled to climb. Even Gayle would have a hard time resisting if it went on much longer. Blast, Owen couldn't get up there by himself, and there was no one else to help him if Gayle succumbed to the song.

As Owen churned and discarded plans in his mind, Gayle sluggishly shook herself and spread her wings. She was three feet off the ground by the time Owen realized she meant to take off, and he was only halfway up the ladder to the shotgun shell.

The rushing air almost tore him away. Gritting his teeth, Owen willed his fingers to unbend and his hand to grab the next rung. The ground only got farther away with each second, and Gayle wouldn't be able to hear him from this far away if he fell. He needed to get to the shell.

Glancing down almost made him lose his grip altogether. Owen was no stranger to heights and had ridden shotgun more times than he could count, but there was a difference between being chained to the shotgun saddle and hanging onto a ladder midflight.

But what he saw almost had him screaming for Gayle to turn back.

Arthur was still on the ground, caught in the same swell that trapped the others. The faint sound of his song melded with the one coming from Aaron's compartment and hung in the air, begging Owen to listen and submit.

Beyond that, past the desiccated ruin of a wall that Gayle had half knocked over when she had taken off, was a group of figures in dirty brown camouflage headed right toward him.

Blood on white sheets, blue eyes staring at nothing, I'm going to see Mom, I'mgoingtoseeMom—he wouldn't lose Arthur, too; he couldn't. Not when they'd come so close and he'd nearly lost Tiffany again.

His foot slipped and he fell. Five feet, ten. The rungs slid through his fingers like butter, and his heart leaped to his throat. Frantically, he scrambled, clawing at Gayle's side, at the saddle and the compartments, and the ladder but couldn't catch anything. His eyes squeezed shut as he dropped into the open air.

The air screamed past and he fell and he fell and he *stopped* for a fraction of a second before whatever caught him launched him up again, straight into Gayle's underbelly. His nose crunched, and warm blood gushed out, but he hardly had time to process before he was falling again, and he scrambled to grab onto whatever caught him.

Opening his eyes revealed a tangled mess of ropes and knots. *The net.* Queen's throne, the net. Gayle and Arthur had tied it around her legs and lower half of the gondola to hold the captives and must've forgotten to take it off. Without it he'd be a red smear on the ground. Taking in deep, gasping breaths, he made a mental note to thank whoever wrote the Corps manuals for their paranoia and started crawling toward the dangling lower rungs of the ladder.

They were too high to go back now. The battlefield stretched below him, and the fae gathered in a circle under Beira, still fighting even as they raised their voices to join hers. And Arthur still sang, oblivious to the figures getting closer every second, but they'd be on him long before Owen could get there.

Blood on white and blue eyes and I'm sorry, Dad, and—NO.

And even if he could stop them, how long would it last? Gayle had barely gotten up the first time. She wouldn't be able to take off again in time to reach Beira. Even now, the light was getting brighter and the singing louder. They didn't have much time. Breckenridge had only taken a few minutes, and going back would mean they wouldn't be able to stop her. He'd save Arthur only to lose him again when Beira died.

Owen swallowed, gripped the netting, and dragged himself up. His body ached with each move, and his blood-soaked hands slipped on the rungs, but every step was one closer. He needed to get to the shotgun saddle.

The scream and the song melded together in an agonizing wail of noise as Owen inched up the ladder. Beira was barely a quarter of a mile away, and Gayle was wobbling like a drunkard. The shelter of the shotgun shell and its promised restraints was tantalizingly close, but each sudden drop or sway to one side threatened Owen's precarious grip.

One more tentative step brought Owen within reach of the chains, and he strained toward them. After three tries and one almost fatal slip, his hand clenched around the lifesaving metal. Then everything changed.

The light pulled back, compacting into a ball around Beira, and crackled with energy. The world seemed to hold its breath as the singing stopped, and a wave of wind like a hurricane cleared the miasma in a single breath.

They were above Beira now, and Owen's breath caught in his chest. Somehow, they'd passed her. If they were going to make a move, they had to do it now, before the light came back. He looked at the chains in his hand, at their promised safety, and almost shouted for Gayle to dive at Beira. The only thing that stopped him was the overwhelming certainty that it wouldn't work. Whatever protection Gayle's battleborn blood gave her wouldn't be enough to withstand a full-frontal order from Beira.

She wouldn't be able to stop her.

It had to be him, Owen realized between one wingbeat and the next. His heart sank, disappearing from under his feet and plummeting to the earth below. He was the only one who wouldn't—couldn't—be deterred by Beira's commands.

Letting the chains slip from his hand, Owen took a deep breath and leaped.

CHAPTER TWENTY-TWO

In Which Death Doesn't Seem So Bad

"I'll never forget the Battle of Breckenridge as long as I live. Beira's scream did something to the rest of us, something I can't explain. It was all of the worst bits of siren song, the most violating parts of empathy, and the soul-shattering pain of the Change all mixed into one horrible sound. The soldiers started screaming once the light died out, and most didn't stop for hours. It was three days before we realized there weren't any humans left. Just us and the battleborn."
—Excerpt from the journals of Lorraine Jacobs, Lady Ailell

There should've been noise. Whether it be wind, screams, or howls, something should've filled the void. But it was just him and the light that was growing ever closer. And within that light, a dark figure with her head thrown back in agony.

He wasn't going to survive this. Whether it was the fall, the light, or even Beira herself, he wouldn't make it home. He wouldn't make up with Jen or hear one of Dorothy's rambling stories or go home to their apartment that always seemed too empty ever again. He'd never finish David's rose or kiss Tiffany or spar with Arthur.

It hurt, but he couldn't find it in himself to regret it. If he didn't do this, there wouldn't be a point in going home. There wouldn't be anyone there, and he'd have lost everything he fought for in the first place. The fae needed Beira—needed a vampire—like they needed air. Without her, they wouldn't survive.

Penetrating the ball of light took his breath away. The wind that pushed against him disappeared and took with it any sense of movement.

Electricity crackled on his skin, leaving flowery burns in its wake, and a rush of air that came from nowhere surrounded him like a vise.

Then he hit Beira, now a dark figure, a shadow in his eyes even when they were squeezed shut. Wrapping his arms around her, he bit back an agonized cry while any part of him that touched her exploded into searing pain. Flames rushed along his jumpsuit and ignited his hair, but he didn't let go.

BETRAYAL HURT PROTECT REFORM, Beira screamed, the words not spoken so much as shoved into Owen's mind with all the venom of a cobra, as her hands closed around Owen's arms and burned like he'd stuck his arm in a furnace. *REVENGE SAVE BECOME.*

"Beira," Owen yelled, unsure if he was speaking or not. "Beira, we're safe, everyone got out."

She screamed again and tore at his hands. Everywhere she touched laid fresh burns down on his skin, and each blow shook Owen to his bones, shattering, tearing, ripping. A blow to his ribs took his breath away, agony lancing down his side as each breath became a battle. A wordless scream tore out of his throat as if chased by the dogs of hell, but Owen didn't let go.

"Beira, listen to me!"

She repeated herself like Owen hadn't spoken, the words growing ever louder and faster, *BETRAYALBECOMEHURTREFORM-PROTECTREVENGE.* Simultaneously, the light grew brighter, and the electricity cracked and struck like lightning. His skin felt like it was peeling up and off, ripping away with each move. A wind came from nowhere and stole the air from Owen's lungs as it ripped the tattered and burned cloth from his skin.

A chant rose above the wind. An ancient, sombrous intonation in a language he couldn't grasp and in a million voices he couldn't understand. Somehow eternal and new, like it had always been on the edge of Owen's hearing, covered by the sound of life.

"Beira," Owen yelled again, her name a nearly incoherent howl over the wind and the voices. "You need to stop or you'll kill me, you'll kill us both." Words disappeared into the whirlwind of agony that consumed him, becoming almost impossible to find. His ribs burned, and he'd long since lost feeling in his limbs. A small plea was all he could muster from a mind on the border of oblivion. "Titania!"

She paused, her rant a sudden absence in Owen's mind, and he felt her agony in addition to his own. *Protect save bring home*, she whispered, *journey keep safe return.*

"Yes," Owen whispered back, a slur that struggled to find the air to be spoken. "We're safe. We can go home now. You don't need to do this."

The darkness wavered, disappearing into the light.

And the light vanished, and with it the wind. Owen dared to crack his eyes open, and his breath caught in his throat.

Beira held him, herself again, no sign of the dark figure that had taken her place. Her face was lined with the exhaustion of battle, and her green combat fatigues were burned black.

Owen wanted to smile but couldn't seem to make his lips move. The muscles had forgotten how. And worse, every inch of him was a mass of pain too knotted together for him to figure out if one part hurt more than the rest.

Beira's voice echoed in the distance, too far away for how close they were to each other. Her hands squeezed his, and he'd have screamed if he could, but she was already calling out to someone he couldn't see.

She kept talking, but her words got further and further away the longer she spoke. The corners of his vision dimmed, and the world turned gray and silent.

Eventually, even that faded away.

CHAPTER TWENTY-THREE

In Which a Wall Comes Tumbling Down

"There are limits to siren song. We can't regrow limbs or revive dead flesh, and we can't provide a guarantee of a complete recovery once we're done. In other words, we can heal a torn ligament, but you might not be running marathons afterward. This is most apparent with injuries that cause nerve damage, such as burns, frostbite, and strokes. Complete recovery is possible but unlikely unless treatment is administered immediately."

—Excerpt from Siren Song: A Complete Study *by Fatima Cunningham*

He wasn't in pain. Which, considering he hadn't expected to wake up at all let alone pain-free, was less of a surprise and more of a subtle confirmation that the afterlife existed after all. Still, as the seconds ticked by and neither Saint Peter nor the Grim Reaper arrived, he figured he should open his eyes.

At first, everything was gray. Blinking to clear the sleep from his eyes turned the endless gray into something a bit more nuanced, but it didn't go away.

He reached up to his face with his left hand—something pinched him whenever he tried to move his right—and confirmed that he hadn't been blindfolded. That, at the very least, was easy to figure out. It didn't explain why he couldn't see, though, and the last thing he remembered . . .

His hand fell back to his side—and he didn't want to admit how much of a comfort it was that his hand was a discernible shadow in the gray mess that surrounded him—and his stomach churned. The last thing he remembered was falling.

The clatter of a clipboard hitting stone and a quiet gasp made Owen jerk his head toward the sounds.

"Who's there?" Owen snapped, harsher than he meant to. If he squinted, he could make out a shadow in that direction.

"You're awake," said a woman with a soft, unfamiliar voice. There was a long pause filled with the sound of fabric shuffling before she spoke again. "Can you see me?"

"No," he said, tangling his fists in his blankets. They'd expected this, he realized as a cold tendril of dread snaked through his stomach. They'd known he wouldn't—no. He didn't know anything yet. He shouldn't jump to conclusions. He swallowed, his throat aching like someone had left it in the sun to dry and then scraped it along a cactus, and forced himself to sit up. "What happened?" At this point, he was mostly certain he wasn't dead, and he needed answers, starting with why, how, and where he was. And whether the gray was permanent.

More fabric shuffled and metal scraped across tile; then the small shadow grew longer. "One moment, I . . . I need to get my supervisor," she stuttered, and her voice shrunk to a fear-loaded whisper. Her chair scraping against the floor was deafening in comparison. "He can answer your questions." She was gone before Owen could think to stop her.

Slumping back down, Owen sighed. A slow dread had been growing in his stomach, and it got worse the longer he was left to his own devices. Supervisors, in his limited experience since becoming a citizen of Tearmann, were rarely a good thing. Most among the fae believed that a person should only be assigned a job if they could do it. Having to get someone better or with more authority meant that something had gone wrong.

He twisted his hands in the blanket and stared into the gray. Everything would be fine. Whoever her supervisor was, they'd explain things. Maybe they'd squirt something into his eye to wash out the gray or they'd have a surgery or—

Or maybe he'd just have to live with it. The thought sank his stomach even further, and he blinked back tears.

Regardless, returning footsteps soon broke the monotony of the gray. Pushing down the twisting in his stomach, Owen took a deep breath, turned his head toward the sound, and schooled his expression into something he hoped looked nonchalant.

"Owen, you're awake." Aaron's blessedly familiar, albeit hoarse, voice filled the room like honey in a mug of tea.

"Aaron!" Owen didn't bother trying to hold back his smile as he pushed himself up. The tangle in his stomach dissolved a little. If Aaron was here—and not openly worried—they must be safe or at least out of human hands. And Aaron could heal humans.

"Careful," Aaron yelled, and swooped forward to push Owen back down. "You'll hurt yourself."

Aaron's grip was unrelenting, so Owen went without a fuss. He caught Aaron's hand before it left his shoulder and used it as an anchor to keep him close.

"Aaron," he said, fingers closed tight. "What happened?" Aaron would tell him, he knew that without a doubt, but it wasn't like him to be this cagey.

A gentle hand pulled Owen's fingers off, and Aaron's shadow moved to sit at Owen's side. "You're in a Siksika clinic a few hours from Calgary." An edge had entered his voice, sharp as a knife. Underneath it was a quiet tapping, claw against metal. "Beira didn't think you'd survive the journey back. You've been here for almost a week."

"A week?" he asked tentatively. Paralyzing dread flooded his limbs, and he took in a deep breath.

Owen may not have expected to wake up, but siren healing was supposed to be quick. For him to have been out that long and still injured said more about how close he'd danced with the Grim Reaper than he was comfortable thinking about.

Aaron shrugged, the movement almost invisible to Owen. "You . . ." His words trailed off into nothing. The edge had grown, and with it, Owen's discontent.

An unfamiliar voice answered where Aaron couldn't. "You were almost dead when they brought you in." The speaker moved forward, a shadow larger than Aaron with a voice twice as deep. "Rodriguez and the other sirens couldn't keep you alive and heal you at the same time, so they left you with me until you recovered enough to go home."

Owen didn't like the sound of that. If he had to be blind for any span of time, he wanted it to be at home—with the people he trusted and the places he knew. "And have I?" he asked, curling his fingers into his blankets. His right hand twinged; they must have given him an IV. He couldn't see it just like he couldn't see the speaker or the room or his blankets or anything but the bloody gray.

The speaker hummed and made a motion with his hands that Owen couldn't make out. "I couldn't say yet. I don't understand the harmonizing process or whatever it's called, so I can only rely on what I'm told and what I see for myself. Rodriguez assures me that the internal damage is healed, but there's always a risk of infection if we aren't careful, and there isn't much we can do for the scars." The speaker paused and leaned down to Aaron to say something Owen couldn't hear.

"You need more healing," Aaron said. The edge in his voice had sharpened to a razor although Owen couldn't tell if it was meant for him or whatever the speaker had whispered. "You can't see or feel it, but you're covered with burns and half your bones were shattered. I had nearly twenty sirens singing with me, and you barely survived. You're not ready to leave."

If it had taken them a week to repair the internal damage, Owen didn't want to know what he looked like. Maybe it was for the best they hadn't healed his eyes yet. He took a deep breath and squeezed his eyes shut. The only difference it made was turning the gray to black. "How long?"

Aaron sighed. His chair squeaked under his weight, so he must have leaned forward. "A week? Maybe two. It depends on how well you react to the delayed healing."

And there was the crux of the problem. Sirens were good—Aaron was among the best, especially with a choir at his back—but they weren't miracle workers. Their song worked best on fresh injuries. After this long, the odds of him making a complete recovery were nil.

But still, there was some hope. Aaron wouldn't dangle it in front of him like that unless he thought he could make some progress.

"Where're the others?" he asked through clenched teeth. Beira wouldn't have left him here in his current state with just Aaron for protection. She was too paranoid for that—to say nothing of what Tiffany would've done.

"We had half a dozen shades here, but we're down to two. The others went home yesterday."

Owen nodded but didn't open his eyes.

"Your wife is here." The speaker's words were enough to make Owen's sightless eyes fly open.

"Tiffany's here?" he asked in a hushed voice, pushing himself up on his elbows. His heart pounded, and the knot in his stomach whirled, tightening and loosening like it couldn't decide if this was a good thing or not. "Why? How?" As much as he wanted her here, her and the kids, she should be at home. The kids needed her. Especially considering how close he'd come to not being able to come home at all.

Aaron sighed irritably, and his shadow leaned forward. "We expected you to wake up at some point today or tomorrow, so we sent for her. She flew down last night with some supplies to refill Dr. Stone's stock."

She'd gone to see the kids first—that was all he could ask. He collapsed back down and ran a hand over his eyes. "Can I see her?" His whole body ached and his hands shook, but now that he knew Tiffany was here, he wouldn't be able to rest until he confirmed for himself that she was safe.

"We need to—"

"Of course," Aaron said, a dark streak briefly connecting his shadow with Dr. Stone's. "I'll bring her in and leave you alone." He hesitated and—after another whispered debate with Dr. Stone—continued, "We'll need to run some tests before you fall asleep again, but we can give you a few minutes."

Despite whispered protests from Dr. Stone and a series of ones that weren't whispered, their shadows disappeared. Owen's eyes drifted along the gray, his ears straining for the faintest sound of footsteps or the whistle of air through feathers. After an eternity that only lasted a minute or two, a single shadow, bigger than any Owen had yet seen, limped into view.

"Tiff," Owen whispered, unable to speak louder over the lump in his throat. There was a chance it wasn't her—that Aaron and Dr. Stone had sent someone in first—but he knew. He'd listened to those footsteps every day for almost twenty years. The feet that made them were different now, but he knew their pattern, and he'd recognize it anywhere.

"Owen," Tiffany said in an equally hushed voice. Her breath hitched, and two lumps that might be her wings slumped down below his line of sight.

He held out a hand searching, reaching for hers, and wasn't disappointed when the familiar weight of her fingers settled between his. His shoulders relaxed as tension spilled off him. She was here and safe, and he could finally confirm that for himself. Without thinking, he raised her hand to his mouth and kissed it. "You're here," he whispered against her fur. "Tiff . . ."

Sniffling, Tiffany pulled their joined hands back and returned the favor. Her whiskers tickled against the back of Owen's palm. Something warm—a tear perhaps—dripped onto his hand as she pulled it away.

"I looked everywhere for you," Tiffany whispered. "Once it was over, I looked for you, but no one knew where you were. Even Gayle . . ." A quiet sob burst from her throat only to be stifled almost immediately. "I didn't mean to stay away," she continued once she'd regained control. Her fingers squeezed his so hard he had to bite back a gasp. "I didn't. I wanted to stay with you, but the kids needed me and . . ."

"I know." It hurt to speak and worse to breathe. Each inhale, each hushed word had become a battle he wasn't sure he'd win. "What happened?"

A hitching gasp—pain and fear and a keening near loss. Then, in a voice wracked with unshed tears, Tiffany said, "I lost you in the rush around the song." A touch of endless, breathless wonder slid into the space between words. A remnant of an ecstasy Owen could only imagine. "When I came back to myself, the light was gone, and the battle was over. The queen . . ."

No fae truly hated Beira, but there was a note in Tiffany's voice that suggested she wished she could.

"She was holding you when I found you. She'd called half the sirens over, and they were singing, but it wasn't doing anything. The burns . . . You were covered in . . ."

A loud, agonized cry ripped loose from a deep part of Tiffany, and she yanked her hand free. Her shadow disappeared into the gray as her nails clacked against the tiles. "You were hurt so bad, I barely recognized you," she whispered, each word raw and bleeding. "The battle sirens kept you asleep while the others tried to heal you, but it was too much, and you're not fae. They didn't think you'd ever wake up."

"It's not your fault," he whispered, the words catching in his throat. "Tiff, it's not your fault." A reaching hand blindly caught her wing, and he followed it to her hand. He tangled his fingers in hers and pulled her as close as he could. It wasn't her fault he'd ended up like this, and it wouldn't be her fault if he stayed like this. He'd made the choices that landed him here.

He didn't ask her any more questions, barely spoke at all. Her hand clutched his like a lifeline as she sobbed, and he stared into the darkness.

"I love you," he whispered, his voice a dry rasp hardly louder than the AC. "It wasn't your fault." It couldn't be. He'd done this to himself, and she had to know that.

He didn't know how long they sat like that, clinging to each other like they were each other's port in a storm, but he wouldn't have changed it for the world.

He still had her. They'd gotten out of that hellhole, and they were going home.

***

It took three more sessions and two weeks before the sirens decided Owen was as healed as he could be and sent him home. He still couldn't see, and his bad leg had developed a limp they all but admitted would never go away. Tiffany assured him that most of his burn scars were gone—not that Owen knew how many or how bad they'd been before—and that he was still as handsome as ever.

"Will you still come to my play next week, Daddy?" Dorothy asked from Owen's left.

"Of course, sweetheart," Owen said in her general direction. If he squinted, he could make out her wings against the lamplight. He wasn't entirely blind—he could still make out shapes if the light was bright enough—but in a place like Tearmann, he may as well be, even if the path was bright as the one to Dorothy's daycare. Give him the open sky instead of a lamp any day.

It was horrifying and cathartic at the same time.

He should've died. Between the burns, the broken bones, and the sheer exhaustion of what he'd done, he should've shuffled off this mortal coil and left the world behind. But he hadn't. He'd woken up, scared and blind, but alive, and he'd pay that price again if it meant he could be with his family again.

Tiffany and the kids—even Arthur, once he escaped whatever punishment detail he'd been assigned in lieu of a court-martial—had been a constant presence at his bedside when he'd recovered enough to go home. Dorothy was in the process of mastering the literary arts and took great pleasure in stumbling through her picture books fifteen times a day with Ashley's help; Jen, tiptoeing around their last conversation, had an endless stockpile of stories about her daily activities; and Arthur griped about his punishments while they played cards or chess.

Owen reveled in it, if not the reason it happened.

Each conversation, each story, and each meeting helped patch a hole in Owen's chest that had been growing since he'd lost David. Joining the Corps may have put a bandage over the bleeding, but it hadn't taken the knife out of the wound.

He had to face the ghost that haunted his footsteps, but he wasn't doing it alone anymore. He couldn't run now and he was glad of it. There wasn't anyplace he could go, even if he wanted to leave. His brush with death had been a firm reminder that his demons needed to be dealt with before they hurt anyone else. He'd go out into the world, even though it was darker than it had been before, and search for the healing he'd been avoiding with the people he loved.

Tiffany never left his side. From the moment she walked in after he woke up to the day he finally came home, she was always there.

He stopped running from her too. And they talked.

About David and the Corps. About grief and who they'd become. About the kids, the haven, and everything in between, and it *hurt* but it was necessary. Owen hadn't been the only one to lose a child that day, and it was past time he stopped acting like it.

Therapy had been a godsend once he'd stopped resisting it.

"Oh, he's coming," Evans answered, breaking Owen out of his fog. Gently bumping into Owen's right leg to direct him around an unseen obstacle, he continued, "He's going even if I have to drag him there myself."

Evans had a new position in the Williams household. Despite Owen's protests that he could find his way around on his own, Tiffany and Beira had teamed up to convince him that he needed an aide until he got used to Tearmann again. As much as it pained him to admit it, they were right. It was nice to have help while learning to navigate blind. Even familiar paths were dangerous if he couldn't tell what or who he was stepping on.

"Drag me there, nothing," Owen grumbled, readjusting his grip on his cane. His leg twinged with pain, constant ebbs and flows that got more severe the longer he was on his feet. He suspected even the walk to the business district might be more than his doctors would like him doing. "You're my live-in aide, a glorified guide gryphon. I could get there without your help."

He probably couldn't, but Dorothy didn't need to know that.

Evans and Owen continued bickering all the way to Dorothy's daycare, much to her delight. That warmed Owen's heart enough for him to smile softly. He couldn't do much anymore—couldn't read stories with Dorothy or play her favorite board games or even look her in the eye—but he could still make her laugh, and that was something to be proud of.

Still, that didn't make it any easier to leave her behind when they reached her daycare. Her little arms wrapped around his knees for a brief moment, and then she was gone, calling her goodbyes over her shoulder as she disappeared into the gray.

The warmth in his heart wasn't enough to ward off the lingering despair that swelled with her gone. With Tiffany back at work and the kids back at school, he didn't have much to do. He couldn't read any of the books in their apartment, his old boss wasn't comfortable having him back in the shop until they worked out what, if any, accessibility aides they could build, and most of his friends had been conscripted to help with the war effort.

As much as it frustrated him, he was at loose ends. He couldn't help with the war preparations, he could barely help out at home—he needed help finding his toothbrush for heaven's sake—and everyone treated him like he'd shatter if he lifted more than five pounds. The day stretched out before him as one great gray blob just like the days before and all days after.

"Owen?" Evans's voice was a sudden reminder that Owen had been standing in complete silence like a lost fool.

Shaking his head, Owen turned to Evans. "Sorry, I was drifting. Did you say something?"

Evans's claws and the odd combination of metal, leather, and wood that made up his prosthetic leg scraped along the ground as he shifted his weight, leaning further into Owen. It was a grounding technique one of the doctors had taught him when he'd agreed to be Owen's guide. Owen was vaguely unsettled that Evans had used it often enough to know when Owen needed it without asking.

"I asked if you were ready to head back." He shrugged, and his harness snagged on Owen's jeans. "I think there's a sale on oranges if you wanted to check it out. You like oranges, right?"

He did. They were his favorite fruit. Doubtless, some kind soul had already thought to leave him some in an unmarked bag outside the apartment or would find a way to slip more than he'd purchased into his bag if he did go. That would fit in with everything else going on.

Sighing, Owen switched his cane to his other hand and walked away from the distant echoes of voices. His mind was too raw to be around people right now and too vast to be alone. The last thing he wanted was to be trapped in their apartment while the others weren't home.

"I'd like to take a walk." He needed to be in a place that felt alive. It ran the risk of running into someone brave enough to speak with him, but if he moved fast enough, he should be able to avoid them. After the battle . . . well, Arthur said people were debating giving him his own statue, even though he'd lived. Few could say they'd managed to stop the annihilation of an entire culture.

If it had been anyone else, he'd have said they deserved the honor. Beira and the fae were still alive by his actions, but the only reason they'd been in danger in the first place was because he'd led his team into a trap. The scars, the blindness, and everything else were the price to make up for that mistake. They should give that honor to Gayle or Ashwind or someone who'd actually done something besides fixing their own mess.

Evans walked silently at his side, occasionally nudging Owen around obstacles and past hallways that would be too crowded to navigate. Owen wasn't sure where they were going, but the sounds of the business district fell behind them. Passersby went from common to rare to almost nonexistent and, despite the growing ache in his leg, Owen was glad of it. He didn't like crowds anymore.

"Owen? We're about to enter the religious district. Do you want to turn around?"

Owen didn't need working eyes to know that Evans was uncomfortable. They'd wandered for at least an hour now, and his prosthetic had to be bothering him just as much as Owen's leg was bothering him. They'd need to rest soon.

Humming, Owen paused a moment and rested a hand against the wall. An unfamiliar carving dug into his palm, and he traced it, trying to decide if the curve he felt was a wing or piece of the landscape. "I'd like to go a bit farther, if you don't mind." The cathedral door had been carved by a blind man, he remembered suddenly. Would it feel different to a blind man than it had looked to a sighted one?

One whispered request later—mindful of any worshippers hidden behind unseen curtains—and Evans placed Owen's free hand on his harness to guide him in the right direction.

Owen kept a hand on the wall as they went, tracing what he could of the carvings he'd once admired and would never see again. A foul-smelling incense burned his nose as they passed one of the curtained entrances, and then a sweeter one a few rows down. They must be getting close.

"We're here." Evans's voice was tired. His steps had been weighted and slow for the last ten minutes, and Owen wasn't imagining the limp.

Owen resolved not to take long and reached out to confirm for himself where they were. He reached as high as he could, tracing as he went, then over until his hands ran into stone. The door was, as far as he could tell, exactly the same when viewed with or without sight. Rough and cracked edges, figures begun and then abandoned halfway through. Still, he might understand it better now.

"I didn't expect to see you here."

Owen was proud he didn't jump when Beira's voice came from behind him. That was something he'd been working on. Still, most people were polite enough to let him know they were coming. "I thought I'd see if it looked different now." His voice didn't shake, and he didn't stumble through the sentence, although it was a near miss.

Chuckling, Beira moved closer on silent feet. "And does it?"

Owen shrugged. "Not terribly. More splinters this way."

The joke fell flat, but Beira didn't seem to mind. Her polite laughter came to a halt near enough to Owen that he felt he could reach out and grab it, but not close enough for him to make anything out in the dim light. She'd received his injury report; she had to know that he couldn't see her from there.

"What brings you here?" Her words were light but carried a faint undertone Owen couldn't quite decipher. Weight without heaviness. Guilt without regret.

Owen hadn't seen Beira since he'd woken up. He'd tried, but he hadn't managed to convince Evans to take him across Tearmann to her office, and she spent almost every waking moment in meetings with the Corps leaders and various ambassadors. "Oh, I was just . . . I wanted a walk. Ended up here."

Beira's shape emerged from the blackness close to Owen, and despite knowing she wouldn't hurt him, he wanted to rear back. It took everything he had to stay still.

"Sounds like you're making a habit of that. I'll admit, most people don't wander the religious district without reason." She moved past him, and the wood under his fingers disappeared as she pushed the door open. "Did you want to come in?"

Owen hesitated. He didn't know the cathedral, and what he remembered of it wasn't enticing for a newly blind man. He'd probably break his leg if he went in there on his own, but he didn't want to stop talking to Beira. They'd been friends once and he missed her. She always knew how to get to the root of what was bothering him, and he could use that sort of clarity now.

"If you don't mind," he said finally, tightening his fingers around his cane. His free hand found its way onto Evans's wing as he took a step back. "But you'd have to help me home. I've kept Evans on his feet long enough."

Beira didn't mind, and Evans agreed after a token protest—he must have been hurting more than he wanted to admit—so Evans left. Owen took Beira's arm, and she escorted him into the unknown. She took him to a pew that, by his estimation, was halfway to the altar and guided him down onto the stone before she joined him.

They sat in silence for a while. Beira on her knees, muttering something in Latin, and Owen sitting at her side, staring at beauty he couldn't see but knew was there.

His mind whirled, underwritten by prayers he couldn't understand, over everything his life had become. The cold stone bit into and numbed his rear, a solid counterpoint to the chaos in his mind.

They were going to war, that much was certain. He might've been unconscious for the aftermath, but the whispers in the market and the halls still reached his ears.

Beira had led an army onto foreign soil, attacked a civilian organization, and fled before telling anyone why. The world waited for the storm to break, and when it did, the fae would break with it.

The Tearmann Accords had been reduced to little more than a worthless pile of paper; Tearmann and Daingneach—really Britain as a whole—were surrounded by armies with their fingers on their triggers; and the Corps, the reserves, and anyone who could hold a weapon had been called into duty. One wrong move, a look at the wrong person, and the havens would turn into bloodbaths.

And Beira . . . she was weak. Even now, she shook next to him, exhausted from the effort of walking here with shuffling hesitant steps. The battle had drained her even before she'd tried to recreate Breckenridge. She didn't have the strength to fight anymore, not even if she drank her weight in human blood.

They would lose. Tearmann and Daingneach would be reduced to rubble and ash. Even if Beira survived by some insane miracle, her body would shatter beneath the stress of her connection to the fae before long. She would die, and the fae would die with her. His family would die with her.

As much as it tore at Owen's heart to admit it, Percill had been right. The fae were going to war, and Beira couldn't lead them to victory on her own. His family, his home, and his friends were hovering on the precipice of destruction. Everything he'd done, every loss he'd suffered had been for nothing, and he was powerless to stop what was coming like this.

"You need to Change me," he whispered, staring sightlessly toward the rose window.

The ceaseless flow of prayers, Owen's companion in his dark thoughts, slowed, then picked up again. He waited a moment and had opened his mouth to repeat himself when Beira uttered a final amen and stood.

"Come with me," she said in a voice like thunder. She tugged him up and led him to the back of the church and through the door without waiting for him to speak.

In the hallway, surrounded by the distant scent of incense and incomprehensible chants, she released him. Breathing hard, she slumped against the door, and a quiet thump made Owen think she'd sat down.

"Beira?" Owen chanced, easing forward. A searching hand grazed the door that brought him here, and he followed it to the ground. His knee nudged hers and he didn't move it.

Beira didn't answer. Her breath took on a regimented pattern, in and out every ten seconds. After ten cycles, she spoke, her words a barely contained maelstrom of confusion, anger, and fear. "Do you have any idea what you're asking?"

Owen turned to face her and arched an eyebrow. It seemed pretty obvious to him.

She'd asked him if he'd let her turn him after the Battle of Tearmann. She'd drunk his blood and said he'd been the second stable vampire she'd found in almost fifty years. Before that, she'd told him she wasn't as strong as she used to be, that she needed more blood as the years went on, that living without the match the other founders had was killing her. Without another vampire, the fae were solely dependent on her, and she didn't have anything else to give.

She needed him. She couldn't fight by herself, and there wasn't anything else he could do to protect the people he loved.

Beira laughed, a harsh, broken sound. "Of course you don't. No, don't interrupt, you think you do but you don't." Her hand brushed Owen's shoulder as she brought it up, presumably to rub over her eyes. "Owen, there's a reason I agreed not to bring it up again. You don't want this, you told me so yourself."

Shrugging, Owen closed his eyes and leaned against the door. It was true; he didn't want to Change. She'd offered to make him her equal, to share her power, and he'd been afraid of it. He still was, if he was being honest, but they only had one shot at surviving this. Despite her protests—and they were legitimate, he couldn't deny that—Beira knew it too.

With each command, each new fae, and each day she lived on her own, some of her power left her and didn't return. The last fight had drained her. Even the last outburst seemed to have taken something irreplaceable. She needed someone to carry the load, or the war would be over before the first battle.

"Owen," she whispered when he didn't respond. "This won't . . . it might not heal your eyes. We don't know what will happen. I've never done it before. You know that, right?"

That hadn't even occurred to Owen, but now that it had, he couldn't stop thinking about it. The Change didn't . . . it didn't fix everything. Scars might not transfer over, but a lost limb didn't grow back. Swallowing, he forced himself to speak.

"We don't have a choice. You know that." His heart thumped and he took a deep breath. He'd give nearly anything to see again, to read with Dorothy or play cards with Jen, and possibility, the slightest chance, was as intoxicating as the strongest liquor. "You're dying, Beira. How much energy did rescuing us cost you?" It was a low blow, but Owen pushed on. "Even if you could win another war, how long would you survive afterward? Would the bloodshed be worth it when you and your people will be dead in a few decades anyway?"

The fae hadn't lost anyone to old age yet. The catacombs were filled with dead, but its tenants were those killed in battle or accidents. Her death would strike down hundreds of thousands in their prime.

Beira chuckled darkly, and her knee pulled away from Owen. Her footsteps echoed down the hall, as regular as a metronome. "We don't—we can't—it doesn't have to be you," she said, her voice tight and quick. "You don't have to do this, Owen, you can go back to your life."

"What life?" Owen snapped, shoving himself up. His cane fell unnoticed to the ground as his fists clenched, and he took a step toward where her voice had come from. "Ten, twenty years alone here if you die? Most of my family is fae—my wife and all but one of my children—and they would die with you. I can't keep them safe like this. Everything I did for them will have been for nothing." His blood roared in his ears, a symptom of unspoken desperation that finally found an outlet. "I'm *blind*," he said hoarsely. "What good is a blind soldier? What good is someone who won't sacrifice a little to keep his family safe?"

He didn't know if he was looking at her, couldn't even find it in him to care. This shouldn't be difficult. She'd said herself that one of the things that made him a good candidate was his desire to help, and here he was—trying to help—and she wasn't letting him.

She sighed, a bit to the left of where Owen had been speaking. "You don't want this," she whispered. "I can smell it on you, you don't want to Change. You'd hate it eventually."

He didn't, he could admit that. Everything would be different. He'd have more power than any person should possess, but he'd be almost entirely alone. Beira had a family but wasn't close to anyone. She couldn't be, not with how tightly she was connected with the fae.

Not when vampires could make fae dance like puppets at the ends of their strings.

If he did this, his relationship with Tiffany, with the kids would never be the same. The thought made his heart ache, and he took a ragged breath.

If he didn't do it, his family and all their friends would die. Tearmann would be a tomb inhabited by ghosts and a few thousand humans.

"I don't," he whispered. His fingernails dug into his palms, biting and aching, grounding him. "But I don't see another way. I won't let my family die, Beira, not when there's something I can do to stop it."

He knew the moment Beira gave in. It was like the air went out of the room as she dropped to the floor and laughed, long and broken. The sound echoed down the hall, filling it and drowning out all other signs of life.

He swallowed back tears and took deep, even breaths. This was the right thing to do, he knew that, but his mind followed the echoes down the hall, down to Dorothy's daycare, down to Ashley's and Jen's classrooms, and down to the training rooms where Tiffany and Arthur were working on forms. Most of all, it followed the laughter down to a small apartment on the second floor that Owen feared would never feel like home again.

CHAPTER TWENTY-FOUR

In Which Owen Revisits His Son

"The grave rose is a custom most fae of the winter court have adopted. Those who live in Tearmann proper traditionally make it from chunks of granite or limestone mined from the city itself, but in the more rural areas, mourners might travel for days to find an appropriate material to work with. The roses will be left at the graves of the deceased once completed as a sign that formal mourning has come to an end."
—An excerpt from Fae Funerary Rites *by Siobhan Albright*

Owen swayed on his feet as Evans led him through the halls. He'd barely slept last night, and all the coffee in the apartment hadn't been enough to properly wake him up. A dark shadow loomed in the corners of his mind, sending him fleeing from his dreams and jolting up each time his eyes so much as drifted shut.

He'd given up sleeping not long after Tiffany and the kids had left for the day.

He should've stayed in bed. His whole body ached from lack of sleep and from the strain of healing, but his limbs thrummed with uneasy energy, and he was going to lose his mind if he had to stare at the same unchanging sea of gray any longer.

When Evans suggested a walk, Owen had leaped at the idea. Maybe moving for a bit would exhaust him enough to nap before the kids got home. As an afterthought, he'd grabbed his backpack and shoved the lump of granite that wasn't a rose yet inside, half a mind to visit David's grave.

He was regretting it now, though. Between the sluggish fog in his brain and the weight against his back, he was fading fast. The chattering and calls of the market flooded through the hall and poked through Owen's mental haze.

"Let's go through the market," he said before he had time to stop himself. That way wasn't faster, but it was loud. He'd spent too much time in his own head recently, and the market didn't leave much room for thinking when pausing could get someone run over by an overzealous centaur. Besides, it had dozens of benches and a turnoff halfway through that could get them back to the apartment if he got too tired.

The sounds and smells of the market washed over them like a tsunami once they passed its threshold. Just past the gate, someone was hawking mittens "special made to order," and a bit farther on, the shadow of a figure Owen thought might be a dragon completely hid the merchant that she was bartering with.

"Wood! Get your winter wood here," came a female voice from Owen's right. The scent of fresh sawdust surrounded her like a perfume, and Owen unconsciously slowed. The merchant didn't seem to notice him. "Half cord or whole," she called, her shadow swaying back and forth to a silent rhythm. "Spruce, pine, cedar, and more!"

A streetlamp positioned almost directly above her stall cast the edges of her table into stark contrast with the shadows beneath them. If he squinted, Owen could make out the barest outlines of her goods.

"Stay here," Owen told Evans without turning around. "I'll just be a minute."

Owen took a step closer and reached out. His fingers drifted over an axe, a few saws, and rough-cut wood samples while the merchant called to other shoppers, and Evans waited silently behind him.

His sleeve caught on something, and he jerked back. The offending object tumbled back to the table with a wooden thunk. Praying no one else heard that, Owen ignored Evans's inquiring noise and searched for what had dropped so he could put it back before anyone else realized what happened. It wasn't with the other goods and obviously wasn't part of the stall, but he wasn't about to leave it on top of the other goods.

It was no great surprise that the offending object was a piece of wood. Admittedly, it was smaller and rougher than the rest of the merchant's goods, but the grain was nice. No warping, knots, or rot. He tossed it between his hands. A good heft to it too. A bit soft maybe, but otherwise a perfect carving piece.

He couldn't remember the last time he'd carved something. Before they'd come here, he'd spent most evenings with a knife and a block of wood by the fire. He'd sold what the kids hadn't wanted at the summer farmers market. He hadn't done that since before he'd joined the Corps at least.

There'd been a time when half of the kids' toys had started life as a block of wood in his hands. Wood made sense to him, and turning it into something as useful as it was beautiful had given him something to do when he'd been young and stupid.

David had been the only one who understood wood like Owen did. He'd sat on Owen's knee in the workshop, asking questions and begging for scraps to practice on. He'd insisted on using his first spoon for three months after he finished it.

Stone was too dead and cold for Owen, but wood . . . He'd always been more comfortable working with wood.

"I'll take it," he said, raising his head toward where he'd last heard the merchant's voice.

"Wonderful!" the merchant said, her voice so perky Owen could hear her plastered-on smile. "Do you want a whole cord or a half?"

"Neither." He pulled out his wallet and waved the wood around. "How much for this piece?"

The merchant sputtered, a half dozen sentences begun and then abandoned. "For my paperweight?" she finally asked hesitatingly. Owen got the distinct impression she was side-eying him, which bothered him less than it should've.

He shrugged. A paperweight. Ah, well that explained a few things. "It's a good piece."

The merchant tittered, the shadows of her elbows moving up and down. "Well, it's not really for sale, but I suppose I could part with it. What do you want it for?"

"A rose. For my son."

The merchant gasped, and her shadowy hands came up to cover her mouth. "Sir, I couldn't. It's not . . ."

Proper, Owen thought as the merchant trailed off. Wood wasn't often used for roses. It had an impermanence to it most fae disliked. It rotted and burned, fading away, whereas stone lasted forever. Using wood was only slightly better than buying a rose outright.

But he wasn't fae. Not yet.

"Is it important to you?" he asked, shifting more of his weight to his cane. His leg twinged painfully. He'd need to sit down soon. "I like this piece."

"Not particularly," the merchant said quickly. "It's just . . . I have much higher quality wood if you're looking to carve a rose. That piece is so small, you'd hardly get started before you ran out."

"It'll be good practice, then." He gestured toward his face vaguely. "It's been a while."

The merchant made a noise that made Owen wish he could still see, and practically lunged toward her cashbox. "Of course, sir, I understand completely,"' she babbled in a voice a whole octave higher than she'd used previously.

Owen chuckled to himself as the merchant hurried through the rest of the exchange. He ended up getting a small whittling knife too—thrown in for free to apologize for "all the trouble" —and the weight of both of them in his hands was comforting, like something he'd been missing for months had slotted back into place.

"Was that really necessary?" Evans asked just loud enough for Owen to hear him over the rest of the market as Owen carefully put his purchases in his backpack.

"Maybe not," Owen said, letting out a breath of laughter. "But it was amusing."

Evans hummed disapprovingly as he tugged Owen's hand to his harness. "Do you need a break?"

His backpack felt lighter now than it had before, even if there was more in it, and Owen set his shoulders. "No, I'm done. Let's go to the catacombs."

He had a lot to tell David, and with something in his hands, he suspected the time would go fast.

CHAPTER TWENTY-FIVE

In Which Familiar Faces Are Made New

"With the exception of the queen, the founders exist in male-and-female pairs. Each pair splits the mental load of the connection to their respective species between them, supporting and bolstering their partner to accomplish something together that neither could do alone. Whether this is some twisted and apotheotic desire of the man who created the fae, as the queen believes, or has some practical purpose is a mystery lost to the ages. Of course, the queen also points out that life rarely falls into such even and pretty categories as the fae are divided into and that many later generation fae struggle with the expectations of their species, so there might be something to her claims that his desires shaped our world more than the necessities of the Change."
— An excerpt from A Study of Fae Governance *by Muhammad Amir*

It took three days for Beira to accept that Owen wasn't going to change his mind and agree to turn him. Three days of chaos, of constant front-line reports worse than the ones that came before, and the universal sense that the world was holding its breath before it jumped off a cliff. Three days where Owen hardly slept, his dreams consumed by a terror half-forgotten by the time he opened his eyes. Three days of walking on egg-shells because he couldn't find the words to tell Tiffany what he'd decided and explain why he was doing this.

And he wanted to tell her. Wanted to tell all of them, but each time he opened his mouth to try, the words fled, and he ended up gaping like a fish.

He'd told David all about it while working on his new wooden rose. He'd spent hours in front of the tomb, slowly and meticulously scraping away excess wood. Talking to him, walking him through each cut and slice was easy. He couldn't move too fast, or he'd risk hurting himself and ruining the wood. He relied on his fingers and the image in his mind's eye to shape it. That might be slow, but he didn't mind. After all, he didn't have much to work with, and he'd have all the time in the world assuming the Change didn't kill him.

Blast, he should've told the others.

He'd left them a letter. Beira had been the one to suggest it and helped him write it. All the words he hadn't been able to say scrawled across that paper in a neat hand that wasn't his, and addressed to the people he loved more than anything in the world.

Beira would probably be upset with him that he hadn't given it directly to Tiffany. That was the idea. If he gave it to her directly, she'd open it. She'd read it. And she'd try to talk him out of it. She'd probably succeed too.

A part of him that sounded like Tiffany called him a coward, and he couldn't deny it. He hoped she'd forgive him one day.

Owen didn't pay much attention to where Evans was leading him. He was meeting Beira in the Changing rooms on the first floor, the reinforced ones meant for suspected angels. Owen had never been there, but Evans knew where to go. Curling the hand not wrapped up in Evans's harness into a fist, he bit back the part of him that wanted Tiffany—anyone—with him. It was better like this, he told himself. Better they weren't here to witness if it went wrong.

He'd been in that position before, outside a locked door listening to three of his children scream, had lost Tiffany when she'd gone through this, and he wouldn't do that to her or to any of them.

Fortunately, Beira agreed with him, if not for the same reasons. She'd decided that even the healers would be sent out, much to their chagrin. If Owen was going to Change, she wouldn't risk having someone who couldn't disobey him on standby, and humans were forbidden for obvious reasons.

Evans slowed to a stop, but Owen only noticed when he walked into him. Apologizing under his breath, Owen untangled his hand and flexed his fingers, squinting to make out what detail he could.

Light flooded the room. It was so bright that Owen could clearly make out the outlines of the chairs, table, and perimeter of the room.

Torches, oil lamps, candles, and even a small electric lamp had been set up to spread their bounty as best they could, and it warmed his heart to see that. Someone had gone to a lot of effort to make things easier for him.

Two figures stood next to the table, and Owen walked toward them while debating which one was Beira.

The figure on the left noticed him first. "Are you sure you want to do this?" Beira asked in a familiar, but tired voice.

Coming to a stop three feet from the figure, Owen clenched his jaw and nodded. "We don't have another choice." Beira had been trying to, well, not talk him out of it, but make certain Owen knew what he was getting into since she'd agreed to Change him.

Beira tilted her head and sighed. "I just want you to know you can back out if you want to." A part of Owen might've been offended that she kept bringing this up, but he knew better than anyone why she was doing it.

Beira's Catholic beliefs bound her in more ways than how she got blood. Doing this, turning him, was only acceptable because she was doing it to save the fae. She needed him to understand the exact consequences of what they were doing, exactly what it entailed, or she risked committing a sin worse than all but the gravest blasphemy.

She'd completely upended her schedule, sitting down with him for upwards of three or four hours a day to walk him through what would be expected of him if he went through with this. Owen had almost faltered the longer that list grew, but he'd made up his mind. He still wasn't ready to become king, and Beira had agreed with that, but it wasn't a responsibility he could set aside either. Once he was turned, he wouldn't just be Owen Williams, father, Corpsman, and carpenter anymore, but he wouldn't become king right away either.

So he drew his shoulders back, trying to channel whatever sense of justice and strength that had led him into the church that day, and smiled. "I know. And I still want to do this, you don't have to worry."

Beira nodded, and Owen was thankful that the light let him see that. She would still worry, she'd be dead before she stopped worrying, but that was beyond Owen's control.

The talking, it seemed, was over. Beira sent the other figure—a siren whose voice Owen vaguely recognized—and Evans away. She guided

Owen to the table, a proper Changing table with restraints and all, and helped him lie down. The restraints went over his arms and legs, then his torso in three places. The angle would make the bite and the drinking awkward, but they'd both agreed it was better to tie him down before the Change started rather than risk him hurting himself.

One final offer to turn back—she'd let him, even now—then Beira knelt at his side, her face lost in shadow. Gentle hands gripped his wrist, turned it up, and brought it to her mouth.

For one stark, terrifying moment while he watched the shadow of his wrist move farther away, Owen wanted to stop. To go home, hug his children, kiss his wife, and forget he'd ever thought he could do this. Terror ripped through his body, tying his stomach into knots, freezing his heart, and cleaving the air from his lungs. The urge to scream was like a physical thing that made Owen's jaw crack as he bit it back.

And then her teeth closed around his wrist, and Owen's anxiety melted away. Distantly, he remembered that Beira's venom kept prey calm, before that, too, disappeared into the abyss. When Beira brought her arm to his mouth an hour, a minute, a year later, he opened it to drink without thinking. Her blood—blacker than pitch, cold on his tongue, and more intoxicating than the strongest liquor—dripped into his mouth and down his throat like a snake.

And Owen's world *burned.*

The blood met the venom already pulsing through his veins and exploded in a wave of agony like no words could say. Like fire, like water, he was doused in something that burned and drowned and froze and seared. A sound that might have been a scream ripped from his throat like it was torn from the very depths of hell.

***

Owen didn't awaken so much as become aware that he was walking. The world he walked through . . . wasn't. A swirling pool of nothing. Not darkness or light or even the gray that had consumed him for the last few weeks. Just a void that existed only for him to walk through.

And walk he did. For hours, never stopping or tiring or wondering where he was going, only knowing that he couldn't stop.

He supposed he was dreaming, but it felt more real than any dream he'd ever had. It was solid and safe in a way he hadn't felt since he was a small child.

He didn't know when he realized he was wearing a blue coat. No, not blue, an oceanic shade that shifted ever so slightly the longer he looked at it. Embroidered sea creatures—sharks, whales, squid, fish, things that didn't even have a name but ruled beneath the waves—intermingled with ornate and ethereal geometric patterns.

Casting his memory back, he debated with himself if he'd been wearing this when he'd woken up here. He didn't think so, but he had enough doubt that he couldn't be sure. A point in favor of this being a dream, he supposed.

Still, the coat was something to look at while he walked. The longer he looked, the more things changed. The colors became brighter, the patterns stranger, and the rest of his clothes shifted to match. His jeans turned into trousers green enough to make a gardener weep, his T-shirt to a flowing white garment that shone like starlight, and his ratty shoes to knee-length boots made of supple black leather. Like the coat, it had been both subtle and sudden.

And still, he walked.

Beira appeared out of the darkness in front of him. She stood, unmoving, frozen midstep. Her face was drawn and wan, and she, too, wore unfamiliar clothes. A long and heavily embroidered green coat, a black shirt, blue pants, and tan boots. On her head was a simple iron diadem inlaid with a large emerald.

As Owen drew near, almost surpassing her, a weight pressed on his forehead, and he knew without having to look that he now wore a similar diadem.

Beira resumed motion when Owen reached her, matching his pace step for step. Neither spoke, but both were aware of the other.

They walked for a long time, longer than Owen could count, and he wasn't certain if he was starting to feel tired because he was or his mind thought he should be tired. Either way, his limbs were aching and his throat was raw.

Beira wasn't much better. Her color had much improved—in fact, she looked stronger and healthier than he had ever seen her—but each step seemed pained. The corner of her lips tightened each time her feet hit the ground, and a deep line etched deeper into her forehead with each passing moment.

The longer they went, the brighter the colors became and the more Owen hurt. Soon each breath dragged through lungs that had forgotten how to expand, and his limbs trembled like he'd walked up Mount Everest.

The pain in his lungs, his throat, and his limbs consumed his attention, almost enough to block out the horizon that slowly shifted from void black to tepid gray. Ahead of them, when he bothered to look, Owen could see . . . something in the distance. A figure, now big, then small, with no discernible features. It flickered like a shade as they drew near.

Owen and Beira stopped three feet from the figure. It turned, flickered one last time, and finally revealed its face.

Owen sucked in a breath and froze, his face white as his shirt. Words became something foreign, lost forever to his tongue, because if he spoke, he'd have to give a voice—a name—to the thing in front of him.

Beira beat him to it.

"Nathaniel," she whispered. Her voice was shot with grief, her words with rage, and underneath it all, love lost on one who hadn't deserved it.

Owen wished he could force himself to turn, to look away and demand to know how Beira could make a mistake like that, but he couldn't. He'd know that face anywhere, had wiped that nose and brushed that mop into submission more times than he could count.

David smiled and opened his arms wide. "Welcome . . ." he said, his voice wrong and ringing. "To Avalon."

The words hung in the air, reverberating like he'd struck a gong, and explained nothing.

"How can this be?" Beira asked in a hushed voice. "You can't be him. I buried him myself. Owen, tell me I'm wrong."

Against all odds, Owen found his voice. "You're wrong." How could she be so blind? "It's David." And it hurt, bringing up almost a year's worth of pain and memories. Countless things that never came to be warred with, a short lifetime of things that had, and each dug into Owen's heart like a thousand daggers. He managed to rip his eyes away, ignoring the silent scream that rang in his ears, and turned to Beira.

Her face was an ashy white, pinched and shrunken with terror. She held one hand in front of her as if to ward off the figure, and the other clutched at her neck, where her engagement rings normally hung.

Owen's eyes flicked between them, unable to face the figure but equally unable to look away for long. This wasn't David; it couldn't be. This was a dream—a nightmare—he never wanted to wake up from.

The figure—*DavidDavidDavid*—tilted its head and frowned. Such an expression didn't belong on a face that had been so sweet. "These forms alarm you," he said, his voice crackling and shifting to one much deeper. "I apologize; I'd assumed you'd find them as comforting as you found their bearers. Please, wait one moment."

The figure shimmered, growing, stretching, and shifting. When the nauseating spectacle ceased, David was gone, and in his place stood a gray-haired man in a simple blue robe.

Owen had never seen anyone who truly embodied the term *wizened* before, but this man managed it. Cracked and ancient hands, riddled with arthritis, clutched a cane that he hardly seemed to have the strength to hold. Shoulders once stout and broad bent so much they practically touched in the middle. And his beard, which almost reached the ground, was a knotted mess of white and gray.

The figure chuckled and, rolling his shoulders, pulled himself as straight as he could manage. "Yes, this will work nicely." His voice creaked like a troll's and scratched like a siren that had sung too long. Looking up, he shot them a toothless grin and continued, "I haven't had to use this form in centuries, but it's nice to pull out the old classics every now and again, isn't it?"

As Beira was still frozen and didn't seem to be in any shape to speak, Owen found his voice, which seemed foreign to him. "Who are you?" Stronger than he felt, and less inclined to weep. Certainly not something from his own mouth. "Where are we?"

The figure raised his eyebrow and gestured again. As he did, the area lit up like he'd shone a spotlight on it. Unknown machinery and archaic electronics filled the dusty and decrepit room, their footprints the only sign anything had been there in millennia. A few of the machines sparked and emitted low whines, a wordless plea for power.

"You're in Avalon," the figure said, "and I am Merlin." The machinery came alive as he spoke, sparking and flaring as lights brightened and fans whirred. Broken pieces found their way back to the whole, and dark screens booted up. The figure crinkled his pointed nose. "A facsimile of Avalon, at least. Not what it used to be by any measure, but I did my best."

"Avalon?" Beira whispered, fear shifting to something closer to wonder. Rubble cracked under her feet as she stepped forward. "It can't be."

Owen glanced at her out of the corner of his eye, and his jaw dropped. The terror that had held her prisoner was gone, and wary curiosity lit her eyes. With each passing second, her courage grew, and she became a version of herself Owen had only seen a few times before. The scholar riddled with intrigue and the historian desperate for answers.

Merlin nodded and looked pleased with himself. "Yes, I've been trying to get in contact with you for years." Scowling playfully, he wagged a finger as if chastising a child. "You didn't make it easy for me. I was beginning to worry I'd failed again."

"Beira," Owen said under his breath. His stomach tossed and turned like a fishing boat in a hurricane. "What's he talking about? Do you know him?"

Slowly, like she was coming out of a dream, Beira nodded. "I heard your voice when I Changed," she said quietly, like Owen hadn't spoken. "In my dreams."

Merlin nodded as he shuffled to a chair in front of one of the machines and gingerly sat. Said machine—and the room in general—was in much better repair than it had been a scant few seconds ago. "Yes, a rather old-fashioned method of communication, but all I've had available for some time. Come, sit."

With a wave of his hand, a plump armchair and a decadent settee popped into existence behind Beira and Owen respectively. A second wave rammed the chairs into their knees, and they collapsed into overstuffed cushions. When Owen dragged himself up, Merlin was smiling at him from less than three feet away.

"All comfy now, yes? Good, let's begin. I'm sure you have questions."

Owen grunted and rubbed at the back of his bruised knees. His head pounded, a drumbeat keeping time to the incessant beeping of the machinery. He grit his teeth and clenched his hands into fists. "Who are you?"

Merlin laughed and gestured to himself. "As I said, I'm Merlin. Who else would I be?"

Beira leaned forward and clasped her hands under her chin. "Was that another thing you pulled from our memories?" If she'd been hurt like Owen was by their sudden sitting, she didn't show it. "Merlin is a legendary figure in Britannic lore. Both Owen and I would be familiar with him."

"Who isn't to say I'm not Merlin himself?" Wriggling his bushy eyebrows, Merlin set both gnarled hands on his cane and leaned toward them, an unearthly gleam in his eyes. "Come now, you must know the stories."

"We've heard them," Beira asked, crossing her arms and leaning back in her armchair in a sort of forced nonchalance. The result was somewhat spoiled because her whole body was as tense as a sailor's knot, and one foot tapped an incessant pattern into the shattered tile. "But so would you if you're in our heads."

Merlin raised both eyebrows, then laughed. "Ah, I've forgotten how little is remembered." As his laughter faded away, he leaned forward farther, eyes burning bright as the sun, and grinned darkly. "Tell me, you know the legends of Merlin, yes? That he was an adviser, sorcerer, and prophet."

Finding his tongue again, Owen released a bark of laughter. "And a madman." The words triggered a tsunami of agony, and it took everything he had to avoid curling up in a ball and clutching his head.

Merlin's face darkened, and he gripped his cane so hard his knuckles turned white. "And a madman, for a time," he said in a voice too conciliatory for the despair hidden behind it. "Faced losses like mine, even the strongest of my kin would've lost themselves to grief."

A screen to their left cracked, repaired itself, then cracked again. A processor somewhere screamed in despair before falling silent. When it did, some of the darkness over Merlin had passed, and he seemed pleased again.

"Foresight was the least of my abilities, but all I had left after Avalon fell."

He turned away and was quiet for a time. Neither Beira nor Owen saw fit to interrupt his silence. The room repaired itself while they waited, and if it weren't for the growing ache in his limbs and his head, Owen would've wondered how. The walls became brighter, covered in paintings and murals in colors and patterns like those on Owen's coat. Cracks and stains disappeared, and a door burst into existence on the far wall.

It was a long time before Merlin spoke again. "I used it as best I could. Guided kings and queens, averted disaster, and tried to contact our brethren." Heedless of his slip into plural pronouns, Merlin continued, staring at Owen and Beira without seeing them. "We lost them, and by the time we learned what had happened, they'd already faded into human myth." He swallowed and his face darkened. "Everything we made—our cities, empires, and sciences—gone in a few measly millennia. Only my brethren, myself, and a few half-breeds remained. And now, I am all that's left." Merlin gestured around them, encompassing not just the room they were in but also the unseen beyond those walls with a single wave of his hand. "This is what remains of our civilization, the only thing untainted by humanity's fumbling."

"A protohuman civilization?" Beira's words floated on the wind of the breath she released. "That's impossible. We'd have found something, a sign—"

Merlin's head jerked up, and he let loose a bark of laughter. "Signs? What signs would be left after millennia under the ocean or an ice age? After a thousand years of earthquakes, droughts, and winters that never seemed to end?" His hands dropped down, clutching his cane like it was the only thing grounding him. "What signs we left were swallowed by the sea, by the earth, and by the wretched flow of humanity that claimed anything left for their own."

Abruptly he shot to his feet, breathing hard. His cane fell to the floor with an unheeded clatter. "Asgard, Tartarus, Olympus, the science of the pyramids—all remnants of a greater past." His eyes blazed like an endless inferno as his great shoulders heaved. He grew, his head inches from a ceiling that never seemed to get any closer, until his shadow surrounded them. "Those are your signs. Humanity leeched out a living in our graves and claimed ownership over the profits of their tomb robbing."

The room shook, the electronics screamed, and Merlin grew, shedding his form for a greater one that staggered description. Spikes and wings and teeth, a roiling, rotting mass that didn't have an end. "We gave you heroes and kings, seers and scientists. It was through our knowledge humanity lived long enough to forget where it came from." His words came not from his mouth, but from around him, bleeding into Owen's mind like poison in wine. His skin faded away to a translucent gray, his teeth grew inches long behind lips that didn't hold them, and his eyes blackened to a shade darker than the deepest abyss. "Hercules, Gilgamesh, Arthur, Hippocrates—"

"Enough."

The voice came from nowhere and everywhere and shook the room. The walls, the computers, and even Merlin himself shimmered, flickering like a shadow eating at a flame.

Owen wanted to clap his hands over his ears, to block out the ear-rending screech of electronics pushed beyond their limit, but could only move his fingertips. He sucked in a breath through his teeth and dug his nails into his legs, hoping—pleading with an unknown force—that he'd wake up.

As quickly as it had appeared, the voice vanished, and everything settled.

Merlin bared his teeth—too long, too sharp, too wrong—then shook his head. Catching a deep breath, he bent reluctant legs back to his chair as his features shifted back to those of an elderly human man. "I apologize," he said once his teeth had retreated enough for proper speech. "I lost myself for a moment."

Owen didn't need foresight to know Beira's thoughts since his were headed that way as well. Both needed answers, but neither wanted to risk a repeat of what had just happened.

Merlin was ready to speak long before either of them were ready to ask questions. His hands—far more gnarled and ancient than they'd been before—clutched his cane, rolling it back and forth across his legs in a hypnotic wave. "Some human minds were . . ." He paused, deliberating over his next words. "They were open to us. We were able to touch them, guide them, and make use of the half-breeds we had. We brought them here and taught them what they needed to know to restore what we had lost."

Owen had more than a glimmer of what restore meant, but a part of him—the part that couldn't look away from car accidents—needed to know anyway. "How?" His voice was raw, and something warm and foul dripped down his chin. Bile surged up the back of his throat, and it almost took more than he had to swallow it.

The computers whirled as if in answer, and Merlin laughed. "How do you think?" he asked between great guffaws filled with nagging despair and exhaustion that chilled Owen to the bone.

Beira finally spoke, and her voice was small and quiet, shaking worse than Ashley had at her first recital. "The dreams." It wasn't a question. It was a verbal confirmation of something she'd known but hadn't thought to pass on.

"Not a dream, but not reality either," Merlin said, glancing at the screens. "Something in-between that we discovered when humanity was young, and we were in our waning years." He leaned in closer, almost to the edge of his seat. "There is an energy to this in-between, the gloaming, one that humanity is only just beginning to rediscover, and we were masters of it."

His smile grew, pulling back until his lips exposed more teeth than should've fit in his mouth. "Our greatest minds—our scholars, philosophers, and alchemists explored it, leaving their bodies to rot behind them. They filled this place with their knowledge so that future generations could learn without needing to study, teach without having to speak, and live on without taking breath."

Now fully paralyzed, his breath rasping through lungs frozen in place, Owen glanced at Beira out of the corner of his eye. She didn't seem to be afflicted the way he was, but she'd always been an excellent actor.

Merlin coughed and shrunk in on himself when neither of his unwilling guests reacted. He stood and limped to a computer. "I never was any good at teaching," he mumbled. "The others were always better suited."

Beira leaped up, proving that she wasn't bound by whatever was holding Owen, and darted toward Merlin, almost out of Owen's sight. "The others? Are there more places like this?" Her voice—a strange mix of wonder, curiosity, and fear fit to freeze the marrow of lesser beings—was barely audible over the growing whine of the machines.

"Hm, Avalon and other sites. Elysium, Aaru, Valhalla." Merlin paused in consideration. "There are others, but I've lost access to them and their caretakers over the years." Shaking himself, he stood and walked around Beira to a quietly humming monitor. "Once we were many, created to watch over our great societies. The greatest minds came together and bound themselves to the machinery. They have fallen asleep over the millennia, and I've had to make use of your crude imitations of my work."

Beira's jaw dropped, and she clapped her hands over her mouth. She stumbled back, face as green as her coat. It took several tries before she was able to speak again. Several painful seconds passed before Owen's mind caught up to hers, and his heart almost stopped.

The battleborn. Percill. Had those been Beira's work or Merlin's?

"Crude imitations?" Beira whispered, swaying on her feet.

Merlin hummed as he gently placed a bundle of disconnected wires in their proper place. "Yes. My blueprints were closer to your consciousness than I intended, but your foolishness in forcing the change worked to our advantage. Now that we have proof your people can survive even without a caretaker, my brethren will awaken."

"Awaken?" Beira didn't move to follow him again. Her face contorted through a medley of emotions, shock and horror and despair as her hands clenched uselessly at her sides. "Caretakers? Are there more of you?"

Merlin hummed, and the screen in front of him lit up. "Yes, hundreds. Some of the old sites have already come online. I've sent them the blueprints for my experiment. Soon they should have the groundwork laid for our return." More screens lit up, listing data in a language beyond Owen's comprehension that tickled at the back of his mind like a barely remembered dream. "Yes, Elysium is already sending out waves."

"Waves?" Owen managed to rasp before Beira could speak. His throat felt like it was closing in on itself, and his limbs had long since gone dead.

Beira had let Owen read Nathaniel's journal once, and he caught on to what Merlin meant only seconds after she did. Waves. Waves like the ones that had created the fae. The waves of Changes that started with the founders. If his legs could move or his throat open, he'd have jumped to his feet and screamed at Merlin until he couldn't ignore them anymore.

Beira surged forward, grabbing Merlin by the arm, heedless of Owen's inability to even raise a finger. "No, no, tell me you're not doing this. We're not strong enough. The humans almost destroyed us the first time."

Merlin frowned as if realizing for the first time that Beira wasn't sitting anymore, and pushed her back. "No, I think I've taken up too much of your time." He paused and tilted his head as if listening to something beyond their hearing. "Yes, there's nasty business back in the world of waking you'll need to deal with." He smiled, and his lips stretched far past their mortal limits. "Besides, your companion won't last much longer if we don't let him wake."

Beira gasped and spun around. Her eyes widened as they landed on Owen and then darted up, and she stumbled back. Something behind Owen hummed sonorously in a register too low to hear properly.

Merlin chuckled, and the sound was closer to a growl. He grabbed Beira's shoulder from behind and pushed her toward Owen. "Have no fear, we will speak again. I need to work, and this is proving more distracting than I'd anticipated." He reached out, grabbed a fistful of air, and—

And something twisted. There was a pull in Owen's navel, in his chest, and in his head, yanking him away from the rebuilding room, into the void where they'd begun, and beyond into a blinding light.

CHAPTER TWENTY-SIX

In Which a New Day Dawns

"It hurt worse than anything I could ever describe. Each of my bones shattered, my blood boiled in my veins, and my skin tore open as anything that might've been human was ripped away. My blood . . . I don't bleed red anymore. Or at all, really. My skin parts, and something else, something black and rotten, swells to cover and close the wound. I see it below the surface of my skin when I go a long time without drinking. The others might not look human anymore, but at least their blood's red. At least they can pretend there's a part of them that stayed the same."
—Excerpt from the journals of Beira Thomson, Queen Titania

Owen awoke with a scream torn from a throat that nearly bled from the effort. A network of leather, nylon, and hemp straps barely contained his thrashing limbs.

An attempt at a second scream sent him into a wracking coughing fit that bruised his ribs. Frantic hands undid the straps before he stopped coughing, their owners talking in rushed voices over his head. They were yelling incoherently to someone behind him as they rubbed his back, their words a hectic rush in one ear and out the other.

"—days. We haven't been able to wake you," said the voice nearest to him as he was propped up. The speaker was agitated, and his voice moved like he was pacing. Wind whistled past unseen wings.

A glass of water touched Owen's lips and drove all thoughts of the speaker away. He drank greedily, heedless of what splashed down his front, to soothe the deep itch in his throat. His teeth clinked against the glass as it was removed—far too soon—and he was able to focus on what was going on around him.

The speaker had stopped. His face was familiar, a Grecian Adonis, and his golden wings even more so. Owen had seen him somewhere before, but he couldn't . . .

No. He blinked. Squinted. And his eyes opened wide, darting around to take in all that was before him. The people, an endless changing hoard of races, species, and generations; the walls, a kaleidoscope of color and life intermixed with spots of blindingly bright lights; and his own hands shaking in front of him.

He could *see*. Those walls, the people, everything that had been missing for weeks. Colors, shapes, clear definition—he drank it all in with the same intensity he'd drunk the water.

One of the nurses—a green-scaled siren with more scars than unblemished skin and biceps bigger than Owen's head—grabbed Owen's head and yanked it around. "Hey," he snapped, "I need you to focus."

Owen grabbed his arm and dug his fingers into the soft blue fabric of the siren's tunic—*hecouldseehecouldseehecouldsee*—and held it tightly. The siren yelped, and the fabric tore as he threw himself back. "What happened?" Owen asked in a harsh whisper.

But Owen didn't even wait for the siren to answer, because he'd remembered how he knew the speaker. "Lord Gabriel," he whisper-shouted. Shoving the siren aside, Owen unsteadily climbed to his feet.

Most of the crowd dove aside as Owen staggered forward. A centaur, a werewolf, and an elf joined the siren in trying to push him back down, but Owen shoved past them like they were made of paper. "Lord Gabriel," he said again, surging forward against the wave of exhaustion determined to bring him to the floor. Gabriel wasn't the person he wanted to talk to, but he was moving toward the door, and with him went Owen's chance of figuring out where Beira was.

Owen needed to talk to Beira. He didn't know how he knew that, but the urge to see her and hear her voice was as overwhelming as the tide. What little he remembered—Merlin, Avalon, and David—turned his knees to jelly, but Beira would know what they had to do.

Lord Gabriel turned, drawn by the increasingly panicked voices of everyone trying to hold Owen back. His forehead crinkled, and he darted forward to push Owen down. "Sit down before you collapse."

Owen grabbed Gabriel's arms and squeezed until bones ground together under his fingers. "Where is she, Gabriel?" he asked, his stomach clenching.

"She's got work to do." Gabriel grunted, trying and failing to pull himself free as Owen squeezed even tighter. "The sooner you let go, the sooner I can get back to helping her."

"It's all right, Gabriel." Beira emerged from behind Gabriel's wings. Whole, alive, and looking just as shell-shocked as Owen felt. She swallowed, and her face, as pale as the moon on a winter's night, relaxed into something like serenity—if serenity was perched on the verge of a breakdown.

Owen tried to push himself up again, and even Lord Gabriel struggled to keep him back. "Beira, we need to . . . we have to . . ." *Days*, Gabriel had said. Days where Merlin had been free to wreak havoc on the world.

Beira nodded and sucked in a breath. "I know. We're working on it, Owen." Her jaw set and she stepped forward. The hand she placed on Owen's shoulder burned like fire. "You need to rest. I'll send Tiffany in when it's safe, and I'll find you when I've assessed the situation."

They both knew what the situation was. Even now, Owen could feel a tickle in the back of his mind. A watching presence. Fear and curiosity that wasn't his or Beira's but belonged to both of them nonetheless.

"I'm sorry," she whispered as she drew back. Owen didn't follow her. "I have to go."

As much as he wanted to, Owen didn't fight her leaving. A distant echo, faint screams just on the edge of hearing, had been growing louder the longer he'd been awake. Screams the others didn't hear. He watched her go, let the nurses pull him back, and tried to quell the roiling storm that was brewing in his stomach.

And as she went, followed by Gabriel who seemed somewhere between relieved and disappointed that Owen had stopped fighting, Owen felt every step she took. Something stretched between them, a connection that was more than just physical.

One step and he could feel the shape of minds beyond those walls. Two and his vision darkened, the colors fading to something less brilliant but still more than gray. Three and four brought tension and aching pain.

Five and every step that came after stretched Owen's mind, bringing him into contact with beings and ideas and energies he'd been blind to even before he'd lost his sight.

***

The halls were dark and empty, the denizens of Tearmann safely in bed and away, and Owen was grateful.

People meant light, and he couldn't see in the light anymore. The healers weren't certain if it was because he was male or if how he'd been blinded played a part, but they couldn't deny it. Anything brighter than a candle shrouded everything in its reach in impenetrable radiance, while he could stroll across a pitch-black room with more ease than a sighted man at noon.

Of course, these weren't the only changes. He was stronger now. His hearing, taste, and smell had been dialed up to eleven. If he concentrated, he could hear someone blink. Taste their sweat from across a room. Smell their last meal on their breath.

They'd done it. Owen hadn't stopped to consider that when he'd woken up, but it was true.

He was a vampire, and that was why he'd been able to push back against the healers and Lord Gabriel like they were strings trying to hold back a tiger. Why, even now, he could feel Beira traveling around Tearmann. Why he could feel the fae he passed even if he couldn't see them.

And why he knew they were afraid of him.

They all knew what he was now. They could feel it. He saw it in the green siren who'd helped him up. The one who hadn't hesitated to tell him to sit back down but flinched when Owen moved too fast. He saw it in the human doctor whose hands hesitated before taking his temperature. He saw it in the werewolf lingering on the edge of the room, taking sneaking glances at Owen when he thought he wouldn't notice.

He was a vampire. It was as inexorable as the sunrise. As undeniable as the passage of time. The hold he had on their lives, on the lives of their family and friends, was as firm as steel and as pervasive as life itself. The ranks of the fae, from the smallest baby to the most wizened grandmother, were his to command, and they wouldn't be able to stop it. Owen would one day sit on a throne beside Beira and make decisions that would impact the fae for centuries to come. They knew it and Owen did too.

The healers hadn't wanted to release him. They'd had tests to run, lists Beira wanted them to check off, but Owen had wanted to go.

He wasn't sure how he had gotten home. No sooner had he left the healers behind than the apartment door appeared in front of him. He didn't have his keys, but the door opened anyway. The haven was a safe place, and no one would even dream of robbing them, but he made a mental note to have a word with Tiffany anyway.

A single candle stood in the middle of the kitchen table, and his head throbbed in time with its flickering. Tiffany sat across from it, her face shrouded in light and shadow.

"Tiff," Owen said as loudly as his still raw throat would let him. Relief pooled in his stomach, easing a worry he hadn't been able to name. "You're . . ." She was still here, a physical and blatant reminder of why he'd done this. If he focused, stringing his muffled thoughts together, he could feel Ashley, Jen, and Dorothy in their room. Arthur was harder, a stretch that threatened to snap the frayed edges of his mind, but soon enough Owen found him in the barracks. They were safe, no matter what happened to Beira now, they'd be safe. A slow smile turned his lips up as he crossed over to Tiffany and kissed her forehead.

His legs went weak as his shaky fingers tangled in the fur on her shoulders, and he almost collapsed into the chair next to her. The clock chimed three times, and in the other room Dorothy kicked her blanket off. The tangled whirl of her dreams—she'd dropped her stuffed lion, and even asleep, it bothered her—tempted Owen to go tuck her and her lion in.

But the greater need was in front of him. Something was bothering Tiffany. He could feel her wrestle with it the longer he sat by her. The twists and turns of her thoughts, all the paths that led her to the conclusion tying her stomach in knots.

"Tiff," he whispered, taking her hand in his. "What's wrong?"

Without speaking, Tiffany pulled her hand free and stood to get a glass of water. While it filled, she sighed and leaned on the counter. Her wings sagged, giving Owen a perfect view of the back of her head. "You're a vampire now?" she asked in a halted voice. Her hands shook as they curled into fists on the counter.

Owen smiled softly and leaned forward. The candle was blinding, but he couldn't look away from its hypnotic dance. "I am." Perhaps it was the giddiness of exhaustion or the comfort of being near his loved ones, but his fear slid away. He was fae now, with all that entailed. "It was . . ." He wanted to tell Tiffany about what he'd seen, about the being wearing David's face and all it implied for the fae, but he couldn't find any words that wouldn't make him sound insane.

His mind searched for an answer, lighting on Tiffany, the kids, and beyond that, to Beira working in her office with a score of people he didn't recognize. The somber touch of Tiffany's thoughts mixed with the carefree dreams of Dorothy and the swirling chaos of Ashley and Jen. Beyond that, a massive tidal wave of unease that consumed the entire haven.

"Could you stop that?" Tiffany snapped, turning so fast half the water spilled from her glass.

Owen's eyes darted up, adapting to the darkness in the span of a heartbeat. "Stop what?" His mind circled around hers in search of clues. Something was bothering her, but the more he looked, the more lost he became in the endless whirl of her mind and—

"That," Tiffany yelled, dropping her glass to clasp her hands around her ears. It shattered on the floor like a crack of thunder. "That digging around. I can feel you doing that."

Owen pulled his sneaking threads of thought back so fast he could've sworn he heard something snap. His exhaustion, the endless cloud covering his thoughts vanished like he'd been dunked in icy water. His chair crashed to the floor, and he tripped over it in his hurry to back away.

Air tinged with the faint taste of Tiffany's distress filled Owen's nostrils. His breath caught in his chest, and his eyes brimmed with tears. He'd caused that. It was his fault.

"I didn't . . . I'm sorry. Tiff . . ." He shouldn't have done that. He knew better than to do that. Elves and sirens could control themselves, and Beira didn't have any problems with the occasional accident, but he should've known better.

"It's . . ." She sighed. Rubbing her face, she slowly slid to the floor. Her foot swept through the broken glass like she didn't realize it was there. "I want to say it's fine, but it's not." Her breath hitched, and she took a moment to gather herself again.

Owen waited with bated breath. The threads that had, until now, been free to do as they wished, fought against his control. They wanted to search, to find, to learn about the world they found themselves in, and reeling them in took all Owen had. Their struggles almost made him miss Tiffany's next words.

"Why did you come home?" She was crying now. Her hands covered her head, and her wings wrapped tightly around her body. He could smell her tears, salty and bitter, without trying. The whirlpool of her thoughts had turned into something foul and consuming. "They told me you were going to stay away until you could control it."

That was right. They'd made a plan. He wasn't supposed to be out until Beira decided he wasn't a threat to anyone. Between everything that had happened, he hadn't even given that a second thought.

He opened his mouth, then closed it again. There were words to describe what had happened, but he couldn't string them together. The threads fought for freedom and kicked apart any semblance of coherent thought he could find.

"I didn't . . ." he managed. He wrapped his arms around himself, a physical cage to hold back the things in his head. "I forgot." He should go back now, he wanted to say. The healers had been right; he never should have left. But something had driven him here. He couldn't describe it, couldn't even begin to, but it was as real as the blinding candle on the table or the threads still desperately reaching for Tiffany. It had driven him away from Beira and all their plans. Driven him toward the safest place he knew. "I—"

"I thought I could handle this," Tiffany whispered before Owen could give voice to the tentative thoughts he'd managed to beat together. She took a quivering breath, and her voice broke. "When they told me, I thought it'd be like with Dorothy or—or the others. They're different now, but I still know it's them." She brought her hands down and looked at Owen with bloodshot eyes. "You're not . . . you anymore, and I don't know who you're supposed to be." The words came like they'd been pulled from her with burning tongs. A tortured, pitiful keen escape her, and her wings pulled in, wrapping around her until all Owen could see was a sea of feathers. "Since David—you've changed. Before this, before the Corps, you never would've put yourself at risk like this. You would've talked to me, and we would've worked something out, but you don't do that anymore, do you?"

"Tiff," Owen whispered raggedly. The threads writhed against his control, roaring louder than the blood pounding through his ears. "Please, just listen . . ."

A harsh laugh erupted from the feathers, and one wing dropped away. "I can't . . . you're still the same, but I don't recognize you." She surged up, climbing to her feet with the grace of a drunken whale. A shard of glass pierced through her foot, but she didn't seem to notice even though the blood was as obvious to Owen as a sunrise. "You're still trying to leave us behind. You still look like you, but you've changed inside."

The threads thickened into vile tentacles, reaching, stretching, and straining toward Tiffany like she was water in the middle of a desert, and Owen struggled to keep them at his side, even as he searched for words to plead his case. He wanted to run, to get out of here before they overwhelmed him, but he couldn't leave Tiffany like this. She was crying and he needed to help and Dorothy was still fussing in her room and Jen was starting to wake up and beyond that, there was a whole mountain of scared people and—

And it needed to stop. It was too much, and he couldn't think. The tentacles found each hole in his defenses, shoving past with all the care of a drunkard trying to thread a needle, desperate to return to their tasks. To watch over the ones that needed him.

"Just stop," Owen yelled. He didn't know who he was talking to. The tentacles, Tiffany, the endless hoard beyond these walls that grew larger with every passing second, or Merlin lost deep in Avalon. His voice cracked, and the tentacles he'd been trying so hard to hold back wrapped around Tiffany like a chain. The swirling whirlpool of her mind ceased to spin, caught in the prison of his unwitting command.

And she stopped. Her mouth clicked shut halfway through a sentence, and she froze in a half crouch. A tear perched on her eyelash, and she scarcely seemed to be breathing.

The clock clicking in the living room was the only sound for several seconds. Owen and Tiffany stared, each waiting for the other to break. And it was Owen—it was always going to be Owen. He'd ordered her to stop, and she couldn't disobey. Dear god, what had he done?

Stammering out an apology he didn't remember, Owen pulled back the chains, tearing, ripping, and breaking their connection to Tiffany as fast as he could.

He'd given her a command.

He wasn't sure if it worked. Tiffany wasn't feeling anything. The constant stream of her thoughts had faded away and hadn't been replaced. She was looking at him with new—*terrified, dear god, what had he done*—eyes and reaching for him, an apology on the tip of her tongue.

Owen ran. Out of the apartment before Tiffany could give voice to her words. Down the halls and up stairways, pushing his exhausted limbs to their limits. He didn't know where he was running or if he had a destination, but he never hesitated, taking turns and stairs like he'd been following this path all his life.

He ended up in the market. It was surprisingly busy for this hour of the night. Men and women of the Corps and what seemed like every member of the reserves rushed back and forth, shouting orders and carrying supplies.

Beyond them all, atop the stage where a lifetime ago Beira had announced how the worst night of Owen's life would be commemorated, stood a group of people that he knew was his destination. In the middle, giving orders in a seamless fashion as she turned from need to need, stood Beira. Her—*our,* whispered a voice in the back of his head that sounded suspiciously like Merlin—generals surrounded her.

Owen's hair stood on end and he slowed to a stop. His limbs shook and ached with the strain of the day and with the weight of his own actions. *"Beira,"* he cried without speaking.

She turned to him, her hair a rat's nest falling loose of her braid and her face drawn and weary. Her clothes were crumpled and worn after sleeping in them for three days, and she looked on the verge of breaking.

"Owen," she whispered back in the same manner.

The silent acknowledgment brought everyone's attention to them. No one else could hear them call to each other, but their eyes followed Beira's to Owen. The generals—wingmasters, alphas, chiefs, and choirlords alike—turned to face Owen in an eerily synchronized move.

The market was silent.

"Beira," Owen said again, curling his hands into fists. He knew he must look more of a mess than even she did, but he didn't care. *"Beira, what's happening?"* Lacking the words but unable to hold anything back, Owen shoved the tangled knot of threads and memories at Beira. His fears, his mistakes, *Tiffany,* and everything else.

Beira frowned, and for the barest fraction of a moment, he panicked she'd break under the weight. The tangled mess consumed her, wrapping around each limb like it meant to drown her.

Her face fell as she unraveled his thoughts in silence and tamed the sneaking threads that even now were reaching toward the fae surrounding them. When she next lifted her eyes to Owen, she was somber. Tears fell down her cheeks as she stepped off the stage, and the crowd parted in front of her.

"I failed you, Owen." Her voice carried until Owen was sure everyone in the haven must hear it. "I should've stayed. This is my fault."

He wasn't sure if she meant what had happened with Tiffany—the horrible violation he'd inflicted on her—the war that drove them here or leaving him before he'd been ready. All he knew was that she was coming closer.

The horrible threads that he had no control over whipped toward her, the wind of their passage almost enough to knock passersby down. He wanted to yell, both silently and out loud, for Beira to dodge, but before he could, threads—beaten and broken, but ten times the size of Owen's—emerged from Beira and beat his back.

The hurricane continued and grew, Beira and Owen at its eye. The threads lashed and fought, Beira's stronger and older ones brushing aside Owen's young and weak ones like they were flies. The air shook with the ferocity of their battle the closer she got.

Beira stopped less than five feet from Owen. Her threads wrapped around his, holding them down, restraining them long enough for Owen to know peace.

"Owen Williams," she said in a voice like thunder. Her threads grew into thick ropes, casting their weight down until Owen thought they would crush him, but that wasn't her intent. Her threads never approached him, only held back the parts of himself he couldn't control. "You are young in our ways. You can provide for yourself and you know our laws, but it falls to me to teach you what you don't know."

The Welcoming. She was welcoming him. Her threads, a quiet strength, wrapped tighter around his as she took another step closer.

"Will you accept my guidance, Owen Williams? Will you allow me to teach you what you need to be taught?"

Owen's threads thrashed, and the Merlin-voice in his head howled. But he forced the voice back and did all he could to make the threads quiet. All that remained was to take a step forward and meet Beira in the middle.

Taking that step hurt worse than anything Owen had felt before. The burning pain when he'd been blinded, losing Tiffany only to regain her when David had died, and the ache his bones remembered but he didn't were pushed aside as the voice in his head screamed and he took Beira's hand.

"I will." Somehow the wrecked and ruined remnants of his voice were as loud as Beira's and carried beyond the edges of their hearing into the world beyond.

And like a switch had been flipped, the threads that had been fighting for freedom lay still but didn't retract.

Beira nodded, her jaw set. A single thread freed itself from the others and wrapped around Owen.

"Then I swear to teach you until you have learned all you need to know to stand by my side. In the name of the Fae Queen's Court, the Founders Council, and my own name, I welcome you to my court."

Owen's threads shook, and Beira's wrapped tighter around Owen. That should've been the end of it, but her fangs descended, and her eyes shone with an unearthly light. This, Owen suspected, was only the beginning.

"We possess powers beyond the ken of others. It is our duty to use them responsibly." A second thread joined the first, wrapping tightly around Owen, followed by each of the others in turn until only one remained and it wrapped around Beira's arm. She continued like she didn't notice them. "Do you swear, Owen Williams, to use your gifts wisely? To refrain from brash and thoughtless commands? To find the balance between restraint and justice for the benefit of all who call this place home?"

His threads writhed. The Merlin-voice in his head wanted him to refuse. It sang silent songs of what he could accomplish if he didn't bind himself now. Of what waited for those who used all their strength to rule.

But that hadn't been why Owen had agreed to be Changed. He'd done it for the fae, for his friends and family. For Tiffany and for his kids. He didn't want them to spend the rest of their lives under the rule of a tyrant wearing the face of someone they loved. He wanted to protect them. To keep them safe from people like Percill who would use them for their own ends and then discard them.

"Yes."

Nothing happened for a minute that passed in silence. Beira arched an eyebrow, glanced at Owen's threads that had fallen silent and still, then at hers bound around her hand.

Owen didn't want to. He'd already lost control, and he didn't trust the threads enough not to attack Beira again, but . . . Taking a deep breath, he focused on one. The others lay as if dead in a ten-foot circle around them, but this one had some life in it.

He drew it up and wrapped it around his arm like Beira's wrapped around hers. As it settled around his hand, it slid across their entwined fingers to join with Beira's thread, and Owen *knew.*

He knew what Beira wanted to do, knew her thoughts and fears in the same way she knew his. The bond pulsed, growing stronger as Beira's other threads drifted toward their matches on the ground.

Beira smiled, and her eyes welled with joyful tears as her heart sang. *Finally,* it said, *I'm not alone anymore.*

"And," she continued, her voice muffled by the raging inferno of emotion passing between them, "do you swear to offer me guidance and teaching as I need it? To remind me of all I've forgotten in my long years?"

Love and pain and sadness and humanity and life screamed into the silent void between them and into the beyond.

After a beat of silence, Owen nodded. "I will," he said, surer of this than he'd been of anything. They couldn't lead together if one of them had to follow. He didn't know what he could do that Beira couldn't, but he would offer his advice freely when needed.

Beira smiled and pulled away. The joined thread stretched between them, forever joining them with an oath that couldn't be broken and a bond that would never fade.

Beira led Owen to the stage. A wingmaster he didn't know helped him up and set a supporting hand on his shoulder as Beira turned to face the crowd that had unbelievably grown.

The people—their people—watched with anticipation. The excitement and wonder of the elves—now a physical form Owen could see—infected all nearby, and life had begun to come back to the statuesque crowd.

"Fae of Tearmann," Beira said in a booming voice. Her threads stretched out beyond Owen's sight, disappearing through the walls and into the great beyond. "Of the Corps and the havens."

The gathered crowd didn't say anything, but Owen felt the course and aim of their thoughts as surely as he knew his own. Wonder and joy and excitement and *Could it finally be over? Could there finally be balance?* fought for dominance as quiet whispers broke out.

Beira smiled, and Owen had no doubt she saw the same thing he did. This was the moment dominion over the fae passed from her alone to shared between them.

"May I present to you . . ." Tears rolled down her cheeks; joy, relief, and wonder mixed into one, and Owen could feel them just like Beira could feel the swirling miasma of fear and doubt coursing through him. "The man who will be king, Owen Williams."

And the crowd roared.

Fae Queen's Court Appendix

Terminology:

Battleborn: Humans turned into fae-like creatures by the queen during the last battle of the fae war.

Change: The process by which humans become fae. It is incredibly painful and can last anywhere from four hours to a day.

Fae Ally/Allies: Any human who helps the fae gets the supplies they need to survive.

Faeborn: Humans with the potential to become fae.

Founders: The firstborn of any species. They also lead the fae.

Halflings: Crossbreeds of any species.

Haven: A piece of land given over to the fae. Currently, there are two in existence: Tearmann in Canada and Daingneach in Scotland.

The Nead: The city of the angels.

Paxton: The city of the battleborn.

Tearmann: The fae capital city. Built inside and on top of a mountain. It is also the name of the haven.

Fae Races:

Angels:

Angels are explosive people bound to their own code of honor. They are unique among the fae in that they produce massive amounts of energy that they can use as a weapon or a tool. The angels established their own city (the Nead) so they could have a safe place to train their young to control themselves.

1st generation: These angels are similar to those seen on church walls. Their wings are large and separate from their arms; however, their chests are larger to make room for the larger muscles and organs they need to sustain flight. They're not graceful, but they don't need to be. Additionally, they have hollow bones.

2nd generation: Their wings are bigger and more developed at this stage. Their eyes also develop a sheen that makes looking into them uncomfortable.

3rd generation: Angels develop eyes like a hawk. They're powerful enough to level a small building if not properly trained.

Centaurs:

Centaurs are philosophers and warriors. In their youth, they look before they leap and their wisdom is hard-earned.

1st generation: These centaurs have human upper bodies with horse legs and cloven hooves. Their hair grows in a line down their backs and their ears resemble a horse's.

2nd generation: At this point, proper back legs develop, but 2nd generation centaurs still tend to be shorter than their parents. They're large enough for small people to ride them.

3rd generation: These centaurs are fully developed. Their horse halves can be as large as Clydesdales or as small as quarter horses. They're usually much bigger than their parents or grandparents. They're large enough for a normal-sized human to ride them.

Dragons:

Dragons are the least common fae race. They are passionate people as equally fond of their friends as they are their hobbies. The hydrogen sacks in their chests enable flight and fire breathing. Males have two spikes on their foreheads and females have a spike at the end of their nose.

1st generation: The scales of these dragons match their hair color from when they were human. Their hair grows in thick spikes like hedgehog quills instead of single strands. They have primitive digitigrade feet, hollow bones, and bat wings fully attached to their arms and their bodies to their waists. Additionally, they have small secondary wings stretching from their hips to their knees that function as stabilizers and rudders. They also have no tails.

2nd generation: In this generation, scale colors start to diversify. They still retain a vaguely humanoid form and size, but they have proper wings and a spiked tail.

3rd generation: These dragons are what an American would consider a dragon. They have four limbs and two wings. They can reach massive proportions, ranging from 20-100 feet long, and their scale patterns are unique to each dragon.

Dwarves:

Dwarves are determined engineers. They seek knowledge to improve the lives of those around them and to accomplish things never seen before.

1st generation: Dwarves of this generation look like humans that have been compressed down. All dwarves can grow thick beards from a young age. Their eyes are best suited for the dark, but they can still see clearly in bright light as well. These dwarves average around 5' 5" tall.

2nd generation: Their proportions smooth out and they look like short and stocky humans, averaging around 5' tall. Their hair becomes uniformly curly and wild. They see excellently in the dark but struggle in normal light.

3rd generation: These dwarves wouldn't be out of place in an epic fantasy novel. They average about 4'-5' tall. They have excellent night vision but need special glasses to see in brightly lit places.

Andrew Stephens – 2nd gen dwarf and First Engineer of the Eyries.

Elves:

Elves are the second least common fae race. Like their kin from fantasy, these are a tall and ethereal species. Elves are renowned for their empathic abilities and their steady hand with animals.

1st generation: These elves look like pointy-eared humans that have been stretched out to make their bodies long and gangly. This leads to most averaging about 6' 6" tall. They begin developing the empathic powers their race is known for, but most can only influence a small sphere around them.

2nd generation: These elves have more natural-looking proportions, but still average around 7' tall. Their empathic abilities are usually strong enough to disable even a dragon at close range.

3rd generation: These elves are the strongest of their kin. They average about 8' feet tall and their empathic abilities are on par with a low-level command from a founder.

Eoire Belfield – 2nd generation elf. A mechanic and engineer in the Eyries. Currently the most powerful empath among the fae.

David Williams (deceased) – 1st generation elf. Jen's twin brother who died in the battle of Tearmann. Formerly the strongest empath ever seen because he attempted to guide the Change.

Gryphons:

Gryphons are a proud species who seek learning for the sake of learning. Offending a gryphon might just be the last thing you do, but they will fight beside their friends no matter what they face.

1st generation: These gryphons are feline in nature. Unlike dragons or harpies, they have wings separate from their bodies and a rudimentary second set of back muscles to support them. Their fingers end in sharp talons and their feet are those of a lion. They walk on two legs and use their tufted tail as a rudder in flight.

2nd generation: These gryphons more closely resemble legends. Their upper body resembles a bird of prey, and their lower body resembles a lion. They are capable of walking on all fours but can easily switch.

3rd generation: At this point, the gryphon usually walks on all fours except when they need their hands. It's difficult for them to walk on two legs as their spines weren't built for it.

Tiffany Williams – 1st generation gryphon and Owen's wife.

Harpies:

Harpies are the social backbone of the fae. They bring news and supplies from one end of the haven to the other and live nomadic lives. They return to their base nests every winter to share stories of the things they've experienced since last they saw their friends and family.

1st generation: Harpies at this stage have wings that end in taloned hands instead of arms. Rudimentary beaks take up most of their face, which makes it difficult to speak normally. That being said, they do have human teeth and almost everyone agrees they look strange.

2nd generation: These harpies have arms and wings. Families begin to resemble various species of bird. Their teeth look like they belong in their mouths and harpies can now speak with ease.

3rd generation: Their fully developed muscles and organs make harpies incredibly fast and efficient flyers. Additionally, they develop a talent for mimicry.

Tony Carson – 1st generation harpy. He was on the team that brought Owen and his family to Tearmann.

Isaac Rueben – 3rd generation harpy. He was on the team that brought Owen and his family to Tearmann.

Shades:

Shades are quiet people. You perceive them only because they wish you to see them. Look away or displease them, however, and you may never see them again. That being said, don't mistake their quietness for laxness. They're very protective of the fae and are known for enacting violent revenge when someone under their protection is at risk.

1st generation: Shades look human. At this stage, they gain their blending ability and can fade into the background if they wish. However, they have little conscious control over it and must practice a great deal before they can use their abilities offensively. Many shades wear little to no clothing to maximize their abilities.

2nd generation: Shades can now control their blending naturally unless in a heightened emotional state. However, their eyes develop a gleam that can be hard to hide.

3rd generation: Blending is as easy and automatic as blinking. They walk silently and produce little body odor or sweat that could be used to track them.

Jason Lucian – 1st gen shade. He was on the team that brought Owen and his family to Tearmann.

Abey Two-Winds – 1st gen shade. She was on the team that brought Owen and his family to Tearmann.

Sirens:

Sirens are the second most common species. They act as the healers of the fae but are also capable of hypnotizing humans.

1st generation: Sirens are covered in scales the same shade as their skin. They possess rudimentary gills that allow them to breathe in water and shark-like teeth. Their hair thickens to small spikes that they can use as weapons when broken off. They remain human-sized and hold onto fat to preserve warmth while swimming. Their fingers and toes elongate and grow webbing. Their song enables them to heal fae or hypnotize humans.

2nd generation: These sirens have slits instead of noses, and their bodies are better suited for swimming. Their song is stronger and families begin to specialize in one branch or the other and they develop poison-tipped claws on their hands.

3rd generation: At this stage, their head spikes don't usually grow longer than an inch or two and resemble fins. Drying out becomes a major health concern at this point in their lives.

Aaron Rodriguez – 3rd generation siren. A siren with the rare ability to heal and hypnotize both humans and fae. He was on the team that brought Owen and his family to Tearmann.

Trolls:

Trolls are shepherds of the earth. They make their homes in the forests and plains of Tearmann and tend to the gardens that keep the population fed. Still, they're slow to trust strangers and unwelcoming toward those who have proven themselves untrustworthy.

1st generation: A troll's skin thickens and cracks until it resembles bark. Their hair grows in thick and stringy, resembling branches or bushes.

2nd generation: Trolls at this stage have better camouflage. Families will begin to resemble particular species of tree and some will have flowers growing in their hair. Having anywhere from 15-30 fingers or toes is considered normal.

3rd generation: These trolls are practically indistinguishable from trees at a distance.

Vampires:

Vampires are the alpha fae species. Their control over other fae is absolute at the cost of linking their very lives to the fae. If the vampires were to die out the fae would die with them.

Vampires look almost entirely human. Looking under the surface reveals that their blood is naturally black, that they have retractable fangs, and that they are incredibly strong–even for the fae.

Beira Thomson – The only vampire in existence and the fae queen.

Werewolves:

Werewolves are the most common fae race. A full fifth of the fae population are werewolves. They are loyal and family orientated to their core. The moon holds no control over them.

1st generation: Fur covers the entire body of the werewolves except for their palms and the bottom of their feet. They have claws, primitive digitigrade feet, a tail, and a short snout. They do not change form.

2nd generation: These werewolves are capable of a slight change from a more human form to a more wolf-like form.

3rd generation: These werewolves can change from an entirely human form to an entirely wolf form.

Garret Abnell – 1st generation and Dorothy's daycare provider.

Jen Williams – 1st generation and David's twin sister.

Battleborn: Various

The battleborn are the formerly human population of the town of Breckenridge and soldiers that were turned into fae-like creatures by Beira during the last battle of the first fae war. They don't consider themselves fae. Most don't trust Beira or natural-born fae, so they live apart from the others in a city called Paxton. Generally, crossbreeding between the two groups is frowned upon.

Each fae species has a group of battleborn that correspond to them, but the battleborn rejected their names and took their own (i.e., dragons became wyverns/hydra/wyrms, werewolves became wargs, elves became orcs, dwarves became goblins, etc., etc.)

The fae refer to them by their species name preceded by battleborn. (i.e., battleborn vampire, battleborn dragon)

Groups:

Committee For Fae Relations – The US government's fae relations department. It is passively neglectful at best and actively harmful at worst.

The Fae – The fae are governed by the Founders Council. The founders are the firstborn of each species and have a similar level of control over their species as Beira does the entirety of the fae. Currently, they are divided between the summer and winter courts.

The Siren Corps – The fae military which is officially an aid group as the Tearmann Accords expressly forbid the fae from having a military.

Society Against Fae Emigration (S.A.F.E) – A highly anti-fae organization founded after the first fae war. They run or otherwise support most of the illicit fae research in the world but do their best to appear above reproach otherwise. There are small chapters around the country that range from people injured by fae who want tighter regulations around their travel to those actively trying to destroy the fae.

About the Author:

Ceril N Domace is an accountant, the owner of a grumpy senior collie mix, and a dedicated dungeon master.

As a lover of fiction works great and small, Ceril has been reading age-inappropriate stories since her father failed to pull The Silmarillion from her grubby little fingers at age five. As a grown-up accountant, her spreadsheet compiling gives her plenty of time to make plans for a fantastic world that isn't plagued by balance sheets . . . and also has dragons.

On the rare occasions she manages to free herself from an ever-growing and complex web of TTRPG, Ceril enjoys taking walks and griping that all her hobbies are work in disguise.

CPSIA information can be obtained
at www.ICGtesting.com
Printed in the USA
LVHW021059140522
718768LV00005B/16

9 781736 430125